BOOK ONE IN THE STARE DOWN SERIES

She swears it's only her curiosity.

He swears it's because she's curious.

A Dom stuck in anger management classes meets his match in his court-appointed therapist. Their attraction is off the charts. Unfortunately though, the timing is bad for both of them. Or, at least it is until he discovers his little vanilla doll isn't vanilla at all. Then it's a matter of timing be damned. He can't keep his hands off her. A definite problem, as she has a past to deal with and he has a goal to attain. So when the present rears its ugly head, they are both blindsided. Now they're forced to stare each other down if they hope to have any chance of a future together...

ROMANCE NOVEL NEWS

"Stare Me Down" by Riley Murphy

This erotic BDSM romance surprised me in a very good way. I'm a fan of Riley Murphy's books, but this one held me in thrall. The banter between Aries, the hero, and Jaxx, the heroine, was delightful, sexy and engaging. Aries is a Dom who is a mindfucker extraordinaire. This will be one of my favorite erotic romances of 2013

NIGHT OWL'S REVIEWS

REVIEWER'S TOP PICK AWARD

The chemistry between Jaxx and Aries is off the chart. I loved the sex scenes. They were so hot. I just wanted an Aries of my very own to wake me up in the middle of the night.

I really liked the author took what could have been a typical doctor patient love story and add enough drama to make not just interesting but a great read. I can't wait to read the next book in the series.

Stare Me Down

Riley Murphy

Copyrights

Dedication

To Ruby Williams for writing, singing and composing the song titled, **In This Bed**, for the book video. I get chills whenever I hear it. I love it! Thanks so much!

And,

To my honey for all the "gold" you've given me for my stories. Believe me. I'm really hoping that one day I will be able to use those nuggets on the pages of my books. Unfortunately, right now there just doesn't seem to be too much call for a massively disfigured, comatose, billionaire hero who gets abducted by aliens the one night his heroine isn't by his bedside. I will concede however, that I thought the twin idea had merit until you ruined it by suggesting it be the heroine's sibling and not the hero's. So for now, I shall toss all your little gems in the vault and only unearth them when I feel the need to share "the shiny" on my blog. Not quite the accolades you were hoping for, but the best I can do until you come up with something that doesn't have me laughing so hard I cry. As, you know, it's hard to type with a soggy keyboard. But this is what I love about you. You make me cry, but in the best possible way...

Acknowledgements

Brooke, I couldn't have done this one without you. You are a saint and a goddess who's been dipped in a whole pile of awesome sauce. Thanks for being you.

Kyle and Kim. What can I say? With you guys in my corner I feel as if I can do anything. I cherish that.

Big hugs to my mom who's one of my biggest fans. I love you, but I think it's time you get your own kindle. Just saying...

A special and big shout out to the real Shawn Alff! He's a very talented writer with Creative Loafing in Tampa Bay. Why, after doing his in-depth interview, where he brought up the "magical vagina" theory in romance, I was inspired to write about the "magical balls" in this story. Thanks for being the smarty you are!

And as always, to my dad...I miss you, but I'll see you after.

Chapter One

"I'm not the enemy, you know."

Ramsey Taylor didn't turn around, nor did he answer, because that statement was debatable. Instead, he continued to watch the angel fish, who was seemingly oblivious to the two oscars fighting beneath her in the tank.

"Please stop tapping on the glass."

Predictably the phone buzzed and he cocked his head to watch his adorable young doctor swivel in her chair to answer as she always did when her nosey colleague rang. This time however, she held her palm over the receiver and said, "The fish don't like it when you do that."

He straightened and turned around, frowning when he spied her shoulders slump and the steam go out of her as she listened to her latest instructions from on high. Two seconds later she whispered, "I know. Yes. Okay. I will." She closed her eyes as if she were doing a mental three count and he held his breath. Would she finally snap? God knew he'd been waiting for the moment. Praying for it even.

So when she quietly hung up he swallowed his disappointment.

"Sorry about that." She took a deep breath and squared her shoulders. "Unfortunately these kinds of interruptions are to be expected when you agreed to join the intern's group. Maybe you should have signed on with my boss."

He ignored that reminder and focused in on distracting her again. "The oscars pick at each other all the time, don't they?"

She looked up from her clipboard and pushed her heavy, black-rimmed glasses against the bridge of her nose. "Yes, they do. I think they're both males fighting for the dominant role."

"Is that your professional opinion?"

She stared but didn't answer. That made him grin.

"I bet you analyze a lot of fish—" he surveyed the room, adding, "—in this studious-looking think tank."

Bingo. Her eyes narrowed as she beat her pen against the metal part of her clipboard. "All right. Go ahead. We may as well get this over with. Ask me."

"What?"

"Why I didn't sign off on your anger management course and why I recommended these extra sessions?"

"I'm guessing you're making things personal."

"No." She looked like she was getting riled. "This is standard professional practice, believe me. What kind of a therapist would I be if I didn't follow my instincts and do my job?"

"Do you want me to answer that? You may not like it."

"It's okay to get mad, you know. It's healthy, even."

He crossed his arms over his chest and sighed. "Really? The last time I supposedly did that it landed me in this current situation."

"Doesn't the fact that I'm making you come to my office for some extra sessions tell you that your constant deflection isn't going to cut it? If you don't get serious, I'm not signing off on this paperwork."

His arms fell out of their cross and he let her see how ludicrous he thought that was. "Is this why I'm here? I wouldn't express myself in front of your band of neurotic misfits, so in privacy I might?"

She took a deep breath. "They are not misfits. They are people in need, nothing more."

At least she had the decency to turn away when she lied. "I beg to differ. One of your people in need set his car on fire when the drive-thru screwed up his taco order."

"I know." She straightened when she looked at him. "Jerry's working on his pyromaniac tendencies in another group of mine."

He shook his head. She was very blasé about the guy he'd labeled The Torch. "And I'm not one to cast stones, but compared to Harriet, who purposely locked her branch manager in the vault over a long weekend and didn't tell anyone all because he gave her a bad monthly review? I decided anything I had to tell them about my purported blowup would pale in comparison which would explain my deflecting."

"Yes, well Harriet is a different matter. She's going through a very emotional time right now and the vault incident? I'm convinced it's isolated within that perimeter."

Perfect. He had a fucking bleeding heart on his hands. "Really? The woman eats the Boston fern in the corner when she thinks you're not looking."

She seemed to be at a loss for words and it occurred to him. "Oh, not to worry though, I checked and the plant isn't poisonous. But her behavior? Passive aggressive if you ask me."

"She's eating it? Son of a...I just paid the pest guy a small fortune to spray the whole building."

He did a double take. "Between your fire-bug and the herbivore bank teller you can see why I was a little taken aback finding myself here."

"I thought it was for the best."

"You thought? I'm thinking it was your boss who insisted."

"You'd be wrong about that. In fact it was just the opposite." She shook her head and frowned. "Are you ever going to have a seat? It's been nearly half an hour and either you're prowling around my office poking at things or sitting on the arm of the sofa as if you're ready to bolt at a moment's notice. I haven't brought it up before as I figured you'd eventually settle in. Can you?"

"What? Settle in? Sure." He ignored her pen pointing, directing him to the couch, and walked right past her, intent upon the leather chair in front of her desk. It was the only masculine piece of furniture in a room packed full of frou-frou shit. Once he was seated, he waited for her to swivel around in the rocker then he held up a hand, adding a wave just to annoy her, "Carry on."

"Wouldn't the sofa be more comfortable?"

"You can call it a couch. As to being comfortable? For you, maybe, but not for me."

"So, what? Is this your way of trying to make me as uncomfortable as you are at the moment?"

Well, I'll be damned. The reserved little doctor was finally showing him some of the backbone he suspected she had hidden beneath her hard-to-crack veneer. "Maybe."

"Why punish—" She caught herself and blushed. "I mean, um, why take it out on me?" Carefully she took off her glasses and folded them prior to dropping them on her lap. "I'm not the reason you're here. I didn't assault anyone."

He leaned forward with elbows on the desk and looked her right in the eyes, briefly noting their unusual color. A light purple-blue. Cornflower came to mind. "Neither did I. I'm here for the court-ordered minimum on principle. You hold the key to my freedom at the moment, so I'll listen to your psychobabble—"

"Psychobabble?" The way her left eyebrow arched up intrigued him. It also inspired him to bait her some more.

"Yeah, you didn't even get the fish diagnosis right. The oscars aren't fighting over who's more dominant. They're pack fish. You either have one or six. Two doesn't cut it, because they'll constantly fight."

She held his gaze. Fascinating.

"I didn't have you come here today to talk about my fish."

"True, I'm here because I have to be here. I need to get my stay out of jail papers signed by you and handed into to my attorney so he can file them with the court."

She examined her clipboard and asked without looking up, "Then I think it's about time we discuss the basics. It says you assaulted a man in a parking lot."

So much for holding her off the topic that had brought him here with deflecting and his pressing-her-buttons antics. With no other patients to act as buffer he was screwed. He'd been trying to keep his distance since the moment he'd walked into that classroom six weeks ago. He'd almost made it, but he should have known his run of good luck was bound to exhaust itself.

Giving her a stealthy once-over, he decided to stick with the truth. Granted he'd still be annoying as that was the only thing standing between her and him carrying out one of his most recent fantasies he'd had of her. The one where he made her stretch out naked over the desk was looking pretty doable at the moment, too doable. "Yeah, I broke up a fight, and when the guy who started it fell he accused me of assault and had his lawyer on my ass for monetary compensation. I was given a choice. I could pay him twenty grand and he wouldn't press charges, or I could stand on principle and let our wonderful justice system protect me. I chose the latter, which obviously didn't pan out so well for either of us. He's still broke, and I'm stuck doing these court-ordered shrink sessions with a woman who can't even analyze her own pets."

She gasped.

Ignoring her, he sat back in the chair. "I should've paid him the twenty grand."

"I don't need to analyze my pets."

"Yes, you do. Because if you had, you'd have known about the oscars. I'm guessing you have a service that sees to the fish?" She nodded. "Fire them."

He checked his watch. It was as if time stood still. Couldn't he catch a break? What the hell were they going to talk about now? The fucking fish were the most interesting things in the room. Besides her, and she was off limits. Way off limits.

"Mr. Taylor—"

"It's Ramsey."

"Mr. Taylor," she began again, "I've been appointed by the court to make sure you get the counseling you need."

Now she went all snippy as she slammed her glasses back on and banged the clipboard. Damn, the urge to drag her over the desk and quiet her some by stealing a taste of those lips was nearly overwhelming.

"I'm very concerned with how you got here and it's time to get down to business and focus on your problem."

Oh, he had a problem all right. Best she knew it. Tilting his head, he bit back a grin. "Great, do you have a way to get me out of these one-on-one sessions? Because right now that's the only problem I have."

"Really?"

He nodded and let the grin rip.

"Don't be ridiculous." She adjusted herself in her chair. "Everyone has problems, Mr. Taylor. After all, we're human, aren't we?"

"And what are your problems, Doctor Gavin? Besides your insecurity, I mean."

She hugged the clipboard to her chest and sputtered. "I-I don't know what you're talking about. You know nothing about me. Besides—"

"I know you prefer tea over coffee. You wear sensible shoes as a rule, but even they bother you and you wind up in slippers when you can get away with it. You use the glasses as cover, the clipboard as a shield and you sleep on the left side of your bed at night."

Her mouth dropped open and she blinked twice before she snapped her lips together. Looking to the right, she examined the wainscoting for a few seconds. It gave him the time to view her profile. It was nice. Delicate. Yes, without those glasses obscuring most of her face, you could see her high cheekbones. He didn't even blink when she turned back and pinned him with an impressive scowl. "Did you hire a private detective to spy on me?"

"No."

Again she held his gaze. "Then how do you know all this stuff?"

"There are teabags in the garbage. Your slippers are here—" he nodded at the floor, "—under the desk. You can read with and without the glasses, the clipboard has nominal information on it and everything of use—your pens, papers, basically all your essentials—are positioned to the left. That tells me you favor your left side. As to you sleeping on that side of the bed? Purely an educated guess."

"Are you purposely trying to make me uncomfortable?"

Trying? She was so not comfortable, he grinned, "Yes."

That got her pen going. Her slim shoulders rocked back and forth as he imagined her mentally flinging, "Oh, yeah? I'll show you!" and for a split second he almost caved to the desire he had to order her to get up on the desk. This was not good. He's the one that should get up, not on the desk of course, but to leave. His desire for her was escalating something fierce especially now that he was sure she was feeling it too. It was inevitable. In this closed space with just the two of them? Thank Christ they only had a couple of sessions. He'd make it.

She continued to jot her nonsense, so he had to ask, "What are you writing?"

"Oh..." she paused and gave him a tight smile before she began writing again, "just my psychoanalysis babble stuff so I can start filling up this clipboard, a.k.a—" she waved it at him, "—my shield."

He chuckled. She was funny, he'd give her that, and as levity was his new best friend, he latched onto it. "Well, make sure you hit all the highpoints. Mention asshole, transference and narcissistic tendencies."

She remained focused as she penned the notes. "So, you have been to therapy before. Good to know..." She stopped and stared at the page with a shake of her head. "I can never remember how many S's there are in narcissistic."

"Three and two c's."

"Thanks," she said and finished writing with a stab of her pen on the paper. "Now." She looked at him. "My shield is sufficiently covered, vis-a-vis, psychobabble. See?"

When she turned it around, he silently read the words, "Mr. Taylor is an arrogant asshole who possibly suffers from narcissistic personality disorder. He mentioned transference, but I highly doubt he understands the factors that drive this condition. If I had to explore a concrete concern about him at the moment, I'd be looking into Parataxis disorder. Clearly his previous therapy had a hand in this."

"Arrogant?"

"Case. In. Point." She threw the clipboard on the desk and it spun in a full circle before stopping. "You just read that whole paragraph and the only word that stuck out to you was 'arrogant'? How ironic."

She smiled. A real smile that lit up her whole face and made the eyes behind those ridiculous glasses twinkle. But then he spotted the gorgeous dimples indented in her cheeks and decided two things. Her attractiveness was subtle. Quiet almost, while it snuck up on a person, and the more time he spent with her the more convinced he was that her kind of beauty would look awesome naked and tied to his bed.

"I've never been in therapy before, so I don't think we can reference an established earlier experience there."

She inclined her head. "Impressive. Did you take courses in college?"

"Yes. I figured the study of the human condition would be a huge asset in my chosen career path."

That had her wheels turning. Her brows furrowed and she said, "You're the owner of a club."

He leaned forward and brought his forearms down in a cross on the desk. "I know."

She stared as his shoulders for a second too long and then raised her gaze to his face. "I don't see the relevance."

"It's a sex club. An establishment that not only tolerates, but encourages all kinds of various kinks. If I didn't take the time to understand what makes people tick, especially kink-inclined individuals, it would be irresponsible of me, don't you think?"

Her eyes widened but her voice was calm. "I think we're far afield from what we should be discussing."

Perfect. Time to keep her out in left field. "Agreed. How about we discuss why The Dragon Lady tries to ruin—I mean run your life."

She didn't miss a beat. "I suppose you're referring to my boss, Doctor Carmichael?"

He nodded.

"That's none of your business."

"Excuse me?"

"I said, 'why The Dragon Lady tries to run my life is none of your business'."

His shock was threefold. Number one, she wasn't surprised by his question which meant she was fully aware of what her boss and colleague was doing to her. Number two, she didn't seem the least bit perturbed that he'd referred to that woman as The Dragon Lady, and number three, she'd point-blank snubbed him, when what she really should have done was placate him with some kind of inane answer so he could have wasted more time. "I think—"

"Mr. Taylor." That address came out as if she were speaking to a child. That got his Dom blood simmering.

His gaze never wavered. "Careful."

This show of assertiveness was what he'd been hoping and dreading to see from her during every minute of those six one-hour classes he'd attended. A little gumption on her part was a good thing, but his instinctive reaction to it? Not stellar if he was going to keep his distance. Before he could help himself, he leaned forward and gave her his undivided attention. Directing the weight of his stare in unspoken challenge, wanting, almost desperate to see how much nerve she had.

"I don't think I need..." Finally caution prevailed and she caught herself while the silence that landed between them was stark and consuming, echoing through the surrounding molecules for a full thirty seconds.

And then there it was. A little shake. A shiver as if a thrill had passed through her. That combined with her pupils dilating, swallowing up most of the cornflower blue of her eyes and turning them onyx, told him many things. The most important? "I know what you need."

She shivered again and the action fed the dark side of his ego until it was nearly full to bursting. But other than that second quiver, she didn't move. Her breathing pattern changed though, and the pulse at the base of her neck picked up speed. He wished he knew what she was thinking. A woman like her no doubt went through a mental list a mile long before she'd admit she was confused and out of her element with a man like him. For the next few moments they stared at each other. Neither one of them moved as the air between them crackled. Any second he was going to reach forward and drag her onto the desk. He'd get those purple eyes to lower beautifully for him before their time came to end, if it was the last thing he did.

"We're not here to discuss my needs. We're here to discuss yours."

Wrong answer. "So you don't want to hear what I have to say about your needs?"

"Again, I think we're far from what we should be discussing."

When she went to pick up the clipboard, he placed his hand over it. "I don't think so."

She let go and sat back. "Well, I do."

"Interesting. Don't you think me being the owner of a sex club is the very reason I'm here?"

"No. I think, unless your career is frustrating you to the point of acting out in an aggressive manner, you being a club owner has no bearing with the circumstances that brought you here. Other than that it happened in your parking lot."

How the hell had they gotten here? He needed to do something else fast. Like pull the proverbial rabbit out of the toy chest or something. When had his plan to maintain distance by being arrogant and insufferable changed into challenging her? Flirting with her? Questioning her about her needs? How was this supposed to keep an arm's length between them? Between her and all he wanted to do with her, to her? He needed to gain back some space. And there was one surefire way to do that. Scare the shit out of her. "I disagree. I think my career has everything to do with why I'm here. If I weren't making buckets of cash, I'd be no good to an opportunist. So yeah—" he leaned back, "—I think I want to discuss my life's work in great detail with a professional who may be able to shed some light. Give me some insight. Offer me ideas even to possibly improve my understanding of things. People. Who knows? You might know better about what makes them tick."

Doctor Jaxx Gavin stared into the steel-grey eyes of her court-ordered patient without flinching. She knew what kind of power shift was at stake here if she didn't hold her ground. Ramsey Taylor, Aries to his friends, was a popular Dom, and she knew why. Not only was he gorgeous, built like a brick shithouse and had a presence that charged the energy in the room, he was also smart. Really smart and that was a shame, because a guy's intelligence was her kryptonite. Looks came in as a distant second to a great brain. And she was sure Ramsey Taylor had one. Not that she'd be pressing to find out. Because even without a great brain he was tempting. Dangerous. Powerful, especially when he gave her one of his "looks" which effectively took her breath away, but his voice? That got her hot and made her heart bash against her rib cage.

"Hello? Earth to therapist. I'm counting on you to be an expert on understanding certain things."

Damn. Busted. One look at him and she gauged his expression. Smug. Was he gloating?

"Understanding of what things?" He'd better not be thinking that they were going to discuss certain intimate—

"The underlying factors that contribute to my specific kinks."

Sex. She should have known that a man like him would stick it to her for making him do the extra three hours. "I don't see how that will help you work through your aggression issue. Maybe we should start with some of your day-to-day stresses instead."

"Boring."

She would have rolled her eyes but she was still trying to win their staring contest, since she'd lost the last one. "These sessions weren't ordered by the court to entertain you."

"True. The court only ordered six. You were the one who added more." Thank God he looked away. She nearly wilted in her chair. It wasn't easy holding her own with a force like him. She was just mentally patting herself on the back when he added, "Be that as it may, if you play your cards right, you might find you're the one who's entertained."

The smooth timbre of his voice melted her insides and she almost smiled. *Smiled?*

Oh, no. He wasn't going to charm her. "I take my job very seriously, Mr. Taylor."

"I know. That's why I think you need to lighten up a little. Call me Ramsey."

She didn't know what to say. It was as if the words got lost from her lips to his ears. "I think you suffer from selective deafness on top of everything else."

His slow grin made her pulse quicken so she added, "And I will not call you Ramsey."

"No, you're right you shouldn't. Call me Aries."

Now he wanted them to be friends? She folded her arms across her chest and glared.

"Oh, come on, don't get mad. Just look at this situation from where I'm sitting."

"I can't help but look." She was going for an even tone, which was hard to maintain while speaking through her teeth. "You're sitting at my desk."

"Yes, and about your desk. Next week I'll bring a cork leg shim for it. I imagine it's annoying."

Not as much as he was at the moment. "Don't trouble yourself. I can pick it up."

He sat back and purposely mimicked her position. The whole scenario would have been laughable if he weren't getting to her.

"Then why haven't you?"

Not that she had to dignify that with an answer, but... "I haven't had the time."

"Yet you've had the time to fold bits of cardboard up and wedge them there? By the look of that mangled piece, I'm guessing it's been there for months."

It was a year, actually, but who was counting? "I'll take care of it."

"Suit yourself. Back to the situation at hand. I'm assuming you read the court transcripts?"

She nodded, trying to guess where this was going. In the time she'd already spent with the man, she knew he didn't say or do anything without purpose. He paid attention too. Close attention. The Dragon Lady, he'd dubbed Maggie, after only briefly meeting her friend what, twice at the most? Worse he had the whole depressing situation figured out.

"So you know that I didn't assault that guy. Surely you saw through the bias of that judge. He didn't like me because of who I was and what I did for a living. That's why I was sent to your class. As to why I'm here for extra psycho duty I have no clue, but since I'm here, I may as well make the best of it, right?"

"How magnanimous. I think you're the first patient I've ever had to accept 'mandated therapy' so well."

"Seriously? Well, try going into the marriage counseling business. I bet you'd have a ton more, as invariably one party or the other is dragged to it."

Hm. Speaking of being dragged. It was clear that he was going to continue to fight her every step of the way unless she came up with a compromise. She supposed he deserved one, as she had read those transcripts. The truth was he hadn't done anything wrong. That much was obvious and the very reason she felt guilty about tacking on these extra sessions. She took a deep breath and let it out loud enough he'd hear it. "All right. We'll discuss whatever you want in the last two sessions on a couple of conditions. First—"

"I'm not good at following orders, but I'm great at giving them. Why don't you let me handle things from here?"

She ignored that chipper offer and repeated, "First off, you will sit on the sofa and not at my desk."

"Couch."

"Fine, couch."

"Why do you let that woman push you around?"

She wasn't going to be sucked into that conversation. "Second, you will refrain from attempting to analyze me during our future sessions, understood?"

He uncrossed his arms and leaned forward. "Why, you don't like to be analyzed?"

"Correct."

"Well, neither do I." His tone dropped causing her adrenaline to rush until her heart fairly hammered with his next quiet words. "Are you going to answer me?"

Even though she knew what he was asking, she said, "I already did. I don't like to be analyzed."

"And I don't like to be ignored or brushed off. Two things that you've managed to accomplish in less than fifteen minutes."

She watched as he slowly dragged a hand across her desk before he smacked his palm sharply against the surface. The move was a clear imitation of a spanking. Was he warning her? The very idea had her tingling.

A man's attention had never made her tingle. Ever.

Breathe Jaxx. Focus. "I did not ignore you."

"So you admit you brushed me off."

She shrugged. She wasn't going to lie. "Yes."

His jaw didn't exactly drop, but the side of his cheek ticked as if he were chewing on it. Poor guy. Women no doubt collapsed at his feet without the least provocation.

A full thirty seconds went by and when he didn't say anything she figured she better.

"Oh dear, are you okay?" She leaned forward and tapped his hand. "You don't look well. Should I get the smelling salts or will we require a coroner?"

Chapter Two

His fixed gaze drilled into her and she stopped tapping when he asked, "Are you enjoying yourself?"

She was. She sat back, stunned at the revelation. She actually was. That never happened to her when she was with a man. Normally guys either bored her to tears or made her uncomfortable. He should be rubbing her the wrong way with his insufferable arrogance and yet, he wasn't. The question was, why?

It had to be his unfailing confidence that wasn't shaken by her intellect that held her interest. Hm. In a way, his massive ego was a great safety net as there was a certain amount of comfort knowing she didn't have to dumb down to mollify him.

Quite simply? He was a challenge.

Unfortunately, he was also funny, smart and gorgeous which put her in over her head, challenge or not, because she was genuinely attracted to him. No matter how much she tried to tell herself otherwise. Shit. Her eyes shot up to his.

Double shit. His look sizzled with—was that lust? No guy had ever looked at her the way he was looking at her now. As if he wanted to devour her. How was that possible? A man like him? All Dom-buff and delicious, lusting after her kind of...what had he called her office? Studious? Yes, her kind of studious stuffy didn't go with GQ BDSM. The two were as similar as chalk and cheese.

She tore her gaze away and whispered, "I'm sorry."

"I'm not. You never answered me about Doctor Carmichael."

"Maggie means well enough."

"That's what would have me concerned if I were you."

The phrase, "He's your patient and you can't screw another one up", played over in her mind until she was calm and focused once more. Straightening her shoulders she took a deep breath and slowly let it out, saying, "Not to worry. I'm taking care of it."

"As well as you took care of the desk shim and the oscars?"

There were a thousand things she could have said, the most prudent being, "It's none of your damn business", but the words didn't form. Instead she found herself admitting, "I'll do better with Maggie." She didn't add that she had to. Just the thought of what she'd eventually have to face there had her stomach tied in knots.

"I find you interesting, Dr. Gavin."

"Oh?"

"Yeah. I think for the last two sessions we should analyze each other."

"What?"

He nodded. "Yes, you set up these extra sessions to learn more about me, but I'm afraid the only way you'll do that is if we do a Hannibal Lector. Quid pro quo, what do you say? It makes sense, right?"

"No."

His smile nearly blinded her. "Sure it does."

Heat—no, steam—fairly percolated beneath the surface. "I'm the therapist here. I'm supposed to be interested in you. It's my job, even if I'm not feeling it, I have to..."

Silence. Oh, God. All she heard was the tick of the clock which sounded like the ominous countdown to a bomb going off. She'd nearly admitted that sometimes she had to feign interest in some of her patient's problems. Not his, certainly, but—

"Yeah, that sentence wasn't going to end well," he whispered and searched her face so thoroughly her cheeks flushed in a hot and telling blush. She had to fight the urge to place her cooler palms against the searing skin.

Unmindful of her mortifying predicament he tilted his head and asked, "Is this why those two other patients complained about you?"

"How did you...?"

"You see? I already have a head start on the analyzing. I heard you and Doctor Drago—I mean, Maggie, having words in the hall earlier. It seems I'm not the only one who needs this paperwork completed and handed in to the court."

"You were listening?"

He shrugged. "No one asked me to cover my ears and being that the walls are paper thin and Doctor Carmichael frequently over-talks you, it was hard not to. In fact, I'll let you in on a little secret." He leaned forward and continued in a mock whisper, "Your little group has a betting pool started. The odds are fifty-fifty. One half is betting you're going to quit the profession and the other half has money on you slaying the dragon and sending her straight to hell."

Jaxx should have been mad. Shocked. Moderately disturbed even, but she wasn't. Truth was she was amused. The thought of a man like Ramsey Taylor being treated to her group of emotional misfits, as he called them, betting on something like this? Priceless. "And which way did you ante up?

"I make it a habit never to bet. Literally that is. I work too hard for my money to piss it away like that. So." He arched a brow at her. "Was it a case of you not feeling them that has you on the bubble?"

"Of course not."

There was no getting around this guy. And hang Maggie and her interfering. On the bubble? Great, now Ramsey knew Jaxx needed to have him complete the mandated sessions to qualify her as a fulltime "court approved" therapist. Attaining that stature was a near impossibility, given that she was mostly dealing with highly emotional patients who thought nothing about taking their imagined complaints of her qualifications back to her case manager. Thanks to Maggie stepping in to "help" she already had two complaints filed against her. One more and she'd be turned down for good. She should have just signed the papers and been done with him. Curiosity be damned. Too late now.

"All right. To get you to open up I'll share a few things about myself, providing you sit on my *couch* and don't try to analyze me."

"I don't want to sit on your *sofa*."

She narrowed her eyes. "Lay on it then."

"With you?"

She gasped. "I'm your doctor."

"I could make a very accommodating patient given the chance."

He winked at her, which was bad, but then what was worse? She blushed again and now he'd know she liked this kind of teasing. She had no business liking it. She was a professional for God's sake.

"I am your doctor."

"You're good at that." He was pointing at her face.

"At what?"

"Talking without moving your lips."

One minute she was melting and the next she was ready to scream. Rip her hair out. Stomp her foot maybe, but then he stood.

"I'll see you next Tuesday."

She blinked and twisted in the chair. "Where—?" The phone rang and she snatched up the receiver and slammed it down. Maggie could wait for once, "—are you going?"

He was at the door and turned around. "Time's up," he said, tapping his watch.

"Oh."

"I liked that," he whispered, nodding toward the phone.

Warmth raced through her and the pleasurable sensation landed right between her legs in a tingling thrill. She did her best to appear normal and unaffected by it. "See you next week, then?"

"Yes, but now that I think about it, would you like to be surprised about the topics I want to cover in our next session when we analyze each other, or should I email you the list?"

"List?"

"No problem. I'll send it along."

She stared at the closed door for a second and then looked around. What the hell just happened here? *You got hijacked, that's what.*

"Son of a bitch."

Getting up, she walked around her desk and put a hand to the leather chair back. It was still warm from him. How did the guy manage to get to her? Every single time? His cologne surrounded the space, and she went to breathe in deeply but caught herself. What was she doing? Sniffing around after him like a...a—

"Careful, Jaxx," she whispered and spun the chair out of her way. "He's dangerous in more ways than one. You should have ignored your curiosity. Strangled it. Killed it. Not given into it by making him hang around you longer." Yanking open the top drawer, she got out her cell and dialed the number as she walked to the fish tank.

"Tropical Sea aquarium service," a voice trilled over the line.

"Yes, I need to speak to someone about some fish. Oscar fish."

*****

Aries examined the collar. It looked beautiful against her flawless skin. He'd been smart to use a combination of metals. Although the design looked lacey and elegant, feminine, it was in truth a weighty reminder that she belonged to him. Drawing his index finger over the gold, silver and copper threads that knitted together in a complex web design, he smiled when she shivered.

She was warm, and the scent of her desire rode the short space between them, filling him with a satisfaction he hadn't experienced in a very long time. He slipped two fingers under the metal and tugged against the band. Pulling until her head was forced back. He wanted her features out of the shadows, but the lighting changed and the ropes that held her in place tightened. The slight shift in position gave him a better view of her back. That expanse of skin was bathed in a pearly-white glow that highlighted the marks he'd made. The swirls of dusky pink impressions his flogger had meted out. Such a nice pattern.

He leaned down and kissed her shoulder. Then the center of her spine as his hand trailed down that solid line of her vertebra. Testing the texture of her skin. Chasing the prickles of gooseflesh away with the warmth of his palm. Until he reached her bottom. He wasn't gentle as he massaged her ass. Kneading the firm mounds with a heavy hand prior to spanking her. Once. Twice. Three times before she listed forward.

"Ass out, beautiful. No shying away from me." He stepped back and waited. "Good. Tilt it up. Very good. I love to see how eager you are to please me. I love—"

A beam of light flared and caught his attention. His heart raced, and blood flooded his cock in a rush of euphoria when he spied the ink. The phrase that was the unequivocal proof that she was his, permanently tattooed across her lower back.

He bent and just as he'd done with the collar, he traced his index finger over the words, silently reading them. "i belong to Ramsey Taylor. my Master, my Love, my Life."

It was true. He was her everything, and the thought was exciting. Challenging. Humbling.

"You're hot, aren't you?" he whispered, squeezing the burning flesh of her ass. Waiting for her to nod before he let go. "Let's cool you down." He reached for two ice cubes out of the bucket on the floor and straightened. "These are going to be cold on you. Don't move. Prepare yourself for it."

She quivered and shook despite his order as he pressed the naked front of himself to her bare back. Wrapping his arms around her as he dragged the pieces of ice from her collarbone to her breasts. Circling her nipples in a series of easy slides until the peaks spiked harder than the ice.

"You're a hot little whore. Too hot," he said and just as he'd promised, he cooled her down. An inch at a time as he trailed the cubes along her rib cage, stomach, belly and hesitated over her shaved mound.

Her shivers only intensified and when her head lolled back against his shoulder, he tried to see her expression. To gauge what was in her eyes. To know what she was thinking, feel what she was feeling, but the pearly-white glow shuttered in successive flickers like the flash of a camera and he couldn't see her face.

After a moment it didn't matter, because she pushed back against him in invitation, and his cock was ready to accept. Both his hands descended between her spread legs. "So open and ready for this, aren't you. God," he breathed and used one hand to tuck both frigid cubes into her heat. Following their path deeper and higher until she flexed against his hand and moaned.

"Relax. I want them to stay put until I get my cock in you. Good. Ass up. Get it up. That's right." He gave one more press with his fingers and then eased out of her. "I can't wait to tumble that ice once I drive into you."

He lifted his cock and braced it right at her opening. "Fuck, you're still hotter than hell down here. How is that possible? Do you burn for me, babe? To be fucked by me? Only me?"

He shifted and when he was met with resistance, he curled down and latched his mouth on to her neck. Sucking. Nipping. Biting until the tension eased and he was able to get into her. "That's better. Open more for me. Yes. Let me—fuck, your pussy is hot and cold and tight. Beautiful," he swore when her inner muscles clamped around him. Convulsing and gripping, as they worked to draw him in deeper and deeper until he experienced the chill of the ice. The scalding end of his cock nudging against the frozen water was heaven. Hell. Fucking excruciating one moment and totally comforting the next that his only thought was getting her to come so there'd be a new rush of heat added to the mix.

His heart thundered as raw lust barreled through him. It took all the effort he had not to give in to it as he pressed his lips to her ear and whispered, "I want you to let go and come all over me. Now." He waited a few taut seconds. Wishing to Christ he could see her through the shadows. "Do it. I'm waiting."

The silence was palpable. The stillness overwhelming. Something was wrong. He peered harder into darkness and brushed her hair aside, saying, "Let me..."

Her head fell back against his shoulder at the same time the shadows turned to mist. Suddenly, the white-pearly glow gleamed bright and brighter still. Clearing the fog and giving him a perfect view of her. Lighting every satin inch and all her feminine curves. He took in the sight until his eyes lifted to her face and he found the prettiest set of purple-blue eyes gazing up at him. He was stunned. "Dr. Gavin?"

"Jesus!" His eyes snapped open and he nearly fell out of the chair.

Knock, knock.

"Come," he called then grinned bitterly at the irony.

"Damn, you look like shit. What happened to you taking some time off? Your infamous catnaps aren't cutting it anymore. I can tell." As usual, Sharon, one of his night managers, didn't mince her words. She was right too. At least about the naps.

"Hey, Shar, what do you need?"

She came in and shut the door. "We'll get to that stuff in a minute. Right now I've come to help. I think I've an idea on a date for you when go to your brother's party."

Aries snatched up his water bottle and unscrewed the top. "Really? I hope it's better than your last suggestion." Although he appreciated that she cared enough to try to find a solution, he was a little leery to listen to her latest plan. Her last one had been laughable. His brother never would have bought Shar being Aries' conventional date for the night. Aside from the gothic clothes and numerous facial piercings, her white-blond hair with various ends tinted navy blue in spots might have given her away. If not that, surely her tattoo sleeves would have.

"I could see where I wouldn't work as vanilla arm candy. But my sister can. She's about as vanilla bean as they come."

He waited for her to collapse in a chair and asked, "Isn't she married?"

"Yup."

"Well, then I'm going to have to pass. I wouldn't want her to get into trouble with her guy."

"He'll never know."

"Shar, you know I don't like deceit in any form."

"But I know how much you want the unit next door, and it isn't going to be available forever. This is the perfect time."

He leaned back and rubbed the knot out of his neck. A remnant from his nap, no doubt. "You're the one who wants me to expand. I've already told you I have no plans to do that here."

"You want that unit for something. I know it. I know you. And if you don't jump on it, you'll miss the opportunity."

"You worry too much. Things will work out the way they were meant to. Trust me. You'll see."

The moment he was alone, thoughts of Dr. Gavin and their last session surfaced. There was no longer any point denying his attraction for her. He was interested the moment he'd attacked and she'd defended. Valiantly. In fact, if she didn't second-guess herself and her conclusions, she might have occasionally won the unspoken battle they waged. Yeah, the little shrink thought he'd been sulking during their group sessions over the last month and half and prowling around her office this morning because he didn't want to be there, but the truth was, at least as far as her office went he stalked around the place in an attempt to keep his hands off her and not put her over that desk and play with her. How messed up was that?

He didn't hesitate. He picked up his cell. The way he saw it, he needed to find an out before he made an in with her. Now was not the time for a woman in his life. Especially a smart one who, consciously or not, was giving off signals unmistakable to a guy like him. She wanted something. Something bad. And bad was just up his alley. A vivid image from his dream came to mind. The collar, tattoo and those eyes... Fuck. He wanted something from her too. Something that didn't bode well for her quiet and conservative lifestyle.

He closed his eyes and thought about The Dragon Lady constantly breathing down Jaxx's neck. *Jaxx needs her confidence bolstered. She needs a dependable shoulder to lean on.*

His eyes snapped open. What the hell was wrong with him? He couldn't afford to be that guy for her right now no matter how much he wanted to be.

Dialing, he put a call in to the attorney who was handling this legal snafu, hoping to be able to finagle his way out of the last two "individual" appointments. The group sessions he had handled, but him and her alone in her private office was a disaster in the making.

As usually his overpriced lawyer was no help so Aries knew what he had to do. He tossed his phone on the desk and plucked up Jaxx Gavin's business card. Spotting her email address, he sighed. Maybe there was a way he could kill two birds with one stone. He could get out of the private sessions and force her to deal with The Dragon Lady head-on. If he had bet on what Jaxx would do he would have put his money on her sending the she-beast to hell. At least that's what he would have been rooting for, so it was a fine line he had to walk as he came up with his present plan.

It was dangerous, he knew, using Jaxx's insecurities against her. This usually wasn't his style, but he was desperate. He needed to take control before they had a situation on their hands. Hopefully, he'd make her uncomfortably squirm enough that she'd give him the paperwork without completing the last of the appointments , but not freak her out so much that it would affect how she felt about her methods, because so far they'd been pretty good. Swallowing his guilt, he turned on his laptop.

*****

Jaxx was up working late when the ting of an incoming message sounded from her computer. It was Ramsey Taylor. No doubt this was his list. Clicking the tab, she spied the one word and frowned.

Rorschech.

Interesting. Although he'd spelled it wrong, she could be just as vague. She typed back.

???

He responded quickly.

It's a kind of test.Do you want me to explain it to you?

She snorted. Very funny. First he was an expert on tropical fish, and now he was going to school her in psychology?

I know what it is.

Great, then we're good for our next session.

What could she say to this? She would have loved nothing more than to tell him not to show up and she'd give him the signed document for his attorney anyway, but she'd made her bed so to speak, and besides, Maggie was hovering.

I'll be ready.

She'd have to be ready for anything, now that she thought about it. It was only two more one-hour sessions. She'd managed this far with him. *Not alone.* Surely she'd survive just two short hours?

All she needed to do was stay focused. But even as she pushed thoughts of how attractive the man was out her mind, she had to acknowledge one thing. Giving a guy like him the Rorschach test was any woman's dream. Therapist or no. Getting a glimpse into a sexy Dom's psyche was a rare occurrence, she imagined. That was the appeal for her. She'd had him for six group sessions and it hadn't been enough. His kind of smoldering, "I'm a man who knows how to be a man" attitude was secretly intoxicating and it was this phenomenon that had her wanting him around longer. Although now that she had him? She'd have to keep him busy and this test might just do trick. Well, at the very least it would keep him seated, and if she picked enough of the right kind of images, he'd be as 'entertained' as he'd wanted to be until she figured out what she was feeling for him. Yes, the more she thought about it, the better she liked the test idea. Insight was always good and where he was concerned the more insight the better.

Goodnight, Dr. Gavin.

Chapter Three

"What's that?"

Ramsey bent and put the small wicker trunk down beside the couch. "My test items."

The doctor's head snapped up and her pretty eyes pinned him. "Your test..."

He nodded, letting her take a moment to get her head around the concept.

"B-but I have my Rorschach Test ready to give to you. And what do you mean by items?"

He looked at the fish tank and smiled. She got more oscars. "I like that." He shot a curt nod toward the tank. "I'm guessing there's no more fighting."

She frowned. "No, there's not. Now what's this all about?"

"I didn't say Rorschach." He pronounced it correctly as Ro-shock. "I said 'Rorschech'." He pronounced it Ro-sheck so she was sure to hear the difference. "I did ask you if you wanted me to explain it to you."

"I thought you misspelled it."

He shook his head, enjoying how one expression after the next flitted across her face. He gauged confusion, embarrassment and finally anger just before she turned and marched to her desk. Snatching up a stack of papers —probably her images for her test— she turned them on edge and banged them on the desk top until they were all neatly aligned.

"I tell you what." He sat down on the arm of the couch and waited for her to sit in the white linen upholstered rocker. She looked great today in her silky blouse and tight little skirt. "I'll conduct my test first, and then you can do yours. Once we're both finished, the saner person gets to decide what we do for the second half of the session. Deal?"

She eyed him over her glasses and scowled. "Do I need to remind you that I'm the doctor?"

"Should I remind you that I'm the innocent sucker who landed on your sofa because of discrimination?"

Her nose pleated up on one side and the accompanying disgusted expression reminded him of a kid facing a bowl of lima beans for dinner. "Um...the closest you've gotten to landing on my *couch* is sitting on that arm."

She had guts. Maybe this wouldn't be so difficult after all. "Should I go first, or would you rather?"

She put the stack of images on her lap and pushed on her glasses. "I think you can go first. But maybe you should explain the rules of your Ro-Shick Test to me."

"It's Ro-Sheck. Sure. Okay, even though there really isn't supposed to be a right or wrong answer to this kind of testing, I know your little secret, and that's what we'll use to figure right and wrong."

Her gaze was leery. "I don't have any secrets."

"If that were true, it would be a shame." He winked at her. "I'm talking about the code."

Now she rolled her eyes at him. "I thought guys were the only ones with a 'code'?"

He pointed at her. "Don't deny it. I've been assured that each therapist has a secret crazy meter. If the individual does this test and says something reasonable and imaginable, the answer is deemed acceptable, so they aren't crazy or, in the case of our test-off, they're 'right'. If however, the individual says something unreasonable and therefore unimaginable, that person is wrong."

"Or crazy," she added so blandly he almost laughed.

"Exactly." Leaning down, he opened the trunk lid. When she craned her neck, almost falling out of her chair to see inside, he angled it with his foot so he was sure she couldn't get a look. "No peeking."

"I wasn't." Her blush told a different story.

"You were, but I happen to like curious women, so I'm not going to mention it again."

She fell back against the rocker with a sigh and he ignored it.

"This is simple. It's basically the same way you conduct your test, only I use items that you have to identify instead of images."

"That doesn't sound too hard."

He grinned. A low-down dirty one. He couldn't help it. She was walking right into this just the way he'd planned it. "It's all in the interpretation. Ready?"

She was slow to do it, but she eventually nodded.

"Good." Ramsey leaned down and rummaged through the trunk. He pulled out the first item and held it up.

Damn, she was easy to read. A virtual open book. She sat up and her eyes sparkled, even as her cheeks turned the prettiest shade of pink. Darker than any blush he'd seen on a woman in a good long while.

"Tape."

Oh yeah, this was going to be a lot of fun. "What kind of tape?"

She folded her arms across her chest. "I'd rather not say."

"Ah, but I insist."

"And I insist we keep things on a professional level, Mr. Taylor."

"I was afraid you were going to say that." He maintained his poker face as he dropped the tape back in the trunk prior to plopping the lid on. Time to tap into her insecurities.

"What are you doing?"

"Getting ready to go." He really wasn't, but this was the fastest way he could think to get her to loosen up a little. "I heard The Dragon Lady loud and clear. I can be reassigned. I'll just tell them we had a difference of opinions."

"Don't be ridiculous. I mean, there's no need for that. I..."

"Yes?"

She drew in a deep breath and let it out in a rush. "Oh, all right. If you insist. It's glow-in-the dark bondage tape."

"Do you mind?" He held up the clipboard, indicating with the pen in hand that he was going to record her answers.

"No, by all means. Although why you asked first is beyond me. You seem to be good at steamrolling ahead with what you want."

"I am, aren't I?" He didn't look up. He just finished writing and then went in search for another item before holding it up as he turned it on.

"Really?" Now both sides of her nose crinkled. She sat forward and moved her head from side to side, trying to get a better look. "Does it have a place for attachments?"

He stared right at her. "Yes. It has a place for an attachment."

"A vibrator."

The way she said it was so blasé, so "meh," he wanted to laugh, which was bad. She wasn't supposed to be getting more interesting by the minute. Far from it. He snapped the off button, put it back and recorded her answer. "Now," he said as he pawed through the trunk. Time to pull out one that would no doubt make her squirm. "What's this?"

He held it up, and when her cheeks turned that deep shade of pink again he got a sinking sensation in the pit of his stomach. He couldn't remember a time when he'd had this much fun with a woman, and she wasn't even naked.

This wasn't the plan.

"I'm not going to—no way. You can't possibly expect me to say."

She shifted several times in her chair. Aww, he almost felt bad for her.

"Just tell me."

Licking her lips, she turned away until she hesitantly looked back with a cringe. God, she was cute.

"Doctor Gavin?"

"Yes?"

He shook the item in question.

"Oh, all right. It's an anal plug or a hook thingy."

He didn't break eye contact. He did swallow. Hard, but he couldn't look away from her bright pink face. "A hook thing-e?"

"This is completely inappropriate," she muttered under her breath, turning her attention to his shoulder.

"I don't think so. I'm having fun. What kind of hook thingy?"

"You want to know?" Her eyes shifted and her chin went up a notch or two as she smoothed her fingers across her unruffled hair from her temple to bun-top. "It gets inserted up the anus, forcing a vict—I mean, a sub to stay still for her, um, Master."

He waited. She was going to say more, he was sure of it. At least he hoped she would as he was speechless at the moment.

"And don't look so shocked. I know a thing or two about your kind of kink, so you're not going to trip me up. I knew you'd pull something like this. Not very innovative. Kind of—" she shrugged, "—boring actually."

Boring? He tossed the item into the trunk and sighed. "Humor me, would you? There might be something in here that surprises you."

She inclined her head, and he inclined his right back before he jotted down her answer and then searched for another item. When he held it up, she said, "Nipple clamp."

He took note and held up the next.

"I don't get it. It's a clothes peg. A wooden clothes peg. What do you do with that?"

He could spend the next twenty minutes running down the list for her, but that would be counterproductive to his plan to make a fast exit, so he asked, "Is that your final answer?"

She studied him and then her eyes narrowed to slits. "Yes, Regis, I do believe it is."

He dropped the item back in the trunk, wrote down her answer and bent to get the last out.

All righty. Time for him to drop the last curtain call. Brandish the piece de resistance, as it were. "And what's this?"

Her eyes locked onto it and she didn't blink. Her lips parted though, as if she were going to say something, but then her gaze lifted and she glared at him.

He popped his brows.

She glared harder.

He was so close to freedom he could almost taste it.

"It's a double-ended dildo."

This time, as he returned the object into the wicker trunk, he worked hard to hide his shock. She was hardcore for a vanilla doll. And how fucking awesome was that? He couldn't let this end here. Thinking quickly he pointed.

"And this?"

He hadn't bothered to write down her last response. He'd do it after she gave him this one because there was no way he'd forget that answer.

"The trunk?"

He put the lid on tight and held it up. "Yeah."

"I don't know." She scooped the papers up off her lap and fanned herself with them. "It's your dirty basket. The trunk where you keep all your toys?"

He dropped it with a thud. He couldn't help it. Her pronouncement hit him like a jab to the gut. If the guys at the club knew a woman in his company thought he could keep all his toys in that puny little basket, they'd laugh their asses off. But she really wasn't a woman in his company, was she? He was more a guy in hers.

"Your turn."

"How did I do?"

He rolled his shoulders and grinned. "How about we'll tally up after I go through your test?"

Once Jaxx concluded she had no choice but to participate in his not-so-subtle way of getting out of the session, she threw all her efforts into nailing his test. The devious Dom tried to stump her, but she was wise to that. She knew about the lifestyle and the props within it. Albeit, some of his "props" looked a little retro, but what did she expect? He was trying to get the best of her.

Which was a shame as that wasn't going to happen if she could help it. She had some pretty awesome images here and could hardly wait to see what he had to say. Even if she was fully prepared for the usual discussion about vaginas, penises and breasts. And as to that, she had a whole slew of relevant "psychobabble"," as he called it, to introduce that was sure to entertain and impress him.

"I'll list my answers."

"That would be fine." She took a deep breath and flipped up the first image for him to see.

"*Tsk, tsk*. Mask of a fox." He shook his head.

Spying his disappointment, she hoped he wasn't going to do this the whole way through. After all, it was only fair. She'd been nice and accommodating when he conducted his. "What's the matter?"

"I told you I studied in college. I got paid to show those images over and over again to other students for course studies. I could ramble off without looking what the most popular non-sexual answers are. I thought you'd surprise me with something new."

His disgruntled expression was so endearing that it was hard to imagine him being a Dom. The idea of him wielding a whip wasn't taking. He looked too normal, handsome and completely put-out at the moment. The dominant alphas she read in her books were usually silent and brooding individuals which he wasn't.

Trying to keep a stern tone and failing miserably, she said, "Okay, hold your horses. I can cut the stack and get rid of the regulars. I do have a few surprises." And boy did she ever. She'd collected quite a number of unique and very stump-worthy images that most test studies had rejected. "Ready?"

"Sure."

"How about this?"

He immediately turned the page over on the clipboard and wrote his answer. When he was done he turned it around and said, "Fat guy sitting on a boulder with legs outstretched and big boots on."

She nodded, having to give it to him. "It does kind of look like that." Must have been a lucky guess. She tossed the page on top of the others she'd discarded and snapped the next page up. "How about this one?"

He wrote as he answered, "Two bears climbing a mountain."

She turned it around, squinted and frowned.

"And this one?"

"Batman kissing a mirror."

No. Way. She flipped it around and had a look. Dammit. "And this?"

He'd never get this one. No one ever did. It was impossible—

"I'd have to say Fred Flintstone spitting at his reflection in a pond."

Jaxx whipped it around and studied the image. He was right. The freaking guy was right. The hair, the nose, the pot belly. Jagged caveman ensemble. Even the spitting thing worked. What. The. Hell?

Wasn't a guy like him supposed to be thinking about other things? Breasts, vaginas or...well, maybe not penises, but still. Fred Flintstone and Batman?

"Are you sure that's all you see?" Now she was the one who was a little disappointed. The rest of what she had planned was fizzling fast.

He turned the clipboard her way and shook it. "I wrote it down."

It would figure. "What's the tally?"

He tapped the clipboard against his knee a couple of times before he stopped and asked, "Depends. How many answers did I get right, according to the crazy meter?"

She frowned, because he said it like she hadn't answered correctly on some of hers, but that couldn't be.

"All of them."

"Nice."

She sat forward in the chair. "Did I get some wrong?"

"Oh, yeah."

She could feel her eyes bugging out of her head. "I did? Like what?"

"Let's see." He pulled out the tape and turned it around in his hands. "You said glow-in-the-dark bondage tape."

She nodded.

He shook his head. "It's neon green duct tape."

"Really?"

"Yep. Came in handy when I helped my buddy's kid make lizard shapes for his book report. Aaron got five bonus points for creativity."

"I bet he did. Does it glow in the dark at least?"

"No." He went to toss it back in the trunk and then hesitated as he eyed her. "And trust me on this. If I go through the trouble of restraining my woman, I won't be enjoying my handiwork in the dark, that's for sure. Even if the ropes are glowing."

"Ropes?"

He dropped the roll in the trunk. "Yeah, or chains, cords, sometimes leather."

She wasn't going to be drawn into asking anything about that. Instead she silently waited until he pulled out the vibrator then said, "I was right about that one."

He frowned and pursed his lips. After a cursory scan of the clipboard only his eyes moved when he looked at her. "Wrong."

She ignored how handsome he was as a lock of hair fell forward to shade an eye and insisted, "How could I be wrong? You said it came with attachments."

"I said attachment. And it does." He angled the item so she could see the hole at the top. "An attachment known as a toothbrush."

One thing was clear. She'd lost a considerable edge here making assumptions and underestimating a man like him. She needed to forget about his made-up game. Put aside the concepts of winning or losing and start thinking about the motivation that prompted this little time waster. Why did he want out of these last two sessions so badly?

"I'm only going to say you're half wrong with this one though, because I've heard from some pretty reliable sources that when a woman's desperate enough...well—" he sat up and shook his head until that sexy wave of hair shot back off his forehead, "—you'd be right."

It took her a moment to realize that maybe he wasn't so much wasting time as he was trying to scare her away. She was going to press him about it, but then he dropped the electric toothbrush in the basket and lifted out the—

"You called this a hook-e-thing for anal play."

She swallowed and just as she was attempting a casual nod, she caught sight of her diplomas hanging on the wall behind him, and it hit her. She was treating him like a man she was attracted to and not the patient he was. She'd allowed him to put her on the defensive while he tackled her over and over again. Just like Maggie. The idea got her back up. "I did."

"You'd be wrong again."

"No."

He nodded and then turned the thing upside-down, which now that she looked at it was right-side up.

"This is an oiled bronze single robe hanger."

She met his challenging stare. He'd learn soon enough that she didn't scare easily. "A what-a-what?"

"A robe hanger. You put it on the back of a door like so—" he held it up, "—and you hang your bathrobe on it."

How convenient that before he'd held it upside-down and had covered the holes where the screws went to attach it. "You purposely misled me. Isn't that cheating?"

His eyes sparkled and lips twitched. "This isn't a game. It's a test. I did say it's all a matter of interpretation. If your mind weren't trolling in the red-light district, you might have seen this for what it was." She went to speak, but he held up his free hand. "Look, I don't want to argue about this. It's your office, after all, and you are the doctor, so we should just carry on. If you think you deserve a point for that one, then fine. You are now the owner of one spanking-new point."

Unbelievable. He bent and placed the hook in the basket before pulling out the clamps. Clearly he expected her to ignore the fact that he'd just used the brush-off tactic with an additional pile of bullshit.

"You said these were nipple clamps?"

"I...ah..."

"They're grips for computer parts."

How the hell was she supposed to have known that? She waited until he took out his next item before saying, "There is no way I got that wrong."

He tossed the clothes peg up in the air and caught it without taking his eyes off her. "If you'd gotten this one wrong, I'd be questioning the court's judgment in making me come here."

That observation was so off-the-cuff and deadpan she almost laughed. But then he ditched the peg and pulled out the dildo. Seeing it, her amusement fled.

"You said this was a double-ended dildo."

She tried to turn away. To not look, but it was like passing by a car wreck. No matter how hard she told herself she wasn't going to, she wound up staring.

"It's a dowel."

She blinked. She'd heard his words, but they weren't computing. Dowel? At the moment she had no idea what that meant. She was too caught up watching as he seductively massaged the glossy ball on one end of the thing. So distracted in fact that it took her a moment to realize he'd bent forward and tilted his head down to her line of vision. Her eyes colliding with his brought her to her senses.

"A what?"

"It's a dow-wel," he pronounced succinctly. "I use it to hang my hand towels on in the guest bath."

That got her attention. "That? You use that?" She pointed.

"Yeah." He held it up and turned it around while he closed one eye, examining it. "I know it looks kind of feminine, but my designer insisted, and when that guy insists—" he stopped eyeing it and turned his attention back to her, "—you have to agree, because he doesn't take any prisoners, if you know what I mean."

No, she didn't know what he meant. Designer? Prisoners? "Seriously? It's not a...you know."

He shook his head.

"It sure looks like one."

He let it roll down his thigh and when it got nearly to his knee, he jerked his leg and the object fell into the basket. "So, you've seen a lot of those, have you?"

She really hadn't. The truth was she never had, but he wasn't going to know it. "Sure."

Now he smiled. A big, you-are-so-full-of-shit smile she wanted to die. "Liar."

"It's true." She didn't know why she wanted to press this. Why she wanted to do something she never did and lie, but here she was, lying right through her teeth. "Just last week."

"You don't say." He crossed his arms over his chest as his head dropped to the right and then left. "What did you do with it?"

"I'm not telling you." She was thankful she didn't sputter. "I'm sure you know all about how two women make use of that." Her cheeks burned and she knew for sure they were the color of the red marker she'd been using earlier to outline her strategy with him. A strategy that had gone full steam ahead in the handcart to hell the second he'd carried in that trunk.

"Oh, I do know, and I'm sure you don't."

"But—"

"Because if you did, you'd know whether it was two women, men or a woman and a man, there has to be some flexibility."

Now he was insulting her? She smoothed her hands over her lap and remained calm. Elegant. She'd show him she was perfectly unflappable. "I'm open-minded and I can be more than flexible when it comes to discussing these types of things."

"Discussing?" Were his eyes twinkling again? They were. "I wasn't talking about discussing anything. I was talking about practical application." He snatched the item in question out of the trunk and grinned holding it out level in front of him. "Tell me, doc, how could two people enjoy this at the same time without breaking it or themselves? Why, they'd have to be a set of book ends to get this to work."

He had a good point there, now that she thought about it...although why she was even thinking about it was disturbing her more by the second. Especially when she saw the big picture. How the hell had he done it? He'd marched in here and taken over. Commandeering the lead role until she'd lost their test competition. The one thing she swore she wasn't going to let happen had. She'd given up ground to him and after examining the particulars, now she knew why. He was trying to unnerve her. Worse, he was using her anger to his advantage. He wanted her to be furious with not only him, but herself. And she was.

"Very clever. Are we done?"

"No." He tossed the dowel in the trunk, plunked the lid over the top and held it up. "Remember what you said this was?"

"Yeah." She pinned him with her best glacial stare. "Your toy chest."

"It's actually my magazine holder. I hate a messy place. This is where I keep them. As for my toy chest?" he chuckled, and the husky sound was sinister. Wicked. Attractive. "My equipment has its own room."

She snorted. She knew all about dungeons. She also knew Ramsey Taylor clearly didn't need a special room or the accompaniment of equipment to torture a person. "Congratulations. I see you've mastered the art of eliciting a cognitive response out of a subject. Impressive, but not very gallant, if you ask me. I suppose desperation to be somewhere else was a key factor? I hope so, at any rate, otherwise you're just plain cruel. So tell me, why was it so important for you to get out of these last appointments?" She reached down and collected the papers from her test. Straightening them, she said, "Clearly you are the saner one out of the two of us, so I'm sure you've got a good excuse at the ready."

She got up and put the stack of papers on the desk, continuing to pack things up without looking at him.

"I cheated."

She dropped her can of pens and whipped around. "You did?" Her heart pounded, even as her mind scrambled to come up with a plausible how.

"Yes. Don't you want to know how?"

She was dying to know. But the more sensible part of her was silently screaming, say no. Say NO. "Yes."

"Sit down, Jaxx, and I'll show you."

It was his tone. It went through her like a hot knife plunging into freshly churned butter. Melting parts of her while it slid in deep. She should have said no. She should have asked him to leave, but the intensity in his eyes, combined with the power that radiated around him, touched her in places that had been lonely for far too long. Parts of her that wanted to reach out and grasp whatever he was silently offering.

"It's Dr. Gavin," she whispered. Hating how soft and feminine her voice resonated in the stillness between them. Had he noticed?

Yes, he had, because he smiled. A real "I can see right through you" smile. "You should have just told me to fuck off and get the hell out of your office."

He was right of course. Clearing her throat she pretended she didn't hear what he'd said. "Show me? Maybe you should just tell me."

"Why? Are you nervous?"

The potency of the moment was gone and in its place came some semblance of reason. She wasn't going to let him run her off. Nor was she going to succumb to her old fears. The ones she'd worked so hard to conquer and he'd unearthed so quickly... *No. You've got this, Jaxx.* She did. She could handle him. "All right, Mr. Taylor." She sat in her chair and pushed her glasses against the bridge of her nose, looking up at him. "Show me."

His grin nearly blinded her. "I'd love to, but first I think it's time you call me Aries.

Chapter Four

Aries may have won the battle, but he'd lost the war. Given this, he had no idea why he was sticking around. His end-game with the test had been to get her riled enough to confront him. When she did he'd win and therefore have his out. It had been right there. Right in front of him and yet, here he was, standing with trunk in hands, ready to what? Mess with her some more?

Abso-fucking-lutely.

"I'm not going to call you Aries. Your friends call you that, and I'm not your friend." Jaxx pushed back against the chair so hard he feared it was going to swallow her up.

"I think someone's a sore loser."

She blew a stray lock of hair out of her eyes and stared at him. "I didn't lose, you cheated remember?"

He stepped to the desk and plunked down the trunk, right over her papers, before he took off the lid. Grabbing the hook and the tape, he turned to her. "Sit up straight, please."

"Why?"

"Okay, grasp this." He ignored her and held out the hook.

She took hold of it, but when he picked up the tape she let go, and his "robe hanger" dropped in a bounce on her lap. "What's with the tape?"

"I was going to do the show before the tell."

"With the tape and that hook?"

He held her gaze. "Yes."

"Normally I'd say, I don't think so, but in this case? I know so. You are not taping my hands to that hook."

"But I have to. It's the main attraction to my show."

"Well, the show's cancelled, as I happen to like my job." She pushed on her glasses and added, "And you know, it would be a shame for me to waste that one year of junior college and four years of regular college I completed in two to get here, just so you can be entertained for an hour."

Sarcasm. Refreshing. "You'd be entertained too. I promise."

She scooped the hook off her lap and tossed it to him. "I already am."

Catching it, he didn't take his eyes off her, saying, "I'm glad, but I can do better."

"I have no doubt of that, Mr. Taylor. You're a very resourceful guy."

She wasn't going to budge, he could tell. Huh. This was new for him. So what did he do now?

As if she read his thoughts, she sat forward and asked, "Why don't I entertain you first. How about, you let me do my show and tell, as it were, of your test results. I believe you said you wanted to possibly gain some insight from a professional like me." She reached around him and grabbed her clipboard off the desk. Checking a page she read. "You said that I could offer ideas and possibly improve your understanding of people because I might know better what makes them tick."

She was fishing. All right, he'd bite as he wanted to see where she was going with this. "I did say that."

She upended the clipboard and slid it between the side of the chair and the cushion. "Well, I can't improve your understanding of other people."

"No?"

She shook her head.

He was fighting hard not to grin. She was appealing in a nerdy, good-looking-woman-trying-to-downplay-her attractiveness kind of way. "Why? You weren't paying attention in class? Don't tell me you were one of those lazy females who slept with their professors to make their grades."

Her jaw dropped and her eyes widened. "I assure you. I came by my honors degree in psychology by conventional methods. No sleeping around for me." She looked away.

"That's a shame."

That had her glaring. "I simply meant that I couldn't give you an understanding of people I haven't met. But I can give you some insight into you, and that may lead you to a better understanding of the people in your life and how you deal with them."

Not exactly what he was hoping for, but he supposed he could work with it. "Okay. You can go first. But I still get to do mine after."

Her brows rose in such a belligerent know-it-all manner his palm literally itched to connect with her ass. And if she thought for one millisecond he wasn't getting his turn, she was in for a rude awakening.

"We'll see."

More like she'd see.

He pushed away from the desk and walked around behind it, landing in a *whoosh* in her chair as he rocked from side to side. "That would be fine. Proceed."

"I really don't understand why you have such an aversion to my couch. It's quite comfortable. More so than that chair."

He stilled and didn't say anything. He just stared at her, which made her squirm.

"Oh, fine. Suit yourself."

"I have." He smiled until he wound up grinning as she pointedly ignored him and carried on.

"Let's have a look at these." She pulled the images out from under his trunk and separated them. "The first was this one." She checked his answer on the clipboard. "You said, 'mask of a fox.'"

"Let's skip that one. It's too easy."

"Do I need to remind you about who's running the show at the present time?"

"No. That's a fine point you make." He inclined his head. "Because I don't want to be interrupted when it's my turn."

She scowled so hard her brows got lost behind the thick frame of her glasses. "Yes, well." Looking down at the image, she traced a hand over it. "A mask in any form represents transition."

"I disagree."

She shot a look up. "You didn't let me finish. But how can you disagree when a person who dons a mask instantly changes into something that they weren't before?"

"In some cultures or tribes, a mask symbolizes the opposite. It's the unchanging face of their ancestry." He leaned forward, encouraged by how engaged she was and listening to what he had to say. "To them, it's a totem of stability. A concrete link to their continuity as a culture. Quite simply, it's tangible proof of solid structure."

She frowned and bent closer. "So, you don't adhere to the belief that masks are the ultimate form of freedom for an individual?"

"I didn't say that. I only said that masks mean different things to different people, and for you to suggest that a mask only represents transition is a little narrow-minded in my opinion. But then, I'm not the doctor. You are."

She sat back. "As I was saying before you interrupted me the first time." She sent him a pointed glare, which he ignored. "A mask frees an individual of his self-consciousness. It gives way for a person to drop social-psychological constraints and be authentic to their nature."

"Amazing." He nodded. "You got all that from the fox?"

"Excuse me?"

"The—" he did an air circle in front of his face, "—fox mask image. And no, I don't think a mask loans itself to an individual being free. I think it's just the opposite. I think a mask gives an individual an opportunity to hide from himself. He isn't authentic when he puts on a mask. It's when he takes it off that he has to face reality."

"Ooh, very good."

She spent the next thirty minutes grilling him on his theory and finally when she stopped making notes, he figured it was a good time to ask, "What did you write?"

"A few things to discuss after we go through the rest of these. Now," she said as she held up the next image. "You said, 'fat guy on boulder with legs stretched out and big boots on.'"

"Yeah."

"Father issues."

"*Buzz.* Wrong. I loved my father."

She hugged the clipboard to her chest. "Issues don't always mean something negative, you know."

"To me, they do."

She dropped a hand on the stack of images and patted them. "With these, they don't."

"Too bad we won't find out until next week. We've gone over by half an hour. It's a good thing I'm your last appointment for the day."

"What? Half an hour? We did?"

"That's okay, but it's a shame to end now because I think I was close to a breakthrough." He put his palms on the desk and made to get up but then stopped. "Hey, why don't we finish the last half hour now? You'll get to pick what's left of my brain with the rest of the pictures, and I'll get to call my time with you as being completed."

She slowly sat back and eyed him over the rim of her glasses. "I suppose we could combine this and make this a two-hour session fulfilling the added requirements. Although—"

"Great." He leaned forward plowing ahead so she didn't have time to change her mind. "So, you were saying? About my issues?"

She hesitated and then blinked. "Right. You greatly respected the male role model in your life. I only assumed it was your father because of the boots."

"Why? They would have been better for him to kick my ass with?"

"No, although you probably could have used a good—I mean, ah..."

"I know what you meant. What I don't get are the boots."

"Oh, that, it's typical prodigal son imagery. You gave your respected male role model big boots. Meaning that you subconsciously know you'll have a hard time filling them while you live up to his expectations of you."

He let his head fall back as he stared at the ceiling. For no other reason than to contain the instant tightness that squeezed his chest. A whole world of grief was edging for some space and he wasn't going to let it in. Not now, maybe never. But then an image of his dad laughing as he thumped Aries on the back came to mind. And with that came a wonderful rush of pleasure he hadn't experienced in so long it made his eyes sting with the memory. A memory of how great he'd always felt when his dad was proud of him. The long missed sensation flooded to the forefront before he could stop it. Damn, it felt good and for just a stolen moment it was heartening.

Taking a deep breath, he let it out slowly. "Very impressive, Doctor Gavin. My father was an honorable man."

"And the third? You said two bears climbing a mountain?"

"I did."

"Sibling rivalry."

He inclined his head. She was right about that one too. Although the feelings this conjured were anything but pleasant.

"Now this one?" She held up the image and looked at it before she turned it so he could see it. "You said Batman kissing a mirror?"

"Yes."

"I'm going to have to change my initial thoughts about this one now that I know your theory about masks."

She was so adorable in her excitement. Her cheeks fused with heightened color, not a blush, but more a stain of pleasure. Those eyes though, they sparkled and shone with anticipation of sharing her thoughts and that had him aching to pull the pages out of her hands. To pluck her off that chair and drag her over the desk. He wanted so much to touch her. To get close to her that he had to work hard to give her a casual response. "Shoot."

"If, as you say, a mask is used to shield who you really are, then I have to say you wear one to hide that person from the world." She let go of the image and let it drop on her lap while she studied him. "You're comfortable doing this because you're fully aware of what you are hiding and why."

His heart rate picked up speed, so to counter it he focused in on breathing nice and even as he straightened. "And you got all that from Batman?"

"Yes."

Her curious eyes raked over him so thoroughly he feared he was going to crack and tell her how right she was. "Ridiculous."

"No, think about it. Batman's a superhero who successfully hides from the world. The mention of a mirror indicates that you're comfortable looking at yourself, even if the reflection isn't a true representation of who you are, but of how others see you."

She was good. He had to be careful. "Psychobabble."

When she smiled the space between them lit up all warm and golden like the dawn on a sunny day. "Well, here's some more for you. From my perspective I see this being directly related to your ah, sexual preferences."

He snorted and fell back in the chair. Wholly relieved that she was wrong in this instance at least. Really wrong.

"Hear me out."

"Why? So you can tell me that I wear a mask to hide the sexual deviant I am from the world?"

"No. I didn't say that. I…"

"You what?"

She seemed to brace herself. "I don't think you're as kinky as you think you are."

He stared at her, stunned. "Get the fuck out of here." He slapped his palm on the desk several times. "You're crazy. No offense. But that's right up there with little green aliens abducting cats and the gruesome ogre who lives under the bridge ransoming them back for his dinner. How the hell did you get this from that?" He jerked a thumb at the picture.

"There's no shame in it," she sniffed. "All kinds of people get caught up in things that snowball out of control. It's quite common to remain living in a lie of your own making. Especially when people depend on you. Oftentimes this forces a person to perpetuate the lie to accommodate them."

He scratched his head. "What does that mean? That I started my club when I thought I was kinky and it wasn't until after I hired people and got my membership up that I realized I wasn't?"

"Exactly. And now you're responsible for people's livelihoods as well as for providing a safe-haven for people of that…persuasion to explore their sexuality."

"Wrong."

"But—"

"Wrong. Next."

She shook her head. "The last one was Fred Flintstone spitting into a pond."

"I know, and I can hardly wait to hear this."

"Your response tells me that you can laugh at yourself."

He blinked. "That's it?"

"Isn't that enough for you?"

It wasn't, but before he could tell her so she shot forward.

"There was something I didn't mention regarding my personal theory of masks."

He plucked a pen out of the holder and beat it against the desktop not sure he was ready for this either.

"Protection."

He stopped beating. "As in armor?"

"Yes. In ancient times, a protective mask helped to circumvent possible physical harm from one's enemies. In these times? I think a protective mask helps circumvent possible emotional harm from society's mores and unrealistic conventions."

"Meaning?"

"Some masks are not only beneficial to the wearer, but to the people who depend upon that individual to wear them."

"Are you talking about my kink again?"

She grinned and he had to hold himself back. He wanted to sink his fingers in her hair and see how silky those strands were. "No, in this case I'm talking about Batman."

"The real Batman?"

"Absolutely. Think about it. If everyone in Gotham City knew Bruce Wayne was Batman, where would the fun, the mystique, the adventure be?" She leaned forward so her forearms were braced directly opposite his on the desk and whispered, "The reason to keep watching every week was to see if he was going to be unmasked." Mimicking the announcer's deep voice, she said, "Same bat time...same bat channel."

It wasn't until her words echoed to silence in the room that he noticed how close they were in proximity. How dark the cornflower blue color in her eyes had turned. How great she smelled and how badly he wanted to lean forward and taste her.

Jaxx felt the sexual pull. The erotic hum that gripped her as they stared at one another. The novelty of experiencing that kind of desire was shocking and before she could stop herself, her gaze dropped to his lips. He'd see her eyeing his mouth. She was sure of it. God, they were so close he'd probably hear how rapidly she breathed.

She didn't look up, knowing, if she did, she might not be able to resist the temptation. "I, ah, better get the paperwork signed. You probably have something important to do after this."

"Yes. Very important."

She nodded and stood, awkwardly waiting for him to vacate her chair so she could see to the form.

She filled in the required boxes and put her signature on it. "There. Here you go." She held it out, feeling more like herself now that their places were reversed and he was on the right side of her desk for a change. "It's all done. Your life is now officially free of my psychobabble."

He took the paper and examined it. "You're no longer my therapist?"

"No, I'm not."

He folded the form and put it in the wicker trunk. When he pulled out the hook, she frowned which deepened when he said, "Then I sort of feel bad about keeping you."

She eyed the hook and then shot a look up. "Keeping me?"

"Yeah, it's my turn for show and tell, remember? I guess we'll be doing it on regular civilian time. I don't mind." He winked at her. "In fact, this might make it more interesting."

Interesting? She gulped.

"Now," he said as he dug through the trunk, "where did I put that tape?"

Chapter Five

"What do you need the tape for?" Her eyes widened and she shook her head. "I thought you were leaving?"

Aries ignored her, knowing if he hesitated for even a second, it would give her the time to think and he was doing enough of that for the both of them right now. And that meant he wasn't going to leave. How could he when he had to learn the truth about her. Was she a fluke? She seemed like the perfect vanilla doll on the outside, but deep down, there was something that tempted him. Drew him. Taunted him in the rawest way possible. Why else was he getting all fox-up in her hen-house?

"You're staying? Why?"

"Yes," was all he said. He wasn't prepared to explain that it was time he confirmed that his suspicions about her were all wrong. That it was just his imagination because someone like her could never actually be a part of the world he wanted to create with the right woman. She wasn't the right woman. She couldn't be.

In order to find out though, he needed her to go along with his spur-of-the moment plan, and not to be thinking. Because even though he'd gotten exactly what he wanted—his freedom and that certificate—he couldn't let the matter go. The moment he'd chosen to stay, he knew he was going to finish this the way it needed to be finished between them.

"No, not like that." He adjusted the hook in her hands until she had hold of the base with the curved part facing down. "Like this." He didn't give her a chance to escape as he held his hands over hers. "Great, now hold your arms out straight, just...a little higher. Good."

"I don't—wait—" she tried to pull away, "—you're going to use the tape?"

He didn't stop but quickly continued to wind it around her wrists and hands, over and over until the hook was firmly held into place and she was unable to get free of it. "Sure. I'm binding your hands around the hook."

"I can see that. Ow. You're cutting off my circulation."

An actress. It was his lucky day. "No, I'm not." He stopped and looked at her. Without saying another word, he waited for the telltale blush. When it appeared, he shook his head because for some stupid reason, he really liked it when she blushed. Her eyes got all glassy and sparkled like raindrops in the sun.

He bent and bit the tape, tearing it before he patted down the edges. "There. Now stand up." He didn't wait for her to comply. Instead he helped her and when she was right in front of him—

"Hey, those are my glasses. I need them."

He twisted and tossed them beside the basket on the desk. "For what? Scaring children?" She opened her mouth, and he placed a finger over her lips. "And by children, I mean the male, six-foot-four kind. Are all the men you know frightened away so easily?"

Her glittering eyes narrowed, and he grinned.

"Fortunately it takes more than Woody Allan frames and a clipboard to run me off. But even if I were ready to bolt, I wouldn't be going anywhere. Not until I get my turn. You promised."

"You can't be serious."

He stepped toward her, and she automatically stepped back. Nearly falling into the chair, but he caught the hook and pulled her into him until her folded arms were the only things between them. Keeping a grip on her elbows, just in case she decided to use the hook as a weapon, he looked down.

"I'm very serious. Tell me, why isn't there a man in your life?"

When her attempt to disengage failed, she readjusted and put as much distance between them as she could. Which really wasn't much at all. "Not that it's any of your business, but there is."

He smiled. Every single time she attempted to lie to him, she blushed like a virgin in a whorehouse.

"I happen to know there isn't and I want to know why."

"I prefer women. The dildo, remember?"

It wasn't the words that made him laugh, but the way she announced them. Confident, emphatic and steady, and yet her face turned the color of a bright red chili pepper. Scratch the virgin analogy. A nun in a whorehouse would fit better. Her blush-o-meter was coming in handy. It gave him one less facet of her he had to figure out. Though, why he wanted to figure out anything about her remained a mystery.

That sobered him. "You preferring women? Is as ridiculous a notion as I only used the duct tape to make geckos."

She hissed in a breath and this time really struggled to break free of him. "I knew it. It is bondage tape."

"Settle down." He chuckled and gave her gentle shake. "The quicker you do this, the quicker we'll be over with my show and tell."

She stopped. "But there's virtually no point to it. We're done."

"You think so? I don't."

She stomped on his foot.

"Hey, hey. Take it easy. By your own admission, I'm the saner one of the two of us."

"But you cheated."

"So?"

"This isn't right."

"You promised." That second reminder got her attention, so he added more quietly, "It's my turn. Let me show you."

He grasped the hook and pulled it up until it was over her head and her arms bracketed her ears. He didn't look at her as he knew she was glaring at him. Instead, he made short work of clipping the computer clamps on the front of her blouse.

She gasped. "How-how dare you?"

"Oh, relax, would you? They're clipped to the material, not your skin. And you're welcome, because I've tested these suckers on myself and they have a bite to them."

"You-you—"

"I'm being careful with the silk. See?" He plucked on one of them that pinched the fabric right over a spiked nipple to show her. Ignoring her growl as he let go of it and felt around inside the trunk for the clothes pegs. When he found them, he immediately lined three to pinch the material across the front of her skirt at lap level.

"What the hell do you think you're doing? You can't to do this. I'm a doctor."

"I can. I'm a doctor too."

"You are not."

"'Fraid so. Honorary degree from Dr. X's school for nymphomaniacs."

"You made that up."

"Unfortunately I did not. It's accredited. The director is a member of my club."

"Let go."

"Why? You wanted me to show you how I cheated, right?" He had the roll of tape around his wrist like a bracelet and shifted to stuff the electric toothbrush in one back pocket and the dowel in the other before he eyed her. "That's what I'm doing."

"Let. Me. Go!" She attempted to yank her arms down.

"I wouldn't pull like that if I were you. You might herniate a disc or something."

"Ooh!"

"Jaxx."

"It's Doctor Gavin."

"Given the circumstances, it should be honey."

"Honey? Have you lost your mind?"

Chuckling, he tweaked her nose. "No, honey, have you?"

When she stilled and stared up at him the chuckle died in his throat. Her bright eyes, pink cheeks and glistening lips were a helluva temptation, but he fought it off. Kissing her wasn't part of the plan. Fuck, he didn't even have a plan. He was just working on instinct. A dangerous thing to do, but he couldn't help it. Between the delicate beauty that she tried to camouflage, the battle of wits that crackled to life between them every time they spoke and his dream, he needed to test the waters with her. See for himself what the hell was happening here. If he was right about her. If... Shit. Although he'd tried to deny it, ignore it, he'd been hotter in her company during these last two hours than he'd been during an intense Scene a few months ago, when he'd had a trio of willing women working in unison to satisfy his every need.

That was the funny thing about needs. One could never predict them.

He didn't say a word, just curled down over her. Bending her back, stretching her, forcing her hips to flex into his while he came in close. He felt the dig of the clamps and the pegs against him and when he pressed her into him harder and heard her moan, he knew she felt them too. This was wrong on so many levels but one, and that was the one he concentrated on now. "You promised I'd get a chance to do my show and tell. Are you reneging, Jaxx?"

She smelled like lemon with an undercurrent of ginger. He fucking loved ginger. He breathed in.

"It's...it's Dr. Gavin."

"Not anymore." He searched her face. "Tell me." He kept his tone soft and encouraging, "Tell me you're not going to break the promise you made to me."

"I..."

He pulled her in even tighter, and she shivered. God, he liked the feel of that little shake against him. It reminded him of his dream. "Don't break your promise to me, Jaxx. Don't."

She swallowed loud enough for him to hear and then closed her eyes, a sure sign she was giving in. "I won't. All-all right. You can have your turn."

The breath rushed out of him and an acute sense of pleasure stirred heating his blood. Christ, this kind of win was epic. How long had it been since he'd had to earn the right to a woman's submission? He couldn't remember. Especially from a strong and feisty woman like her.

She was so close to him. Only a mere inch separated their lips. His weight shifted and all he wanted to do was go with it. Dip down. Taste her, but he didn't want to scare her too soon. She might be smart and strong, yet there was an underlying edge to her. She was a woman who needed to be pushed. Carefully. With that in mind, he straightened and before she had a chance to regroup or he could change his mind, he pulled her to the closet. He let go of her for just a second and opened the raised panel door to look inside. Spotting a lone pair of shoes, he grabbed one of them and wedged it under the door until the door was stable.

"What are you doing?"

"The show part before the tell." He grabbed the hook and pulled.

"Wait, I—oh, no you don't. I'm not going to be hung like some Christmas wreath."

"Stop fighting. You're going to hurt yourself." He brought her arms up and gave her an encouraging push toward the door with his hip. "I'm not going to hang you. I'm placing you. See?" He set the hook over the top of the door so she was effectively captured and then stepped back. "You're still touching the ground."

"Barely," she spoke against the wood. Her warm breath fogged the high polished grain, while she teetered on tiptoes. "You completed the sessions. You don't have to do this. Really. I get the point. You can stop now."

He wished he could. In fact, he really wished he hadn't started this at all, but it was too late to turn back. Between him fantasizing about her and their conversation today, he was the one who was hooked. That brought him up short as he wondered what kind of psychoanalysis field day she'd have with that one. *Just get her out of your system.* And in the process he'd scare her enough that she'll be forced to push back and they'd both be free of this odd attraction. It was as simple as that.

Simple?

It was this kind of spur-of-the-moment shit that got him into the numerous problems he currently faced. He should have participated in group sessions. He should have made shit up to satisfy her until the six sessions were up. That was what he should have done. One look at her squirming ass, and he was reminded why that wasn't possible. From day one he wanted her all to himself.

Fuck.

Jaxx tried to stay focused on the moment, but remembering how he'd felt against her kept distracting her. She'd burned from the inside out. She'd never experienced anything like that before. Brief though it was, it had been an electric embrace that sent currents of lust through flesh, blood, down deep to bone. It had a power all its own that had wrapped around her. All consuming. She wouldn't have believed the simple action could turn so complicated in the blink of an eye, but it had.

He might not be her patient anymore, so that was one huge stress over with, but now she faced another—her modesty being challenged at a time when she could least afford to be tested. And yet for all of that, her only thought was of how great he smelled and how good the hard parts of him felt when he pressed into her. Parts of him as hard as the door, only much warmer. Much more inviting.

"Stay still."

She heard the screech of tape being pulled and automatically stiffened. "Now what are you going to do with the tape?"

"You'll see. Lean forward."

Forward? If she went any more forward, the computer clips and clothes pegs would make perfect impressions into her skin, despite the material between them. "I can't—hey!"

His hand splayed flat on her ass and he pushed while he stretched a length of tape from the edge of the door across the empty width to her right, over her ass, to the width of door on her left until he reached the other edge.

"You can't tape me to the door."

"I think I can."

"But—ow." She'd tried to turn her head to see if he was getting another length of tape and banged her chin so hard her eyes watered. Then she heard the tear of tape being unwound and forgot about her pain. "I'll scream."

"No, you won't." He spoke low from right behind her. She felt him stick this second length of tape right over the first one. "You're going to be good." That soft statement made her shiver. "Besides, your neighbor, Dr. Dragon Lady might hear. I'm no expert, but it could be awkward for you both."

She frowned. "What about you?"

"I'm pretty much shameless, so no need to worry about me. Scream away. You wouldn't be the first female in my company to make noise."

Closing her eyes, she pressed her cheek against the cool wood and tried again. "Okay, like I said before, you made your point." More tearing. "Oh, for the love of God, stop with the tape already."

He didn't, and by her count there were five lengths pinning her tightly into place.

"One more for good luck."

"Seriously?"

He got the last length stretched over her, patted it into place on the door but smoothed it with a lazy and intimate hand-drag over her ass. "There. Now what do you think the point of me doing this is?"

Finally, he was going to be reasonable, and maybe she wouldn't wind up doing something with him she'd regret. "I'm insecure, which makes me a poor therapist. That's the point of this, isn't it? I let you control the sessions, and now you're driving your point home. In your mind, if I weren't so unsure of myself I would have stuck with my original answers and called bullshit on you. Like I should have done." The last part of those words came out in an unintentional grumble.

He remained silent while he rubbed his hand back and forth over the tape on her ass several times. Heating her up so badly, if she weren't glued into place like a bug on a pest strip, she would have shifted into his touch.

"*Tsk, tsk.* You give me far too much credit. Those are valid thoughts, but they're not mine."

"No?"

"No." He pressed his body against her, the heat of his chest branding her back. "The point of this little show and tell was to render you helpless. Do you want to know why?"

She swallowed hard as her mind raced with possibilities. "Why?"

The whisper of his breath against her ear sent a shiver skating through her. "So I can make you come."

This time, when she turned her head and banged her chin on the corner of one of the raised panels in the door, she didn't even blink. He didn't really just say that, did he? He couldn't be that bold—her heart pounded—maybe he was, or... "Come where?"

"Here."

She gasped when he slid the barrel of the electric tooth brush between her and the door. Pushing it down and down some more until it was wedged tight and horizontally across her groin. The tops of the three inline clothes pegs acted as shelf. He was clever and creative, and bold didn't even begin to describe what else he was.

"You coming for me wasn't far from every thought during group sessions. But now that we're alone? You coming for me again and again is all I can think of."

"Y-you can't do this."

"By now you should know I'm a can-do kind of a guy."

He sure was. In a flash he found the on switch and flicked it. She was shocked, outraged, speechless and instantly aroused. The heavy vibrations beat straight through her. Right to the core.

She tried to move to dislodge it but couldn't. "Turn it off."

"Say please," he breathed into her ear.

"Please."

"No."

No? He was denying her after he'd told her to say it and she did? "B-but I said please."

"Yes." The heat of his lips penetrated the skin at her nape. "And I loved hearing it. Say it again."

"No...I—"

"Stop thinking. Stop fighting your instincts. Just breathe. Relax and breathe."

He pushed into her in such a way that her breasts rubbed against the computer clamps and her nipples tingled and puckered even harder than they were before.

"I shouldn't—"

"Shhh."

When he pressed his mouth into the fine hairs at the back of her neck, just below her upsweep, her knees almost buckled. Her legs shook and before she could stop herself, she moaned. The desire she'd be denying for so long was dying to show itself.

"Close your eyes. That's right. Breathe."

She quivered as he dipped his head and licked the pulse point at the base of her throat. And when he opened his mouth and softly bit her there, she lost what little control she had left.

"Please..."

The vibrations skittering through the muscles between her legs, combined with the heat of him pressing into her back was bad enough. But then he forced her legs to spread and used the dowel. Rolling a glassy end up, from the inside of her one knee to her upper thigh, before he switched sides and did the same on the other limb. Going so slow and coming so close to her center on each upward draw that she trembled and ached with anticipation of that touch arriving higher. Over and over he stroked in an unhurried pace, melting her insides as she burned. And when his mouth opened again and he tasted her skin and his teeth softly bit into her...she couldn't breathe. She couldn't move. All she could do was sink deeper. Fall faster toward the craving of wanting, no needing more.

Her pulse raced and her heart beat just as furiously against her rib cage. A flutter that turned more to an ache rolled up from her toes, to her knees, landing in a crash of mind-blowing euphoria deep inside her. Deep, but low in her belly, where it spread and stroked until she let go of every thought, every care, and rode the swelling wave upward as it pushed her higher and higher.

"Oh, God..."

"Breathe, honey. Don't forget to breathe."

His husky whisper sounded like a dream. The words penetrated her consciousness, making her shiver and then, when she did comply and drew in a rush of air, her whole world opened up. Light came into her from all sides warming her. Until a swell of raw lust crested, causing her breasts to tingle almost as if they were being stroked by his hands. The flesh between her legs ached and wept, wanting—dying for his touch.

"That's right."

He used his hand, the flat of his palm against her bottom, and pushed in a motion that mimicked a pump or a flex. Whatever it was, it was enough. Too much. On the third press, her tightly wound muscles were ready to unravel. They convulsed once, twice and then let go.

"Ahhh..." It felt good to give in. To breathe. To let nothing in but the light and the pleasurable sensations as her whole body shook.

And when she came, it was hard. Hot. And very, very wet against the satin of her panties.

She didn't want the floating sensation to disappear as she drifted back to earth, so she kept her eyes closed and continued to relax. Enjoying the ebbing tide of adrenaline as parts of her sputtered and sparked with need of wanting more. Those lonely parts of her still ached to touch and be touched by him, despite the release he'd just given her. And she was so caught up examining those things she barely noticed he'd unwound her hands and taken away the hook until her arms slid down the cool wood. Until her fingers laced together, and she tucked them under her cheek as cushion.

With the computer clamps and clothes pegs gone, she sank fully against the door. Sighing with a mixture of relief and despair as the steady vibrations suddenly ended. She didn't even protest from the zip of the tape being removed. She was too caught up in amazement. She'd just had an orgasm with a man— a staggering enough occurrence, because she had difficulty bringing herself to orgasm—but more stunning was the fact that Ramsey had gotten her off in less than five minutes. Probably closer to three.

"Are you all right?"

Her eyes snapped open, and the one word that came to her was no. Because now that she knew it was possible, she wanted more.

Chapter Six

Aries forced himself to turn away. He had to put his stuff back in the trunk. Fast. And when he did, he noticed how steadily his hands shook. The urge to get them back on her was nearly killing him. None of this was supposed to have happened. Not him staying. Not him pushing and certainly not her allowing him to push her. She submitted and so beautifully too. Just like in his dream.

But this wasn't a dream and if he weren't careful it could turn out to be a nightmare. Right. *Deep breath and deal with this the way you should have from the beginning.*

He turned, expecting to be greeted by a confused and possibly pissed off woman, so when he saw Jaxx still hugging the door, he frowned. Come to think of it, she hadn't answered him either. That wasn't good.

"Jaxx?"

Not good was the perfect description of the intense expression on her face when she pushed off the door and came at him. Her slight frame crashing into him barely ruffled his shirt, but when he realized she was trying to be amorous, he had no choice. Fuck choice. He had no strength to deal, so he went with it. He fell back against the desk and pulled her with him. A good thing, because she began climbing him.

"Whoa, that's skin." He tried to get her attention before she drew blood. It was no use, though. She was too busy pulling at him. "If you—"

Before he could get the rest of those words out, she latched on to his mouth. If he had to describe what she was doing to he'd say devouring it. Then after a moment he wasn't thinking at all.

Crisp lemon and hot ginger assaulted his senses. Warm silk and delicate satin wrapped around him. Her desire poured over him. The frantic pulls, desperate tugs and sweetly surrendered hug tempted him like he'd never been tempted before. Her fingers sank into his hair while she massaged his scalp. And when that didn't seem good enough for her, she shifted and pressed into him tight, while her mouth sliced over his again and again. At one point he was afraid she might swallow his tongue. Damn, she was aggressive. Needy. Fucking spectacular as she ate on him.

He didn't even wince when she repositioned. Now her hands were braced against his chest, fingernails digging into his pecs as she shimmied all over him. That sexy little dance got him even harder, and that occurrence clearly had her curious. She flexed and felt the hardness with her hip. He could tell because she pressed against him twice before she angled a hand down to frantically find the outline of him with her palm. When she did, she closed her hand around him at the base and traveled in a series of graduating touchy-feely squeezes along his length. One, squeeze, two squeezes—she hesitated—three squeezes and when she went farther and reached the end of him, her whole body stiffened before she tore her lips from his, whispering, "I want to feel it again. Please."

At first he thought she was talking about the length of his cock, but then her meaning registered. "You want to get off again?"

"Yes."

That groaned-out word almost got him coming. "Spread your legs around me." He hauled her up higher until her knees bent against his hips. His hand had barely gotten beneath the hem of her skirt when she smacked his shoulder.

"Oh. It's not working."

"Not working?"

"Don't do it like that. Do it like…"

He didn't mean to. It was instinct when he speared a hand in her hair and sharply pulled back to gain her attention. No woman in his arms ever made demands or directed him to do things differently. "What?"

"Mmm," she purred, and he realized she'd gone languid with the hold he had on her. "Yeah, like that."

He tightened his grasp and sucked in air when he saw it. That fucking sexy tremble. He looked at his white knuckles buried in her hair, and adrenaline bolted through him. One last test to make sure he was right about this. He lifted, straightening his arm, which forced more painful tension on her skull.

She closed her eyes and moaned in such a way it left not a doubt in his mind. The attraction was real. She wasn't a vanilla doll. She was his kind of chick.

He drank in every line of her face. Noticed every subtle nuance as she purred for more and that was bad news for him because he really couldn't resist.

She moaned again. Oh yeah, she liked it.

Another moan.

Screw just liking it. She loved this kind of attention. No wonder she hadn't screamed bloody murder when he'd ambushed her earlier. "Jaxx."

Trill.

Her eyes popped open and she blinked. As the haze lifted, he read the dawning panic loud and clear. If he didn't let go of her, she'd probably scalp herself running away.

"The bell. The door. I mean, there's a delivery." She leaned and snatched up her glasses, shoving them on. Only she braced her elbows into his solar plexus to do it and the action caused him to grunt.

"Sorry about that." She had her Woody Allens back on and awkwardly pushed off him in a half-roll stumble move.

By the time he stood and readjusted himself, she had her back turned toward him, and that's when he noticed her hair. Long. It was really long. Down to the center of her back. She'd had it clipped up before he'd dug his hand into it, so even then it was hard to gauge, but now it wasn't. It was thick and wavy. Threaded with gold, copper and silvery blonde highlights. Beautiful. He willed her to turn around so he could see those cornflower blue eyes framed by all that rich, unobstructed brilliance. Jesus, he bet she'd be stunning.

"Jaxx?"

"It's—" she cleared her throat but didn't move, "—Doctor Gavin and our, um, time is done."

"Don't be shy. Turn around and talk to me."

"Why, so you can tell me what an awful therapist I am?"

"Jaxx."

She shook her head, and the action sent those ribbons of silk swaying. It was hypnotizing.

He waited for the swinging to stop. "I realize you're upset."

She shook her head.

"You're not upset? Mad, then?"

She nodded.

He tilted his head. "At me?"

She shook her head again and reached out to peel a bit of leftover tape from the door.

"At yourself?"

She nodded, and he grinned. He loved a woman who took responsibility for her actions. But what action was she mad at? Caving into him when he had her hooked, or diving on him the first chance she got? Didn't she know she had no choice? He'd stacked the cards in his favor and played them. Now he felt bad.

He went to her. "Honey," he whispered, grasping her by the shoulders. His plan was to make her turn around so they could talk and he could explain, but then she sank back against him and he forgot all about the plan. The action was so reminiscent of his dream, he nearly stepped back.

"Please. Please don't call me that."

"Why?"

"Because it makes me want to ask you to stay, when what I'm going to do is tell you to go. It's best if you leave before we have a complicated mess on our hands."

He had nothing to say to this because she was right. This, whatever it was between them, was a complication he didn't need in his life right now. And judging by her firm resolve to not turn and face him, she felt the same way. Shouldn't he be experiencing a sense of relief that she wasn't looking for more from him? Shit. It was precisely because she wasn't that he was bothered.

"Yeah, I'd better go."

She nodded and leaned away from him, and illogical though it was, he had the desire to pull her back against him. To continue where they'd left off. The need to do that burned like a bitch, so he was glad that she hadn't turned around. It was safer for both of them this way. He was beginning to think that dream had been a warning not to mess with her, and what had he done?

The bell rang again and he noticed her shoulders slump. The fury he felt over this surprised him. It also made him realize he couldn't leave without saying his peace. "That's not a delivery. It's Carmichael sending you a message, isn't it?"

"Yes." Her voice was barely a whisper. "She's probably wondering why you're still here."

He thought about all the phone calls during sessions and now the ringing bell and scowled. "Before I go, promise me one thing."

"What?"

Her shaky tone made him feel like absolute shit. "Promise me you'll deal with The Dragon Lady sooner than later."

Silence.

"Please."

"I-I will."

"Goodbye Jaxx."

Jaxx nearly wilted when he was gone. Taking a deep breath, she calmed her racing heart. What the hell was she doing? No, what had she done? Some therapist she was. She bent and pulled the shoe out from under the door throwing it inside the closet harder than she intended. It bounced off the interior wall then came back and hit her in the shin.

"Ow!" Without hesitation, she kicked the runner in and slammed the door with a resounding bang.

"Bad session?"

Spinning around, she scowled at Maggie, who had just come into her office. "The worst." She wasn't going to sugarcoat things. She'd meant her promise to Ramsey. It was high time she dealt with her friend. "After more than a month of doing as you suggested and denying my attraction to him, I folded. Gave in. Gave up." She nodded. "And I'm pretty sure I broke a couple of personal tenets and even if I didn't, I'd definitely lose your respect if you knew what I did on that desk."

Maggie stopped short and stiffened. "Did you have sexual relations with Mr. Taylor on it?"

She reminded Jaxx of a slightly younger Diane Keaton. She had the same kind of hair and always wore a turtleneck, regardless of the time of year. "Well, no, but I almost did, so I think that counts."

Maggie inclined her head and walked in that elegant way of hers. The royal glide that Jaxx envied. When she got to the upholstered rocker, she eased into it. Slow and measured movements. "Tell me everything. And for Pete's sake, fix your hair. No one is going to take you seriously when you look like a gypsy."

Jaxx shucked off her shoes and bent under the desk to grab her slippers. When she stood with them in hand, she used one as a pointer and said, "I'll tell you one thing. I'm never going to see that guy again. No way. It's completely insane. Even now I'm aching in parts of my body that are—it's not good or decent to be feeling tingles... So when he comes back here, you're going to have to handle him."

"How do you know he'll be back?"

She plunked a hand down on his trunk. "He'll be back for this."

"All right. Then it will be my pleasure to see that he gets it. So tell me what happened."

"I'm not sure." She dropped her slippers in front of her and wiggled her right foot into one. "One moment we were swapping Rorschach tests, and the next I was stretched out against the open closet door, and he was..."

"Yes?"

She got her second slipper on and scowled. "The guy's fast and clever. I, um, you know, and then when he un-taped me—"

"Un-taped?" Maggie sat up straight

"Yes, it's a long story. But all you need to know right now is that I screwed up. That little voice in my head? You know the one. Well, it was very convincing this time and you know how hard I've been working to silence that chatter."

Maggie nodded and frowned.

"Not to worry, though. I think it's safe to say I ripped out its tongue before I almost ripped out his with my teeth. Oh, God." She thought about her hand traveling along his length and what she'd said to him, and fell into her desk chair with a wail. "I made a huge fool of myself."

"How?"

"I lost control. I lost my head. Worse? I'd do it all over again if I could."

"With the sex club owner? I knew this was going to happen. I told you not to do the one-on-one sessions. Jaxx." Jaxx heard her disappointment loud and clear.

"The man is—he's...too hard to describe."

"In my day, we used to call a guy who looked like him a heartthrob."

"Oh, God, don't remind me of his looks."

"So, it's his tall, muscular frame that's attracted you?"

"Ugh, don't add more fuel to the fire I've already got going on over him. I was trying to forget about his to-die-for body."

Maggie sat forward. "If it isn't his looks or his body that you're attracted to, what then?"

"His brain."

"Oh, dear."

"Exactly. He's got a fabulous mind. I can only imagine..."

"Yes?"

"You already know I've been fantasizing about him since after our first session. And now that he's no longer my patient? I want him." She felt the burn of her blush all the way from her forehead to her breasts and cringed.

Maggie scowled and looked away.

"More than anything. Anything else." Jaxx hoped Maggie would understand what she was saying. Admitting.

"Oh." Then her friend did a double-take. "Oh, no."

Despite how nervous Jaxx was about tackling the issue, she knew it was now or never. Aries was right about her needing to standup to Maggie. And, the more she thought about this, she came to see intentional or not, he'd given her the perfect excuse to open a dialogue. "I'm sorry, Maggie. I've made a mess of things, haven't I? The hard work and all your planning? Ruined. I can't—"

"Now don't get ahead of things. And don't be too hard on yourself. Gunther's not here yet, so not to worry." Maggie reached out and patted her hand.

"There's something else."

Maggie drew back. "What?"

No sugar-coating it, Jaxx. "Things were very intimate between us."

Maggie's eyes narrowed. "How intimate?"

"Very."

"Jaxx."

"I had—" she braced herself for the fallout, "—an orgasm with Ramsey Taylor."

Maggie didn't blink. "Are you sure?"

What kind of question was that? "Of course, and now that I know I don't have a problem that way? Well, it changes everything. You see that, don't you?"

Maggie held up her hand. "Wait. Before you commit to making a decision based on one little—"

"It wasn't little."

"On one encounter, I urge you to think about this. While the sex therapist in me is glad that you've had an epiphany of some sort, the woman in me wonders whether this little miracle had anything to do with Mr. Taylor at all. Maybe your subconscious forced it to happen so you wouldn't feel guilty if you didn't like Gunther. You've been stressing about his arrival for months now."

Leave it to Maggie to save the day. "Well, do you blame me? You've been talking me up to that guy. He probably thinks I'm Sofia Vergara's twin. I can't compete with that."

"Don't be ridiculous. We just need to get you settled, is all." More to herself than to Jaxx, she said, "Quickly, by the sound of things."

This is what Maggie always fell back on. Jaxx settling. And she knew why. Maggie held the belief that children were a product of their upbringing and as such she was determined to make things right. In Maggie's mind, Jaxx had grown up with her adopted family, learning and taking on some of their behaviors. Mostly from her father, why else would she be attracted to the wrong kind of men? And, since Maggie had known her birth mother she was set on Jaxx being more sensible like her, and less head-strong and foolish, like the people who wound up raising her. When Jaxx thought about what she'd just done with Ramsey? She was almost ready to concede that in this instance maybe Maggie was right.

But then she thought about the last time she did that and scowled. Letting Maggie push her into being with the "right kind of guy" had been disastrous. Yeah, agreeing to settle had cost her all right. Two years wasted on mundane and boring and how had that eventually ended? She winced at the recall and then said, "I appreciate you trying to help me out, but I don't think I'm that desperate, that I need to dangle the prospect of obtaining a green card in front of guy just to get him to like me."

"He's not just a guy. He's the perfect man for you. You'll see."

Jaxx did what she usually did when Maggie was pushing her in the wrong direction. She remained silent and just stared.

Maggie may have waved offhandedly, but Jaxx knew she was anything but over the topic. "All right. You're getting your back up so we'll talk about Gunther later. Instead, tell me more about Mr. Taylor."

"I think I've said enough."

"Nonsense. I can tell you're worried about something and I know what it is. He gave you pleasure when no man ever has. So what?"

"So what? It happened, okay? And in the process, I made a huge fool of myself. I actually dove on him. What a desperate ass I am."

"No, you're not. You just overcompensated. You're inexperienced when it comes to men. This kind of thing is bound to happen from time to time."

Jaxx sagged forward and banged her head on the desk. "What was I thinking?"

"You weren't. That's the problem."

She sat up, and tried not to grumble, "He's a really good—he's got a great mouth. What am I going to do if I can't get him out of my head? You have no idea how hard it was to let him go and then not to go after him."

For the first time in their conversation Maggie looked worried. "Out of your head? You're that attracted to him?"

She nodded. "I can't even think straight."

Now Maggie scowled as reached out, only this time to pull a small piece of tape off Jaxx's blouse. She brought it closer to examine, started rolling it up and then looked her right in the eyes. "Well, fortunately my thinking is crystal clear. I will be the one to make sure he gets his stuff back while I make the much needed arrangements."

Jaxx knew what that meant. "No. No more plans, okay?"

"It's a simple one to cure your inappropriate crush so you can put the dread away."

Jaxx thought about why she'd responded to Ramsey, and that truth scared the hell out of her. If Maggie ever found out she'd be looking for Jaxx to do therapy which wasn't going to happen. "I don't think there's an easy cure to what I have."

"Then there's nothing to lose trying. It's nothing crazy. When I meet with Mr. Taylor and give him his things, I'll arrange for a vanilla's version of exposure therapy. It's bound to solve the problem."

Jaxx's heart skipped a beat. Maggie had come close to nailing what really had her worried. "You know about vanilla?"

"I know a lot of things that might surprise you." She dropped the tiny, balled-up piece of tape on the desk and sighed. "One thing I'm fairly positive about is that this attraction of yours has more to do with the stress over Gunther's imminent arrival than Mr. Taylor being 'the one'. And I'm going to prove it to you."

"How?"

"You need to spend more time with him."

"Oh, no." She fell back in her chair and when she swiveled she immediately got a visual of him doing the same thing and stopped. Damn.

"Just a few hours. A time where you're not in charge and he's not charming you to get that certificate. Clarity is what you need. These other issues were in the way, clouding the experience. Trust me."

Jaxx wasn't sure about that, because he really wasn't very charming. Especially when he was taping her up—but then, maybe there was a certain charm in a guy being that confident. "I don't know. I'd be surprised if he'd agree."

"He'll agree. Don't worry about that. Just leave it up to me."

It was this that had Jaxx worried.

*****

Aries turned his phone on as he got into his Escalade. He had three missed calls. All from Shar. No doubt she wanted to discuss her ludicrous plans of setting him up with her married sister. That wasn't going to happen. At the end of the month, if he had to go it alone to the company year-end and beg Gabe to agree he would. That is if his brother didn't lock him out again.

Slowly he reversed out of the duplex drive, but when he saw a shadow pass behind the frosted double front doors, he put his foot on the break. Was that The Dragon Lady heading down to Jaxx's office? What would Jaxx tell her about their extended session? What would she share?

Probably everything. Dr. Margaret Carmichael had some kind of hold over her. When Jaxx was herself and not kowtowing to her boss, she was a refreshingly unusual woman. But the fire-breather was into crushing—maybe crushing wasn't the right word, controlling her, which was bad enough, but she was also attempting to turn her into ordinary. Which was a damn shame.

Recalling their banter, he found himself smiling. A smile that turned to a grin when he remembered how dramatic Jaxx was with the "ow's". But then he imagined the feel of her hand squeezing the length of him and slowly that length even now began to grow. He went with his lust-fueled thoughts until a visual of her savoring the tug he'd given her hair arrived and suddenly he wasn't smiling anymore.

Jaxx wanted to explore and he wanted to let her.

Fuck. This wasn't the time. He had things he had to do.

He hadn't said anything to Shar, but he did want that warehouse space next to The Egyptian. In fact, he'd already conditionally purchased it. Not for the purpose of expanding the club, but to complete the ownership of the whole twelve-unit parcel that was zoned as flex-space. With this last piece in his portfolio, he'd be able to do what he wanted with the complex providing his brother signed off, and he had big plans. Huge plans that came with a price that even he couldn't afford without leveraging most of his capital. So, although he hadn't needed to tap that for the purchase itself, he'd definitely needed to draw on it for what he wanted to do with the conversion. These plans were what he needed to concentrate on now. Not a blonde-haired brainiac with purple eyes.

This decided, he mulled over various business ideas until he turned the corner on his cul-de-sac and saw his neighbor's grandmother cutting through his yard toward the golf course.

"Shit." Putting his foot on the gas, he hurried onto his drive, parked and cut the engine. There was a pond right behind his house, and as this wasn't the first time she'd escaped her caregiver, Aries knew she couldn't swim.

He shot out of his car and jogged around the side of the house. When he got close enough, he called, "Ms. Hannover? Betty?"

Finally she stopped and turned around. "Yes?"

"How are you? It's a nice day today, isn't it?"

"Do I know you?"

He bent his arm and offered it to her with a smile. "The important thing is that I know you."

"You do?" She beamed.

"I do. I also know..." He bent down closer to her while he talked. He noticed last time that she responded better when he was more familiar-like. "There's a big, fat, spoiled Siamese cat named Durante waiting for you to come home."

"He is spoiled, isn't he?"

He nodded.

"I fed him most of my tuna sandwich. I hate tuna."

Okay, this was totally messed up, because he barely knew the neighbors and yet, he was so well acquainted with this neighbor's grandmother that he knew this fact about her. Why the hell didn't her caregiver know it? He wasn't one to blame someone, given such a difficult job. He knew firsthand how trying it was looking after an Alzheimer's patient all day, every day. But Jesus Christ, every time they tried to feed the woman the fish, she ran away. It wasn't that hard to connect the dots. Surely.

"How about I make you a deal? I'll tell them to stop making you tuna fish sandwiches if you promise me you won't go near the pond."

She tripped to a stop and looked up at him. "But I love to swim."

Her earnest, almost contrite expression cut deep. Poor thing. God, he hated this disease. Patting her hand he knew there was no sense trying to convince her of the truth that she couldn't swim; her family constantly tried to do that, and the most it accomplished was to stress her out. That was why he tried a different tactic. "Yes, I know you love to, but you see, the pond is dirty and they just sprayed it for bugs."

"Oh, I hate bugs."

He squeezed her hand. "I know. So I wouldn't want you to go back there until it's safe." Or he got the homeowner's association to put a wrought iron fence around it. He'd have to send them another email.

They got to the front door, and he rang the bell.

"This is nice. Is it your home?"

"No sweetheart, it's your home. Yours and Durante's."

When her caregiver looked through the side panel window, her eyes widened and she whipped open the door. "Betty. Didn't I tell you to stay in the family room while I was on the phone? I'm sorry, Mr. Taylor, I don't know how—"

"You see, Betty," he said as he pointed to the cat basking in the sunlight that streamed in through the living room window. "There's your fat cat posing for you."

He waited for the older woman to let go of his arm. After she picked up the cat and walked off, he gave her caregiver his undivided attention. "I don't want this to sound like I'm accusing you." But he was now that he knew she was on the phone. She was always on the damn thing. Even when she took Betty out for a walk, she was texting or talking. Whether she was with a dementia patient or not, the fact was, it was disrespectful and in this case dangerous. "I just want you to be aware that I'm going to have to tell Mel and Angela this time. Did you make Ms. Hannover tuna fish for lunch?"

"Y-yes."

"I wouldn't do that again if I were you. Betty doesn't like it. That's why she sneaks out. Who knows why these things get triggered this way. They just do."

"I don't think it was the sandwich. She's not having a good day today. She's been very stubborn. Not doing the things I wanted her to do. Including eating lunch."

"Candy moments. Remember that."

"I beg your pardon?"

"When my dad was going through a rough patch, I'd ask him if he wanted some chocolate. He never said no to that, and once I had him saying yes, his whole day got better. And so did mine."

"I'll, ah, give that a try next time. Thanks."

By the time Ramsey got through his own door, shot off an email to the association, marinated his steak for dinner and got on his workout clothes, he was calmer. And after dealing with Ms. Hanover's attempted escape, he was more convinced than ever that his future plans were valid, but to accomplish them he'd need to focus. And that meant free of all distractions. Especially the female kind. If he hoped to get Gabe's support, he needed to make this court shit disappear as quickly as possible and find a way to convince his brother about said plans when he got the chance.

He thought he was well on his way to making all this happen until he went to call his attorney. That's when he realized he'd forgotten the trunk. And inside it? Was his get-the-court-off-his-back paperwork. Damn. Now he'd have to do the one thing neither of them wanted. He'd have to complicate things and see Jaxx again.

Chapter Seven

Aries figured the minute he sat his ass down in the ladder-backed chair in their front entranceway, he'd lose his edge with Doctor Carmichael. Screw the dragon analogy, the woman was a cerebral shark who hunted using any means necessary to gain the advantage. And right now the only advantage he'd had over her, his intimidating height, was diminished when she'd ordered him to sit. Fuck.

"I think you knew exactly what you were doing, Mr. Taylor."

"I'm sorry you feel that way." He didn't mean it, and they both knew it.

"I'm not. I'm relieved by the discovery." She rested her arm on the top of the trunk she refused to give back until they "spoke" and added, "To hear Jaxx talk about you, you're the perfect mix of brain meets brawn with a side order of sensual. We know that can't be true. Man wasn't created that way. If he were, I'd be out of a job because everyone would be happy."

"I said I'd hear you out, but if you're going to sling bitter insults aimed at my half of the population, I think I'll pass."

The older woman's eyes roved over him before she said, "I can see why she's so attracted to you. Maybe she was right about a fabulous mind."

"She said that?" For some reason, he liked the idea.

"She said a lot of things, and now that I've met you I'm beginning to understand why. But let me be clear, Mr. Taylor. Doctor Gavin is on the fast track to becoming a very well-respected psychologist. She graduated top of her class. That's top, not second or third out of two hundred and forty, but first."

"I know. She's a smart cookie."

"Cookie? Cookies are for the Keebler Elves, Mr. Taylor. Doctor Gavin is an intelligent woman who needs an intelligent man. And if I have my way she'll find one at which time they will have equally intelligent children. That's her path, and you are not on it."

He was getting hot under the collar here. And he didn't know why. The truth was, that path she was talking about? He'd already decided a week and half ago he was going to stay the hell away from it. "I understand. Now if you let me have my stuff I'll be on my way."

She stretched to her full height and glared down her nose at him. "You don't understand because you have the attention span the size of a gnat. I'm trying to tell you that she needs to get you out of her system before I can make those plans for her future happen. You came at her with all your playboy ways, and now she thinks she's infatuated with you. You can't just abandon her because then she'd never get over you. I'd be competing with a memory of who she made you out to be. I don't know what you did during your last session, but I do know it has her questioning a number of things."

Even though she'd just insulted him, that wasn't why he felt like shit. Jaxx was doing exactly what he feared. She was second-guessing herself because he'd pulled a fast one on her with those test items. *You knew there was a risk she'd think she'd failed at her job.* "If I made her think she did some wrong—"

"Well, you did."

"I never meant to."

"No real man would do such a thing, I'm sure. Are you a real man, Mr. Taylor?"

Perfect. She had him by the short ones as there was only one answer to that. And once he gave it, he'd be obligated to do whatever she had in mind to make the situation right. "Yes."

"Good. Now don't scowl. It's not as if I'm going to ask you to do something that will be too taxing on you. All you need to do is dinner. One evening at a nice restaurant. A meal. That's it."

Like hell. There had to be more. Didn't she want him to apologize? That was the first thing he should do. "I don't get it."

She let out a relieved breath and clapped her hands. "Finally, that fabulous mind is not so fabulous."

He blinked.

"And not so fabulous? That's the objective. Just be yourself for two hours, and she'll get over you."

He was going to laugh, but then he realized the woman was serious, so he stuck to glaring at her.

"Oh, don't take it personally." She plucked an imaginary bit of lint off her sleeve and pretended to study it. "It's a curse being smarter than average. As such Jaxx needs to be stimulated and if she's not, she's easily bored."

That got his antenna extending upward. *Not good.*

"No run-of-the-mill for her."

His antenna tinged, fully extended. *Pretend she didn't just say that.*

"She needs a man who can compete with her on a deeper level."

He could do that. *Not gonna happen.*

"One who has new and interesting ideas to share with her."

He had a whole dungeon full. *Get the fuck out with those kinds of thoughts.*

She looked at him. "Quite frankly, Mr. Taylor, the one thing she needs above all these others, you can't give her."

"And that is?"

"Loyalty."

If she were trying to drive him away from Jaxx, she was failing. "Why? Did she have a bad experience in a relationship? A boyfriend cheat on her or something?"

"God, no. Jaxx has only had one, what most would call a 'real relationship' with a man and that ended badly."

That got his adrenaline jacked, even as he decided the woman wasn't just failing. She was miserably failing. If he were going to make things right with Jaxx, Carmichael needed some help in the driving-him-away department. Because right now? He was raring to go forward. He needed a stumbling block fast. "Then why is loyalty an issue with her?"

"That's not for me to say. But..." He'd call the look she gave him calculating. "Let's just say her parents weren't the best role models for a successful marriage or proper behavior. Jaxx doesn't want to be like them."

Couldn't he catch a fucking break here? This was one more aspect of Jaxx he could totally relate to. Family issues. "I don't think you want me to be myself as that—" He was throwing her a bone here. Ready to come clean about how he'd already been an asshole which hadn't deflated the attraction between them, when Carmichael made a mistake. A big, no, huge mistake.

"For your part? There's no thinking to be done. That should be easy enough for a guy like you."

He tried not to glare. "Let me get my feeble head around this. You want me to take Jaxx out for dinner and be myself, correct?"

She sniffed and curtly nodded.

"You're sure about this?"

"Absolutely."

"Fine. Will Friday night work?"

He stood and reached behind her to grab up the trunk. Adjusting it in his hands he said, "I heard you the other day. You know, if you eased up on her occasionally she wouldn't be so quick to doubt herself in the workplace. She's a very talented therapist."

"Talented? She's brilliant. And doubting herself in the workplace? Who said anything about that?"

Aries halted at the door and then spun around. If this wasn't about him righting Jaxx's angst over what they'd done in her office, what the hell was it about? "This—you wanting me to spend time with her so she can get me out of her system isn't about Jaxx's feeling bad about her career?"

Carmichael shook her head.

Genuine relief flooded him, and with the fear that he'd shaken Jaxx's confidence in her job off the table, there was virtually nothing the Doctor could say to stop him from cancelling the forced-upon-him date. There was nothing—

"I was talking about her being frigid."

Except that. "Frigid?" An image of Jaxx on that door and then off it when she dove on him came to mind. "She's not frigid." He shifted the trunk and tucked it under the other arm, ready to defend his statement, but the doctor spoke first.

"She is, or was. Or thought she was, actually. But now she's questioning that. Who's to say? All I know is that until you came into her life, she was on-point and focused. On track with her career and the perfect wife material for Dr. Gunther Kreizeger."

"She's engaged?" He nearly dropped the trunk. He was totally stunned because the answer mattered to him for some reason.

"Not yet, but when my illustrious doctor friend comes from Germany at the end of the month, I'm hoping that will change. I know it will. Combining their genes would be magical."

Now this was irony at its finest, because this therapist was nuts. "Tell me, Doctor FrankenMicheal. Is Jaxx aware of your plans for her?"

"Of course...to a certain extent. She wants a family and since she hasn't had any success in the relationship area of her life, she has to be practical about it. I think she was prepared to be until you showed up. Didn't you pick her off the list because she was the youngest doctor in our group and you figured you could get around her?"

Actually, it was just the opposite. Not that he'd share that with her, but he'd chosen Jaxx off the list his attorney presented to him because he'd recognized her name from the byline of the monthly column she wrote. He'd read it for years so he assumed Jaxx was far older than she was. "No."

The doctor sighed, "Oh, come now, Mr. Taylor. I know what you were doing even if she didn't."

"You think I was doing something?"

"I know it. You were overly wonderful just so you'd get the paperwork you needed from her."

"You think so? I assure you—"

"I know you were. Yes." She seemed to be talking to herself here. Maybe she was nuts. "Before you, she was perfectly happy with the Gunther idea. Now she's confused and with all the fantasizing she does about you, we have to deal with this little hiccup before it gets out of hand."

She shouldn't have said it. "She's fantasizing about me?"

"She is, but only because she thinks you're smart and clever." Now she looked at him with a scowl. "And a good kisser. Well, she also thinks you're gorgeous, but that's obvious, and it doesn't hurt that you're built like—" she gave him the once over, "—a Calvin Klein underwear model, either."

Was she for real? "Never wear the things."

"Mr. Taylor."

Oh, she was for real, all right. So it was kind of hard to justify a smart woman like her—he'd seen all the letters after name or her door—stupidly giving him the means to take advantage of the situation.

"I wanted to put all my cards on the table Mr. Taylor. I'm on to you. You may have pulled the wool over Jaxx's eyes but not mine. And just so you don't have it in mind to take advantage of the situation with all that I've shared, I'll be going with you."

She should add "mind reader" to her titles. "To dinner?"

She nodded.

If she had any idea how much she'd misread the situation between Jaxx and him she'd be begging him to stay away. "Why, so you can help me play dumb?"

She walked to the stairs and then turned back. "Don't be ridiculous. You don't need my help for that. Good day, Mr. Taylor. Oh, and," she called over her shoulder as she descended the stairs, "we'll both be ready at seven. Don't be late, and wear a tie...and underwear."

A few minutes later, Aries leaned into his car and dropped the trunk on the passenger seat before he got behind the wheel. Frigid? He snorted. With the way Jaxx had purred and climbed all over him on the desk? No fucking way. An image of her drawing her knees up and digging her nails into his chest surfaced, and he ignored his body's instant reaction to it. But then he recalled her saying, "Yeah, like that" when he'd tugged on her hair harder that day, and damn—he looked down and shifted to make the much-needed readjustment—he was the one hooked. Again. Then. Now. Shit.

She was fantasizing about him? His dream came to mind, her naked, tied, collared, tattooed and hot for him. Did she have the same kind of thoughts about him?

"Christ." His head fell back and he banged his skull against the rest a few times as he ignored the heavy ache in his cock. Think. Plan. This is what you're good at. Forget about the shitty timing of things, and do Jaxx a favor. Do yourself a favor.

Sitting up straight, he ran a hand through his hair and pondered. A dinner date where the esteemed Doctor Carmichael was going to tag along and chaperone?

Not going to happen.

Oh, he'd take Jaxx for dinner, because now that her mentor had shared those interesting tidbits about her protégée, how could he not? The situation needed to be corrected. Things put into proper prospective. He'd told himself he wasn't going to be the shoulder for Jaxx to lean on, but clearly she needed someone other than the dragon for support. Perfect wife material? How about husband material? If this guy was "so right" for Jaxx why was Carmichael so worried?

Frigid? He shook his head and chuckled as he whipped out his phone to dial. Jaxx was far from it, so he'd do her a favor and save her from making a huge mistake. But first he needed Carmichael suitably entertained during his impending play-date.

"Hey, Q." The older Dom's name was Quentin, but he went by Q. "It's Aries. I need a favor. What are you doing on Friday night?"

*****

"This is beautiful," Jaxx whispered. When Ramsey had picked them up, he'd been very hush-hush about where they'd be dining. She'd asked him if it was a popular place, and he'd assured that it was. So when she spied the home he pulled up to, her curiosity outweighed all the nerves she'd been dealing with, because this...this mansion was something else.

The sprawling Spanish colonial had wheat-colored plaster walls drenched in burnished gold tones cast from numerous gas lanterns. The red barrel tile roof and repeating arched windows really gave the large property a Mediterranean feel. It was open, with tons of fragrant plants, trees and shrubs. An oasis. No wonder Ramsey had chosen to have dinner at his friend's house rather than at a restaurant.

"Don't get too attached," he said, stalking on ahead of them, up the interlocking walkway to the door.

Jaxx's stomach clenched as she shot a look at Maggie out of the corner of her eye. Had she heard that comment? It could only mean one thing. They weren't here to stay. Were they here to pick up a date for her friend so they could double? In all the years she'd known the doctor, she'd never seen her romantically involved. They reached the curved stairs that lead up to the doors. "After you." Jaxx swept an arm. She was going to hang back out of firing range when Maggie cut Ramsey off at the knees. Who knew? A dinner and a show.

"Hi, Q. This is Doctor Margaret Carmichael."

The man who opened the door was tall. Almost as tall as Ramsey, and he was built for an older gentleman. If not for the thick white hair and naturally tanned and weathered skin on his face, he could pass for someone twenty years younger.

"Q?" Maggie slapped her clutch impatiently against her elegant silk pants. "That's your name?"

"It's Quentin." He smiled, and Jaxx imagined she could see a flashing gleam, like from an actor in a toothpaste commercial, bounce off his eye-tooth. "You may call me that if you like." He leaned forward and took hold of her arm, bringing her inside before anyone had a chance to say another word.

Her friend was the first to recover. "Quentin Reed? The Quentin Reed from that seventies soap opera?"

"I am."

Even though Jaxx had no idea who the guy was, Maggie did. She seemed momentarily star-struck. She had to be, because she wasn't yelling. Ah, but then the shock disappeared as she twisted and called over her shoulder, "Mr. Taylor?"

Curiosity got the best of her, and Jaxx leaned around Ramsey, craning her neck to see the stunning interior.

"You two kids have fun. Thanks for babysitting, Q."

"Mr. Taylor!"

"You're in good hands, Doctor Carmichael. The best. Q taught me everything I know."

Jaxx heard Maggie's gasp. But it wasn't until she saw her yank her arm out of Quentin's grip that she held her breath. Maggie was going flip out on the poor guy. Famous actor or not.

"Quentin, I'm not staying."

"Oh, don't say that, darlin'." He took her arm. "I have champagne chilling. You can tell me all you know about the show episodes you watched. You did watch Realms Of Reality?"

"Yes. And I...I appreciate the trouble you've—"

"No trouble." He leaned down and added, "For a beautiful woman like you."

"It's tempting but, I don't want Jaxx—"

"Jaxx is a big girl, and Aries is the finest man I know. Let them have their dinner, and we'll have ours."

"Jaxx?"

"It's okay, Maggie. We won't be long." Jaxx had no idea about the plans, but she did know one thing. She was feeling relieved that she wouldn't have the dragon breathing down her neck tonight.

"If you're sure?" When she let Q lead her up the hall, Jaxx knew her friend had conceded. Q was quite the charmer. Speaking of charmers...

She straightened and tugged on the back of Ramsey's shirt. "Ambushing Maggie like that wasn't very nice. How did you know she'd have a thing for an actor?"

"Every woman does. And as for not being very nice, neither was she trying to crash our party."

"I'm going out on a limb here and making the assumption that Quentin's a trusted friend of yours, yes?"

He turned so quickly, she stepped back and was treated to his scowl. "Of course he's a good man. The best. The doctor is probably going to get a better dinner than we will. Q's a class-A chef." He took her arm and led her down the stairs. "Not one of those French-tidbit kind of chefs either. She'll probably be eating grilled steaks—"

"Maggie's a vegetarian."

He whistled, as if to say "oh, brother," then asked, "Is she a pescatarian?"

"Yes, but a picky one."

"Never mind. They'll work it out. Working it out is Q's specialty."

Halting just before they reached the car, she asked, "You're sure about this?"

"Positive."

She was just about to slide into the passenger seat when she stopped and looked up. "Ramsey?" The moment she had his attention, she asked him the question she'd been dying to speak since his visit with Maggie Wednesday afternoon. "Why did you agree to this?"

His smile lit up the space between them and he answered, "You'll see."

*****

A few hours later, Aries waited until the last dinner dish was cleared before he answered Jaxx's question. "How can you say I have an aversion to talking about politics and religion? I answered you, didn't I?"

She laughed. A full throaty laugh that snaked through him like a sultry caress. "Yes, but you prefaced answering that rhetorical question by saying in the immortal words of Fred Flintstone as dictated by Batman."

"That was meant to be rhetorical?" He deadpanned.

This time when she laughed harder, her head fell back and he didn't deny the urge he had to examine her wonderful attributes.

He'd thought his monumental attraction to her stemmed from her Woody Allens, but he'd been wrong there, because tonight she wasn't wearing them. And with her hair down and that short pencil skirt wrapped around her so sweetly? God, he'd sucked in a breath earlier when she got out of the car and walked in front of him. Being treated to that tantalizing horizontal pull across the tuck of her ass was exhilarating. Especially when he recalled the afternoon he'd smoothed the tape over her curves. He had all he could do to keep his hands off her before they were seated and now? All he wanted to do is reach across the table and drag her over it until they were close. Tight. Until he felt the warmth of her breath on his skin.

When she quieted and looked at him he grinned. "So, how about we smash every first date taboo and talk about soul mates? If as you say, romance is overrated, what happens to the prince and princess at the end of the fairytale?"

She didn't hesitate, grinning right back at him. "There's a reason they call it fiction."

"A realist and a cynic." He leaned back. "I dig it."

"Okay, I'll bite. How would you explain the happily ever after syndrome?"

He loved how she continually caved into her curiosity. Smiling, he popped his brows at her. "Since you asked. Magical vaginas."

She inclined her head. "That's a topic that sounds noteworthy."

"It is, believe me—" he checked his watch, "—but we don't have time. I promised Q I'd be back to pick the doctor up by midnight, and it's nearly eleven now."

"Eleven?"

He nodded.

"Time just seems to..."

"Fly?" He offered, because oddly enough it was the truth tonight. He'd been prepared to wade through the evening until it was time to initiate the part of the plan that entailed doing her a favor with a little "I'll teach you something about yourself" session. The sole purpose he had in mind was to free her of the notion that she somehow needed Krum-head or whatever the German guy's name was. If the idea that she was frigid was the only thing holding her up from finding a real relationship, well, he was going to magnanimously lead her to the promised land of smut, but then they'd sat down and everything changed.

No preconceived thoughts. No plans put in motion. It had been just the two of them in real time. In the moment without other distractions so they were free to talk about substantive stuff. Topics that were interesting and surprising. If she were a song, he'd say her river ran deep.

"Yes, fly is a good analogy."

He motioned for the waiter and paid the tab. "Thanks. Keep the change. But could I trouble you for a cup, with a little water and lots of ice to go? Just tell Angelo that Aries wants to steal a glass. I'm sure he'll be okay with it."

"Yes, sir."

Before Jaxx asked about the ice, he spoke, "Why are you so interested in figuring yourself out?"

"I am?"

He wasn't going to let her duck out of the question. "Yes."

"I guess I want to be like everyone else."

"Why? Wouldn't you much rather be unique? It's your flaws that make you different. You should embrace them."

"I think I do to a certain extent. There are just so many."

When she couldn't escape one way she tried to verbal escape another, but he'd already figured that out about her so he was prepared. "According to who? Maggie?"

"No." She took her napkin off her lap and threw it on the table. He was surprised then that she eyed the exit instead of him while she admitted, "I have my critics. Mom, dad, Maggie—" she turned to look at him, "—my fifth grade teacher who told me I was a silly twit for Christmas treeing the middle school placement test."

"I gather you wanted to be like all the other kids?"

She shrugged. "It didn't matter. My grades landed me in those AP classes in the new school so my little defiance that I was caught in, was for nothing."

"So why are you smiling?" Her smile made him want to smile too.

"For a kid who was purported to be smart I was a complete ass when it came to that test. I took the term Christmas treeing it literally. It's no wonder I got caught. I put a star on top of the darn thing."

An image of her taking the time to do that made him laugh.

"Yes, well, enough about me. Are you going to tell me about the magical vagina?"

With the check paid, his ice on the way and forty-five minutes to spare before he had to be at Q's, he'd be cutting it a little close taking her to heaven, but what the hell. "All right. Do you read romance novels?"

The waiter arrived and handed him the glass.

While he waited for her to answer, he wrapped his hand around the tumbler to gauge the temperature, because the colder, the better. He was fully expecting her to deny it. That's what most women did, but then, she wasn't most women.

"Of course."

He grinned. "Then you should know the prevailing fantasy theme. Invariably the hero is usually tamed by the heroine's 'magical vagina,' which makes him want to give up his bachelorhood and dedicate himself to paying homage to that special vessel for the rest of his life as it completes him."

There was that laugh again. Genuine and totally seductive, because he could tell she didn't know how great it sounded and that, more than anything, piqued his interest. Not that his interest needed piquing. He was on a mission. Hence the ice, but after spending these few hours with her, the little goodnight interlude he'd had planned was expanding. Rapidly.

"Ha, that's a good one."

He crossed his arms over his chest and leaned back to study her. The candlelight did awesome things to her skin and made the lavender color in her eyes stand out. "You don't agree?"

She tossed her head in a shake. "No. But I do give you credit for coming up with an eloquent definition of a guy being pussy-whipped."

"Oh, that wasn't me. The credit goes to my buddy, Shawn Alff. He's an up-and-coming writer out of Tampa Bay and whenever he's in town we shoot the breeze over world changing shit like this. The conversations are riveting. Shocking. Mind-blowing even."

"Oh, I bet."

He eyed her and decided. Since she said the 'P' word first, to his mind, she was now fair game. Time to see how deep her river ran. He leaned forward and held her gaze. "Do you like pussy-whipped guys, Jaxx?"

"I'm not going to answer that."

He waited for her to cross her arms and settle back to glare at him before he asked, "Why not? It's a simple question. Do you like a soft man? Or would you prefer a man like me?"

"You're not so hard."

"I can be, and we both know it. Answer the question."

"I don't think I want to."

"Sure you do." He was relentless. He knew she wanted to look away but he wouldn't let her. Instead, he challenged her. "Do you like a man who knows where he's going? A man who commands his space? A man who cares for the things he loves?"

She uncrossed her arms and leaned forward. "Put like that, I'd be crazy not to say yes."

Now he had her. "Yeah, but that kind of man comes with a price. I'm that kind of man."

Silence.

"Come on, Jaxx." He reached out and took hold of her hand. "I know you're dying to ask."

Energy crackled between them until she chickened out, closed her eyes and whispered, "What's the price?"

"Loyalty."

Her eyes snapped open and she frowned. "Loyalty?"

"Absolute. I want one hundred percent fidelity and I demand a steadfast commitment from my woman. I'm possessive. Selfish. And totally single-minded in my pleasure of her."

She gulped and unfortunately for her, he saw it. The hunt was on.

"Do you think you could handle that?"

A full thirty seconds past before she stammered, "I, ah—are you asking?"

He nodded. Not quite sure how they'd gotten here, but now that they were in the thick of things, he was going with it.

"Why?"

It was his turn to frown. "Why what?"

"Why me? Why now? Just..." She shrugged.

He had no ready answer. He certainly couldn't tell her that his original plan was to show her she wasn't frigid so she didn't have to waste herself on a dried-up old genius. "I don't think I have an answer, other than to say, life. I wasn't looking to start a relationship now. Far from it, actually. And I don't think you were either, correct?" She nodded. "But sometimes what we want and what we get are two different things. As in this case." He squeezed her hand. "I think a start of a relationship found us."

When she didn't say anything, he let go of her and sat back. "Unless I'm the only one feeling the attraction."

"No."

He was glad she was quick on the draw with that denial. "Great."

"But..."

"Yes?"

"I may only be feeling this attraction to you because of external forces. Newly discovered ideas that have me curious. I want you to be aware of this just in case it doesn't...and then I have to...I just want to be totally honest and above board."

"External forces?" He was thinking about her imminently arriving German sperm donor. Was this what she was referring to?

"Books, to be exact."

"Excuse me?"

"You have cited the magical vagina as the traditional fantasy theory in a romance, but I'm afraid women's lib has demanded that fantasy be met and trumped with the onset of mainstreaming kink in stories. Currently, anyway, and I'm also afraid I've been swept along for the titillating ride."

He had no idea what she was saying, but whatever it was it was killing her, because her face was as red as the rose in the bud vase. "I'm not sure I'm following."

"The magical balls."

He blinked.

"It's true." She nodded. "When I read the kind of romances I do—BDSM, by the way—it's the hero's bold and less-than-heroic actions, for the sake of the heroine's pleasure, that gets my pulse beating."

"Ah, I see." Did she know what she was admitting to him? Was she that savvy or completely naive? He poured the water with the additional melted liquid out of his ice into another glass until there were only cubes left. Time to see. "You could have just told me you're into consensual non-consent. I'm rather a big fan of that myself."

"I said no such thing." She picked up her purse and clutched it against her belly. "I was just merely stating—"

"That a real guy should have the balls to give his woman what she wants, even when she doesn't know what that is?"

"No, that's not—"

"That a real man has the strength to face his woman's fear and help her walk through it?"

She frowned. "Well, no, but that does sound sort of reasonable."

"How about that you want a real man who won't let guilt rule you because he rules you. He makes you, so if there's any guilt involved, it's his. Only he doesn't have any, because he's selfish and single-minded in his dealings with you." He stood and held out his hand. When she stared at it, he whispered, "Take it."

Nothing but her eyes moved as she looked up at him.

"Come on, Jaxx. It'll be fun. Your magical vagina up against my magical balls. While they duke it out over supremacy, you and I will be enjoying ourselves. I promise."

"This is crazy." She might have said that, but she still took his hand.

"Trust me."

She hesitated, and he held his breath. After a charged moment she nodded, and the air escaped his lungs. He was relieved. Ecstatic. So when she pointed to his glass and changed the subject, his relief increased tenfold. "You dumped out all the water."

Time to mess with her. "I sure did."

"Don't you need it?"

"No." He didn't add, not for what I have planned. "Let's go."

Chapter Eight

Jaxx was trying to keep it altogether. This hadn't been hard until the end of their dinner, when they'd veered off quick-fire topics of the day onto more intimate subjects. She'd just about slid under the table when he'd asked her if she could handle a guy like him. Handle him being possessive and single-minded while dealing with her.

Dealing? That word was fraught with all kinds of titillating ideas. Each one of which got her tingling. "I thought the restaurant closed the maze at ten?" she asked. This was not the place to go, especially at night, when the only guides were cozy gas lanterns swaying from tall Sheppard's hooks that towered over the ten-foot-high manicured ivy walls. "I got lost in here once with my dad. Are you sure you want to chance it?"

Ramsey didn't answer. He just pulled her along.

"If we need to pick Maggie up soon, this isn't a good idea."

He didn't even slow down. He made a right, a right, a left, no a right again. Jesus.

"Ramsey?"

He stopped so abruptly she nearly walked into him. "When are you going to call me Aries?"

It wasn't until that moment, as he looked down and she looked up, that she realized how tall he was. Oh, she'd known it, but she'd never seen it. Really seen the discrepancy and how it related to her. Maybe because like he'd said, a relationship had found them, so now things like that mattered. She needed to pay attention to them. "You're a giant." That thought came out of her mouth unedited.

"And without the heels, you're what? Five-four?" They took off again.

"Yes. Do you know where you're going? You seem to."

"We're going to the middle."

"Middle." She snorted. The one time she and her dad had tried to do that in the daytime, they'd given up after an hour and rang one of the "come save me" loser bells for the maze keeper to come and lead them out. "That's the equivalent of finding a needle in a haystack, isn't it?"

"I don't know about that." He pulled her closer. "But I do know there's a bench there. The back is carved in an image of two horse's heads with flowing manes."

They made another turn. "It sounds beautiful."

"It's something to see. Especially tonight."

He was right, of course. The moment they got to the circular middle, which was odd in itself, after traveling through nothing but straight lines to get here, the bench looked surreal. Bathed in the light cast from the full moon, the intricate design seemed ancient and yet ageless at the same time.

Ramsey went right to it. He sat down, put his glass to one side and motioned to her. She almost wanted to pinch herself. Not that she was one of those females who got all giddy or, God forbid, giggly, but she was feeling very light. That was the best way to describe it. The last time she'd felt this way was when she'd tested out of all her first-year and some second-year college courses.

"Okay." When she got within a six inches of him, she tossed her purse toward the end of the bench and was going to ask, 'what would you like to do now', but he spoke, and she had her answer.

"I want you to take off your blouse. Bra too."

Her heart skittered. "This is all a little sudden, isn't it?"

One side of his face was in shadow and the other was bathed in the glowing moonlight. From that half profile, he looked hard. Set. Determined. And when he didn't answer, she shifted under the weight of his solemn stare and asked, "Exactly what kind of relationship are you looking for with me? A consensual non-consent one?"

"If I were looking for that kind of relationship with you at the moment, I wouldn't have politely told you what to do. I'd make you do it or I'd have done it for you myself."

She peered, trying to gauge what was in his eyes. No use as a cloud drifted in front of the moon.

"Take off the blouse, Jaxx. Do it."

"Why?"

Now he sat forward, bending with his forearms braced on his knees. His whole face came into the bar of gold-tinted light from one of the lanterns, and she saw his eyes. He wasn't fooling around. "Because I told you to."

A thrill went through her and she found herself undoing the buttons. One by one until she was done. She shrugged out of it and tossed it on the bench.

"Now the bra."

If anyone had told her this morning that she'd be doing this tonight, she would have called the person a liar. Even now, as she unhooked the clasps at her back, she wondered how he'd gotten her to comply. She placed an arm over her breasts and threw the bra on top of the blouse.

"Arms down."

The fact that he hadn't moved and his drilling-into-her expression hadn't changed was unnerving. She was wary to do as he asked, but more wary not to. That little voice inside her head said, "own the moment," so she did. She dropped her arms to her sides, shook her head and straightened. Thrusting her breasts forward so he'd see her bravado.

"Are you ready for different?"

"I think—yes."

I think yes, too. Now I want you envision a set of traffic lights. There's a green light for go, a yellow light for proceed with caution, and a red light that forces the driver to stop. When we're together, if there's ever an occasion I'm driving you too hard, you let me know just like the traffic lights guides safety on the road. Does that make sense to you?"

"Yes."

"Go to the tree."

"W-what?" She'd expected him to call her to him, not send her farther away.

He sat up. "Here's how it's going to go. I tell you what to do, and you do it. For the first little while, I'll tell you why I want you to do these things, but once you're comfortable with our arrangement I'm going to stop telling you why, and I'll expect you to do them."

"What if I don't want to?"

His tone dropped an octave or two as he stared at her breasts and said, "You'll want to."

Her nipples gave her away. He was right. "You're making me feel uncomfortable."

"I'm not going to let you talk your way out of this, Jaxx. I know what you need. Uncomfortable?" She nodded, and he grinned. "Feeling uncomfortable is not abnormal. In fact, it's very normal. Everything new is awkward. Put your fear aside and work with me here."

She was going to compliment him on his eloquence, but then he ruined it with that last half of that sentence. "Okay. Why the tree?" She turned and walked over to it before she swung back around to face him.

"It's the perfect backdrop."

"For?"

"You. Your white skin shines beautifully against it."

She didn't know what to say to that, so she said nothing at all. Only shifted to push the flats of her palms into the deep grooves of the oak when he stood and came to her. He stopped right in front of her and with less than four inches of space between them she had a hard time looking up.

"Are you going to ask for it, Jaxx?"

"For what?"

At first she thought he was going to put his hand on her breasts, but then he extended two fingers and used them to tilt her chin up. "This is what your problem is."

"Problem?"

"Your guy problem. Why you lack a man in your life who can satisfy you."

"I hate to be the bearer of contrary news, but me standing half naked against a tree is not the problem I have with men. I know—"

"I know about you." His expression got hard and unreadable. Which had her all hot and restless. "You like to be kept on edge. You need to be, but for the most part you're not willing to do the work required to get that kind of reward from a patient man."

He gripped her chin now. Cupping it tightly in his hand as he squeezed and pulled up. Not too high and not hard, but high and hard enough that she was paying full attention as she rolled up on her tiptoes.

"I-I'm willing to work."

He bent and dragged his chin across her forehead. When he straightened, he sighed. "You can't expect to get what you want if you don't ask for it."

She closed her eyes unwilling to look at him. If she did, she'd have to admit that he was right...about her.

"Courage is its own reward. Are you ready to explore different with me? Do you want to experience something unique or would you rather immerse yourself in ordinary?"

Her eyes fluttered open. His tone, those words and her vulnerable, forced position had her ready to scream "Yes, I want what you're offering". Yet for all of that, she remained silent.

He gripped her chin tighter. "If you're afraid to say the words, Jaxx, that means you have to voice them. You have to let go of the fear."

Swallowing to ease her rapidly drying throat, she dug deep and whispered, "It's not fear. It's shame."

"There's no shame in honesty. Nin got it right. 'Shame is the lie someone told you about yourself'." Leaning down, he kissed her. Consumed her. Using the grip he had on her chin to his advantage, he shifted, slanted, pressed forward until she was forced to open her mouth and let him inside.

The feel, the intimacy, the ferocity of the embrace was like nothing she'd ever experienced before. She wasn't prepared for it. She would have tried to escape, but he slammed his hips into hers, pinning her against the tree as he steadily ground on her while the bark bit into the naked flesh of her back. And...

And her insides melted. Because the pain, the force and the power he exerted over her had her breathless and wanting more of him. His biceps were hard and bulged beneath her fingers as she kneaded them. The rest of him was equally as hard when she crushed herself against him.

Their mingled breath sounded loud in the quiet space. Raspy and needy. He tasted so good. So damn good, she couldn't fight the burst of adrenaline that shot through her and made her want to attack. Finding an opening between the buttons on his shirt, she shoved her hand in. But before she could stop herself, her fingers curled and nails met skin. With one long, hard rake, she scratched him. It was a heavenly form of release.

"Fuck." He tore himself away and leaned back, looking at her. He didn't even blink, only grinned as he let go of her chin and said, "You like it rough. You're going to be fun to play with."

She was too stunned to move. Breathe, even. Never had she acted on her baser impulses. They were wild and inappropriate, but then, so was he. "I'm sorry, I shouldn't have done that."

He put a hand to his chest, no doubt testing the damage she'd done, and then stepped back. "You're right, but not the way you think you are. No." His command was sharp enough to stop her in mid-action from crossing her arms over her breasts. "Put your hands on the trunk like you had them before. Beside you with palms flat."

"All right."

"Good." He relaxed his stance and said, "You shouldn't have done that because you weren't invited to do it. There will be occasions I'll invite you to do what you want. But not many, as I'll keep that kind of play between us sparse. I know you like it. And things you like should be kept special."

She scowled and looked down at herself. Then she looked up. "This really isn't how I envisioned ending the night with you. Can I put my blouse back on so we can talk?"

"The night hasn't ended between us. Not yet. And I'll be doing the talking. You'll listen. As for the blouse? No. It stays off until…"

"Yes?"

"I'm satisfied." He ran his bent knuckles down her cheek. His touch was warm and inviting. But then he grasped her hair in one big hand, tugging and pulling. Forcing her head to tilt to one side as he took hold of her mouth again. And although this time he didn't have a grip of her chin, his fist buried in her hair prevented any thoughts she had of escape. Not that she wanted to. His kiss was brutal. Consuming. Branding, and the pleasure that sizzled through her with his arrogance made the butterflies in her stomach take flight.

She was getting—her heart pounded—getting—it picked up speed…wet. *Don't think about it. Let it happen. Concentrate. Pay attention. Don't spoil*—great, now she was thinking about the reports she had to write tomorrow and wondering whether she'd fed the oscars. Maybe she'd feed them a few pellets before she went to bed tonight.

Aries drew back the second he felt her disconnect. He'd had her there for a moment. He knew it, but the second he'd eased up on the aggression, she'd retreated. Lost focus. So much for patient Mr. Nice Guy.

He used his grip in her hair and slowly forced her to bend. Holding her at an uncomfortable angle, he leaned down and bit her neck. Ignoring her gasp he bit her again harder. She half-gasped. He bit her harder still, and she moaned. Perfect.

"Here's what we're going to do moving forward." He spoke harshly in her ear and made note of her body language. She was breathing fast, trembling, clutching on him as if he were her last lifeline. In an odd way he wanted to believe he was, because without him to show her how good things could be for her, she'd probably settle for ordinary with fuckwit egghead.

"You're going to give me a key to your house and I'm going to use it. Anytime I want." She made to struggle, and he pressed in more. "I'll never interfere with your work, but before and after those hours? You're mine when I want you. You'll never know when I'm going to be there. You're always going to have to be ready for me and what I want from you. Do you understand?"

She was almost hyperventilating.

"Jaxx?"

She closed her eyes, licked her lips and said, "I understand."

"Good." He gave a sharp pull, amazed when she didn't cry out. "I'm going to require certain things from you from time to time. Things that will make our time together better. Always know I have a purpose. No matter what I ask you to do."

"What kind of *certain* things?"

He followed the rim of her ear with his tongue until he got to her lobe. Then he gave that a tug with his teeth before blowing a breath in ear. "We'll cover the full scope of what I want as we go. For now? I'll keep it simple. I want you to shower every night before you go to bed, and when you get in your bed? I want you naked.

Always. The only exception is when you're menstruating. At that time I want to be told so I can make use of your mouth."

She hissed in a breath, and he tightened his grip in her hair. "Does that honesty shock you? It'd better not, Jaxx, because that's all there'll be between us. Get ready." He eased his grip out of her hair and added, "I'll give you the night to think about this, but to help you decide..."

"What are you doing?"

"Stay still and I'll tell you." She stopped so easily he wanted to give her hug. But it was too soon for hugs with her. She needed the hard before they got to the soft. "I'm going to bite your nipples."

"No, you're not!"

"Yes, I am. Uncross your arms." He helped her reposition with her palms flat on the bark. "And after I'm done making them all hot and sensitive, I'm going to turn you around and make you stick your ass out invitingly." He bent getting closer to her breasts, brushing his thumbs over the rapidly hardening peaks. "When your ass is angled just the way I like it, I'm going to lift up your skirt." He dragged his gaze away from her pert breasts and looked up. "I love this skirt, by the way. It's tighter than your black one. It reminds me of the duct tape. Damn—" he concentrated on her breasts again, "—you were one hot wreath on that door."

"Ramsey."

"Shh." He played with her. Teasing and pulling at her nipples. Loving how her whole breast bounced when he let go of the areola. "When I have your skirt up, I'm going smack your ass hard. As hard as I intend to bite your nipples so that those parts of you will ache when you go to bed tonight. You'll be aching while you think about how we move forward from here. Because if you decide to say yes, your only thoughts when you're in your little bed from now on are of me. What we've done or are doing or what we will be doing. Nothing else invades that space. It's mine."

He went after her then. Pinching, sucking and then biting her nipples. First one, then the other. Hard and then harder still until she sank back against the tree trunk and speared her fingers through his hair. Massaging his scalp, drawing him closer as she moaned.

He was careful not to hurt her. That wasn't the purpose of this little interlude. Actually, his only purpose when leaving the restaurant was to reenact his dream. With the ice, anyway. But that turned to shit at the same time the ice turned to water. Jaxx was complicated. Wary. In need of a man like him, and *he* hadn't been needed this much in a long, long time.

He used his teeth and grazed her delicate skin. Over and over, he teased one breast and then the other. Biting and nipping, and when she flexed her hips forward in a continuous plea for more of his touch, he gave it to her.

"Open your legs. Wider." He slid his hand up her inner thigh and when he got to her panties, he didn't waste any time. He wasn't sure which one of them was more eager to draw that silk down. She wanted to be touched, and he wanted to explore. Would she be wet for him?

His fingers slid into her hot steam and he had his answer.

"Ahhh..."

 She was shivering, and he hadn't even gotten to the good parts yet.

"Aries," she groaned out when his index finger slipped into her. "Ohh..."

"Stop flexing. Stay still. Very still. That's right." He took hold of her nipple between his teeth and tugged on it before letting go. "Let me move you."

Her clit was swollen. Pulsing against his knuckles as he pressed and circled it. Over and over, harder and harder as she clung to him. Panting and moaning.

Sighing.

Until he pinched that bundle of nerves between his bent knuckles and squeezed her with graduating pressure.

"Aries..."

This time, when he clamped her delicate flesh, he didn't let go. He stayed still and ordered, "Now move. Slowly. Rock forward and back."

She was unsteady at first but then got the hang of it.

"That's right. A little more. Now..." He eased his grip from her and waited. He knew what came next. Or who, more accurately.

The second all the blood rushed back into those starved nerve endings. "Oh my God! Mmm..."

He held on to her tight as she shivered and trembled, coming hard as he rocked her in his arms. The scent of her desire, mingled with the cool evening air, wrapped around him, and he want to beat his chest in primal satisfaction. Being in control with a woman he liked and respected for other things than just sex, offered a new layer of contentment for him. A new brand of satisfaction.

When she let go of him and he saw her intent, he bent down and whispered, "Don't. Leave your skirt up. Panties down. Turn and face the tree for me."

Her eyes were languid but wary.

"It will be okay. Remember the traffic lights and you'll do fine. I promise. Turn around and let me see your ass. Now."

She nodded and did as he told her. The second he saw her gorgeous ass, he sucked in a breath. Round, firm and as white and pristine as new fallen snow...for now. "Arms up." He helped her. "Good, only..." He pulled her hips toward him, which gave her back a sexy sway. The position also put her ass on greater display. "That's better."

He'd thought to use his hand, but with such a beautiful canvas? "I'm taking off my belt. It's older, so it's nice and worn. Flexible. It's going to sting and then burn. Are you ready?"

"Yes." Her sigh was more a groan.

Jesus, with her answer she changed position. Normally he would have made her move back the way he had her, but her way was better. Much better, as her breasts connected with bark. Her cheek connected with bark. Hell, even her splayed hands lovingly pressed into the rough surface.

She was more than ready, and there was nothing hotter than the sight of her prepared.

He started off with a series of graduating taps. Light, then successively harder.

"You can go do it harder than that if you like." She didn't open her eyes when she spoke, but she did do a little ass wiggle.

Oh yeah, she was going to be fun.

He continued to tap the leather against her while he leaned down and said, "Quiet. I'm warming you up. I don't want to bruise your beautiful skin. I suppose now would be a good time to remind you that I'm in charge." He gave her a good tap and then returned to moderate ones. "I know what to do and how to do it." He tapped her hard again. Only once, but she jerked. Good. "Which is fortunate for you, because you don't have a clue about what you need." This time, he pulled back and gave her a full whack across both cheeks with the leather.

She didn't complain, so he did it again. And again. Careful not to hit the same spot too many times. He wanted her whole ass hot and tingly. The ripples the force of the belt created were mesmerizing. Stunning, because she didn't tense up. She didn't clench. She embraced the experience, but then, even martyrs had their limits. She was getting to hers and when he gauged she reached that threshold as he spied her biting her lip, he lightened up. Landing the belt on her in lesser degrees until he finally stopped.

"Are you good?" He helped her to stand straight and then pressed himself against her. Forcing her into the tree trunk. He leaned, but not too heavily as he whispered, "Your ass is burning me through my pants."

"Mmm..."

He slid a hand between them and took hold of a scalding cheek. Firmly, he kneaded it until she groaned and tried to move.

"Don't ever shy away from my touch." He waited for her to still and then said, "You did good, Jaxx, but don't forget. Tonight while you're lying in bed and your ass is all tender and itchy and your nipples are aching to be sucked by me, think of this." He squeezed her ass cheek so hard she cried out. "If you agree to our arrangement, I control what you feel and how you feel it. Right now we're concentrating on your needs, but soon we'll be focusing in on mine. I have very specific needs. I like to take things. I'm going to take you. Whenever, wherever and however I want. Does that excite you?"

She shivered and then whispered, "Yes."

"Are you wet?"

"Yes."

He smiled because that admittance was so soft he had to strain to hear it. Slipping his hand between her legs, he spoke equally as soft in her ear, "Let me see........."

When she came this time for him, it was fast. So fast he wouldn't be surprised if she handed her house key over before they got to her doorstep.

He waited for her quivers to stop and then helped her with her clothes. When she was dressed, he pulled her in for a hug. "If I had your key tonight, I might be tempted to pay you a visit."

"I don't think I could take it."

This was nice. Just the two of them bathed in moonlight with nothing but the rustle of ivy leaves swaying in the breeze to break the silence. He closed his eyes and enjoyed the moment.

"Aries?"

"Hmm."

"What were you going to do with the ice before it melted?"

"I was going to make you come over it."

"Oh."

"Hey," he said as he kissed the top of her head. "Congratulations."

She leaned back. Damn, she had the prettiest eyes. "For what?"

"I think your magical vagina scored round one. Enjoy it tonight, because come tomorrow? She's going down."

He let go of her, but when he noticed her smile falter he frowned. "What's the matter?"

"I don't want tonight to end."

There was no falter in his smile as he mentally calculated how many more minutes would tick by before she caved and gave him the key.

"But then the quicker I get home, the faster I can start thinking about whether I should agree to this. And about that. I have a few questions. You can answer them on the way to get Maggie, okay?"

Okay? No it wasn't okay. "Sure."

And the magical vagina won again. Fuck.

Chapter Nine

Jaxx sat on the edge of her bed and stared down while she nervously wriggled her toes. Should she do it? Could she do it? Who would know?

Aries.

To him, it was probably a foregone conclusion. She tilted her head and peered at the master bathroom as if she hadn't seen it before. Well, she hadn't, at least not in her current state, with nerve endings vibrating in a sexual hum especially the sensitive ones in her breasts and bottom. He certainly knew what he was doing in that regard.

This was crazy. She stood and went to flick on the light. Looking down, she noted the defining line between the wood and tile at the threshold. She wasn't going to step on the glossy black and white checkerboard floor while she debated, because the ceramic was cold. Just the opposite of her.

"You want to do this." She had to say it out loud so she'd believe it. She'd just had two mind-blowing orgasms with the man, and all he had to do was kiss her goodnight and tell her what he wanted from her and she was ready to give him anything?

She recalled his quiet words. They replayed in her mind. Seducing her. He had a great voice. Firm, but husky. Hell, the guy could read the phone book, and it would be a thing of beauty. She closed her eyes and let them penetrate. *"If you decide to give me that key tonight before you fall asleep, I need you to text me. Let me see the phrase, 'I want you to fuck me anytime you want to' and after you do that mark the occasion by going into your shower and when you're all soapy and warm under the water, I want you to get yourself off with your hands. Nothing else, just your hands while you fantasize that it's me touching you."* Opening her eyes, she flipped off the light. Who was she kidding? She couldn't do this. It was too—one word echoed within her—awkward.

She snapped the light back on and scowled. Hadn't they already established that everything new was awkward? And if she wanted to experience something new as in unique she'd have to get over feeling awkward about it.

Five uncomfortable minutes later she stopped debating and tore her gaze away from her cell, where she'd typed out the phrase he'd asked her to text him. Releasing a deep breath she cringed, closed her eyes and pressed the send button. When no telling thunder clap sounded and the sky didn't fall down, she opened her eyes.

"Well, that wasn't so bad." She put her cell phone on the night table and went to the bathroom doorway. Peering in she muttered, "A promise is a promise." One foot touched the cool tile, then two, and before she knew it her robe was left behind as she went straight for the shower. She walked into the L-shaped enclosure and bent to crank on the water. As it heated up, she faced the truth. Once she took this step, there was no turning back. She was smart enough to know that. She was also smart enough to know that this may simply be sex for him, but for her it was much more. This was a chance for better understanding and possibly some enlightenment into why she had a hard time responding to normal stimulation. She'd look at like an experiment. An opportunity for self-discovery, but could she trust him? She still had no idea why a man like him would want a woman like her. It made no sense.

"Stop overthinking. Even if this was only about sex, enjoy it for fuck's sake. Why not? Yeah," She nodded and then nodded even more resolutely. "Hell, yeah."

And now she was like a crazy person, talking to herself? She took a deep breath and turned the dial until hot shots of water beat down on her. It was simple. Until she felt she could trust him, she'd remain emotionally distant from him. It would only be about sex for her too. How hard could that be?

She grabbed the soap and lathered herself. Her breasts tingled and hardened and, just as he'd predicted, begged to be sucked by him. She dragged the soap in languid circles over her stomach and belly, closing her eyes as a wave of desire coursed through her. This new physical phenomena was one she could get used to. She angled her head back, letting the water shower her chest and drain down to wash the suds away. Then she shifted her head forward so the water rained across her back. Slowly, gently, she pushed the glycerin bar over her sensitive bottom. Back and forth and up and down, until she wasn't thinking anymore. Only doing.

She let the soap slip over one hip and slide between her legs. Dipping in between her thighs. Skating over her flesh so smoothly, she sighed. She didn't even notice when she'd dropped the bar because her fingers were just as slippery. Moving over her clit, circling, pressing and pressing some more. "Mmm."

"I think you dropped this."

"Aries?" She snapped her eyes open and immediately closed them against the blasting water. Which was a mistake, because she couldn't see where she was going, but she needed to go somewhere. "Is that you?"

"Stay still. Careful, I don't want you to slip."

His arms wrapped around her, and that was when she got her second shock. He was naked. "But how?"

"I got your text."

"What? Were you waiting outside my door or something?"

"Yes." When he answered it was in whisper against her ear, "I want to fuck you now."

He pulled her back against him so deliciously, she sighed. Until...wait, was there—she flexed her bottom back to double-check—latex covering his very hard...? "Are you wearing a condom?"

"What color are the lights?"

"What lights?" She wished he didn't have her arms pinned to her side, because she was dying to wipe the water out of her eyes and see what the hell was going on. Was that his jaw against her cheek?

"The traffic lights."

It took her a second and then she realized. "Green. No yellow."

He laughed. It was soft and surprisingly comforting. "Don't tell me you're one of those drivers."

She scowled with her eyes closed. "Hey, I'm a good driver."

"Then make a decision. Green." He softly kissed her ear, jaw and neck then abruptly stopped. "Or yellow?"

Her skin tingled everywhere his mouth had touched. Damn, he was good. "Green. But tell me how did you get in without a key?"

"We'll talk about that in few minutes. Right now I want to talk about how pleased I am with you. How beautiful you are and how happy you've made me with your choice."

Those words swirled right around her heart and gave it a hug. She literally felt all the tension rush out of her as she relaxed in his arms.

"That's better. Did you get yourself hot? Are you ready for me?"

More moisture slid out of her with his words and she nodded.

"Let me check. Oh, yeah." He was bold in the way he touched her. Spreading her as he examined. "You're ready."

Without warning he let go of her and pushed her up against the wall. Gently forcing her forward until her cheek met the tile and her arms were up over her head with hands flat and fingers spayed. She barely had time to breathe before he crushed into her. Everything happened so fast then. With one hand at the back of her neck and his other grasping her hip, he entered her. Hard and deep. There were no pleases, thank-yous or hesitating to give her time to get used to him. Instead, he steadily plunged into her over and over until his breathing became hers. His rhythm became hers. His desire became hers as she gave herself over to the intensity of moment.

When he threaded his finger through her hair and pulled, she went with it. She let her head fall back on his shoulder and moaned while he kissed her. The feel of him invading her body, owning it and commanding her was as exhilarating as it was frightening. He was rough one moment and excruciatingly tender the next. The two extremes played out over and over again until somewhere deep inside it came to her that this experience was touching her in places that weren't physical. He had tapped into a need. A secret desire she had to be used and he wasn't disgusted by it. He wasn't shocked. Instead he was feeding into it and it was tearing her apart. Stitching her back together. Holding her under the heavy waves only to lift her out of the torrents so she could breathe.

He ended the kiss and stopped moving. He still had hold of her hair, so she blinked the rivulets of water aside and looked at him. Both of them were breathing heavy and if she thought the frantic coupling of a moment ago was intense, this moment was more so. The silence brutal. But then he shattered it with a whisper.

"Put your hands between your legs and make yourself come. I want to watch."

She did as he asked when she closed her eyes and leaned into the comfort of his arms. With the water pelting down on her and him breathing husky words of encouragement in her ear, she relaxed.

"That's right. Make it good. Breathe."

She stroked herself, applying pressure on her clit just as he had done earlier, and when the rush built, she followed it. Riding the waves that crashed up her calves, over her thighs and landed with bursts of hard tingles between her legs. She trembled, doing as he instructed, and breathed. Deep and full. The adrenaline climbed, taking her higher and higher. Lifting her so her heart had to race to catch up. The squeeze, God, that muscle-gripping squeeze was heaven as she pulsed around his hardness. The contractions getting stronger.

"Breathe."

It felt good with him inside her. She flexed and panted and flexed again as his name was torn out of her. "Aries."

She came so hard, her muscles clenching him so tightly, he groaned, which catapulted her over another crest so swiftly she reached back to grab one of his hips as anchor.

"Put your hands on the wall, Jaxx. Yeah, like that. I'm going to bend you—fuck, you have the tightest little pussy."

She was bent over as he hammered into her. Over and over he pumped. In and out, while he caught her bouncing breasts and played with them as he ground against her bottom. Both sites, sensitive from the earlier attention he'd given them, were on fire now and made her ready to climb the walls. But then he slammed home one last time. Going deep and holding his position there as she experienced the branding heat of him and all she could do was relish the hard tremors that intimately pulsed against her while he came.

"Damn." He growled, disengaging and was gone by the time she stood up on trembling legs. She was monumentally disappointed and just about to slam off the tap when she heard him behind her.

She turned and leaned back against the wall. Her eyes devoured him. Hard rope-like muscles shifted as he walked toward her. His features were sharper, more intense with his hair slicked back and plastered against his skull. The sight calmed her racing heart. "I thought you'd left me."

"No." When he smiled her knees went weak. "You're going to wash me. Right here." He cupped himself with one hand and held the soap out to her with the other. "On your knees. Two hands. You can touch but only with your hands."

Jaxx didn't hesitate and it was the oddest thing, but she suspected she found a piece of herself while doing the task. There in the shower, on her knees, intimately bathing him while he had a hand in her hair. Not tugging or pulling this time. More like holding. Owning. Possessing some part of her she could never seem to hold on to herself. She would have stayed like that forever, but then Aries took the soap from her and let her rinse him off. When she was done, he helped her stand.

"That was nice. Now let's get you dried."

*****

By the time Aries tucked her into bed he had to fight the urge to climb in there with her. If he stayed, he'd be all over her again. It was too much too soon. She needed time to process this.

"Mmm," she purred. "Not that you'll use it, but the key is on the dresser. How did you get in, by the way?"

"I could have picked the lock. Given how ancient it is, a five-year-old with a fish hook could break into this place. But I didn't. I took the key out of your hide-a-rock."

"No."

"Yeah, I'm a pretty resourceful guy, remember? And FYI that wasn't fooling anyone." He got up to get the key. "I'll only need this to lock the door tonight. Tomorrow I'm sending my locksmith over to change that front reception deadbolt. He's going to fix the bedroom window locks as well." He sat on the end of the bed and put on his socks.

"You don't need to do that."

"Yes I do. It's one thing to have shoddy security, but when you invite the crazies to your place? As in, they know where you live?"

He tilted his head and stared right at her. "You need to Fort Knox this sucker at night."

She came up on elbow and smiled. "Last time I checked, it wasn't a crazy person who broke into my place tonight."

He grinned. "So I am the saner one out of the two of us. You admit it and this time I didn't have to cheat."

She fell back on to her pillow with an *ack.*

"What?"

Her head came up and she said, "You know very well. I walked into that one. Tonight you got me."

She flopped back against the pillow, and he laughed. "No." He stood and moved to the head of the bed. When he put a hand to her cheek and she leaned into it, the ease of her action made him smile. "I got you, period."

"Hey, wait." She grabbed his hand when he turned to leave. "Before you go, tell me why."

"Why what?"

"Why me? Oh, don't look at me like that." She came back up on elbow. "I feel as though I'm waiting for the other shoe to fall. I'm not a woman who needs constant reassurance either, but—"

"You could have fooled me."

"I just want to understand."

He took in her wide purple-blue eyes and mass of scattered hair and nodded. "Okay, understand this. If you had any idea what kind of gorgeous, sexy mess you look like right now, you'd be using it to your advantage instead of throwing such a colossal advantage away."

She sat up. "Are you kidding me?"

Shaking his head, he reached forward and plucked up a fat curl, rubbing it between his forefinger and thumb before letting it go. "No."

"Really?"

He just stared...at her breasts. Waiting for her to notice that when she'd sat up, the duvet had folded down and she was naked to the waist.

"Oh." She scrambled for cover, and he figured it was a good time for him to make an exit.

"No goodnight kiss?"

"Now you're learning," he called over his shoulder without stopping. "And? No."

He heard her *harrumph* and chuckled until he saw Maggie waiting in her doorway across the adjourning front hall. "Carmichael." He nodded. "I thought you were exhausted. Shouldn't you be in bed?"

"And I thought you went home."

Aries swiveled and locked Jaxx's door. Turning back, he said, "And I thought when I'd picked you and Jaxx up tonight, your turtleneck was right-side out. Yet when I picked you up from Q's, it wasn't. Are you sure you want to have this discussion?" He hiked a thumb toward Jaxx's door. "I could call her down here, and we could all clear the air about things."

Carmichael's eyes narrowed. "You think you're so smart. What happened tonight with her? I thought you were going to lay off the playboy charm?" Her chin went up a notch and her arms were already crossed over her chest. Clearly she'd been waiting for this pissing contest.

"I did exactly what you asked me to do. I was one hundred percent myself tonight. Too bad for you, as clearly she likes me."

"Unacceptable. She's not one of your—your...troglodytes."

That comment brought him up short. He didn't like that the term. Especially in the same reference as Jaxx. "I'm not in the habit of dating those kinds of women, I assure you."

She gasped. "You're dating now?"

Aries didn't like how the color drained from her face. He wasn't Caligula for fuck's sake. "Yes."

"No."

He made to step around her but she stopped him. "Don't do this to her."

"I'm not doing anything to her."

"I've got a decent man all lined up. Unlike you, he's perfect for her. And he's—"

"An egghead?"

"Single."

He did a double take. "What's that supposed to mean?" He wasn't?

"She deserves better than a *sex* club owner."

He took a deep breath and let it out slowly, counting to three before he said, "I'm a decent man."

"That's yet to be seen. What is it that has you interested, anyway? The fact that she brings respectable to the table? Being with a doctor? Does this make you feel important when you're with her?"

Carmichael was nervous and grasping at straws here, he could tell. She was still pulling on her turtleneck, so when she glared he couldn't help himself. Grinning, just to annoy her he answered, "Yeah, you hit the nail on the head there, Maggie. Jaxx brings class to the table and I bring what the classy people do below it, that's the draw between us. It's a fair exchange, don't you think?" He was going to let that sit for a few seconds and then tell her to fucking relax and have a little more faith in her friend, but he wasn't fast enough.

"This is real life, Mr. Taylor. She has patients and a practice. She's expected to be classy at all time. Remember that or you'll deal with me."

He nodded and before he could say anything to that she whispered, "You'd better not hurt her."

Hearing those words, Aries studied her for a moment. The concern marring her brow was real. The dragon had a heart after all. Finally, a redeeming feature. "And just when I thought I wasn't going to like you, you go and say something I can respect. Good night, Doctor Carmichael. And I'll do my best."

*****

An hour later while Aries waited for Shar to look over the plans, he braced himself. She wasn't going to be happy. He knew how much she prized her short commute, but he was going to counter the prospect of a longer drive to work with a promotion and pay raise. He figured that would soften the blow. Not that he wanted to have this conversation now. He was bone-tired.

He'd been more than ready to go home after leaving Jaxx's, but since he'd passed by the club en route, he'd stopped in to speak to his locksmith, who doubled as his head dungeon master. It was right after he'd done that Shar cornered him.

"This is what you've been working for the last year? I thought you were planning to make this complex into the next BDSM play park."

"As you can see by the plans, I'm not."

"It's pretty ambitious. You sure you don't want me to ask my sister to go with you? After your recent court shit you're going to need someone acceptable in Gabriel's eyes to balance out all that crap."

"I've got it covered."

"You found a date?"

He wasn't having this argument again so he shrugged and gave a vague answer, "It's all taken care of. Don't worry."

"Yay. Your brother's going to be so surprised when he sees how much you've changed. I wish I was going with you."

Aries tried not to scowl as he collected the preliminary plans and folded them in half and then quarter. It always struck him as strange when Shar made comments like this because they were all wrong. When Aries thought back to the first year of owning the club and meeting Shar, among others, he wanted to groan. He also wanted to tell her those weren't the old days. In fact they'd been "the new days" where he had no caretaking responsibilities, tons of cash and a grief that he couldn't cope with. It had taken him nearly a full year to snap out of his self-destructive rampage, but by then he'd pretty much burned the bridge back home to his real "old days" and the only family he had left. His by-the-book and uptight older brother, Gabe.

"You're going to need some impressive vanilla arm candy to pull this baby off. No tattoos, no piercings. A woman who's snobby and stiff. Just like him. Otherwise, you'll never get through the front doors to talk to him."

He stifled a yawn. And not wanting to turn this into a huge discussion, he sighed. "I know. No worries, I've got it covered."

"You've got a way around his bouncer?"

"Steven's not his bouncer. He's a house manager. And I told you before he had every right to bar my entry that night. In fact I'm glad he did."

"What are you going to do if he doesn't let you in? Have you thought about that?"

He'd been trying not to. Surely enough time has passed that Gabe would be reasonable. "He'll let me in as I'll give him no reason not to." He leaned around her, tossed the plans inside his safe then spinning the dial. It was time to throw her off the topic. "Did I mention that when I relocate the club, you're getting a promotion and a raise?"

"Cool. How much is the raise?"

His ploy worked as she focused in on this. But it wasn't until he held his office door open for her to leave five minutes later, that he knew he hadn't been a hundred percent successful when she hesitated in the doorway and cocked her head.

"Are you sure you're all set with things? With your brother's shindig, I mean. You're usually on edge when his year-end approaches, but you're calmer now than I've ever seen you over it. It's the woman, isn't it? Do I know her? Is she vanilla?"

"Shar."

"I'm going. I'm going." She took a step and then stopped. "I'm glad you've got this all worked out. I know that once Gabriel sees the personal changes you've made and what you want to do, he'll agree. But on the off chance he doesn't let you in? I'm here for you. Just remember that."

Aries nodded and once she was gone he closed the door. Running a hand through his hair, he thought about the "what ifs". He needed to see Gabe in order to pitch the complex. Did he chance showing up on the doorstep alone? Despite telling Shar they wouldn't lock him out this time, he wasn't so sure. Gabe was a stubborn hard-ass. Aries knew the only reason he continued to get the annual invites was because he owned stock in the business. That was one thing his brother had no control over.

He'd have to think about this. Inviting Jaxx might better his chances because Shar was right about one thing. Gabe was too much of a gentleman to embarrass a woman he deemed worthy. And Jaxx was worthy. *Yeah, too worthy to be dragged into this shit.*

He stalked to his desk and sat down.

Right now all he could do is hope to Christ that Gabe was past the disappointment and anger enough to admit him. But then if they did let him in would Gabe be reasonable, or would he continue to shut him out of his life?

It seemed a lot of people wanted him out of their lives these days.

He plucked up a pencil and beat it against the chair arm as he thought about Carmichael. She most certainly didn't want him around. And her words tonight? They'd cut him deep. But what did he expect? She'd be happy about Jaxx and him dating? She had a point too. Jaxx needed respectability and no matter which way he sliced or diced it, the owner of a sex club just didn't cut it in that department. Fuck, the sooner he got his future plans in motion the better. Becoming a silent partner was the first step. He dropped the pencil and watched it roll back and forth before it stopped and he made his decision. Tomorrow he'd start the process.

*****

Jaxx had been awake for about five minutes or so, not quite ready to give up the comfort of warm sheets, when she heard the beep. Snatching her cell phone off the nightstand, she squinted to check the text.

Damn, it was a long one. Probably from Aries. That got her pulse rushing. She'd need her glasses for this. She cleaned the lenses with the sheet. "Better," she said before she slipped them on. "Now..." She was smiling until she started reading. And reading and reading some more. Was he crazy?

Good morning, Jaxx. I trust you're up. Sam Tremmal is coming by at one o'clock to change the locks. I hope you can accommodate him. I know you said you were free this morning, so I have something I'd like you to do. Go to Brockelman's market and shop for these items. Only these items. If you need something else, go at another time. Ready? I want you to get a cart and go to aisle eleven.

"Aisle eleven?"

Pick up a three pack of white terry serving cloths. Make sure they're white. They're on the second to last shelf by the oven mitts. Put the stack on the top seat level of the cart then go to aisle six. There are two items in this aisle you will need. On the left toward the back of the store you'll find KY jelly. Get the largest box and put it on the terry cloth vertically. That's with the bottom of the carton facing you and the top facing the seat back. Then go to the right side of the aisle toward the front of the store. There you'll find condoms.

"Condoms? He wants *me* to buy the condoms?"

Yes. I want you to purchase these.

She gasped. Then looked around. Once she was satisfied he wasn't remotely watching her somehow she read on.

Get the Magnum XL. A thirty count, and place this vertically on the terry as well. Now this is the fun part. Head over to the produce section and park your cart right next to the cucumber wicket. I want you to take your time here, Jaxx, and find a good, long, thick and firm one. I mean it. Don't just pick the first one you put your hands on. It has to be of a good size. Once you have one chosen, put it right between the two boxes. Don't cover them up. I'll know if you do.

She reread this last bit and felt the blush burn from her chest to her forehead. She couldn't do this.

Then I want you to walk up and down each aisle from number one to twelve. No skipping. If you do, I'll find out. So no cheating. Now when you're done, go to checkout number four. I don't care if there's less of line-up at any of the other cashiers, you go to four, okay?

No, it wasn't okay. She wasn't going to do this. She scrolled down to see the end of this seemingly never-ending text.

When you get home put the KY, condoms and cloths on your nightstand. The cucumber can go in the fridge. Oh, and I'm buying dinner tonight. I'll be at your place at five. It's going to be a casual night, so no need to dress up. Make me proud today, Jaxx. And remember, Sam's coming at one. I'll see you at five. -A.

She blinked. Just like that. *You go mortify yourself in front of a pile of strangers, and I'll see you at five?* She snorted.

Make me proud today, Jaxx.

She groaned.

Beep.

It was another text from Aries. No saga this time, just four to-the-point sentences.

Hate me all you want. I can handle it, but what I won't handle is you dragging your feet. No disguises, either. Just go and get the task done and be home in time for Sam.

Jaxx bit her lip, staring at her phone. The thought of doing this scavenger hunt was ludicrous. But now that she thought about it? She should be less worried about purchasing the items in question and more concerned over what he intended to do with them.

Don't just pick the first one you put your hands on. It has to be of a good size.

Her pulse picked up pace and her heart followed suit. That sexual hum was back full-force, making the spot between her legs tingly and wet.

A completely normal feminine reaction to a very abnormal request. She closed her eyes and savored the thrill. A minute later, she came back down to earth and tossed her phone on to the nightstand with a sigh.

"Brockelman's it is."

Chapter Ten

Aries waited for Jaxx to open the door. "Hi."

"Hey, I'm ready." She went to step by him, but he blocked her way.

When she looked up at him, he smiled. "For what?"

"Dinner. You said you're buying."

"Yes, and I did." He held up the grocery bags. "I'm cooking for you tonight, so we're not going anywhere."

"Here? At my place?"

He nodded.

She didn't budge, and he could only image what thoughts were dancing in her head. But when she peered up at him, he knew for sure she was worried about the stuff she'd purchased today. Christ, she was fun to play with. "Problem?"

"No. I just expected to be going out. Are you sure you don't want to? I mean, it's a tough job cooking, and the mess—"

"I love to cook, and we can both pitch in for the clean-up." She still didn't move, so he added, "Besides, I want to have a look at the items you picked up at the store. I'm most interested in the cucumber."

"Why?"

"You'll see, but first I want you to tell me all about your shopping trip. I bet it was a blast."

"Are you a tortured soul, by chance?"

"I don't think so."

"Hm." She stepped aside and indicated for him to enter. "Normally it's the tortured who turn the tables on the unsuspecting and become the torturers. Tortured or not, you've got talent in this area. No wonder you're a Dom."

He went into the reception area and then waited for her to unlock her front door. "You mention this because...?"

"You're good at games. The first—" she shut the door after he stepped inside the house, "—was your Ro-shick test. I've never been so humiliated in my life until today."

He chuckled and put the groceries on the counter. "It wasn't that bad, was it? Your hair looks, great by the way. I love it down."

"Thanks. I—you see? There you go again. You make it hard for me to call you a jackass when you preempt my insult with a compliment."

He grinned. "I know." Delving into the bags, he began unpacking.

"Can I lend a hand?"

"Thanks, but I got this. Sit right there—" he nodded to one of the barstools at the counter, "—and you can tell me all about your store adventure while I prepare dinner."

She launched into a whole huge production with the telling. Describing people's faces, the stares, glares and leers, depending on their gender. He actually laughed at one point. Almost to tears when she told him about Janet. Brockleman's worst cashier, who always worked the four spot. Just imagining Jaxx standing there with the poor older woman who'd never mastered the use of the scanner, calling over the microphone for a price check on condoms. Then KY. She said it wasn't until Janet got to the cucumber that Jaxx had stopped her by putting her hand over the mic.

"So how'd she get the price?"

"I asked the bagger to go check on it."

"Poor kid."

"He was sixty-five at least and he insisted on helping me out to the car with my bags."

Aries couldn't stop grinning as he gathered the ingredients for dinner. "Well, that was nice of him."

"Oh yeah, it sure was. Considering I could have fit everything in my purse."

"Hey, where are the pots?"

"Oh, over there." She pointed. "Second cupboard to your left."

He grabbed her outstretched hand from across the counter and turned it over to kiss her palm. "I'm glad you did it."

Her gaze didn't falter. Nor did she pull back when she whispered, "Why?"

"You'll figure it out. You've got Keebler elves in your corner."

She withdrew her hand and frowned. "Keebler elves? Did you buy cookies?"

He found himself smiling ear to ear. She perked up so quickly, he almost wished he had bought some Oreos. "No, sorry, I got that from something Maggie said. I just meant you're a smart cookie. You'll figure it out."

Jaxx thought she already had. The humiliating exercise had one profound side effect. It built a resistance. Actually, she had started off on her little trip a nervous mouse and by the time she was done, she was like a roaring lion. She went from thinking, "Oh God, I'm sorry. This is so bad" in the housewares aisle to "look out, move out of my way. There's nothing to see here, people. It's my business, pay attention to your own carts" in the checkout.

"That smells good already."

"I'm making beef stroganoff over basmati rice. I thought we'd have a side salad too."

He could have said he was serving black-death soup and curdled capers and she would have smiled and nodded anyway. He looked so good, standing in her kitchen. All tall and muscly. His dark wavy hair and steel-blue eyes took her breath away. Half the time she wanted to pinch herself to make sure she wasn't dreaming.

He leaned with elbows on the counter right in front of her, and she couldn't stop herself from staring at his biceps. They were huge. Thoughts of his arms around her last night in the shower came to mind, and she let out a heavy breath. Blinking, she tried to calm her heart rate. It was increasing as if she were going to take the stage and talk in front of a thousand people. But this wasn't stage fright gripping her. This was lust. Raw and real. It made her ache between the legs and caused her nipples to become more sensitive than they were a few minutes ago.

"Jaxx?"

"Yeah?"

"Go take your clothes off and lie on the bed."

She could barely breathe. The energy and power that poured off him washed over her in the most scintillating way, she knew she couldn't, wouldn't refuse him. She didn't say anything, just nodded and slid off the stool. She probably should have asked him if his stroganoff was going to be ruined, but she didn't care about that. All she focused on was walking, not running, to her room.

Of course, once she got there and pulled off her top, she spotted the KY and condoms, but it was the cloths that bothered her most. Then she spun around.

"The cucumber..."

All kinds of nasty images came to mind. Dirty, disgusting, awesome and exhilarating things that made her hands shake. Shivering, but not from cold, she took off the rest of her clothes and lay down.

Aries put the beef on low, got the rice organized and chopped the salad stuff. He'd given her plenty of time to sweat it out. He wasn't worried about her not doing as he said, because she was hornier than shit. He'd seen the signs. Her breathing pattern changed and her pupils dilated. She practically devoured the sight of him when he'd leaned on the granite. God that had done it for him. He was as hard as the counter top and ready to go after her then and now.

With all his prep work done, he grabbed a glass and filled it with ice. Plucking out a chunk, he shoved it in his mouth and chewed the cube until it was crushed to shards as he made his way to her room. Images of his dream weren't far from his every thought. He couldn't wait to get this coldness into her heat.

But it was him who got heated the minute he saw her. On the bed and ready. Well, almost ready for him.

"Now although the sight of you lying naked on the bed appeals to me, you lying on that bed the way I'd like you to appeals to me more."

"What do you mean?" She remained motionless, with her head on the pillow, arms crossed over her chest and her ankles locked.

"I mean—" he bent and put the glass with ice on the nightstand, careful to use a magazine as a coaster, "—if I wanted a corpse, I would have visited the morgue. What are you doing?"

She lifted her head and looked at him. "I'm waiting for you."

He stood over her and gestured toward her torso. "Like this? You think this is sexy?"

Her head fell back to the pillow and she readjusted. "I'm naked, aren't I?"

That snarky comment made him smile. It also got him itching to tan her ass, but he was going to ignore the impulse. She was still learning about herself, so he was giving her some leeway when it came to her attitude. She needed the space, and he'd give it to her.

"All right. Since you can't figure this one out on your own, let me help you. I want you lying across the bed with your legs open. Not just spread, I want them bent and open."

"Why?"

Deep breath. He'd had enough with that word. She used it far too often. Bending, he grabbed hold of her hair. With his finger speared through the golden silk, he whispered, "Because I told you to. Move."

She looked like she was going to argue, so he gave a tug and raised his brows. Hopefully she'd get the message. He waited. After a few charged seconds she did, so he let go, which allowed her to scoot down in the bed. He was happy she did as he asked. Well, almost as he'd asked. "Bend your legs." After she complied, he said, "Good. Now put your arms up over your head."

"Like this?"

"Yeah. Keep them there until I tell you to bring them down."

This time he was determined the ice wasn't going to melt, because there'd be no more talking. Only focusing. Him on her and her on him when he went right for the gold. Bending, he licked so hard up the length of her slit that her folds parted, giving him his first taste of her clit. Beautiful.

"Jesus! Your tongue is cold."

He pulled her closer to him. Closer to the edge of the bed as he came down on his knees, pausing to nip her inner thigh.

"Hey."

"No more talking. Bite your tongue if you have to. Got it?" He nipped her again.

Silence.

"Jaxx."

"What?"

"Quiet."

Jaxx nearly came off the mattress just then, because he latched on to her sensitive flesh and sucked hard. Firm, but good. Oh-so good. The tingles started in that area and spread out. Warm waves of heaven penetrated all her muscles. She was sinking. Slipping until—

She couldn't help it. She mouthed the phrase, "Jesus Christ" and jerked when it touched her.

Ice.

I wanted to make you come over it.

She remembered those words he'd spoken in the maze. But was it possible? The chill had pulled her out of that languid space, and now all she felt was the frosty burn.

But then he sank his teeth into her clit. Soft at first and then successively harder, and she focused in on that instead of the ice skating over her belly and thighs. Those tingles were back. The waves. The heaven...

She flexed into his mouth as her fists crushed the sheets. He was killing her. The cold. The hot. So open. So ready. Her adrenaline surged. Pulse pounding. Insides melting.

"Aries."

The sides of her knees hit the mattress. Blood racing. Muscles trembling as the breath was lifted out of her. The light. So close. The tingles rode over her thighs, hips, belly and crashed with a mighty grip on her center. Almost there...almost...there.

She cried out when he took his mouth off her.

"I want you to come on this."

Her first instinct was to complain, but then she felt the slide. The chunk of chilling ice that penetrated her. And then his hand—

"Oh, God." She drew up her knees as two of his fingers chased the ice but detoured to play with her g-spot. It had to be her g-spot, because she couldn't lie still. The acute sensations demanded she move. Flex, pump, and beg for more.

And he gave it. "I can't get enough of you."

The second his teeth grazed her clit and he took up where he'd left off, nipping and biting, she was pushed right to the edge. Because now she had the ice melting inside her. His fingers strumming against her to perfection, and she couldn't hold on.

With her grip strangling the sheets. Her breath coming out in heavy pants. Her hips pivoting. Pushing. Wanting more of all he had to give, she let go. Heat. Ice. Pain. Pleasure.

This time when the waves came, she rode them. As hard and as fast as she rode his hand and mouth. Heart hammering. Blood rushing. She was lifted. And lifted more. Higher and higher, until the air got thin. She moaned. Groaned. Closed her eyes ready to scream. When suddenly her inner muscles squeezed, convulsing against him and the ice and...and...

"Ah, God!"

The small muscles let go with an exhilarating burst, and she did what he wanted. She came for him with stunning tremors that rocked her to her soul.

It took her a few moments to come back to earth but when she did, she pushed the hair out of her eyes, licked her lips and frowned. He was using one of the terry serving towels to wipe his hand.

"That's what you wanted the cloth for?"

"Sure." He turned and pressed it intimately against her.

"I—the towel—don't do that."

He brushed her hand away and continued to use the cloth on her. "Only in movies and your romance novels are things clean. Sex is never clean. Especially with me, so keep the stack in the nightstand drawer, okay?"

She was sure she was blushing all over the place. "All right."

"There. I'm going to go finish getting dinner put together. Why don't you get dressed and see if there's a movie we can watch."

She grabbed for the duvet the second he stepped back, but she wasn't quick enough.

"Don't cover up."

"But it's..."

"Awkward?"

She nodded.

"I told you about awkward." He walked to the door and just before he exited through it, he said, "So let's make you being naked around me so old that it's normal."

Could she do it? She looked down. *You already did.*

A minute later, she was bending to pick up her top when she heard him.

"Where's the cucumber?"

She snapped up straight so fast, the action sent her hair flying in a cartwheel. It hadn't finished falling around her when she stammered, "W-what d-do you want that for?"

His eyes danced and he grinned. "The salad."

"Salad? But I thought—"

"Go on," he said, crossing his arms over his chest and leaning against the doorframe. "I'm listening."

She didn't reply at first, and he tilted his head, so she decided to own another moment and answer him. Half naked and being teased, she snapped her top out twice. It wasn't that she needed to air it or anything. The action was more for dramatic effect. "I thought you were going to put a condom over it, slather it with KY and then screw me with it."

That'll teach him.

She'd pulled her shirt down over her head and went completely still when she heard him say.

"That was my original plan until I saw your fridge had an ice maker in the door."

Her arms were like two snakes in a sack, trying to find an exit. Where the hell were the sleeves? Success, finally. She spun around, but the retort died on her lips when she spotted him. He had his arms stretched up over his head while he hung onto the doorframe. He was so big and handsome. No, sexy. *Too sexy for a woman like you.* What was he doing here?

"So." He tapped a rapid drum-beat against the trim then stopped. "Do we have a GPS on the cucumber? I didn't see it in the vegetable crisper."

She lifted her chin up a notch. "Maybe I lied and didn't buy one."

His arms came down and he smiled like the cat that ate the canary. "You bought one."

Great. Another staring contest. Damn, he was good. She blinked and looked away. "Oh, all right. It's on the second shelf."

"I'm sure I looked there."

She scooted past him and headed to the fridge to get it herself. "You probably missed it. I put it into a large freezer bag after I scrubbed—" She nearly fell into the fridge when she realized what she'd almost admitted.

"Well, I hope you left some skin on it. That's where all the nutrients are." He reached around her and opened the door.

Before she could stop it a groan escaped.

"What?" He wrapped his arms around her and gave her squeeze. Leaning down, he whispered against her cheek, "Did you have your heart set on the cucumber?"

She closed her eyes and took a deep breath. "No."

"Well, then." He let her go and playfully smacked her bottom. "Get out of my kitchen so I can finish making my girl dinner."

She was lightheaded and practically floated to the sectional. When she turned on the television, she barely saw the movie list. She was too caught up in the euphoria of hearing the phrase "my girl" from him.

"Score. You have zucchini. I can do great things with zucchini."

Zucchini? There he was, holding up a large one. She was going to say something, but then he winked at her. That put her mind at ease. He was only teasing her.

"After all, it'd be a shame to waste the KY."

She turned her head so fast she almost fell off the couch. But he wasn't paying her any mind as he sliced the cucumber. The zucchini, however, had a place of honor on the counter. Right where she'd be forced to look at it all night.

"Quit staring at it and find us a movie."

Did he have eyes on the side of his head? She'd find them a movie, all right. "Oh, here's a good one. It's older, but I think you'll like it. It's called *The Piano* with—"

He chuckled really low and downright dirty as he said, "I know who's in it. If you want to watch it, go ahead."

"Really?" She prayed he said no, because she didn't want to watch that cry fest.

"Yeah, I won't be doing much watching anyway. I have a zucchini to prep."

It wasn't the implication that pressed all of her lust buttons, because let's face it, where was the sexy in a giant vegetable? It was his look that totally melted her.

She'd never make it through dinner.

Chapter Eleven

Jaxx stretched and then scowled. What time was it? She rolled over and checked the clock. Seven-thirty. It was the second Sunday of the month, so she wasn't on call. This was a day of rest. She flopped over on to her back and wondered why she was awake. Maybe she...could...just close her eyes and fall back...

Beep.

Her eyes snapped opened. Who? Oh, yeah.

Aries.

She grabbed her phone and squinted.

Good morning, Sunshine. Feel like hanging with me and a few of my friends today? Would have asked you last night, but after the zucchini, I lost you. You need to get more rest.

She sat up. "Ha, this coming from a guy who just woke me up?"

A buddy of mine is having a birthday party. It's for his son. I like the kid, so you want to go? Burgers and corn on the cob. Oh, don't worry, I have the gift thing all worked out. I got him something that will make us look like rock stars. And in his world, that means I'm the Beiber and you're Swift.

That made her smile. How could she refuse? *I guess. Time?*

What? No good morning? I'm crushed after the good night we had last night.

She fell back on the pillow and stared at the text. She dropped her arms, stared at the ceiling and then brought her hands up again. Okay, what could she say? *Had an okay time last night...*

No. She backed that out. *Last night was terrific...*

Overkill, even though it was awesome. *You have mad skills...*

God, no, his head was big enough. *Good morning. Sorry about falling asleep. I was tired.*

She held her breath.

I loved watching you sleep.

Her heart skipped a beat and she had that floating sensation again. What was she supposed to say to that?

I'm coming by at four. Wear jeans, a tight little T-shirt and sneakers. You may have to help me out with the sport of the day.

This she could handle. *Tight little T-shirt, huh?*

Sue me.

She was still smiling when she got out of bed. It wasn't until she went into the kitchen to put on coffee and saw Maggie out back that she wanted to punch someone. Sometimes living in a duplex with a shared patio was inconvenient. Like right now when Maggie spotted her. Damn. She had to wave back and she knew that would be seen as an invitation. Sure enough.

"You're up early for a weekend off. Are you making a habit of leaving your hair down? When Gunther comes, you have to remember to wear it up."

Jaxx finished putting the water in the coffee maker and turned it on. She was determined to ignore Maggie's sniping. "Are you ready to tell me what happened with you and Q the other night?"

"Why do you think anything happened? Did Mr. Taylor say something?"

"About Q?"

"His name is Quentin. And did he?"

Jaxx had been straightening up items that Aries had rearranged when she took note of Maggie's tone. She's been making small talk, and Maggie was sweating big time. What. The. Hell? "Maggie?"

Her friend wouldn't look at her.

"Out with it. You wouldn't tell me before, so tell me now. What's bothering you?"

"Bothering me?" She fiddled with her turtleneck and looked away. "Nothing." She looked back. "Well, nothing to do with Quentin. It's just that..."

"Yes?"

"I was sure *that man* would be out of your system by now. That's why I arranged for you to have a date with him in the first place. He can't be that interesting."

"But he is."

"Don't be foolish. He can't give you what you want, and I told him so."

Jaxx forgot about the coffee and walked over to the breakfast nook to sit down. "You told him something? About me? What?"

"That you prized loyalty, and a man like him can't give it." She let go of her turtleneck and reached out.

Jaxx barely felt the pat on the hand. She was too invested in processing that bit of knowledge. The whole reason Jaxx had fallen in with Aries' magical vagina versus ball plan from the get-go was because he'd brought up loyalty. He'd insisted on it. And now?

Don't jump the gun here, Jaxx. Don't let self-doubt rule you.

"Since my plan of you being bored to tears with him has backfired, I think it's time for a little tough love. Ramsey Taylor is beneath you. He owns that establishment, for heaven's sake. He has women all over him, day and night. He's not the man to give you what you want."

But he was the man who'd so far given her what she needed. "Like Gunther?"

"Yes. With him it's a matter of likeminded individuals coming together. He's into quantum physics. He has more degrees than both you and I put together, and he's single. He's a...oh, what's that creature that's very rare? He's that, and you can bet a man like him would be loyal to you."

Jaxx turned and looked out the window, thinking one thing and saying another. "It's a chupacabra." Had Aries purposely used the concept of loyalty to get to her? She took a deep breath.

Even if he had, she couldn't complain. Off-the-charts sex with a guy who could put Joe Manganiello to shame? Oh yeah, Aries blew him out of the water, so why was he with her? She thought about what Maggie said about him being beneath her, but in her mind it was the other way around.

"Chubra what? Never mind. Enough of this kind of talk. Just think about what I said, okay? And be careful. A man like him is dangerous." She leaned back and smiled. "So it's a good thing you're more attracted to the male mind. I'm sure you'll find Gunther to be a better intellectual match for you."

She wasn't so sure about that. Aries was a pretty smart guy. "We'll see. Coffee's ready. Do you want some?"

"That would be lovely." Jaxx was just reaching to take down a second mug when she hesitated, hearing Maggie's next question. "Are you still going to the movies with us this afternoon?"

She'd forgotten about that. Maggie and two of her friends always went to the movies on Sundays, and she usually joined them when she wasn't on call. "Not this time. I have plans." She poured the steaming coffee into the mugs and tried not to cringe.

"With him?"

Good thing she hadn't served Maggie yet, because her frosty tone was icy enough to freeze the java. *Deep breath, Jaxx.* And here she was, prepared to own another moment. "Yes. There is something else too." No time like the present to bring this up she supposed. "Why am I the only therapist in our group that's on call three weekends in a row?"

Maggie blinked but didn't say anything so Jaxx added.

"It's not like it's that much of a burden as we hardly get any emergencies, thank God, but it does limit what I can do and where I can go on those days, you know?"

"You're new. All new doctors that join our group are required to do this kind of internship."

"That's what I thought. But I've been with the group for over a year so I think I've paid my intern dues, don't you?"

"Has it been that long?"

"Yep. I think it's time I went on one weekend a month, all right?"

"I'm sure I can arrange that." She nodded. "I'd better try Gunther again. Maybe he can change his flight."

Jaxx slid the mug to her, put her own down and then took a seat. Finally Maggie was making sense. "You're going to tell him not to get his hopes up about me?"

Her friend held her mug and blew off the steam. "No, I'm going to tell him to hurry up and get here before it's too late. With all the life changes you're making right now, I'm afraid you'll decide to go backpacking in Paris or something." She gave a mock shudder."

"So what if I did?"

"What?" Maggie's cup made a loud bang when she plunked it down. "You've worked so hard to get where you are. And what about wanting a family and a man to settle down with? Mr. Club Owner can't help you with that."

Jaxx felt like dragging her hands down the sides of her face. Normally she could handle Maggie's well-intended meddling, but lately? It was really grating on her. "It's not right that you're more interested in my life than your own. Maybe we should have that talk now, or do you still think I'm not ready for it?"

Maggie gasped, "You're just like—"

"My father and we've already gone over how unacceptable that is to you, but some things can't be helped. I'm sorry. I've tried very hard to be the better person you want me to be. I really have."

"He's gotten to you."

It was Jaxx's turn to do the hand pat. "Yes, in some ways, I suppose. Good ways, because now I'm sure I have options. Choices I never had before. You should be happy for me."

"I want to be." Maggie sighed, "That's all I want for you." She paused as if she were trying to hold her next words off. Unfortunately she couldn't contain herself. "But I just know a man like him won't make you happy."

Jaxx sat back. This time she was going toe-to-toe with her. "Well so far I'd have to say you're wrong about that."

"Because of the sex?"

"If only it were that simple. No, there's an element of..."

"What?"

She wasn't sure what to call it so she said, "Mystique that surrounds him. I'm attracted to it."

"Mystique?" Maggie repeated.

"Yeah," Jaxx nodded trying for a better explanation as Maggie's confused expression called for one. "I would have said danger, but I didn't want to scare you as I don't mean like the traditional concept of—"

This time when Maggie gasped it came out as a half choke just before she abruptly stood. Her usual elegance deserted her and her hip knocked the table sending both their mugs into a teeter.

Jaxx grabbed the cups, careful not to let the hot and sloshing contents burn her while she steadied them.

"I—I forbid you to see him anymore."

Jaxx looked up. Not quite sure that she'd heard her correctly. "Excuse me?"

"I don't want you to get hurt and I just know you're going to. What about our plans? Gunther?"

"There was no *our* to *your* plans. I should have said something about this sooner. I should have told you how I felt about all your plans."

Maggie's hand shook as she reached for the table. When she gripped the edge for support Jaxx didn't miss how her knuckles turned white while she demanded, "Tell me now."

This really wasn't how she wanted to start her Sunday, but it was clear Maggie wasn't going to let the matter go. "All right. I've been falling down on the job of me. Brushing my needs aside and doing things that *other* people wanted me to do." The inference was clear and she could tell by the dawning indignation that Maggie got the message. "I think it's time I explore the things I want to do. For me. So if you want me to be happy, please be supportive of my decision."

"I can't support this."

Jaxx tried not to get mad. She tried and failed. "Why not?"

Maggie let go of the table and stepped back. "He's no good for you."

"Oh, but all your picks for me were?" Jaxx took her time pushing her chair back before she stood. "I suppose now you're going to tell me how perfect Gunther will be for me?"

Maggie blinked and Jaxx continued, "Walter was your choose remember? He was the decent guy who was going to be good to me. Remember how you said that. Do you recall how that turned out?"

"Jaxx." Maggie went to put her hand on her shoulder, but Jaxx shied away from it.

"No. I'm doing this for me. Trying it my way for a change. I know your intentions are the best, but even good intentions turnout bad."

Although it looked like it killed her, Maggie curtly nodded. "All right. Try it your way, but if it doesn't work out promise me you'll consider Gunther. There's always the chance you'll be attracted to him."

Jaxx doubted it, but Maggie seemed convinced as she plowed forward with singing the guy's praises.

"It could happen. Gunther writes beautifully and his accent is more French than German, thank God. And when he says *Cheri*?" She placed her hand over her heart. "You never know."

She looked so hopeful, Jaxx felt compelled to say, "I can't know for sure, but truthfully? I highly doubt it."

Maggie waved that off. "In any case, I just want you to have first crack at him before another woman beats you to him. He's a good catch, and you're, well..."

That hanging sentence was like a punch to her stomach. "I'm what?"

"Never mind."

She went to turn away, but Jaxx caught her by the arm. She wasn't going to let Maggie's well-placed digs get to her. Not anymore. "I want to hear what you were going to say."

"You're not ready for the kind of relationship Taylor is offering. I know it's exciting, but look at how you handled yourself that afternoon. The desk, remember? You're completely inexperienced when it comes to a man like him. That makes him dangerous. He's already a bad influence. You've looked like an unkempt rag-a-muffin since you've taken up with him. And, quite frankly, I'm mystified as to what the sex club owner is doing stringing you along. He must have dozens of willing women tied up somewhere calling him Master or Sir. It's deplorable."

Jaxx instantly regretted pressing to hear all this. In a flash she was reduced to the inexperienced and stupid little girl Maggie was accusing her of being. Oh, she knew exactly what Maggie was doing and why, but it still hurt. It also shook her new found confidence to the core. She wasn't going to let her see it, though.

"I can handle Aries."

"Aries? I thought his name was Ram— oh, how clever," she quipped and then her expression turned serious. "He is not husband material. Can you see a man like him being a father? Aries?" She shook her head in disgust.

Jaxx swallowed and her hands started to tremble. She was getting hot. No, but she was sweating. Suddenly it was hard to breathe. The air in her lungs wouldn't go deep enough and she began to feel light-headed. Dizzy, while Maggie stared at her. When Maggie called her name it sounded drawn-out as if it were spoken in slow motion.

No.

She hadn't had a panic attack since...since that night-from-hell. Her graduation when Walter was a no-show.

"Jaxx?"

This time when Maggie spoke Jaxx heard her clearly. Thank God. One breath, then two. Better. "H-husband material?" She wiped a hand across her damp brow and focused. "I suppose there was a time I may have wanted the white picket fence but thanks to one of your choices I've been cured of the notion."

"Are you talking about Walter? I told you to forget about him."

Jaxx tried to hide how shaky she was and reseated herself. By the time she looked up she felt stronger. "You think because you told me to forget about him I did? You of all people should know emotions can't be turned off like that. I was devastated because the whole life I planned with that asshole was snatched from me in an instant when he left me for that...that—"

"Woman with her Master's Degree in engineering?"

"Witch."

"I see."

"Do you?"

"Yes. Obviously now when it comes to the matter of men and their prospective gene pools you aren't going to be very selective."

That comment got under Jaxx's skin and rubbed her raw. "Whether I am or not—when the time comes—is none of your business."

"Of course it is. If you think for one minute I'm going to sit by and let you waste your education—"

"That you paid for." That popped out of her, but she didn't care. It felt great to finally say it.

An awful silence fell between then, until Maggie whispered, "I wasn't thinking that."

"But you've been thinking other things. Aren't you tired?"

Maggie clenched her fists and stiffly knocked them against her outer thighs. "Tired of what?"

"Running two lives."

In the wake of that comment the steam went right out or her. She was calmer when she sat down and put her hand over Jaxx's. "Is that what you think I'm doing? I'm sorry you feel that way, but I realize how hard our relationship is for you sometimes. Half the time I'm compelled to be the parent and the other half I just want to be your friend. We're not mother daughter, but we're more than friends." She shook her head and assured, "Just know all I've ever wanted to do was help so you wouldn't make the same mistakes—"

"I'm making your mistakes. Don't you see? If I continue to allow you to make all my choices for me. Good or bad. The results aren't mine they're yours." She put her free hand over Maggie's and squeezed. "I know. I know you have my best interest at heart, but it's time I make my own choices and live with the success or failure those decisions bring me."

Maggie didn't like coming up against this kind of resistance. Jaxx could tell. Her features went back to being unreadable when she pulled her hand away and sniffed, "What do you intend to do with the sex club owner?"

Jaxx could be equally as stubborn. She braced her palms flat on the table and narrowed at look at her. "Stop calling him that and anything I want."

"It's the truth. He owns a sex club where the dregs of society—"

"Stop!"

"Please don't see that man anymore."

Jaxx wasn't going to back down like she usually did. This was too important to her. And now that she'd extended the olive branch and Maggie had tossed it away, she figured she had it coming. "This is ridiculous and...and I should have said this before." She straightened and looked her right in the eyes. "This is my life and I'll see whoever I want. Whenever and wherever I want."

Silence. Then?

"I agree with one thing." Maggie stood. "You could have said that before, but you didn't. Why?"

It was a damn good question that Jaxx had no answer to. "I don't know."

"I do. Until Mr. Taylor showed up, you had absolutely no prospect of a man in your life and you didn't care because you thought you would never physically respond to one."

As painful as that was to digest, she had to, because it was the truth.

"You're making the wrong choice Jaxx. Choosing sex over our relationship is not the right decision to be making."

Jaxx sank back in her seat totally at a loss. "Is that what you think I'm doing?" She shook her head. After everything she'd just said to Maggie this was what she focused in on? "Even if I was, it's my decision to make. It's my choice. Right or wrong. Not yours."

Maggie inclined her head. "All right. Have it your way." She stalked to the door and then turned back. "I'll leave you with this. The way I see things? Ramsey Taylor is a mistake waiting to happen. Mark my words. He wants something more than sex from you. A man like him always has an angle. You'll see and when you do we'll talk about your poor decision-making process, because unlike him? I'll always be here for you. No matter what."

Jaxx held her breath until Maggie left. Then, she let out the pent up air in a rush. She should be feeling a sense of relief knowing she'd handled the situation, yet all she felt was sadness that they couldn't be honest with one another. It was fear that kept them from speaking the truth.

Mistake waiting to happen.

She'd sounded so confident that Jaxx sent a silent prayer skyward. *Please let Maggie be wrong.* At least in this instance because Jaxx didn't know how she'd handle it if she were right.

*****

Aries spotted Maggie peeking through the blinds on her side of the building. This was a new one. He'd fully expected to be confronted by the dragon before he got to the front door. But then Jaxx appeared and he decided not to question his good fortune. Damn, she looked great. And she'd worn the tight little T-shirt too.

He smiled. "Hi."

"Hey." She closed the door and turned to lock it. This gave him a chance to check out her ass. She had the best walking away ass.

"Ready."

"Yeah." He took her hand and whispered, "We have an audience." He led her down the steps and when they reached the bottom, he waved without turning.

They weren't even to the car before Jaxx sighed, "Maggie's a little upset with me today."

"Oh?"

"Yes, I sort of gave her the Cliff's Notes version of my theory about people with masks."

"Hm. Woulda liked to catch some of that one."

She gave a mock cringe. "Um, I don't think so."

"God you smell great. Like lemon and ginger. I happen to love ginger."

She slid into the passenger seat and laughed in a real husky 'don't I know it' kind of way. "I bet you do."

He slammed the door shut and made it halfway around the back of the car when it hit him. She knew about ginger. Well, this was interesting. Now he had another item to add to the list of things he'd have her to pick up this week. Beautiful. He really did like surprises and as he got behind the wheel he decided Jaxx was great at surprising him.

"Why don't you tell me what you know about figging?"

And when she explained in detail, he was sorry that he'd agreed to go to the party. He'd rather have gone to the grocery store to pick some up and then take her home to give her a practical lesson. He was harder than rock by the time they pulled into his friend's the drive.

"Damn, I can't go in there like this."

"Like what?" She turned mock innocent eyes on him. That's when he knew she'd been so explicit on purpose.

"You're going to be punished for this later."

"Great, can't wait." She opened the door and had one foot on the running board.

"Hey, I wasn't joking."

"Neither was I. Where's the gift?"

"In the back. Normally I'd like you to wait until I came around to open the door for you, but today I'll make an exception." He pressed a button and the back door opened. "The present is under the blanket."

"I thought that was workout equipment or something. What did you buy?"

He shifted and tried to readjust himself in his pants. "You'll see."

Two seconds later, she did. "You bought the boy this?"

She looked adorable in the review, standing there owl-eyed holding up the blanket, that he smiled. He'd been on the fence about her wearing her hair pulled back, but now examining her reflection, he was sort of liking it. "Yeah. You don't approve?"

"I didn't say that. It's just it looks professional. How old is he turning?"

"Ten."

"Do his parents know about this?"

"No." He got out and shut the door. "I want them to be surprised too."

"Oh, they'll be surprised, all right. How are we going to carry it?"

"We aren't." He took the blanket and placed it back over the set before he leaned in and pulled an envelope out of one of the side pockets near the wheel well. "He'll have to come find it. I left instructions in the card." He tapped it against her nose once and grinned. "And you made it sound like Dan and Marsha's surprise will be bad."

"They're the parents?"

He nodded.

"Well, I'm no expert, but all my friends with kids warn me every Christmas. They say if I buy their kids anything that breathes or makes noise, I'm axed off their guest list for life."

"Aaron wants to start a band. I'm giving him a leg up."

"By buying him a full drum set—with cymbals, even?"

"Sure." He pulled her out of the way and pressed his fob so the door closed. "The poor kid can't carry a tune to save his life, and every guy knows when it comes to groupies, the drummer is the next in line after the lead singer."

"I have to disagree. My friend Christine is married to a bass player. She has assured me on several occasions that he gets hit on more than the drummer or keyboard player combined. It drives her nuts."

He took her hand and headed up the walk to the house. "Hm. What's the guy look like."

"Totally gorgeous."

He shot a look at her when that came out with absolutely no hesitation. Before he got a chance to reply, she spoke.

"I think good genes trump good pipes, even. So maybe using Chris's stud wasn't a fair indicator."

He was just about to say *"fuck good genes and pipes and tell me about the stud"* when Dan opened the door.

"Aries how are you, my man?" Dan turned his attention to Jaxx with a warm smile. "Hello."

"Dan this is Jaxx. Jaxx, this is Dan Vancello. We went to high school together."

"Man, don't bore her with that crap."

One minute Aries was standing at the door with his girl by his side, and the next she was being pulled around by the host as he introduced her. It might be Dan's job as host, but Aries was having none of that.

He caught up with them. "You're right. We don't want to bore her so I've got the introductions. Why don't you go get changed for the party."

"Ouch." He looked down at his shirt and frowned. "What's wrong with what I have on?"

Aries grinned. "The shorter answer would be what's right."

Dan mimicked being stabbed in the chest, but Aries ignored the show. "Pay no attention to him, babe, he's juvenile. And speaking of kids, I see the birthday boy's out back. I want to introduce you to him."

"What about the card? Shouldn't you leave it with all the other gifts?"

"Nah, let's give it to him now. I want to see his face light up while his dad cries."

She knocked her shoulder into him as they walked. "You are mean."

"You're just figuring that out about me?" He squeezed her hand. "I'll have to step up my game." Leaning down he whispered, "And your punishment for later."

She shivered in a good way. The best way. God, he loved that.

Chapter Twelve

"I don't see it," Jaxx said as she searched the last corner of the shed. "Are you sure Dan said it was in here?"

"Yeah, it's right here."

She spun around and found Aries directly behind her, balancing the football in the palm of his hand. "Great. The boys will be happy."

He put the football down on the seat of a ten-speed bike and said, "But I'm not happy." His eyes darkened, and she recognized the look. "Are you going to make me happy, Jaxx?"

She searched his face before she dropped her gaze to his chest. He couldn't be serious? They were at a kid's birthday party. In a smelly old shed. With cobwebs and dust and the hot lust that poured off him and owned the space and air between them. Damn.

Don't look up. Not in his eyes. Don't. Just—too late. The steel-grey was intense. Powerful.

"Get down on your knees and suck me off."

She should have gasped or denied him. Maybe even stormed off, because logic called for her be outraged. Embarrassed. Ashamed of him. Yet the moment she got wet between the legs, the shame was all her own. Increasing tenfold when she found herself making note of the locked door and being glad for it before she stepped forward.

She was back to staring at his chest, afraid that if she didn't, she'd see the triumph in his eyes. Without a word, she sank to her knees and undid his belt and then the button on his jeans. Being this close to his quietly restrained power was exhilarating. It wrapped around her, giving her courage while taking the shame away. Suddenly she couldn't wait for the time it would take to bring down his zipper. The length of him straining under the denim was too much of a temptation.

Instead of using her hands, she leaned forward and traced the outline of him with her chin and cheek. Rubbing and brushing against the hardness.

"Now this makes me happy."

He took hold of her ponytail and lifted, pulling just hard enough to get her focused, more wet and ready to do anything for him. To him. Her heart beat against her rib cage and her pulse raced. Was that her panting?

She slid her hand up his thigh and took hold of the pull on his zipper, but when she went to take it down he put his hand over hers. "That's enough. Refasten the button and belt." When she didn't move, he gave her hair a light tug and said, "Jaxx."

She wasn't budging. He'd put her in some sort of trance-like state and then expected to snap her out of it in the blink of an eye? She stared at his groin. "I want to suck you off."

"I know you do. But I said no. Now do as I told you," he ordered and let go of her hair.

She refused to look up and continued staring at his tempting package for no other reason than it gave her a modest amount of satisfaction, knowing he was as uncomfortable as she was. "Is this a test? It'd better be some kind of a test, otherwise—"

She fell silent and closed her eyes the second his large hand landed on the top of her head. Just the weight of his warm palm on her while she was in this position calmed her somehow. And then when he spoke, she was back to being breathless.

"It is." His tone was firm, but soft too. "Now please do as I asked."

Once he removed his hand, she opened her eyes. With shaking fingers and heart, she did up the button. When she buckled his leather belt, all she could think about was the night in the maze.

As if he'd read her thoughts, he said, "This is the belt I spanked you with in the maze. Do you like it?"

"Yes."

"Kiss it."

Her head fell back. "Wh-what?"

His expression was dark and unreadable, but his eyes? His eyes burned like steel-grey fire while he waited for her to do it. The silence rained down around her, and she knew she had no choice. Leaning forward, without putting her hands on him, she pressed her lips against the leather.

"I'm very happy now."

He helped her to stand, and a need to fill the awkward moment with something came to her. Grabbing the football, she tossed it up and caught it, asking, "So what was the test? Did I pass?"

"You had to, because there was no failing allowed." He swiped the ball from her and held it up high so she couldn't get it.

"Hey, that's not fair." Smacking him playfully in the chest she repeated, "The test?"

"Oh, it was just to see how long it took you to do what I told you to when you're horny."

This time when she smacked him there was no playfulness about it. "You're evil."

"And you're adorable." She gasped the second he dropped the ball and scooped her up for a bear hug. But then he nuzzled her neck and kissed her there, and she was back to being horny all over again. Especially when he slipped a hand between her legs and kneaded her, right where she was the most sensitive.

Tingles skated all over her as he whispered against her cheek, "Are you happy?"

"I'm shameless," she answered and to prove the point, she flexed into his fingers.

"Shameless is exactly how I want my woman to be."

He kissed her, and her whole world spun away. She was sinking. Fast. So she wrapped her legs around his waist and buried her hands in his hair to hang on to him. She loved the way he made her feel small and light, when she knew she was neither. God, the power of him was the best aphrodisiac of all.

Bang, bang, bang.

"Uncle Aries? Are you in there? Dad says you took Jaxx out to the woodshed, but this is a garden shed. Hello?"

She tore her mouth away from his and panted, "Fuck, we've been discovered."

"Such foul language coming from—" he kissed her quick, "—such a pretty mouth. I like it." He let her slide down him and once her feet touched the floor, he made a grab for her breasts.

"Aries. Don't do that. The birthday boy is at the door." She craned her neck to see over some lawn equipment making sure Aaron didn't have a key to get in.

"So what? It's not like you'll be burning up with shame. You didn't suck my cock or anything."

She hissed in a breath. The guy was incorrigible. "Aries!"

"Oh, relax. The kid's ten. He has the attention span of a hooker who's been paid up front. He's probably checking the house by now."

"He'd better be." She bent and snatched up the ball. "Is touch football like tackle, only you don't tackle?"

"Yes." He brushed his knuckles down the side of her cheek, and her toes curled. "We call it flag though. I guess you haven't played before."

She took his offered hand and headed for the door, careful to step around the numerous stored items along the way. "Nope not football, but basketball, volleyball and golf."

"Golf?" He swung around to look at her after the door was unlocked and creaked open. "Are you any good?"

If she weren't mistaken he sounded worried. Was this a weakness? "I can beat you, I bet."

"Hm." He eyed her. Trying to figure out if she was serious. Wow, was the mighty Dom worried that she could beat him at golf? "I've never played a woman before."

"Ha! Tell me another one, Lothario." She sauntered past him and was nearly through the exit when he smacked her ass. "Ow. Not fair. I was only teasing," she said and dramatically rubbed her butt cheek, hoping to make him feel bad. She should have known better. A guy like him would never feel bad about that because he knew his own strength and how to wield it.

"Did you happen to take acting classes in college? You're quite proficient. And I was only teasing too." He leaned down and added, "But just so there's no future confusion about this—" he reached around and gave her ass cheek a squeeze, "—I'll show you the difference. Tonight. Maybe I'll bend you over my knee."

When he walked off all superior-like, she thought hell, no. She threw the football at his back, hitting her mark, because he was too dang big to miss.

He didn't even stop. Not even a flicker of an acknowledgement that her throw had connected. But then she heard him say, "Was that a little bee sting at my back? It sure felt like one. A tiny, wee little one."

He was such an ass. She shook her head and walked forward to pick up the ball, thinking she could get used to spending Sundays with him.

"Yeahhhhhhh!"

"What the?" She looked up and saw six ten-year-olds barreling out of back door. They were gunning right for her. She didn't even think. She just threw the ball aside and put her hands in front of her face, waiting for the tackle...that never came.

"Thanks for finding the ball, Jaxx," Aaron said, smiling from ear-to-ear. "We really weren't going to tackle ya. Uncle Aries said just to make it look like we were. Are you playing?"

She glared and pointed toward Aries, who was leaning against the doorframe, arms crossed and smiling. "Depends. Is he playing?"

"Yep."

"Then count me in."

"Awesome!"

*****

Aries stood, waiting for everyone to get settled for the last quarter. Jaxx was on the opposing team, and he saw she had a couple of fans. He watched Aaron inch closer to her as they talked. The kid was a snake-charmer just like his dad. He shook his head over that one and was going to look away, but then he saw Jaxx smile and Aaron stand up straighter and, son of a bitch, he was jealous of a ten-year-old. Not that he blamed the kid. Jaxx's dimples, combined with that laugh, had the power to nearly bring him to his knees.

She's beginning to matter to you.

Beginning to? There was no beginning about it. The minute he went into that shed to mess with her he knew it was game over for him. She was coming out of her shell. Responding to him in such an open way he was humbled by it. He thought about that and realized he was in too deep not to be completely honest with her. But first he needed to be honest with himself. Truth was he'd been straddling two lifestyles for the last few years. A concept that had worked for him right up until he'd met her. But now it was different.

She was the link. The connection he'd been missing while he'd been silently battling which way to lean. Before he always thought he needed to embrace one way of living over the other, but now he knew for a certainty this wasn't true. With a woman like her he could have the best of both worlds and that suited him just fine. His own little vanilla doll who wasn't really vanilla at all. He loved keeping that secret from the rest of the world. In his mind it made their relationship that much more special and unique.

He caught sight of her. Damn, she looked great. With most of her hair loose from the clip, her cheeks pink from playing the game and her T-shirt smudged with dirt and grass from when he'd tackled her earlier—it was worth the penalty—there wasn't a snowball's chance in Hades he was giving that up.

She waved to him, and he waved back. Even as he thought about how he could make this work for them. That's when it hit him. If he wanted this kind of special he'd have to cut all ties with the club. And how did he feel about that?

Right then a part of Jaxx's summation during their test came back to him. *You're not as kinky as you think you are.* On the one hand she was totally right, but on the other where it really counted to both of them, she was very, very wrong. And yet none of that had anything to do with the club. He was almost shocked when that came to him.

"We're up, buddy." He'd been so distracted that when Dan punched the ball hard into his stomach, he sucked in a breath.

"What the fuck?"

His friend banged him on the back a couple of times and said, "Oh, that's for the drum set, you rotten motherfucker. We have a two-year-old who barely sleeps as it is."

Aries took a deep breath and nodded. 'Cause yeah, maybe he hadn't thought the whole wannabe-the-rock-star-gift giver thing all the way through. He'd forgotten about their little one.

"What's a matter, *babe*? You worried you're going to lose?" Jaxx said as she sauntered past to switch sides.

"No." And he wasn't, because he was going to tackle her again. Screw the penalty. The win for him came every time he broke their fall and propelled them into a roll. With her hair wrapped around them and breasts crushed into him as she laughed? Hell, if that wasn't a victory, he didn't know what was.

"Uncle Aries! You're phone's buzzing!"

Aries frowned. There were only two people who had his cell number and since Jaxx was here that could only mean Shar was calling with a problem at the club. He hated problems and lately they'd been drowning in them.

Aaron snatched Aries phone off the picnic table and said in a teasing sing-song voice, "It's Wild Shar!"

Damn.

*****

The following morning, Jaxx listened to the newest member of her group and made the occasional note as she was determined to stay focused on her class instead of Aries. She put aside the doubt and anger that surfaced every time she thought about how quickly he abandoned her last night. With little to no explanation after he got the text that had effectively left her high and dry after all the verbal foreplay about spankings and punishments.

They'd barely finished their ice cream and cake when he'd announced he was taking her home. And once there she was left alone with her suspicions and disappointment. They nearly strangled her until she consciously decided she didn't want to be that woman, so she'd swallowed all the hurt and fears she had, that maybe Maggie was right about him, and did the grown up thing. She ate more ice cream and wallowed in self-pity until she fell asleep with a stomach ache.

"But I'd rather not say."

Jaxx's pen stilled and she looked up. Lisa Monreo, her newest patient had clammed up part way in the telling of what incident brought her here. This wasn't good, but before Jaxx could coax her to share, she caught sight of Harriet at the back of the class covertly stuffing a piece of fern in her mouth. *Son of a bitch.*

"Harri—"

Trill.

The phone buzzed and she knew it was Maggie. She held up a finger in Harriet's direction and answered, "Hi Maggie."

"There's a delivery for you. I've sent him down."

That's all she heard before the phone clicked in her ear. She blew out a sigh over Maggie's terseness, but didn't have time to even think about it when the knock sounded.

"I'll just be a second." She announced to the class. Hanging up the phone she tried to ignore the whispers. By the time she got to the door she guessed they were all placing more bets on that pool they had going.

"Good Morning, Dr. Gavin. Just sign here."

Jaxx eyed the large cellophane wrapped package with the attached card and got that floaty feeling again. She knew it was from Aries. Who else would be sending her something like this? She signed on the dotted line and then asked, "Could you leave it on the hall table, next to my office over there?" She pointed to the door on her right as the bigger room between her and Maggie's office was where she held her group sessions. "I'll see to it after class."

"I can do that, but the instructions were for you to open it right away. That's what I told the other doctor when she suggested the same thing."

No wonder Maggie broke her silent treatment to call. "Oh, all right then. I'll take it. Thanks."

When she got back to her desk she plucked the envelope off and said, "Sorry about this, guys. But I'm supposed to see what's in here right away."

There was a picture of a funny little mouse wearing a cardigan on the front of the card and when she opened it there was only one sentence.

I hope this helps saves the green. A.

She thought he was talking about money until she undid the blue and green cellophane and found a large glass bowl shaped like one of her Oscars filled with penny-sized Swedish fish. On a fin he stuck a Post It Note with the words, *Put this on the plant stand, and save the green. The fern will do better on the window sill.* She almost laughed out loud as she did as he instructed. Feeling infinitely better about things with him now. Yes, she was sure it had been legitimate business that had dragged him away last night. Otherwise why would he have taken the time to be so thoughtful this morning?

"All right." She sat down and checked her clipboard. "Where were we? Lisa," She eyed the young woman and said, "It's imperative you share honestly with group. No matter how painful that honesty is. Now you were saying you caught your boyfriend cheating on you and you—" she checked her notes to make sure she had the right phrase, "—wigged out?"

"Yeah. I beat him with a garden gnome."

Jaxx snatched her glasses off and fell back in her seat. "A...?"

"I felt bad afterward. The poor guy."

Lisa had a smirk on her face as she looked around at the other patients in the room. She liked attention. Not a good sign. "I'm glad you felt bad, did he forgive you?"

"Who?"

"Your boyfriend."

"I was talking about the gnome."

Now that smirk stretched into a deep grin while the rest of Jaxx's patients laughed. Even Harriet and she never laughed at anything. Taking a moment to digest the news, Jaxx had to admit it was kind of funny, but she couldn't let on that she did. Instead she asked, "Did you break him?"

"Oh yeah. He cried like a baby when I threw the dwarf through the windshield of his nineteen-sixty-five Mustang. You might say it instantly became a dual convertible."

The room erupted with more laughter and Jaxx knew this was going to be a long, albeit entertaining session. So when it finally ended and she was alone, she picked up her phone and spied a text from Aries waiting. Smiling, she eagerly read it.

I want to make up for last night. I'll pick you up at six. Italian sound good?

She didn't hesitate to text back.

Great. And thank you for the fish bowl! The green is saved and currently enjoying a spot on the windowsill.

Perfect, but I wasn't referring to the fern. I was referring to your wallet. No more expensive pest control to order.

Oh.

Jaxx?

Yeah.

Wear something tonight you know will please me. Something my hands can get into or up without too much of a struggle.

She blinked when she read that. Who said shit like that?

Make sure it's comfortable though. I've been thinking about you on your knees in the shed. God, I fucking loved your cheek rubbing on my cock. You loved it too, didn't you?

And there she was standing all by herself in the classroom blushing up a storm. To have his kind of bold honesty would be—she closed her eyes and took a deep breath—wonderful. She deserved wonderful, didn't she?

With shaking hands and before she could change her mind she text back,

I would have loved to have sucked your cock better.

When the beep of a return text sounded she cringed, closed one eye and narrowed her open one as she read,

Now you're learning.

He inserted a smiley face with devilish bracket above the half colon eyes.

See you tonight.

*****

Aries stayed close to Jaxx. Insisting they sit on the same side of the huge booth together even though they were the only ones in this private dining room. He'd known last night that she was hurt and possibly unsure about the change of plans to their evening, but it couldn't be helped. His conditional purchase of the warehouse unit had to be solidified as there appeared to be another interested party sniffing around so he didn't want to take any chances. And thanks to Shar's quick thinking he'd begun the process. Now all he had to do was wait for the returned documents showing that the kick out clause was removed.

"I answered your question. It's only fair you answer mine." He waited for her to stop fiddling with her wine glass and look at him. Then he coaxed, "Come on. It can't be that bad."

"All right, here goes. My parents handed me a hundred bucks when I turned eighteen and told me to have a happy life."

That pronouncement was the last thing he'd been expecting so he wasn't prepared for the instant fury that surfaced when he wanted to jump to her defense and find the fuckers to make them suffer.

"I don't understand." He took her hand and squeezed it. He wasn't one to shy away from the tough topics. No matter how awkward. "Why?"

"I probably should have told you first, that on my sixteenth birthday my father shared his philosophy with me. He said, since my mother insisted they adopt me so he'd stop screwing around on her and my arrival hadn't change that, he or rather, they shouldn't have to continue paying for me once they weren't legally responsible anymore. When their marriage fell apart and they went on to separate lives I was sort of on my own anyway." She shrugged. "It made for one hell of an eighteenth birthday bash."

"I didn't know you were adopted." But now that he did a lot of things made perfect sense.

She snatched up her glass and took a large gulp of wine. When she returned it to the table she stared into it, saying, "Yep. My birth mother had me when she was young, but I wasn't put up for adoption until she died."

"I see." He let go of her hand and sat back. "How did you meet Maggie?"

"It wasn't a matter of a chance meeting. She knew my birth mother and when...well, when she was able to, she found me. Things weren't very good with my adopted family by then, so Maggie stuck around and when she found out that my parents were basically cutting all financial ties to me, she stepped in. She didn't like any of the colleges I applied to so before I knew it, a few months later we were both living in Colorado. I attended the college of her choosing and spent the next two years immersed in studies while she started her practice. It was a foregone conclusion that once I graduated I would join her group."

"Interesting." The dragon wasn't so much as burning Jaxx, as she was suffocating her like a guilt-ridden parent. "Are you aware that she's got her heart set on some Germany guy coming stateside to knock you up?"

Her eyes widened in such a comical way he almost laughed until she whispered, "She told you about that?"

Now his eyes widened. "Is it true?"

"No."

"Good. I'm not going to lie. The concept kind of freaked me out."

She blinked up at him. "Why? There's nothing wrong with a woman being a single parent."

"I wasn't referring to that. I was talking about Carmichael's idea of skimming the crème de la crème sperm off the conception pool.

Apparently the Kraut is a dried-up old egghead who would have helped you conceive the next Einstein."

She scowled. "Dried up? Maggie never said that. You're exaggerating." She hit her shoulder into his and laughed, "I think she's trying so hard with Gunther because of Walter."

Recalling Maggie's words just before she arranged his and Jaxx's first date he asked, "Was Walter your one long term relationship?"

"Wow, you do have all the news, don't you? Yeah, I guess you could say he was my first boyfriend. I met him sophomore year in college. I think I was too young for him."

"That's why he broke up with you?"

"I wish."

The way she muttered that sentiment had him curious. "What happened?"

She was back to fiddling with her wine glass until he moved it away from her. Then she looked up and said, "I think he needed me to shoulder him through his courses and when those courses were done? So was our relationship. On graduation I learned he'd gone back to his ex. Who probably never was an ex, if you know what I mean?"

"The guy must have had shit for brains."

That made her smile. "Maybe he was just angry that I graduated with same degree he did only in half the time."

Aries had another idea. "Or, maybe Maggie ran him off."

Jaxx shook her head. "No, she loved Walter. She was the one who set us up."

"She seems to make a lot of arrangements for you, doesn't she?"

"Yes, but—"

"I hear an excuse at the ready. Are you actually going to defend the dragon?"

She squirmed, took another sip of wine and looked at him. "There's something about Maggie you don't know. She was supposed to adopt me when my mother died, but that didn't happen. And when she finally found me and saw...well, learned how my life had been with my adopted family she felt guilty."

"Maggie told you that? And how bad was your life with them? Were you—?"

She held up a hand. "Not, abused. More neglected and to this day I'm not sure which is worse. And as far as Maggie telling me? That's a negative. We don't talk about that part of the past. She thinks I'm not ready, but I know it's her that needs to come to terms with it, because I don't blame her. She was young. Too young at the time to take on my care."

Aries considered for a moment. "So this is why she wants to run your life?"

Jaxx shook her head. "No. When I was eighteen she called it 'keeping the reins on me' and she hasn't let up since. You're the one who calls it 'running my life'."

"Really? You don't need reins. Christ, it's just the opposite, if you ask me."

"Well—now this is according to Maggie after she found me—I needed to stop behaving like the people who raised me and start being more sensible like my real mom. Not an easy thing to do living up to a ghost." She scooped up her wine glass and shot back the rest of the contents. "But enough about all that. I just wanted you to understand she's not so bad."

Aries took the glass from her hand and grinned as he returned it to the table. "If you say so." Taking her cue he changed the subject. "Now I've been wondering…"

"Yes?"

"Why don't you ever pull the doctor card?"

"What do you mean?"

"I mean—" he tucked a stray chunk of hair behind her ear, "—if you told people you were a doctor you'd get good seats. A better table. Maybe some free shit once in a while."

Even though she laughed there was an aura of sadness buried in the sound. "I don't know. I don't really feel like a full-fledged one, you know? I'm more like an intern."

He pulled back. "An intern? No you're not. You graduated. I saw the diplomas on the wall. Besides, as fucked up as our justice system is, it's not that screwy that they'd put you in charge of the criminals unless you were qualified."

"I don't deal with criminals. People in need remember?" She shrugged. "I guess I'm waiting for Maggie."

"To what? Baptize, anoint or promote you? Come on, sweetheart. Maggie is not the boss of you."

"You don't think? Why?" Her dejected kick-the-can expression had him grinning until she said, "You want to be?"

This made him scowl. "No. I'd like you to be the boss of you."

"Oh."

He tipped up her chin and lowered his voice so she'd focus. "Tell me, did you like the berries we had for dessert?"

"Yes."

"Good, but I want another kind of sweet." The server came in and Aries waited for him to collect the check. After the guy left, he pulled her into his arms. "Finally. I've got you all to myself."

"Aries!"

He ignored her laughed-out protest and pressed her down into the cushioned upholstery. "I seem to remember a ballsy woman who texted something about wanting to suck my cock."

"You can't be serious? Here? The waiter might come back in."

"He won't. I tipped him fifty percent. In the land of waiterdom that's code for 'I own this room for as long as I want it'."

She gasped. "What are you doing?"

"I'm putting my—God you have the softest thighs—hand up your skirt. Now I'm taking these down. They're silky. Are they the black ones?"

"Aries."

He stuffed her thong in his pocket and nuzzled her neck. "Spread your legs for me. Come on. Get them up. Wrap them around me." He was glad when she did and he flexed into her. "Fuck I can feel your heat right through my pants. It reminds me of the night in the maze. Of your hot ass burning me."

Some of the tension left her so he pressed his advantage. He bit the side of her neck, her earlobe and nipped along the line of her jawbone as she angled to give him better access. "I want you to talk to me. Tell me what you want."

"Oh yeah..."

This time her voice was a hoarse whisper as her grip on his shoulders tightened. He could tell she was trying to focus in on the moment and go with it, but she needed help.

"Is this what you want?" He sank his hand in her hair and pulled. The soft strands felt so fucking good in his palm that he groaned, "Open your eyes. Very good. Now tell me what you want." He tugged until she shivered.

"I want you to put your mouth on my nipples."

He'd been expecting her say she wanted to suck his cock, so when he heard that breathy plea his pulse kicked up speed. "You just want me to put my mouth on you? Are you sure? Think and be specific."

"I-I want you to suck on them."

"How?"

"Wh-what?"

"Hard. Soft. How?"

"I want...I want—"

"Tell me," he breathed in her ear. "What do you want?"

"I want you to bite them."

Now this was... "Very good. What else?" he whispered as he slowly undid the buttons of her blouse with his teeth. Pausing mid-pop on the second to last one to repeat, "Tell me."

"Oh, God, I want—"

"I'm sorry sir. I didn't know—sorry."

Aries leaned over Jaxx to cover her until the maître d turned and left. Then he sat up and raked a hand through his hair. "Fuck."

"Not here. I told you someone would come in."

He did a double take. There she was calmly buttoning up her blouse and yanking on her skirt. It was hard to tell whether that color on her cheeks was from a blush or the heat of passion. Either way it didn't matter. She was gorgeous and looked so fuckable right now that he stood and held out his hand.

"Come on. I know somewhere that's totally private and close to here."

She let him pull her up. "Your place?"

He took one look at cock straining the fabric of his pants and shook his head. "Too far. I have another place in mind."

Chapter Thirteen

A few minutes later Jaxx stared through the open hatch of Aries Escalade and frowned. "What do you mean get in? You want me to crawl through the back way?"

He stepped behind and wrapped his arms around her. Resting his chin on the top of her head he said, "What I want is for you to climb into the back. You can see I put the seats down so there's plenty of room." He bent and continued to whisper in ear, "You'll take off all your clothes for me and fold them before handing them over. Then when you're naked I want you to lie on your stomach with your right cheek pressed into the carpet so you're facing the passenger door on the driver's side."

"Why?"

"I told you to."

"But—"

"Trust me."

"I..."

"Do it. For me. Please."

She was just about to say okay when he sucked in a breath and said, "I love your little shiver. It tells me you like what I'm doing with you. I'll help you up. Come on."

She nodded not sure if she could speak. This was so weird, but in a good way she didn't want to spoil it by saying something normal.

"All your clothes off."

She was on her hands and knees waiting for the hatch to close and when it didn't she shot a look over her shoulder at him. "Aren't you going to close the door?"

"No."

She scooted around so fast she nearly got rug burn on her knees. "But someone might see."

"I definitely know of one person who intends on seeing." His smile almost blinded her through the darkness.

"This is crazy." Even as she said it she was undoing her blouse and peering out the window to scan the parking lot."

"Hey, Eagle Eyes, pay attention. You missed one."

She looked down and realized he was talking about one of her buttons. "Oh."

"I'm thinking if you concentrated on the task at hand it will get done quickly and maybe the couple I see currently waving goodbye to the maître d won't wander past."

She had her blouse and bra off so fast her breasts bobbed. Unfortunately her skirt presented a challenge. She tugged and pushed, nearly ripping the material at the zipper seam as she shimmied out of it. "There."

"Wait. No tossing. I asked you to fold them."

She felt like growling. His congenial tone had a tendency to grate on her in situations like this. How could he be so calm? *Well, for starters he wasn't the one getting naked.* And when that came to her she wanted so badly to look out the window to gauge where that couple was, but fought the urge opting to attack the job of more-like wadding up her clothes than—

"*Tsk, tsk.* Neatly."

"Ugh!" She finished and then patted the small stack. "There. Hurry up."

He leaned against the side frame of the door and crossed his arms over his chest. "Hurry up, what?"

Oh, for the love of God. This was no time for him to be waiting for her to be polite. "Please."

"No. I didn't mean that. I literally meant hurry up and do what?"

Were those footsteps approaching? Was that a woman's laugh? Coming closer. And closer. "Hurry up and shut the door!" She put a palm over each breast and tried to duck behind the driver seat.

"Jaxx?"

"I don't—" she squashed up against the back of the seat and squinted to look between the seat top and the bottom of the headrest, "—see anyone. You?"

"Jaxx."

"What?" She shot a look at him and then turned back to keep an eye out on the lot. "Why haven't you shut the door?"

"I'm waiting."

"For?" She stretched up and strained to get a better look of the parked cars around them. Was someone there?

"For you to position yourself the way I asked you to."

When that pronouncement sank in, she frowned. He couldn't really think that she was just going to carry on with his smutastick plans when they both knew there were people milling about, could he?

"You're wasting time."

Well, that answered that. Slowly she turned to look at him. Taking in all of his six-foot-four, totally gorgeous and completely serene inch of him, she whispered, "What if someone walks by?"

"I'd shut the door."

Of course he would. *Deep breath.* She needed to get a grip here, but then, just as she moved to do as he asked she heard him softly murmur.

"Maybe."

"What?" she grabbed for her blouse and straightened so much, her head bumped the glass sunroof. "I know this is normal for you but I'm a doctor."

His lopsided grin had her heart rate speeding until his voice sounded and her pulse shattered that record and made one of its own as it sped. "Now you pull the doctor card?"

"I—yes."

His expression went all serious when he leaned forward and braced his arms, shoulder width apart with palms flat on the carpeting and looked at her. "And I'm a Dom, but more specifically I'm your guy who has asked nicely for you to do something for him because he has a plan in mind. So unless you have a better one, I would like you to do as I asked. Please."

She was stuck back on "I'm your guy" so the rest of what he said was just a blur as she nodded like a bobble-head and assumed the position.

"Thank you," he whispered as if to himself before his hands pressed against each of her calves. "Your skin is so soft."

Jaxx squeezed her eyes shut and bit her lip. A thrilling zing coursed through her from toes to shoulders and back again as his warm palms stole upward. Over the backs of her knees and thighs, landing with an intimate rub on her bottom.

"Beautiful. Just relax. That's right." His voice was soft. Encouraging. "Arms out stretched and hands flat to the rug. Good. "Perfect now..."

Her eyes flew open and she gasped, "Aries."

"I want them open," he told her while he slowly spread her legs wider and wider still. "There. This is the way I want you to stay while I'm driving. There will be—" he slipped his powerful hand up the inside of her left thigh stopping right at the top, sliding his index finger into the sensitive crease between her leg and center. "—no moving. I want you thinking though. Think about these words. Are you listening?"

"Yes," she breathed.

"All right." He leisurely stroked her. Back and forth. Slow and steady. "Naked," He pressed against her to emphasize. "Exposed." He pushed into that crease with unspoken promise of better things to come. "Taken." Her teeth practically chattered. "Chained, given and used." Her heart fluttered. "I want you to silently repeat them. Explore what they mean to you and what you think they mean to me." He gave her one last stroke. "Close your eyes. I'm going to shut the hatch and come around to the passenger door. When I open it the interior light is going to come on so you'll need to wait for a few seconds for it to go off."

She heard the door open and then felt something touch her forearm. Light or no light curiosity got the best of her. She needed to see what he'd put beside her. Blinking rapidly she'd almost focused when the light went out and now her eyes had to readjust again.

"I want to leave this here so I can reach it when I get to where I'm taking you."

Finally she was able to make it out. It was a small black canvas bag. It looked like a tool bag with yellow piping around the formed handles at the top. She didn't ask him, but she did go through a huge mental list of what could be inside, when suddenly all those dreamed up items scattered. It couldn't be helped as he reached down and brushed a hand through her hair, whispering soft and husky in her ear, "I have something in there you're going to love. It's smooth and made out of metal. Can you guess what it is?"

"No."

"No? Are you sure?" He tugged on her hair and her insides turned to jelly, but then he took up whispering again and that jelly flowed to liquid, "I'd like to climb in here with you. Right now and lick every inch of your body from ankle to shoulder blade. Damn," he released a warm breath in her ear, "With your legs spread wide for me like this I'd be able to plunge my tongue so deep into you you'd scream and pant."

"Mmm..."

"Are you pressing your hips into the carpet? Are you aching for my touch?"

"Yes."

"God, you tempt me." When he kissed her forehead, cheek and then ear, she moaned, but before she could beg him to give into the temptation and join her, he'd closed the door and was in the driver's seat. Now she was left staring at the black bag again. It had yellow piping. It was canvas.

And it was filled with his things.

She was shivering inside out by the time he exited the parking lot and it had nothing to do with the cold. *Naked, exposed, taken, chained...* he'd said that last one before when they were doing their test, yet now it affected her in a different way. A deep way. Right to her core where she burned and ached for him. Yeah, she wanted him so badly that she physically ached.

But then he opened the sunroof and the cooler night air rushed in and over her. Caressing and teasing. Touching her more profoundly than his words. She felt free and alive. Exhilarated and sexy as she pressed her hips into the rug for better contact. Here again, she realized that Aries had touched a place inside her no one else had. He'd found a spot she never knew existed.

"Are you doing okay?" he called.

"Yes," her voice was so low he probably didn't hear it. "Yes," she said louder wanting to say so much more. But then how could she, when she little understood all the feelings coming to life within her.

Some were physical, while others were much, much deeper than that. Flesh and bone was one thing soul-tapping another.

The air, the quiet, the vibration of the vehicle put her in a floating space. Time and reason deserted her as she let everything else go.

"I'm going to make a turn, I'll go slowly though. I like to go slow."

That last gruff comment swept through her so fast she groaned.

"Did you say something?"

When the car shifted she automatically pushed her palms into the carpet even as she heard the crunch of the tires chewing up gravel. *Taken. Chained.* The words echoed in her mind causing her to nearly hyperventilate. "N-no."

Uttering that denial was the last coherent thing she did before she gave in and sank into the tempting avenue of escape Aries was offering. With the wind sailing over her and her excitement trumping her fear she relaxed and enjoyed the ride. Evergreen and the rich scent of evening dampened grasses surrounded her. The fragrance intoxicated her to such a point that she barely knew it when the car stopped.

Aries had intended to go to Monroe Park as it was only a short distance from the restaurant, but the minute he turned on Bell Street he kept heading north until he realized where he really wanted to go. It was to a place he hadn't been in years, and somehow it seemed fitting to revisit that clearing with Jaxx tonight.

After he parked and cut the engine he said, "Close your eyes, sweetheart." Getting out of the car, he added before he shut the door, "Remember, the interior light has a delay so when it shuts off I'll let you know."

By the time it had, he had the hatch fully opened and was standing in the dappled moonlight enjoying the view of her. "Damn, I'd love to kiss every bit of the moonlight I see dancing on your skin. Every last inch of it."

"Aries." She not only opened her eyes, but sat up and turned around. The sight of her naked in the moonbeam shadows, pushing her hair off her forehead as she stared at him was an image he'd carry with him forever. Poignant and beautiful. Devastating in its intensity.

He couldn't decide how he was feeling. Maybe needed? Or maybe he was wanted in a way he hadn't been wanted in a very long time. If ever. "This is what I love. You focused in on just me. Just us. This—" he leaned in and slid his hands under her ass cheeks, dragging her to him, "—does it for me. Do you know how much?"

He lifted her and when she wrapped her naked legs around his hips, her silken arms around his shoulders and pushed her face into the side of neck to steal a taste his skin, he knew life didn't get better than this. He was sure of it.

"Hey, look at me."

Spying her languid expression in the moonshine his pulse picked up speed and even though he didn't think he needed to ask he did anyway. "Are you ready to get in the back of the car with me? Will you let me touch you? Taste you? Drive you wild and make you scream?"

"Yes," she breathed. The husky sound rocked him to the core until she half moaned which sounded more like a groan, and said, "I'd do anything for you. Anything."

Then it was his turn to groan as he pulled her in tight and spoke in her ear, "I'm going to take you up on that. Surely I will." He bent and put her down. So her ass was on the carpet, but her legs dangled with thighs over the bumper. "Give me a taste of you."

He fitted his hand in her hair as his mouth slanted over hers. Forcing her lips to part until he captured her need. Her desire. Her pure and honest reaction to him and it was humbling. It fed him and gave him a sense of power that was wicked and extreme as there were no barriers. Nothing between him and her and what he desired. Exactly what he was hoping for. He slipped a hand between her legs and parted her.

"Aries..."

"Oh, baby, you're so wet. So hot." His index and middle finger slid through her warmth. First going down and then up before he repeated the process. "Does that feel good? Flex forward. Come on. Yeah, good. More. Mmm..." Sharply he bit her earlobe and then licked the sting away before he stopped touching her and said, "Scoot back. I want you to lie down for me. The way you were before." He leaned away and she tried to follow him but he held her off. "Jaxx, please do as I said."

She opened her eyes and frowned. "Why? I thought we could..."

He brushed her hair to one side off her forehead and whispered, "Babe, I'm the one with the plan remember? I think you'll like it if you give it half a chance. Lie back down on your tummy. Arms out with palms flat to the floor."

This time there was no hesitation as she turned to do as he'd instructed.

He had one knee on the carpet when she asked, "Will you shut the door?"

He paused and drank in the sight of her. "Why, are you cold?"

"No, just nervous."

She wiggled. No it was her little shake. The one he loved and he grinned. "Of what?"

"Things in the forest. Where are we?"

"Some place safe." Even though it was the truth, but because it would make her feel better, he got in and used his fob to close the hatch and lock the doors. After all, they still had the huge opening in the roof to enjoy the evening through.

He stretched out beside her and pushed her hair off her shoulder. "Your skin is like velvet." He bent and kissed her arm, shoulder and base of her neck. Smiling when she trembled. "Did you think about those words?"

"Yes."

"And?" He softly nipped at her collarbone.

"I want you to take me," when she whispered this, her lower half ground into the carpet. Fuck what a turn-on. "Use me." She flexed again and his cock thickened and filled even more than it was a few seconds ago. The skin so tight it burned. Swallowing the urge to do exactly what she'd just said, he kissed a path across the top of her back and reached for his bag. Slowly he retrieved it not wanting to break the spell.

"Did you think of an item that's in this bag?"

"Yes."

He rested his jaw on her shoulder blade and blew a lengthy breath down her spine. "Tell me."

She shivered and quaked as she groaned, "A dildo."

He blew another breath then said, "You can do better than that, can't you?" When he put a hand on her ass, she jerked so he stroked her until she settled. "Relax. It's just me and you. No one else. Talk to me. Tell me what other items you think I have in the bag."

"Clamps."

He smiled and made a circle with his mouth as he blew. When he was done he asked, "What kind of clamps?"

"N-nipple clamps."

"What else?"

"I don't—tape."

Finally she was catching on. His smile widened as he blew several more times down the vertical line that split her back. "I do have all those things in there, but there's one more, and that's the very item I want to use on you. Tell me what it is."

"A...plug."

"Yes," he kissed her back, "Only this one isn't a hook. It's small and slender and made of metal." He kept his jaw resting on her while he undid the bag and searched for the oil and plug. When he had both in hand he kept his tone even and low. "I'm going to put plenty of lube on this. I'll go real slow. Would you like that?"

"Yes—no. I don't know."

"I think you do." He placed the plug in the dip at the bottom of her back and snapped the bottle lid up with his thumb. "Is it a yes or a no?" He tipped the container and drizzled the oil over the metal until it skated down the curved sides and landed to create various puddles on her skin. "Tell me."

While he waited for her to get over her embarrassment, he pushed his index finger through one of the oil spots in a circular motion before he headed south. Creating a gleaming line from one of the two dimples at the base of her spine to the middle of a rounded cheek. "I love your ass." He gave it a tap and added, "I can't wait to heat it up some."

"Yes."

"But not now. Tonight we have other things to do. Can you take a deep breath for me? Can you relax while I..."

"Aries."

"Stay still. Breathe." He placed the tip of the plug against her opening and curled down wanting her to feel protected. Fenced in. Controlled when he encouraged, "Push back. It's okay. I'm here. Relax."

She drew in air and did as he told her. He almost came watching the metal slid up into her and when she let that indrawn breath out in a guttural moan his cock was dry heaving for the need to get into her. "Very good. It will take a little while to get used to the weight and fullness, but once you do, it will be good. So very good." He skated his palm through the excess lube on her back and rubbed it all over her ass. "I promise. Now..."

She moaned again when he rolled with her until she was lying on top of him—her back on his front—and he had to steel himself. He was so close to ditching his plan it was a wonder. He prided himself in self-control and tonight, but especially with Jaxx, would be no exception.

"What are you doing?" She tried to shift to the side to look up at him but he held her still.

"I'm going to show you the stars." Capturing her chin he adjusted her. "Look."

Both of them were quiet as they lay there and viewed the Big Dipper through the open expanse of roof.

"It's beautiful."

"Yeah, but not as beautiful as the other stars I'm going to show you. Drop your legs for me. Leave yourself open. Wide open. That's right."

The second Aries' arms wrapped around her and his hands descended to play, she was lost. He did nothing more than draw circles over her clit again and again and again until, this time, her teeth did chatter and the urge to be penetrated overrode her desire to do as he commanded when he told her to stay still.

"I can't...please."

"We're going to have to work on building your patience. You're too eager."

He moved his hand and she cried out, afraid that he was taking away his attention, but then she was left gasping and flexing some more as he pushed that metal object deeper with one hand and slipped two fingers into her pussy with the other.

"Ahhhh..."

"I want you to see stars, babe. Come on. That's it. Push down. A little...a little..." he groaned in her ear and she almost shattered when molten heat slipped out of her. "Oh yeah, make it a lot."

"Oooooh..."

"So wet. That's right. Fuck my fingers. Take them in deep. Deeper."

She pivoted and flexed, gasped and groaned. Panted and cried as she rode the tide of euphoria that started at her toes and rolled upward. Scintillating waves that vibrated through her. Pushing her. Pulling her. Taking the air from her lungs before blessed oxygen rushed back in to sweep her away in a universe filled with bright stars that hung suspended in thin air before they fell with her to earth. Spiraling and careening.

"Aries...Aries..."

"It's okay, baby. It's okay. Let go. Let—"

"Oh, God! Oh, my fucking God." The orgasm that rocked her was so intense she would have slid off him sideways to double over if he hadn't held her in place. Those stars exploded in bright pinpricks of light and shadow that took her very breath away, as her muscles pulsed and trembled in the aftermath of the crash.

"Beautiful." She barely felt the tug when he removed the metal. She was too focused in on how intense the previous moment had been. "Breathe a little deeper, babe. That's it."

She was still sprawled on top of him. Naked to his completely dressed. Exhausted to his massaging her arms, and belly, and thighs. Oh, she wanted to move. To give back. To tell him how wonderful, no how beautiful he'd just made her feel, but she couldn't. Not at the moment. Thankfully he seemed to sense this because he pulled her in for a hug and sighed.

"I think you need a song."

Admittedly of all the things she was expecting to hear from him this would probably have been dead last on her list of possibilities. She shifted against him to snuggle. "I have a favorite song."

"No, that's not what I mean." He rubbed his cheek on the top of her head and she melted. Just a little. "Not a favorite song. You need a song for your soul."

She drew circles with her fingers on his forearm while she thought about what he meant. "Something that touches me deeply you mean?"

"It's something that touches you totally. The one thing you can count on. Like those stars. It can light you up from inside out and make you shine brighter than you ever have before."

Her finger stilled and she frowned. "A song, huh? You're kind of putting me on the spot here."

"No," he chuckled and gave her a squeeze. "You don't have to come up with one now. But you do need one. It makes me sad to know that you haven't danced. Very sad."

She didn't like where this was going. She wasn't a woman who cried and yet she could have easily turned in his arms and let out a whole world of hurt. How the hell had he done it? Maggie had spent hours analyzing her issues, heck, she'd spent a year's worth of nights working through all the things that troubled her to no avail. And then? Along comes Aries Taylor with his tantalizing tool bag and husky voice and she was touched deeper than she'd ever thought possible. She wasn't sure she liked that idea because it meant he was coming to mean something to her and she couldn't let that happen until she trusted him. And it was too soon for that.

"Don't be sad." She squirmed in an attempt for him to let her go. Finally when he did she slid off of him and sat up. "I want to make you happy."

"What are you doing?"

"I'm unbuckling your belt."

He came up on elbows and watched her. "I got that. Why?"

The leather flicked and slapped on her thigh, but she ignored the sting. "I want to suck on your hard cock until you see stars, as I happen to agree with you."

They stared at each other through the moonlit darkness and then he whispered, "How so?"

"When you see them they do light you up from inside out and you do shine brighter." She wrapped her hand around the thick, hard length of him and stroked steady. Up and down while his eyes darkened and gleamed. "What do you say? Can I make you happy?"

She didn't wait for an answer. She just bent forward and drew him deep into her mouth. Over and over. Up and down. Knowing she'd won the second he fell back with a husky groan of pleasure.

*****

Jaxx tip-toed to her door after saying goodnight to Aries on the front step. She winced as her heels clacked against the tile, wishing once again she hadn't bought into the duplex with Maggie. Sometimes, just like last Sunday morning, it was a little close for comfort. Hopefully Maggie was sound asleep and would remain none the wiser about what time Jaxx was finally getting home. Sliding the key in the lock she bit her lip and turned.

Snick.

Perfect —she turned the knob and eased the door open— she was almost home free.

"Do you know what time it is?"

Dammit. That chilly question stopped her cold. Not only was Maggie up, she was livid. There was only one way to play this.

"Of course I do." Jaxx spun around and grinned. "I had the best time tonight."

"You look like a gypsy." Maggie eyed her from head to toe and back again. "Why is every time you are with that man you wind up looking like...like...?"

"I'm happy?" Jaxx offered in the hopes Maggie wouldn't continue with that sentence. By the sheer contempt in her expression she knew whatever was going to come out wasn't going to be encouraging.

"I was thinking unkempt and disheveled. Where are your glasses?"

Jaxx didn't want to fight over that topic again, so she said, "In my purse. Why are you up at this hour anyway?"

"I've been waiting for you to get home. I was worried. You were only supposed to be going for dinner, but by the look of you—"

"Stop. Stop right there. I asked you for space, remember?"

"You did, but you don't understand."

After their last tiff, Jaxx understood better than Maggie thought she did. Maybe it was time they cleared the air a little so her friend would know Jaxx was old enough to handle some of the truth.

"I know you're carrying a sense of guilt that's making you stick your nose into my life. Into places that you don't belong and stepping over boundaries which you weren't invited to cross. Just tell me. Are you harboring guilt over the past? Is this why you continually treat me like a child? If so, we can leave it at that and I'll forgive you. If not? I think we may have a problem on our hands."

Maggie gasped and plucked at the jersey fabric wrapped around her neck. "It's not what you think."

"At this point does it matter? The past can't be changed, but the future can. Think about that before you give me your answer."

Maggie took a step forward, but Jaxx held up a hand. "I'm not a gypsy. I hate when you say that. I like it even less when you make comparisons. I've held back speaking to you about this because I didn't want to add to your guilt. But now that you—not me, are bringing it up, I'm putting it out there. You want to know what it was like for me as a young woman living with those people before you came into my life? It was lonely and—"

"I'm sorry—"

She held up her hand determined to finally tell her the truth. "When they weren't ignoring me, they were crushing my self-esteem and undermined every good feeling I ever had about myself because they were bitter and they took that bitterness out on me. Just like you're doing."

"No, Jaxx."

Jaxx didn't know where all the words were coming from but she was glad for them. "And now that one good thing has happened to me and I'm actually feeling and enjoying myself again, you can't stand it."

"That's not true. Please tell me you don't believe that. I just don't want you to get hurt and you're going to be. If you dance too close to the fire it may keep you warm for a time, but eventually it's going to burn you."

Jaxx shook her head even as she hated. Absolutely hated that Maggie had brought up dancing, tonight of all nights. "What the hell is that supposed to mean?"

"I wasn't going to say anything because I thought you'd come to your senses before things got—" she swept a hand indicating to Jaxx's less than tidy attire, "—too serious between you. I should have told you the other morning when we had coffee."

Warning bells went off in her head and a tiny voice inside screamed to be heard. *Leave. Don't listen to her.* But then that other voice. The voice of reason chimed in. *She knows something you don't.* Her heart pounded. "You should have told me what?"

"Ramsey Taylor is using you."

She could breathe again. "I know that's what you think, but it's not—"

"That's what I was told."

The surety in her voice had the alarms blaring again. "By who? What did they say?"

"He told me himself." Maggie shook her head. "Don't look at me like that. It's true. He said you bring class to the table and he brings the things that go on below the..." If Maggie hadn't looked away Jaxx could have doubted what she was saying. Unfortunately, her discomfort only lent credibility to her words because she believed them."

Jaxx opened her door and tossed her purse on the hall table. She was going for casual on the outside. Inside she was a nauseous mess. "Okay, I'm listening."

"He said it was a fair exchange."

Jaxx felt light-headed. "Exchange?"

"Yes." she whispered.

Although the last thing Jaxx felt like doing at the moment was putting Maggie's mind at ease, she nodded and did it anyway. "No problem. Aries and I are on the same page so you don't have to worry about me, okay?" But it wasn't okay. There was no page. Same or otherwise. He never mentioned an exchange to her. Suddenly she was hot and cold at the same time. And when the inner trembling started she wished she hadn't pushed to hear this. Was it true?

"Jaxx, he wants something. A man like him always does and when he gets I predict he'll leave you. Just like…"

"Like what?"

"Like Walter left you the moment his engineer said yes."

She gave herself a mental shake and then sighed. "Good night, Maggie."

"Wait, I don't want to leave things like this. Tomorrow…well technically today, is the holiday, remember? We're doing the quilt show as they're calling for rain. Say you'll come with us. We can talk some more there. Please."

Jaxx shook her head and repeated, "Good night. Thanks though."

By the time she slipped between the sheets she'd come to some conclusions. First and foremost? She wasn't going to jump to any conclusions just yet. She pushed aside all the nagging doubts and determined to trust—not Maggie, but her instincts. Aries was right. It was time she found her own song as listening to someone else's all the time was deafening her.

Tomorrow when she got the chance she'd simply ask him. There was a concept.

This decided, she had nothing to do but smile when she woke up at the break of dawn to his husky whisper sounding in her ear, "Good morning, sunshine." Aries slipped his cold hands under the covers and rubbed them over her breasts until her nipples spiked. "I need to catch some rays on this dark and stormy day. What do you say we shut the thunder out and make some of our own in your cozy bed?"

Just then he slid his hand between her legs and pressed up. Lust roiled through her and all she could do was breathe, "Yes."

Chapter Fourteen

Aries stretched and reached for Jaxx. "Okay, sleepy-head we need to get up."

"Why?"

"It's nearly noon." He scooped her in against him so they spooned, smiling into her hair when she groaned. One thing he'd learned about her? This woman liked her sleep and she didn't like to snuggle which was a shame as snuggling was one of his favorite things to do with a warm and naked woman. "We have to get ready."

"For what? It's still raining and besides I don't think I can move a muscle. You've exhausted me. One more nap and then I promise. I'll make you lunch and we can watch one of your awful movies and I won't even complain."

"Maybe you should complain so I can spank you. That way you'd know what my kind of punishment feels like."

"I think I'd like that."

He laughed and then growled, "I'd be careful if I were you because I'm pretty sure you won't."

"Now you'll have to show me. I'm curious."

"Mmm, sounds tempting, but since my golf game with Dan got cancelled I agreed that we'd meet him and Marsha at Alley Eight at twelve thirty. Best two out of three."

"So, no spanking?"

"Not now, but tonight, I promise."

"Nice." She'd been squirming and stopped. "Wait, you want to take me bowling?"

"Yeah. You any good? I'd like to win. Loser is buying ice cream at The Slab."

She turned over and smiled. "I'm pretty good. Not as good as I am at other sports, but I'm decent in the lanes." She smiled and then frowned. "Twelve thirty? What time is it?"

She didn't wait for an answer when she slipped out of bed and made her way to the bathroom. He didn't mind. Damn, her ass had a nice sway. He was mesmerized.

"Aries?" She'd disappeared into the bathroom but then poked her head out the door. "Are you coming? We can conserve some water, right?"

When she grinned and popped her brows, he grinned right back, "Absolutely. Let me get a condom."

"I meant coming into the shower with me."

He flicked off the covers so she'd see exactly what he meant. "Yeah, that too."

By the time he dove for a condom in the drawer and pushed off the bed she disappeared again, but he heard her. Her laughter echoing in the small room made him smile. Then he hurried up.

"Aries!"

"Gotcha. Come on." He picked her up and carried her to the shower stall. "Come hard. Come all over me."

He was going to tickle her but then he spied how serious she was and he hesitated. "What?"

"Did you tell Maggie that we were doing some kind of an exchange? As in, I was bringing the class to our relationship, while you brought the déclassé?"

He curled down and bit her shoulder. "Oh yeah, I love it when you talk dirty."

"Aries?"

"Yes, I did say something like that." He kissed her nose and pulled back. "But in my defense, I would have promised her my left nut that night just to escape. Seriously, she had me cornered. I'm wondering? Would you still screw me if I only had one nut?"

"You are bad." She relaxed for a moment and then went full on serious again.

"Now what?"

"I was just thinking we could switch things up a little. How about you come on me?"

His heart pounded.

"We'll be in the shower."

His pulse raced when she pressed her lips against his ear and whispered, "I think I'd like it. Wouldn't you?"

"Oh yeah. I know for sure I'd love that."

A few hours later at the bowling alley, he and Jaxx were tied one-all with Dan and Marsha. While Jaxx was striving for a spare to pull ahead, Aries was distracted, still thinking about how good his cock had felt pressed between her breasts. How she'd pushed the rounded globes together, making some serious cleavage as she slid the soapy sides up and down his length. Angling occasionally to tease his balls with her hardened nipples and making him—

"Okay, big guy, now that I nailed the spare we need either another one to move forward for sudden death or give me a strike and they'll be toast. No offense." She shot that last sentence out of the corner of her mouth to Marsha when she sat down next to her.

"Well I'll be damned, Aries. You finally found a woman who can rival you in the competitive department," Marsha laughed and shook her head.

"Could spell trouble." Dan patted his wife's shoulder and looked over at Jaxx. "You don't happen to play golf, do you?"

Aries didn't like the way Jaxx crossed her arms, resting them on the table before she smiled and leaned in. It was as if she were warming up to the subject and, being that the subject was golf, he wasn't sure he was going to like what came next.

"Why, yes, I do. I play that better than I bowl."

Dan gave out a low whistle while Aries tried to keep his expression unreadable. The last thing he wanted was for Jaxx to find out he had this thing about his golf game. Yeah, she could beat him at anything. Everything. He'd even help to make that happen, but when it came to that particular game? It was sacred. Indian burial ground sacred.

He stared at Dan and Dan stared at him, while he saw Jaxx out of the corner of his eye splitting her attention between them.

"Gee, did I say something wrong?"

Marsha burst out laughing. "I want to be a fly on the cart when you guys play your first game. Please, please, please."

Aries ignored her and focused in on Jaxx. When she turned to look up him he felt like an ass. She was adorable with her hat on backward—well, it wasn't a hat per se, it was one of those fancy French cap things. A beret, he thought they called it. It was grey and looked totally awesome on her. Yeah, with the band that was supposed to be in the back, cleanly stretched across her forehead and beautifully framing her face, her eyes appeared to be twice the size they usually were. The sight made him forget all about his golf fixation for the moment.

"Wrong? No." He shook his head. "It's all good. So we need a strike, do we?"

"I can taste that mint chocolate ice cream already."

"You know what I taste?" he asked as he scooped up a ball and got set. "I taste victory."

He winked and she blushed. God, he loved that. It gave him just the boost he needed to hurl that ball dead center down the lane to take down every last pin.

"Yaaaay!"

He spun around knowing he was grinning like a fool, but one look at Jaxx beaming as she clapped and he didn't give a shit what he looked like. He just opened his arms wide and caught her up high when she launched herself into them. Turning around with her as she laughingly chimed, "We won. We won. We're so good, we won."

"What do you mean no rematch?" Jaxx was teasing Dan he ate his sundae a half hour later at The Slab. She was having so much fun she didn't think anything could spoil her good mood until...

"Is there a problem?" This was the third time she'd asked Aries in the last fifteen minutes. She'd just finished her cone and, if she didn't misread his body language, Aries already had one foot out the door. And, damn it all to hell, she knew why.

"No. I just think it's time I drop you home."

"I thought you were coming back to my place?" She wasn't going to say more than that, although she wanted to. From the moment he got his "urgent text," she was suspicious. She'd heard him tell Marsha it was Sharon, but when she'd asked him about it, he just said it was work. Yeah, right. He'd already told her his club wasn't open on the holiday. Clearly he'd forgotten that fact.

No wonder Maggie's words began to echo repeatedly in her mind almost deafening her. Then when Aries excused himself and went outside to make another "private" call she saw red. She barely heard what Marsha was saying but when Dan spoke up she paid attention.

"It's nice Aries has found himself a normal gal for a change."

"Dan!"

Dan tossed his napkin into the waste basket and said, "What? It's the truth." He looked at Jaxx and asked, "You have any tattoos?"

"No." Jaxx grinned and shook her head because she was pretty sure Marsha was going to brain him.

"Dan Vancello. Normal women have tattoos."

"Not all over their arms, neck and God knows where else."

The look on Marsha's face was comical. Her expression went from shocked to completely mortified. "It's okay, Marsha, I won't judge you the way I'm judging him right now." Jaxx grinned so they'd both know she was kidding, well...sort of.

"What?" Dan blinked. "What did I say?"

Marsha smacked him and Jaxx laughed, "Although I'm not a big fan of tattoos for me, I've seen some beautiful ones on other women."

He made a "So there!" face at his wife and said, "See? Normal." Then he turned and leaned forward to loudly whisper, "We'd almost given up on him."

Jaxx should have been pleased that they approved of her. She should have said something, but Marsha's rebuttal stopped her.

"What the hell is wrong with you today? That's not a nice thing to say either." To Jaxx she said, "Dan shouldn't be speaking about other women that Aries—" she turned and smacked her husband on the arm again, "—you're such a jackass."

"It's okay."

"What's okay?" Aries came and slid in beside Jaxx, but before she could answer him big mouth Dan did.

"Jaxx was just saying how much she hates tattoos."

"I was n—"

"And I was telling her how great that was as the last girl you brought bowling looked like a walking atlas."

Aries stood as if they weren't in the middle of a conversation. In fact his face was so expressionless, Jaxx kept a speculative eye on him. Interesting. Was this another one of his weaknesses? Girls with tattoos?

"We have to go."

"Listen man," Dan stood and held up a hand, "I was only yanking your chain. It was a joke. Shar was great."

Shar? He'd brought her bowling too? Probably on a rained out golf day as well. Had they spent a lazy morning in bed fucking their brains out? What if they had?

Those thoughts made her swallow hard.

Now Maggie's warning was gaining power until it haunted her so badly that by the time they left and she got into the car with Aries, she was now convinced he was going to see wild Shar, probably his ex-girlfriend, instead of coming to her place like he promised. She might not be all that wild but she'd taken steps, done things and said things all because she believed in him, and now?

"Is this a family matter?"

"No. Business. Did you have fun?"

"Yes." The polite thing to do would be for her expand her answer or be a little more enthusiastic as she'd had a blast right up until he got that mysterious text, but she was feeling like shit and she wanted him to know it. If she had the guts she should come right out and asked him, but she was too afraid to hear his answer.

"You're a good bowler."

She didn't say anything to that. She just stared out the window.

"Did you like the ice cream?"

"It was okay." Which wasn't true at all. It was the best. Here again, she didn't feel like saying anything was enjoyable at the moment.

"Do you always sulk when things don't go your way?"

Now she turned to glare. "No I only sulk when a man breaks his promise to me." She didn't add 'and ditches me for the rest of the day to be with another woman'.

"Ah," was all he said and she wasn't going to press him further.

He'd had plenty of opportunity to tell her who the woman was and to tell her truthfully where he was going. Clearly he didn't want to.

And she had plenty of time to think about that as things remained quiet between them until she couldn't take it anymore. "I was really looking forward to that spanking. You remember about the promise you made this morning, don't you? Maybe we can reschedule that when you're not so busy."

"It's not that I'm too busy. I told you, I have to deal with something at the club."

She bit back the bitchy retort that came to her of "the club isn't even open today" and offered, "Well, if it's that important, drop me off at the nearest bus stop. Look, there's one now." She pointed.

"Jaxx."

His deep tone sent those familiar warning sirens blaring in her head. Crossing her arms over her chest, she sank back in the seat and fumed. She had absolutely no idea why she was behaving this way. *Yes, you do. You were looking forward to spending the evening with him and now he's cancelling on you to see another woman. Just like he'd done that last time after the football game. You knew this was too good to be true. A guy like him interested in a woman like you. Maggie was right. You're going to be hurt. Bad.* She took a deep breath in an attempt to ignore that little voice inside screaming, *You're not important to him, but wild Shar is,* and looked out the window. They'd be to her place soon. Maybe she should do the grown-up thing and apologize despite how awful she was feeling. He wasn't to blame for all the personal shit she carried. *He's contributing to it though.*

"Why are you turning here? My place is three streets up."

"I know."

A shiver ran through her at his husky tone. She recognized it. It was the one he'd used in the shower that night.

"Where are we going?"

"You'll see."

When he pulled into Monroe Park, her pulse rushed into high gear and she couldn't help herself. "I thought you had to deal with something important at your club?"

He parked and then turned off the car before he eyed her. "I have to deal with something important here first."

She couldn't breathe. Too late, it occurred to her that she'd just behaved like a child starving for attention. Even the bad kind. One look at him as he walked around the front of the car, and she decide to analyze that thought later. Right now she needed to have all her wits about her when he opened her door.

The second he did she blurted, "Who's wild Shar?"

He scowled and stepped back. "I don't like this, Jaxx." He looked away and ran his hand through his hair, staring off in the distance while he probably plotted a way to end things with her.

"I'm sorry." She turned and scooted toward him in the seat but didn't get out. "I had no right to ask that. It's just that…"

He looked down at her. "What?"

"What are you doing with me? Really? Even Dan and—"

"I'm going to forget you asked me that as you should know the answer already. You need to have more faith. In yourself and your choices. You need to have faith in me. No man wants a woman who questions her own judgment. A real man wants a woman who knows her worth."

"I trust my judgment."

"If you did, you wouldn't keep asking my why I'm with you. It's as if you're two people. You're a confident, adventurous and sassy woman when I give you my attention, but the moment I step back you go into yourself and start doubting. Be careful, Jaxx. You have people in your life who like the self-doubter in you. That side of you makes them feel all-powerful."

"You mean Maggie? I've dealt with her over this already."

"I mean anyone who lets you behave the way you just did without calling you on it. I'm not one of those people, so I'm definitely calling you on it."

"You're calling me on it? I'm not the one at fault here. You're the one who's breaking plans."

"For business. It can't be helped. You know I wouldn't if I didn't have to."

She snorted.

"Jaxx."

That sent a shiver right through her and she figured it was time to come clean with what was really bothering her. "I can't help it. I'm jealous of wild Shar."

"Wild Shar, huh? I gather you got that nickname from Aaron? He's the only one who calls her that." He took off her cap, brushed her bangs to one side and tossed the hat on the dash. "Now out you get." He held the door opened for her and when she exited, she suddenly felt shy and excited at the same time. Maybe he was right about when he gave her his attention. Good or bad. Here she was excited on some level and if his demeanor was any indication to the attention she was going to receive from him, it was going to be all bad for her.

Yes, he was so calm and purposeful, tight-lipped too, because he still hadn't shared who wild Shar was. *Right.*

"Are you going to tell me who she is?"

"No."

So she remained quiet as they walked until the silence got to her again. She hated it. "It's secluded and still around here."

"Yes, it's very private at the best of times and with the earlier rain it's even more so. That's why I brought you. I never understood why they built this children's playground. It's surrounded by three separate retirement communities. No kids ever come to play. Not unless someone brings them."

He led them over to the merry-go-round and stopped. The dreary afternoon shadows made it seem later than it was but there was plenty enough light to see the free-standing squared-off bars that dotted the platform of the ride. The bars were bright yellow, while the base was Bubblegum pink.

"Get on."

She didn't move. "Why?"

"Look at me."

She really didn't want to as she knew his expression would heat her up or piss her off.

"Jaxx."

Own the moment. "Yes?"

"I don't want you to ask me why anymore. You can form a full question when something bothers you, but don't ask why. It's wearing on me. You never ask it at the appropriate time."

She pointed sideways to the ride but kept looking at him. "This isn't an appropriate time?"

"No. You know what's going to happen. You've spent the last fifteen minutes making sure it was going to happen. Get on."

She inhaled deep and then exhaled. "Fine." After she stepped on the platform and grabbed onto a rail she asked, "Do you want me to bend over it?"

"In a minute. Right now just hang on and take a ride for me."

He grabbed hold of the end of the bar and pulled back and then pushed forward so the platform spun at a rapid rate. After one quick turn she was dizzy, but it kept on going. The wind whipped her hair and the storm-darkened landscape whirled by in a blur.

"Don't close your eyes," he called. "You'll get dizzier."

"I'm already dizzy." She tried to focus in on one thing to help her stay grounded, but that didn't work. Her head was spinning as fast as the merry-go-round.

"All right. Hang on tight. I'm going to slow you down and when I do you're going to be tipsy."

"I'll be fine." Of course she wasn't. She nearly fell sideways when he stopped the darn thing. Fortunately he caught her in time.

"Easy there, tiger. Now let's bend you over the bar."

She gasped because she felt like she was falling, even though she knew she wasn't. "I'm going to fall."

"Just hang on to these." She was bent over the squared-off bar, and he helped to place her hands on either side of it, but she still teetered. Then he undid her pants and pulled them down, and she wasn't teetering anymore. She was totally focused and very quiet.

"Ah, I see now I have your attention."

Before she could answer he—well, rubbed would be the wrong way to describe it...chaffed, maybe?—her bottom with the palms of his hands. The caress was hard and got her hot, not in a good way, and made her itchy. Again not good, so she tried to move.

"No squirming."

The first smack with the flat of his hand was shocking. Strangely more shocking than the belt had been to her. Probably because he'd talked to her that night in the maze and now he didn't. He was strict. To the point. A little heavy-handed, to her way of thinking. This wasn't fun. This was...the punishment she'd pushed him into administering. Taking the time to compare this to the experience she had in the maze, she now knew the difference between erotic play and corporal discipline. Both affected her physically and stung, but the latter touched her on an emotional level that stung worse. After he was done, he helped her to stand and pull up her pants. He didn't say anything to her. Not one word as he handed her back into the car. She thought the short ride to her house was bad, but bad didn't compare to how awful she felt when he walked her to the door, fit her cap on backward and said goodnight. No kiss. No hug. No smile. Just polite reserve that hurt her more deeply than any spanking could.

She didn't even hesitate. She walked right to her bedroom and undressed. Once she was under the misted spray of the shower, she closed her eyes and ignored the heat of her ass. Because unlike the first time, this time there was nothing to relish about it and it had very little to do with the physical aspect of things. Despite her best efforts, Ramsey Taylor had found a way to connect with her emotionally. Maybe his methods borderline on the bizarre, but there was no denying her response to them. Why else would she have texted him the second she was dried off.

Have a good night.

She waited nearly an hour to see if he'd respond, and he didn't. Suddenly she was thinking all kinds of things. She never should have agreed to explore things with him. She was out of her element and even when she was in her element, she wasn't in the same league with a man like him. Why did he make the offer that night in the restaurant? And why did he bring up loyalty? Was it true he was playing at an exchange? She thought about Dan's comments this afternoon at the ice cream shop. *It's nice Aries has a normal gal for a change.* Oh, she knew Aries was tired of the word, but she had to ask herself, why would he want such an ordinary woman when he lived such an extraordinary life?

Ramsey Taylor is using you. He's going to leave you just like Walter...

She couldn't bear something like that. Not now that he'd touched places inside her that no one else had. Not her parents or Walter, and what had she felt like when they abandoned her? God, she didn't want to think about that.

The second he gets what he wants he'll leave you.

Maggie's words rang with stark clarity, but then she recalled what Aries had said. Maggie liked to feel power over her. The irony of this coming from a man like him didn't escape her. And the longer she waited for a return text that didn't come, the worse she felt. Her disappointment turned into a physical ache, manifesting in her stomach and seeping into her heart. If she was ever given to cry, she probably would have done so tonight. But then, she didn't have any tears left. Her parent's colossal fights and her father's cutting words to her had wasted a lifetime of them years ago.

With a huge sigh, she settled in to fall asleep and hugged her pillow, wishing to God their day together had ended better.

Chapter Fifteen

Aries signed the last document and handed it to Shar. "That takes care of that."

"Consider it sent."

When she was gone, he fell back in his chair and rocked. Whoever wanted to beat him out of that unit certainly played hardball. And the next time he put a kick-out clause in a contract, he was going to make sure he gave himself more time to respond.

He picked up his phone and read Jaxx's text. She'd sent it hours ago, and he'd decided not to respond to it. She needed time to think, and so did he. He wasn't used to dealing with an insecure woman. Normally he steered clear of them. Too much work, but with Jaxx it was different. What he'd told her tonight was true. She shined when she was with him because he set the boundaries. There was no second-guessing for her to do. No doubting. Was this what she needed from him?

What about what you need from her?

He sat back, steepled his fingers together and tapped them against his lips while he thought. He'd have to be careful introducing her to his needs, and he wouldn't be doing it at all if he couldn't break through this block she had that she wasn't good enough for him.

The second she'd asked about Shar tonight, he understood her better than he ever had. Oh, he'd covertly tried to figure her out right from the beginning. Watching and gauging her during those classes. That was how he learned about Carmichael's far-reaching influence over her, which had to stop. Especially now that he knew what motivated that woman to interfere. It wasn't healthy. The way he saw it? Jaxx needed to stand up for herself and not cave into her fears. He was of a mind that a person had to face those demons and with Carmichael trying to run the show, Jaxx was never forced to do that. He hadn't missed how quick she was to offer up "Maggie" tonight when he'd mentioned the prospect of some people in her life liking the self-doubter in her. That told him she was aware of the problem on some level. Which was good. But it also told him she might be immune to it. Which was bad.

He dropped his hands and decided. He needed to be her everything. All-consuming until those two facets of her became one. Until there was no self-doubter for her family and friends to connect with and only the confident and sassy woman remained. When the idea began to take shape, he winced. It wasn't going to be easy. So maybe this small rift tonight was the perfect jump-off point for what he had planned.

Jaxx was still embracing the pillow when she awoke. Rolling over, she blinked from the glare of the bathroom light clicking on and then sat straight up.

"Aries?"

"Turn over."

His expression was serious. Dark. Sizzling in a thrilling and sexy way that had her heart fluttering and her pulse careening. She didn't even nod. She just did as he said.

In one quick move he had the sheet and duvet off the bed. He took the pillows off too. Now there was only her, but apparently he wasn't satisfied. He slipped an arm between her waist and the mattress and brought her over to the middle of the bed. He smelled so great and his skin was cool against hers that she shivered. His muscles were unyielding as he positioned her as if she were a living doll.

"Get up on your knees. No. Not kneeling. I want your ass up and shoulders down."

She did as he instructed, almost afraid to breathe, but then she saw him take off his belt. He leaned on the bed and buckled it on her headboard. Bringing the long, flat strip toward her.

"Use two hands and hold on to this. Move up some more. I want your chin above your hands so you'll be able to rest your cheek on my leather."

Here again she did as he asked, feeling totally exposed and yet completely grounded this time, because she had a hold of something tangible that was his.

"Spread your knees. Ass up. Shoulders down. Cheek pressed on my leather above your hands. That's right. Stay like that."

Jaxx closed her eyes, thinking she was going to have a hard time getting over the embarrassment of being displayed this way, while he did what? Got undressed? But she fought off the discomfort. And it was a good thing too, because he may have stripped naked but he didn't come to her right away. He sat in her overstuffed lounger and stared at her. Heat rode the distance between them. Burning her up as she gauged his interest, knowing his eyes were on her... and she loved it.

The longer the minutes took to tick by, the hotter she got. Thoughts of him coming behind her anytime he wanted fired her up. She was there for him. Prepared. Ready. Available in the most basic way possible and he didn't rush it. That was the best part. The anticipation. The build. She found herself breathing heavy and when he spoke she almost came.

"Kiss my leather."

She did, and the simple act made her tremble. Quiver. Want him so much she moaned.

By the time he came onto the bed and got behind her, she was in that hazy trance-like state. Euphoric almost. So when he easily slid into her and whispered, "Just what I like. Hot pussy." She didn't blush, move or moan. It was as if she were outside her body. Floating above it. Watching closely as he flexed into her.

He pressed a hand to her back, not that he needed to, because she was his to command. "Kiss my leather again."

She moved to do this. Kissing, then sliding her cheek up and down the worn hide. Matching his rhythm. Up and down and in and out. Nothing but sensations. The heat and hardness. The pressure. God, it was consuming. Stroking and working her over until her hands slipped some on the belt.

"No, don't let go. Get a better grip."

His steady rhythm never changed as he spoke and that more than anything got her adrenaline surging. The tingles, when they came, were deep. The inner squeeze, long and tight as her lungs filled with air and she breathed and breathed some more, as the urge built inside her. Higher and harder. Faster.

"Not yet."

She panted through the need. Trying to hold on. Trying not to come because he didn't want her to, but...

"Almost."

She kissed the leather even though he didn't ask her to, over and over, until he ran a hand down the length of her spine, pushing all the way into her.

"Okay, babe. Now you can come."

She sucked in a deep shot of air and then let it go. "Yes!"

"Fuck, I love your pussy."

Her inner muscles tightened around him, and the friction this kind of invasion created was heaven for her. Hell. Until those clenching muscles let go, only to constrict again. Over and over they danced around the raw power of him and when she heard the telling sounds of all that moisture as he continued to ride her hard, she buried her face against his leather and hung on tight.

It was much later, after he'd put the bed back together and tucked her into it, that she smiled. It felt good to be snuggled up against him. Nice as he stroked her hair. She didn't even want to examine how glad she was that he wasn't mad anymore.

Truthfully, Aries had been expecting a hissy fit, and what did he get? A wonderfully subdued woman who was ready to be mastered.

Recalling how she'd purred all over his leather got adrenaline jetting through him. He wanted more than just acquiescence from her. He wanted it all. He wanted her locked in his collar and marked by his hands. The way she'd just surrendered was an encouraging start.

"Do you feel better?"

"Yes. I don't like it when you get mad."

"I wasn't mad. I was disappointed."

"Worse."

He grinned. "Don't test me, and we'll do fine."

"You test me."

"I know."

"Not fair." Even though she was grumbling, she still rubbed her cheek against his chest. She really was contrary.

"I have something I want to talk to you about."

She tilted her head back and looked right at him. "Okay."

"I want to do a Scene with you."

She stiffened. "At your club?"

"No. At my house."

She relaxed at the same time she let out a breath. "I'm glad to hear that. Sex clubs are not my style."

And neither were tattoos. One he could deal with, the other he couldn't, but they'd cross that bridge when they got to it.

"I'm going to be giving you instructions over the course of the week in preparation for it. Tomorrow I'll send you over a list of limits, and I want you go through and take off the things that would be intolerable for you. The rest can be rated from one to five. Five being you hate it to one being it's okay."

"I think I can do that."

"I'm going to buy what you'll wear."

"Are my choices on the list?"

"No. I'm also going to tell you what to eat for forty-eight hours beforehand."

"That sounds ominous."

"It's practical. Women usually do stupid things before they have a big night with a guy. Like skip dinners and lunch so they can get into that fancy dress. I don't want you fainting when I'm in the middle of—" He caught himself.

"Yes?"

He lowered his voice, "Giving you my undivided attention."

She snuggled back down and sighed, "I'd like that."

But he was smart enough to know that she wouldn't. At least not a hundred percent of the time.

"So you'll have to be on your toes this week, because I'll have a lot for you to do." He felt her nod against him and figured now was a good time to start. "The week starts now, Jaxx. I want you to go in the bathroom and shave yourself."

"Shave?" Her head came up and she frowned. "My legs, you mean?"

He shook his head.

She swallowed hard. "All of it?"

He nodded.

"I've never done that before."

"Well, do it now and make me happy."

"I'm not even sure I'd really know how to go about doing it."

He took hold of her hair and pulled her over him. Until they were nearly nose to nose. "I know how to go about it. Would you like me to take you into the bathroom and do it for you?"

"No. I can do it."

As soon as he let go of her hair, she slid off him and jumped up. He'd never seen anyone exit a room so fast. Unfortunately she was going in the wrong direction. He sat up. "Where are you going?"

"I'm getting my laptop."

"Why?"

A minute later she sauntered through the door with a big white terry towel wrapped around her and had her laptop in hand. "This isn't an appropriate time to be asking why."

"Jaxx."

Her chin came up a notch. "What? I'm going to look it up. There are probably a few good tricks to doing it."

"You have ten minutes and then I'm coming in after you."

"Ten minutes?" She rushed into the bathroom. "I'd better get going on this."

"Do a good job, because when you're done I'm going to be checking."

She leaned partway out and made a face. "Okay, ew."

He looked at the alarm clock. "Nine minutes." She didn't move, so he slid the sheet off his lap. The sight of his hard cock was sure to back up his words. "I'm dying to get in there and do it for you, so waste all the time you want."

Her eyes widened, then she gasped and disappeared. So adorable. He gave a soft chuckle before he eased back down and put his hands behind his head content to listen. He heard running water, the sound of shaving cream leaving the can, a few goddammits, one Hail Mary and a promise to Bart Simpson that made absolutely no sense before she came out with seconds to spare.

He rolled to his side and came up on elbow. "Take off the towel."

"I don't want to."

"Okay," He frowned as he sat up and moved to the edge of the bed. A strip of the sheet lay over his lap when he spread his legs, making a V. Patting his thigh he said, "Come over here and I'll take the towel from you."

Amazing. She had no problem with that. She sat on his lap and when she was comfortable, he undid the towel. "Let me see."

She averted her gaze which made him smile. He also took hold of her chin and brought it around until she was looking him right in the eyes. "Did you do a good job?"

"No."

He was trying hard not to grin. He could tell she was pissed. "Why?"

"I didn't have my glasses."

"Hm. I'd better take a look." He kissed her neck and shoulder and breathed in her ear, "Spread your legs, honey. That's right. A little more. A little..." When he caught sight of her delicate skin, he sucked in air. "Damn, I never thought your pussy could get any sweeter, but now it is."

"Aries."

"I want you to lie back." He shifted her so her upper half was on the bed and the lower half across his lap. "Stay still. I'm going to show you a trick that will blow your mind."

He had to do this just right. Jaxx responded to heavier sensations almost to the point of pain. Otherwise she lost focus.

He pinched her clit between his forefinger and thumb. Harder than he normally would have, but for her benefit. He wanted the blood momentarily cut off from this bundle of nerves while he slid two fingers into her, going deep.

"Oh, God!"

He'd warm her up first. A simple finger-fuck until he had her hot and restless. "Does that feel good?"

"Oh, yes."

"No flexing. Only I'm allowed to move." When she stopped, he whispered, "Good girl. I love when you do things for me. You're going to do things for me when I tell you to, aren't you, Jaxx? You're going to do everything I want you to, won't you?" He pushed in deep and wagged his fingers.

"Yes," she panted.

"Promise. Promise me. Say you're going to do it. Everything. All I want. Say it."

"I promise...oh God, I'll do anything you want me to do. Anything."

"Very good." He readjusted and held her clit hostage while he reached up deeper inside her and searched. He knew it was just... There. "The mind-blowing? It involves stimulating this spot. Then..."

She gasped.

"This spot."

She groaned.

"And this one."

She screamed. And screamed some more when he released her clit so blood could circulate again. While she enjoyed the residual effects of what he called a sexual trifecta of several orgasms, he was free to examine her cleanly shaven slit that eventually gleamed with a gorgeous pearly shine.

"Fuck this is the prettiest, wettest pussy. It's just begging to be tasted." He shifted and repositioned her. Lifting her hips and spreading her wide until he got his mouth fully on her.

"Aries, I'll do anything for you. Anything..."

That sighed-out promise was one he was going to hold her to. Damn, tomorrow couldn't come soon enough for him.

Chapter Sixteen

The next day, Jaxx had just finished with the last of her morning appointments when Aries texted her.

Hi, get a pen and piece of paper. I'll wait.

She read that and blinked. What, no "good morning" or "how are you after my little visit last night?" She bit back a grin as she tapped out the short response on her phone.

Who is this?

I'm waiting...

Hm. Someone was no fun today. She blew out a sigh and grabbed a sheet of paper from her desk.

Ready.

Two Hundred and twelve Penton Street, suite five. Find Everything Retro. That's the name of the store that has your outfit. I want you to go there and pick it up today.

She had a rough idea where it was. She checked the time. If she hurried, she could be there and back before her next appointment.

Okay.

But don't skip lunch to go. Speaking of lunch, eat more than a salad today. Why don't you splurge and have a sandwich.

She said she would, but how could she when she was dying of excitement to see what he'd picked out for her? In the end she wound up eating a half a sandwich and her usual salad. Then she had her two afternoon appointments and left for the shop.

The place was one of the newer stores in this up-and-coming part of the city. So much building was going on in the downtown core, she barely recognized it as she drove in, but this older section remained the same. Waiting at the front desk while the clerk went to get her order, she eyed the merchandise that lined the walls from floor to ceiling. There were gowns reminiscent of the forty and fifties Hollywood glamour displayed side by side with Harley Davidson-type leather gear. The merchandizers certainly knew what they were doing. The place had an eclectic vibe that drew a person in.

"Here you are, Ms. Gavin."

"Thank—what's this?" She pointed to the Post-It note on the top of the box and scowled. Not that she needed confirmation. The words "Do not open" were clear enough. She just wanted to make sure they were meant for her.

"Mr. Taylor packed the box himself. He was the one who left those instructions like that. I know they weren't meant for me or my staff."

The inference being clear. Perfect. Now she couldn't say she'd opened it by mistake because she thought it was meant for the sales people. "Thanks. It's all paid for?"

"Ah, yeah, sure thing."

By the time she got home, she was absolutely dying to see what was in the box. She put it and her purse on the counter and texted Aries.

I have it.

Who is this?

Very funny. Can I open it?

No, put it on the coffee table.

And?

Nothing. Leave it there. What are you having for dinner? I can't come by tonight, but I was thinking you should make that chicken. Either that or freeze it.

Chicken? She went to the fridge and sure enough, there was a small package of free-range boneless breasts right there on the second shelf. Huh.

What are you, the grocery police or what?

I'm the dietary police. Make some grilled chicken, and there's some leftover rice in the Tupperware container. I'd say slice some zucchini for a vegetable but...

The blush burned a path from her chest to her cheeks. She shook her head and was just about to tell him she'd be going with the baby carrots tonight when another text arrived.

I love it when you blush.

She gasped and then scowled as she shot off a reply.

I'm having carrots and I'm not blushing.

Liar.

After dinner she sat on the couch. With elbows bent and braced on her knees, she laced her fingers together and rested her chin on the bridge they made, staring at the box...willing it to open of its own accord.

What did he buy? Leather. God, she hoped it wasn't satin. Satin wasn't good for her curves. Spandex was pretty good though. What if it was one of those hokey costumes? Like a nurse uniform or French maid outfit? She'd die. What if it didn't fit?

She sat up and dropped her hands. That would be a real shame. It would ruin the whole night. His whole Scene with her would be ruined. Guys didn't think about things like this. He probably hadn't.

She leaned forward. She'd better—

Beep

Her phone. A text from Aries.

Don't open it. I'll know if you do.

She sat back and glared at the phone in her hand. She wasn't going to answer him. Instead, she tossed her cell and let it bounce beside her on the couch. He really was evil.

Beep

She wasn't looking.

Beep

Not looking.

Beep, beep, beep

"Evil and relentless." She snatched it up and read.

Don't be mad.

Be patient.

Jaxx, answer me when I text you.

And he was telling her to be patient?

Geez, I was in the bathroom.

Are you blushing?

Did he know everything? She was blushing.

Yes, how did you know?

Because you're lying. You weren't in the bathroom.

She scowled and typed back,

Did you want something?

Yes, your list. You remembered to fill it out, didn't you? I'm waiting for it.

The list. She wished she had the list. This morning she was running late and didn't have time to turn on her desktop computer to print it. She'd thought to get to it at lunch, but then she'd gone shopping. She knew he'd been expecting it before this.

Didn't I send that to you this morning?

LMAO. No. Go do it now and get it over to me.

She tossed the phone on coffee table and shot up. She'd taken no more than two quick steps when it beeped.
"Oh, for fuck's sake." She marched back and picked it up.

Tea?

Now what was he trying to pull?

I only drink coffee. Naked. In the moonlight.

All I have is tea. Jaxx, are you okay?

What the—oh no.

Sorry Maggie, I thought you were someone else.

Don't tell me.

So she didn't. She did, however, race to her desktop and sit and wait the ten minutes it took to load the ancient thing. Finally. Rubbing her hands together, she logged into her email and clicked on the attachment he'd sent. Three words into the list, and she was beyond gasping or blushing. This shit was right up there with the instructions on the how-to list of making someone die of embarrassment.

Cunnilingus and clit torture? Oh yeah, she was dying here...

*****

Aries was happy with Jaxx's list, with the exception of one item he'd been expecting an issue with. Tattoos. She was totally adverse, as in struck a line right through the word and added exclamation marks next to it even. That hurt. His one non-negotiable was going to be a sticking point with her. Well, not right away. Fortunately he had some time to convince her, if they got that far. And as of right now it was looking as if they would.

She'd done well today. She hadn't told him to go fuck himself when she'd realized she wouldn't be allowed to see her outfit. That was good. But then, when she'd sent over her list, she'd ended her email with, "and don't bother to text me for the rest of the night. I've turned my phone off because I'm tired." That was bad. He didn't like not being able to reach her and he was going to tell her so. Right after he woke her up to make him happy.

He didn't say anything, just shook her awake.

"Mmm?" She yawned and rolled over. "Aries? What time is it?"

She was getting used to his middle-of-the-night visits. She didn't startle. He liked that. "I want you to get out of bed and come to the chair with me."

She sat up and rubbed the sleep out of her eyes. "For what?"

He sat in the lounger and said, "I want you to kneel right here. Right between my spread legs and undo my belt."

She nodded and got up from the bed. Seeing her in the pale light cast from the hall got his adrenaline pumping. She had a woman's body. With real curves and some padding that did great things for her tits and ass.

"Right here, that's right." He leaned back to give her access to his belt and when she had it unbuckled, he whispered, "Now take it off me."

She had to tug a couple of times, but eventually she got it and when she went to drop it, he said, "No, hand it to me."

She probably thought he was going to use it on her. Well, he was. Just not the way she thought. "Look at me." Her eyes always seemed larger right after she woke. "I want you to trust me, okay?" He waited for her to nod and then said, "I'm going to buckle this around your throat. Not too hard—you'll still be able to breathe. But hard enough so you'll know my leather is wrapped around your throat and holding you while you suck my cock. Hold up your hair."

He leaned forward and drew the belt around her neck. "Lift your chin. A little higher," he said as he threaded the leather through the buckle and tightened. "See? Not too tight." When the prongs engaged in the holes so that it wouldn't tighten anymore, he wrapped the excess leather around his hand and pulled. "Now undo my pants."

When she had them undone but didn't move to do any more than that, he gave the belt a tug. "You know what to do. Make me happy. It's that simple."

His grip remained tight on the leather as she worked. He wasn't going to help her. This was up to her and how badly she wanted to satisfy him. In no time at all she'd gotten his cock out, but instead of going right to it and taking it in her mouth, she did something totally unexpected. She used her hands and fingers to explore him. Petting and rubbing. Squeezing, which pleased the fucking hell out of him. Because watching her discover him this way was a different kind of turn-on. A more meaningful experience that touched him deeply. It was slow. Thorough. Bordering on bliss-filled torture.

Already he was harder, longer, thicker and ready to explode the moment he gave himself permission to, and she hadn't even gotten her mouth on him. That was the amazing part. A heaviness settled in his belly and lower, branching out. Rolling and reaching as he watched her. With one hand holding his leather tight around her neck, he rested his other on the top of her head. He'd noted before how she'd responded to the gesture, and he hadn't been wrong. The second he did it, it was as if she dipped on cue, but instead of her mouth taking him inside, she licked him.

From the base where his cock met his ball sac to his tip, she dragged her tongue. He wasn't a man to say he shivered, but it was something fucking close when she dragged her tongue back down. Only slower, and not on the same path. She made a new one, which left the old one to chill in the air after she abandoned that saliva thread. Over and over she did it. Teasing with kisses to the top of his dick until he almost lost patience and demanded she open up and take him inside her mouth. Would she ever?

Oh, fuck, yeah. Her mouth opened and opened some more as he slid over the cradle she fashioned her tongue into and went deeper to the back of her throat. There was so much he wanted to say. Do. Command, but that wasn't the point of tonight. The belt around her neck was, and yet? He'd nearly forgotten about it. He nearly forgotten about everything as she surrendered to the moment and focused on him. On giving him pleasure. He reached down and felt between her legs. Soaked. She was soaked. He grabbed hold of his dick and gently pulled it out of the suction of her mouth. If he didn't have hold of the leather around her neck, she would have dove forward for more.

When she was six inches from him, panting but not trying to hang herself any longer, he let go of the belt and ordered, "Turn around and get on all fours."

Thankfully she did, because he needed a few seconds to regroup. Get the condom out of his pocket and—fuck. She dropped her shoulders down toward the floor and lifted her ass toward the ceiling. Just the position he loved. Closing his eyes, he took a deep breath then opened them and said, "Spread your knees. Wider and keep that ass up. Is your pussy aching? I bet it is."

He tugged on the condom and kneeled behind her. Astounded when, with one arm and shoulder to the floor, and cheek turned sideways against the wood, she used her free hand to reach back and give him his strip of leather. He wound it around his palm and decided she deserved to come twice for that.

"Do you love the weight of my leather around your throat?" He slid his cock into her slowly, going halfway in and stopping, wanting to hear her answer. "Do you?"

"Yes." She tried to push back but he stopped her.

"Say it."

She moaned and attempted to move, but he held a firm grip on the belt so she couldn't. "Say you love my leather around your throat. You love the way it makes you feel. Owned. Needed. Wanted."

"I..." He felt it. That shiver. The one she did when she truly enjoyed something and his heart beat like a drum against his rib cage. "I love it. I do. It makes me feel safe and protected."

Her words were better than his. So much better. He leaned over, reaching for her clit, whispering once he got hold of it, "Do you want me to show you another trick I know that will blow your mind?"

He was careful as he slammed into her, making sure the tip of his cock beat with steady precision against her G-spot. Over and over and over.

She gasped. Moaned. Groaned and then screamed when he gave her back-to-back orgasms before he hammered into her to find his own with a growl.

"I don't think I can move," she finally said.

"Do you want me to help you to the bed?"

"No, that's okay. I can manage."

Aries watched her get up. She didn't take any notice of his belt, which was still locked around her neck. It looked great against her skin. And with the slack length of it falling down to the apex of her thighs, all kinds of ideas came to him. Like what he could connect to the end of that before he—

"Are you coming to bed? You're going get cold lying there."

He didn't think so. His heated thoughts warmed him. "Yeah, I'll be there in a minute."

He got up and went into the bathroom and by the time he came out, she was sitting up in the bed. She always looked sexy after he'd fucked her hard, but tonight with the belt wrapped around her neck? She was the prettiest he'd ever seen her. Albeit a little

neck? She was the prettiest he'd ever seen her.

neck? She was the prettiest he'd ever seen her. Albeit a little pensive at the moment. That could only mean one thing.

"You look great." He dove over her and spread out beside her with arm bent and chin propped in his hand. "Is this going to be a long discussion, do you think?"

She shook her head and smiled. A deep smile that showed off her dimples and made her eyes sparkle when she looked down at him. "No, I don't think so. I just wanted to ask you one thing."

He picked up the end of the belt and played with it. He was feeling something. Something good. Really good, with his hand on the end of the leather and the other end wrapped around her throat. "Ask."

She looked him in the eyes. Her gaze was deep. Penetrating. This was important to her. Whatever she had to ask him he knew the answer he gave was going to mean something to her. "Do you want to take the belt off...or, um, should I?"

"I don't want to take it off," he said and could almost feel her disappointment as she sat forward. When she brought her hands up, he whispered, "Don't touch my leather, Jaxx. If I put it on you, I'm the only one to take it off, do you understand?" He sat up and after she nodded, he added, "What I meant was I didn't want to take it off you just yet. I like it on you. Come here."

He opened his arms and when she leaned into them, he fell back in the bed with a sigh. She was a handful. Smart. Too smart and stubborn, didn't barely even cover it, but he wanted her. He wanted her all to himself.

"You're crushing me."

Her playful growl made him grin and when she poked him in the ribs to get him to loosen his grip, he chuckled, "Okay, easy there, tiger. Relax." He opened his arms and let her slide off his chest so she was lying beside him. Then he dug the belt out from between their bodies and took hold of it.

He should take it off her and go, but he didn't want to. It felt nice. Better than nice lying next to her. He closed his eyes as he rubbed the leather with his thumb, thinking about how great it was going to be to Scene with her. She was going to be a pleasure. An absolute joy to master.

"I think I'm cut out for this," she whispered and God love her, she tugged on the leather. "I do. It's not like I want you to tell me what to do during the day or anything. Actually, when you do, it annoys the shit out of me because I have things I need to get done that don't involve you. There are people I work with and decisions I make every day that you can't help with, but that said?" She snuggled up to him. "When we're like this, I'd do anything for you. Anything."

"Do you know how glad I am to hear that?"

She was walking her fingers over his chest then stopped. "So, you're not bothered by the fact I find you annoying occasionally?"

"No, but just so you don't feel bad about that, on occasion, I find you're no peach either."

She snorted. "Well, at least I'm not trying to rule the world."

He leaned back and popped his shoulder to make her look up. When she did, he said, "You could have fooled me."

"What? Why? Because I challenge you?"

She was staring, so he stared right back. "Maybe."

"Bullshit."

"Do you kiss your mother with that mouth?"

"No, I kiss you, and I don't hear you complaining."

He held her gaze while he wrapped the belt around his palm until there was no slack left, much like in the atmosphere around them. It got heavy. Quiet. Intense as he whispered, "The only time I'm going to complain is when you displease me. Right now? I'm enjoying your feistiness because you need it, Jaxx. Somewhere along the way something happened. I think I know what it is, but until you do, I'm not going to say. Use the elves. They're in your corner, and when those guys come out, they're swinging."

His grip eased while he waited for her to say something. He expected something sarcastic, so when she laid her cheek over his heart and whispered, "For a smart cookie I'm pretty dumb. I can help other people understand their problems but when it comes to my own life it's like I'm swimming in pool of water locked in a body bag."

He drew her in closer. This was his opening. The perfect time to ask her again. "Why do you have to figure yourself out?"

She stopped rubbing her jaw up and down his pec, and said, "So I know."

Her breath fanning his skin felt calming. Right. "Why you are the way you are?"

She nodded.

"And when you discover the answer, what are you going to do about it?"

She leaned up on elbow and stacked one hand on top of the other on his chest before resting her chin on them. "What do you mean?"

"I like who you are, don't you?"

She frowned while she thought about that, so he'd give her more to think about.

"I see a woman who's growing into her future because her past, no matter what happened there, isn't holding her back. She just needs a little confidence and maybe a spanking once in a while to set her straight." She blinked, and he couldn't help himself. "I wasn't going to gossip, but word is? The elves are exhausted."

She got up on her knees, and blood drained to his cock. The sight of her naked, hair all mussed from their playing and his belt around her throat had his adrenaline revving. But this wasn't the time. She needed him in a different way right now.

"You know? I'm more myself when I'm with you. It's like I know who I really am and I think...I think I like who that person is more than the other ones."

He shook his head. "Other ones?"

"Yeah, there's the Jaxx who tried to be the best daughter so her parents would like her better and then there's the Jaxx who tries to be sensible and calm so she won't disappoint Maggie. I just want to be me and with you I can be that. There's no stress."

His desire was all but forgotten. She'd just given him the best compliment. Now more than ever he knew things had to work out between them, because if he weren't mistaken, Jaxx Gavin had just wrecked his chances with ninety percent of the female population.

"Come here." He pulled her by the belt down to him and kissed her deeply. "I like who you are too. So if there was bad shit along the way you had to deal with? I'm not sorry about it, I'm thankful for it. It made you who you are. And I repeat. I like who you are."

She combed her fingers through his hair while she looked to be digesting this. Then she stopped. "Could you put a good word in for me with the elves? This is no time for them to be exhausted."

He pulled her down. Close. Searching her face and then eyes. "Fuck the elves, babe. You have me now."

He wasn't expecting the response he got when she wound her arms around his neck and squeezed tight. He knew she hadn't meant for him to hear it. He was sure of it when she whispered softer than soft.

"I need you..."

But he heard it. He heard it loud and clear and he hoped he wasn't wrong about being her everything. He prayed he was doing the right thing. God, if he wasn't? He didn't want to think about that.

Chapter Seventeen

Aries had a full night ahead of him and he was working on little sleep. But who could blame him there? Jaxx was a temptation no guy could easily walk away from, and last night with his belt wrapped around her throat? He never wanted to leave her. But right now he had to do his weekly inspection of equipment and make a few needed adjustments in this regard. It did occur to him that even without the epiphany he had that afternoon at Aaron's birthday party he would have eventually realized that the club scene wasn't his style anymore. Jaxx's presence in his life proved this.

"Yeah, move this one over there and then do something with this. What the hell happened to it? Did someone bring a dog in here?"

"Draco. He likes to show off the power of his custom-made finger cuffs. I don't know how he hasn't maimed any of his subs with those things."

Aries bent to examine the damage to the spanking horse and then stood. "We're not paying for this."

Shar followed along behind him. "I know. I already told him. He's cool with it. Aries? Hey? What happened? Did your date crap out on you?"

He stopped and spun around. "My date?"

"Doctor Gavin. For your brother's thing."

"How do you know her name?"

Shar stuffed a bar-cloth in her back pocket with one hand and pushed him away with the other. "Q. You could have told me. I've been worried about you going, but with her by your side it'll be all good."

He blinked and then sighed, "Look, I'm going to be honest with you. I haven't even decided whether to invite her. This is my shit, not hers."

"Shit? This isn't *shit* it's the future of the club you're talking about. Are you afraid she won't go? Should we find someone else?"

"No. No, if I ask her I know she'll go."

"Well then?"

He didn't like the way Shar had her hands on her hips. Clearly now that she knew there as an opportunity for her to have her own stake in the club she didn't want to take any chances, but she needed to know that until that time came, he was the one who made the decisions.

"I'll handle this. Are you going to deal with the spanking horse damage?"

"Yes, but—"

"Make sure Draco doesn't wear those vampire finger-cuffs around here in the future unless he's willing to leave a deposit."

He didn't let Shar respond. He was tired of her prodding. Although he appreciated that she had his back, he wasn't ready to be pushed.

When the door was shut between them he relaxed. With the prospect of realizing one dream within reach he knew soon he'd to have to face the reality of all he wanted with another dream of his. The more important one. And when he did, it would be a private and intimate discussion between him and Jaxx. No one else, as the topic was uniquely theirs. At least he hoped it would be. That was the funny thing about special. You never knew when special was going to happen, but when it did, you wanted to protect it. Keep it close and not let others know you were experiencing it, for the fear it would disappear.

When you tell her what you want for your future together she may disappear

He wasn't going to think about that as he snatched up his cell and texted her.

Get a pen and paper. I'll wait...

Good morning to you too. Why yes, I had a great night, thank you for asking.

He was like a teenager with his first crush. Every time he texted her like this, his heart raced and he felt...good. Damn good. "It's the weekend with nothing to do" kind of good. That's what she was to him.

13 West Henshaw Street. Stripper Land. This is where I want you to go to pick up the shoes I bought you.

Stripper Land?

He could just imagine her body language. She was so easy to read, he didn't even have to be in the same room with her.

And after that I want you to go two suites over. To 15 Henshaw and pick up our order.

Take out?

Hm. If she weren't being so sassy he might let it slide, but after their conversation in the early morning hours?

No, I'd say most of the intimate items to be picked up there require you to take them in. Do you have any more questions for me?

No.

He waited, and sure enough.

Yes.

He smiled.

Do I get to see the shoes at least?

Of course.

Several hours later he was in the middle of a meeting with his architect and contractor when his phone vibrated. Normally he wouldn't check his text. It was rude to do so mid-meeting, but in this case he excused himself and went out to the hall.

Golf shoes? You bought me golf shoes for our Scene?

Great, she was off balance and had no idea what to expect.

The shoes weren't for that. They're for our golf game. You said you can beat me, and I want to see it happen.

And I wanted pretty shoes for our Scene. I CAN beat you. Who's worried about that?

This didn't sit well with him. Not at all. What if she could beat him? Nah, that wasn't possible. Images of Erica Sorensen started to surface, and he scowled. That chick could definitely beat him, but Jaxx wasn't a pro. She couldn't be that good at golf, could she? He needed to stop stressing about golf and get his head back in a different game.

Fucking golf gods. They messed with your shit, even when you weren't on the course.

Trust me. You'll have the perfect shoes to go with the outfit I bought. I mean it.

He should get back to his meeting but he couldn't help himself. He wanted to spend as much time with her as possible, even if it was only via text.

OKAY, let's talk about the bag of stuff I picked up from "Virginia's Vag Emporium". I don't even want to discuss the name of the store. Forget that. My question is, are you organizing a sex party I'm unaware of?

Hm. He looked at that text and decided. This wasn't about quantity, it was about quality time spent with her, and if he got dragged into answering that? There'd be no quality, because he'd have to call her on her snark. Best to ignore it. He stuffed his phone in his pocket and reentered the boardroom. "Sorry about that."

His architect turned and the look on his face was scary. "There's a modification here that impacts the whole project. In a big way. You didn't tell me you wanted an outdoor lift on either end and in the middle of the complex."

See? He could handle this no problem. But one stubborn woman who kept insisting she could cream him in golf? That had him worried.

*****

Jaxx was glad it was Thursday. She'd accomplished everything she needed to do today. She'd finished with her appointments, handed in her monthly "Grin with Granny" article to the local newspaper and gotten her hair done. All in preparation for their coming Scene. Last night he'd invited her to his place on Friday and she wanted to look her best. She'd just gotten into the car when her phone beeped.

How's the hair look?

Great.

I'm doing dinner.

Where?

Your place.

When?

I'm there now. Waiting for you.

That gave her a thrill. Her hands shook as she typed, *I'll be home soon.*

Jaxx sent that off and leaned back in the seat. She had a lot to think about and yet she hadn't done what she usually did by overanalyzing it. In fact she hadn't analyzed it at all which was really odd. As she pulled out of the parking lot she had to admit it was as though everything was skewed in her life at the moment. The one man who shouldn't be making any sense made all the sense in the world, and the woman she'd been trusting for years was suddenly unreliable.

Go with your own instincts.

It was hard doing that when she had Maggie in the background just waiting for Aries to prove that she was right about him. Maggie probably hoped this would happen before her friend arrived. As to that, Jaxx knew she still hadn't given up on that idea. She'd taken the time to slip a note under Jaxx's door yesterday to say that Gunther would be arriving first of the week. She just couldn't let go and Jaxx knew why.

Guilt.

Jaxx was so engrossed in her thoughts she nearly missed her street. Making the turn she decided from now on she was going to be patient with Maggie instead of getting angry. Living with that kind of guilt was a terrible burden and she supposed it could make a person act out and do crazy things like trying to sabotage a relationship by saying hurtful things. Not that Jaxx was going to put up with this forever. She planned on talking to Maggie about all this and when she did she'd tell her that she wasn't responsible for Jaxx's upbringing. It was Jaxx's adopted parents who were solely to blame as they both knew going into the process they didn't want children. It wouldn't have mattered who that child... As she pulled in, the car all but rolled onto the drive. The shock of that logical deduction echoed in her mind as understanding dawned. Searching for Maggie's truth she'd inadvertently discovered her own and for the first time in her life, it was right in front of her. Clear as day. Jaxx had spent her whole life blaming herself for not being the daughter her parents wanted when the truth was they never wanted a child at all. It wasn't a matter of her not measuring up. She measured up all right, it was them who didn't.

Her heart pounded as a small rush of what? Happiness? Soared through her. It was as if a dark part of her heart had been let into the light. Why hadn't she'd seen this before?

Spotting Aries car she had her answer. He'd given her the confidence and courage to face down her shame. Yes that's what it was. Shame that she wasn't good enough to be wanted by the two people in her life that were supposed to love her best. For years she'd believed that to be true. But now that Aries had entered her life? She knew for a certainty she was good enough. Her pulse raced as she got out of the car and headed up the steps.

She'd have the necessary conversation with Maggie eventually, but right now all she could think of was Aries.

Once through the reception doors she took a deep breath and decided she felt lighter right now than she had in years.

Standing at her front door, she determined she wanted to give back. She wanted to do something solely for him. Something different and imaginative. Something he wouldn't forget. It took her a minute to come up with a plan, but when she did she went in, balls-to-the-walls.

"Hi, your hair looks great."

The scent of rosemary on a crisping chicken greeted her, and she breathed deeply. "Smells great in here." And the scenery was just as tantalizing. His dark hair was mussed and he had a speck of flour on his nicely tailored shirt. Totally dreamy, and she was more committed now to giving something back than she was before. "Thanks. Is there anything you're cooking that could be ruined if I stole you away for...say, fifteen minutes?"

He eyed her, but she didn't give up any territory. She was doing this. "I'm intrigued and I do have forty minutes on the clock."

"Great." She grabbed his hand and pulled him into the bedroom then stopped. "I know you're used to running the show or the Scene or whatever, but I want to do this. Just this once. Before tomorrow."

He lifted her chin, and she melted a little. "Are you worried about tomorrow? Is that what this is about?"

"No. I'm ready. Even if I don't know what to expect, I'm good. This is..." She looked up at him. "It's special, Aries. Only for you. I want to do it."

He gave her a measuring look and then agreed. "All right."

"I want you on the bed and stretched out, waiting for me."

"Jaxx."

She grabbed one of her sleep masks out of the drawer, plucked out two tennis balls from her bucket-full of unused workout equipment, and then scooped up her iPod. "Here's how this is going to work." She handed him one of the tennis balls. "You are going to grip these magical balls—" she handed him the other, "—in your palms so you won't be tempted to sink those hands in my hair. This is my way of putting you in bondage without any restraints."

"Have you been drinking?"

"Not at all. This is going to be a game-changer."

"For who?"

"Both of us. Let me put the blindfold on you."

He frowned.

"I want to do this, but I can see you don't. How about I give you three strokes when we play our round of golf?"

"You're that good?" He looked more worried over that prospect than he did over being blindfolded. *Men.*

"Is it a deal?"

When he nodded, she didn't hesitate. She got the sleep mask on him before he had any second thoughts. "Now I'll help you to the bed."

Aries let her put the mask on him until he couldn't see. He was all right with it because she was making a point. Any minute she'd come out with it. He was sure.

When he sat on the bed, he heard her say close to his ear, "Just lie back and relax. That's right."

What he wasn't sure about was what to make of all this. What the hell had happened at that salon today?

"I'm going to unbutton your shirt. Keep your arms at your sides and grip the balls nice and tight."

He did as she told him. Odd, but nice, because he was doing it for her.

"Now I'm going to undo your pants." Her hands were soft as she slid them into his jeans and pushed his pants down. Slowly, she moved the fabric down in a sexual shimmy that had him visualizing her staring at his cock when they came all the way off.

"I love looking at you."

She moved his shirt, and his muscles tightened.

"Your stomach is like a washboard. All ribbed and rippled." She kissed his abdomen, and he sucked in a breath. "You have a magnificent chest too."

He felt vulnerable and exposed and he wasn't sure he liked it. To counter his discomfort, he asked, "Do you want me to sit up so you can take off my shirt?"

"Shh, no talking for you. The shirt can stay. I can see all the good parts."

He grinned at that as she was using words he'd used with her before. But then she stroked his dick, and his grin disappeared as a bolt of lust snaked through him. She continued to stroke him like he stroked himself if he wanted quick relief. Was this her plan? Get him to come fast?

He was staring into the blackness of the mask and wondering about that when her hand stopped pumping. She still had a firm grip on him but—Jesus! Silky hair cascaded over his thighs, balls and groin. Tickling and teasing until her velvet lips pressed against the head of his cock. Right over the tiny opening—

He flexed up. He couldn't help it when her tongue connected with the spot. Licking against him in the most intimate way. As though she wanted to commit this part of him to her memory. Savor it. Just the thought got his adrenaline spiking and his heart hammering in his chest. If she kept going in this direction, he was going to come.

"Not yet," she said as she laid his cock down and patted it like she would a good pet. "I want you focused."

He was going to have to start keeping his thoughts to himself when he played with her. She was too smart and obviously paid close attention—shit, she was naked. The second she reached over him and the tips of her breasts skimmed his biceps, he knew it. And knowing it got him hotter than fuck and ready to throw the tennis balls aside and rip off the blindfold. But then her hard, beaded nipples brushed against his skin, a sure sign that she was as turned-on as him. Any moment he expected her to climb on for a ride and he couldn't wait. This wasn't so bad. He could let her lead.

"Stop thinking," she whispered in his ear just before she fitted earphones on him with music already playing loud enough to deafen all other sounds around him. Kings Of Leon. Oh, hell yeah, "Sex On fire".

And when she rubbed herself up against him, used her body as a brush and stroked him good, he closed his eyes behind the mask and gave up the reins. For this ride he'd gladly be the passenger.

Her nails digging into him felt great and reminded him of that afternoon on the desk when she—damn, her teeth grazed first one nipple and then the other and when they hardened, she leaned in for a bite. Nipping each of them to the point of almost pain. But then her hair skated over him as she slid down south and he forgot about the pain. He forgot about everything but the feel of her all over him. Her softness against his hardness made his hands grip the balls tighter and tighter still. With the way she dragged her tongue over his abdomen, going lower and lower. Slow, but firm. Nails raking him as her tits pressed into his thighs, she'd be lucky if he didn't crush the balls to dust. And when she finally took hold of his cock and drew it in deep, he was toast. She licked, sucked and fucked him with her mouth from every possible angle. It was heaven and hell, while his hands were no good to him, his eyes closed in darkness and his ears filled with music. Life didn't get any better than this.

At least he didn't think it did until a few minutes later when he came so hard he thought his heart was going bust right out of his chest. "Fuck that was good."

Jaxx took the earphones out of his ears and lifted the blindfold up to rest on his forehead. He didn't want to open his eyes just yet. He was enjoying the peace until she said, "You can let go of the balls now."

The light made him blink, but otherwise he remained immobile. "I don't think I can."

She grinned. "Why, did I exhaust you?"

He grinned back. "No I think I squeezed the fucking things so hard they're embedded in my palms."

"Do you kiss your mother with that mouth?"

He let go of the balls and grabbed her, hauling her up until he could nuzzle her neck. She laughed and squirmed, and he loved it. "That reminds me, babe. Who gave you permission to use my stuff?"

That got her attention. She stopped trying to escape and asked, "What stuff?"

"My stuff. You're quite the little parrot when Topping."

"Did you like it?"

He looked her right in the eyes and said, "Yes. I liked it very, very much."

She smiled so wide her dimples made an appearance. Damn, he loved those. Rolling over, he took her with him and whispered, "My turn to copy you." He slipped off the blindfold and handed it to her.

"What about your dinner? Don't you have to stir it or add something to it or something?"

"It can wait. Put the blindfold on."

"But I—"

"Hm." He brushed a thumb over her nipple and frowned. "I can see you don't want to do this right now, so how about I give you back the three-stroke lead you were going to give me on the course. Deal?"

"All right." She put the blindfold on and added, "But I predict you're going to be sorry you gave them up. I know how you hate to lose."

He nipped her breast and said, "Stop talking. They'll be no more talking for you." Then once he found an album on her iPod he thought would work, he leaned down and spoke in ear, "And I bet you're soaking wet between your legs. I know how sucking my cock really does it for you."

He put the earphones on her and spread her legs to check. So much heat and it was all his...

Chapter Eighteen

Jaxx refused to think about tonight. She'd made a pact with herself that she wouldn't start worrying until after she got through her appointments today. But now as she ushered her last patient through the door, she was regretting that pact because all her pent-up nerves hit at once.

She went to her desk, opened the top drawer and checked her cell.

Good afternoon, sunshine, guess what you get to open?

The box? I'm just packing up and I'm going to head upstairs.

You're still in the office?

Yes.

Text me when you open it.

Ten minutes later, with shaking hands, Jaxx opened the box. She stared and stared again. Snatching up her phone, she punched out her text to him.

I can't wear this.

You don't like it?

I didn't say that, but there's nothing for me to wear in the box.

I know.

Jaxx looked down at the collage of balled-up colored tissue paper and frowned. Was it glued in place? It was, and the design took up the whole box. She squinted and held the box at a distance. Focusing like you would on a hidden three D image. Why, it looked like...

Is it supposed to be a frog holding a big red heart?

It's a Gecko. Only Aaron and I didn't have enough green tissue paper, so we made him yellow and used the red for the heart. Do you like it?

Aaron helped you with this?

Yeah, I helped him with his art project and he helped me with mine. We were going to use the green duct tape but decided against it. Hey, he got a gold star for his. What do I get?

She stared at that last question for a full thirty seconds. With hands trembling and butterflies fluttering in her stomach she typed,

Me.

And she was sure he had no idea what that really meant. But she did as she placed a hand over her heart and drew in a deep breath.

I'm honored.

She read that response and thought maybe he did know.

I'll pick you up at five. Wear whatever you like, because tonight after we have dinner you'll be wearing nothing at all.

*****

Aries could tell that Jaxx was totally overwhelmed being in his house, but now that they'd entered his playroom and he'd instructed her to take off her clothes? He gauged she was trying to keep it altogether. He waited and when she took the last item off, folded it and placed it on the bench, just as he'd instructed, he smiled. She was nervous.

He saw her hands shaking and frowned. "Come here."

She stood right in front of him and whispered, "My palms are sweating."

"I'll have the rest of you sweating soon enough." He brought her to the square table he usually reserved for wax play and lifted her to sit on it. "I'm going to position you for our session this time, but next time I will want you to do this yourself. Prepare yourself for me and our special time together. So pay attention." He pulled out an elastic band from his pocket and reached out to gather her hair. Once he had it tied back, he looked down at her. "Are you warm enough?"

"Yes."

"Good, now lie back." When she did, he helped to position her with her arms up, fingers laced together behind her head and legs bent and spread wide open. "This is how you'll present to me in this room."

He trailed two fingers down the center of her chest to her navel. "I prefer this position because I can see the heart of you when I come through that door. Now I want you to stay like this until I'm ready, do you understand? No moving. I don't care how uncomfortable you get. And remember, if there's pain you can't endure at any time, I want you to tell me. Traffic lights, okay?"

"All right."

Aries set about getting all that he needed. He'd purposely waited until now to gather the items so she'd have time to get used to her position. The sight of her spread on that table had his cock hard and thick. Throbbing to get into her.

Opening the top drawer of his cabinet, he pulled out the collar. It was huge for her slender neck and it was leather. Not to his personal tastes. He preferred metal. Lacy tri-colored metal, but that would come later. Tonight he wanted her to feel the weight of the training collar when he locked it around her neck. He wanted her to be aware of it as keenly as she'd be aware of him.

He tilted his head and checked the corner of the room where she waited. He'd bet her heart was pounding and her breathing shallow. He knew how well she responded to the wait. Some women dreaded this time, imagining all kinds of difficult things that would be put to them. Not Jaxx. He'd learned the second night into his late evening visits that she relished the wait. She was always wet and ready.

He turned back and opened another drawer. Choosing his newest addition he bought just for her and examined it. It was a high-quality riding crop with a nice flex and delivered a good sting. He had two perfect stripes on his upper thigh from where he'd tested it.

Jaxx liked pain, he knew, but how much was the key. He liked the marks. The proof of what had been endured for him, and he found the crop left the prettiest marks. He was dying to put some stripes on her ass. She had a nice, rounded ass. He spotted the paddle and decided maybe he should use that on her too.

The nipple clamps were a no-brainer. He was going hardcore here. He wanted to push her to the edge. Find her near-breaking point and bring her back from there. He selected the ropes he'd tie her with, and then spied the marker. Thick, black ink. Perfect for— no he'd already decided it was too soon for that. He didn't want to push her. Or scare her. Maybe...? Screw it. He'd been fantasizing day and night over this. Ever since his dream he'd been burning to get his name on her any way he could. This way he could ease her into the idea. Get her thinking about it.

It's too soon.

He ignored that silent warning and purposely made noise as he deposited the items on the table between her legs. The marker rolled and brushed up against her calf. "I want to talk to you about one of your hard limits. You crossed off tattoos from the list. I was disappointed, because I want my woman—" What could he say? "— I'll...I respect your boundaries. So I'm going to ask. May I write on you with marker? If it's in a place that won't be seen by anyone but me?"

"I-I guess. Yes," she breathed.

"Good. This is it." He held it up so she could see it. "I'm hopeful you'll to get used to the words I write on you. I want you to get used to wearing them on your skin...for me."

He walked to the side of the table and took hold of her arm. Straightening it, he rubbed from shoulder to wrist and back again. Then he placed it at her side. He did the same with the other and looked down. "There. Now I want you to stay very still." He picked up the clamps. "I'm going to put these on you, and then you're going to come up in a kneeling position."

He didn't have to work her nipples; they were already spiked. He was paying close attention to her breathing too. They hadn't even started, and she was excited.

"Oh." She sucked in a breath.

"I know they're cold."

"They pinch."

"You'll get used to it. Open up." She automatically went to turn her head away, so he grasped her chin and pulled her back until she was looking at him. "You're going to hold this chain that's connected to the clamps in your mouth. Every time you jerk or move, those clamps will tighten. You'll be punishing yourself if you fuss." He dropped his tone and ordered, "Open up. Please."

She did, and he laid the chain over her tongue.

"The only time I won't punish you for dropping that chain is if you need to use your safe word. Otherwise, you suck on it."

He moved his items aside and told her to kneel. "Very good. Knees spread wide, hands behind your back and breasts out. Yes, like that."

He stood, facing her, and picked up the collar. Holding it up in front of her, he said, "This is the training collar we're going to use for our session. I'm going to lock it around your neck, and you see this O-ring? I'm going to thread some rope through it when I bind you so you won't be able to move. I happen to like collars. I'm hoping you do too, because that would please me."

He buckled the leather around her throat, mindful of the dangling chain of the clamps, and locked the collar into place. Wishing to Christ that this was his metal she was accepting. Metal or not, she was calming. Easing. Just as she'd done with his belt around her, she committed herself more to the moment.

"You like to be Mastered, Jaxx. You like to feel the power someone else has over you. You give into it so beautifully. Look at you. Are you wet?"

She closed her eyes, and he didn't hesitate. He slipped a hand between her legs and cupped her. Kneading her hot wet flesh almost roughly. "Oh yeah, you're a dirty little thing, aren't you. So ready to be fucked. But you don't get that yet. First we need to warm you up so I can introduce you to a different kind of caress. One that I think—" he pinched her clit and tugged on it as he spoke, "—you're going to love."

Saliva pooled in Jaxx's mouth but she was holding off swallowing. Every time she did, the clamps tightened. Any second now she was going to have to bear it; otherwise she'd be drooling.

He tied her hands together behind her and just as promised, he threaded that rope through the collar so was unable to move her head down. She didn't dare move it up because of the clamps.

She felt a tug and realized he was tying the end of the rope to table leg.

"Beautiful. Now let's bend you over. You're completely helpless right now. You have to rely on me to position you."

Her heart pounded as she shifted forward. She had no way to break her fall if he let go of her.

"I've got you. This is my favorite sight of you. With your cheek pressed to the ground. Well, in this case the tabletop and your shoulders down while your ass is up and presented. I love this position for you."

She closed her eyes as he put his hands on her. Pinching and rubbing, tapping at times, hard then soft until he got to her bottom. Then he wasn't soft at all. He took hold of her cheeks and squeezed. Rolled. Pinched there too, until her skin and muscle tingled and burned.

"Did you see what I bought you in honor of my little art project? No?"

She couldn't turn her head to look even if she wanted to, and at this point she didn't want to. There were too many warring sensation rippling over her at once.

"What do you think?"

He held a stick with a little red leather heart on the top of it. She blinked and tried to focus, but when he smacked the heart in the center of his palm, she jerked and pain shot through her.

"Jewez Crips!" She nearly lost the chain, but managed to swear around it.

"Careful, babe. Those nipple clamps are a bitch, aren't they?"

She closed her eyes and took a deep breath. In and out, she imagined the air moving through her lungs as she tried to find that place inside herself.

"Oh, no you don't. You're not going anywhere."

The first strike landed across both ass cheeks, and her eyes popped open. That wasn't too bad. Then the second strike landed, and that wasn't too bad either. Maybe there was something wrong with her, because this should be painful. It should be stinging or something and it was just like he'd described her throwing that football at his back. A wee little bee sting.

Of course a few seconds later, when she realized he was gradually increasing the force of each strike, she started to pay attention.

"That's better. Now we can begin."

Jaxx was expecting more of the sensations she'd experienced when he'd used the belt that night in the maze, but this was different. The strikes were sharp. The sting from them lasted longer and when he got into a steady rhythm, something began to happen to her. It wasn't from the external thing he was doing to her—this was more internal. Her state of mind was being altered. Everything had a new meaning. All the sensations gathered together and pushed upward.

She couldn't hear the strikes as they landed anymore. All she heard was the sound of the ocean. All she felt were the waves of cool water lapping at her legs and washing over her breasts. This was heaven. This was where she was always meant to be. Floating on the edge of nothing.

Chapter Nineteen

Aries had never Topped a woman like Jaxx before. One who committed to the experience on a cerebral level. He was sure it brought her in deeper to center, because when she surrendered it was unequivocal and complete. Her body opened at the same time as her mind, and it was something to be a part of. Watching her slip into sub-space took his breath away.

He'd worked her in a slow and steady rhythm. Increasing force in a gradual but measured pace. Over and over he connected. Watching and waiting. Pausing every few strokes to test the heat on her skin. Gauging her threshold while he waited for her to react. He wanted her to let go. To laugh or cry. He knew she needed that kind of release where the genuine emotion was hers alone, but she remained quiet and still.

He leaned down and angled his jaw over her shoulder. Breathing with her. Pacing himself with her every breath and when he did he knew he wouldn't see her let go that way as she'd already let go another.

"So beautiful." He kissed her cheek and stood back to admire the blush colored marks on her ass. The sight of her was humbling. "Gorgeous," he said, positive she'd never know what kind of a gift she'd just given him. Conscious or not, she'd put herself into his hands which meant on some unseen plane she trusted him more than she trusted herself.

"Here, babe." He kept his voice soft and his movements unhurried. "I'm going to take the clamps off you. Open your mouth." She didn't, so he gently forced her lips apart and unhooked the chain from her teeth. "This is going to feel good soon." He dislodged the clamps and rubbed each nipple with his palm. "When the blood rushes back to them, they're going to be hot and tingly. Maybe I should get some ice. Would you like that?"

He spoke as he worked, knowing that she probably heard one tenth of what he was saying if anything at all, but he didn't care. It made him feel as if he was more connected to her when he talked.

"There. All untied." He rubbed her hands and wrists. Bringing them down slowly before he picked her up and carried her to his chair. He sat and tucked her up against him, good and tight. The heat from her ass burned through his leather pants warming him and wrapping around his cock while he gently rocked them. Damn, it felt good with her in his arms as he waited for her to come back to herself.

Curling his knuckles he stroked her cheek and thought about all the things she had to learn. The first thing he was going to teach her was not to check out on him so soon. He wanted to play with her some more, and she dove the first chance she got into the abyss. Had she been more experienced, he would have continued while she drifted, but not now. Especially when he wanted to get his words on her. Right above the ass he'd just marked.

When she shivered he hugged her close. As she trembled he rubbed his palms over her to create warming friction. The moment her teeth quietly chattered he drew her in tighter and touched his cheek to hers, whispering, "You're amazing. So special. I love the way you got lost for me. Only me. Shh…"

He placed gentle kisses on her lips until eventually she calmed. Then he adjusted their position so she was folded nice and safe in his embrace. With his chin resting on top of her head while her slow and even breathing bathed his chest, he enjoyed the overwhelming satisfaction he was experiencing. Never in his life had he had an occasion to want a moment to be perfect, but now that it was he wanted it to last a lifetime.

"Take your time, babe. We have all night." He kissed her forehead and murmured, "I'm here." He held her close. "I'll always be here."

It was sometime later that she stirred.

"Mmm…" She stretched against him like a little cat waking from a nap. "That was remarkable."

Her eyes were so bright now. Wide and alert when she tilted back to look up at him that he grinned and shook his head. "You know most women would have cried or begged, being caned like that."

"Why?" At her frown, he realized she was serious.

"I don't know. It hurts."

"It does?" She wiggled her bottom against him and said, "It feels right somehow."

His heart skipped a beat. "Why?"

"It makes me feel closer to you. Does that make sense?"

"Oh, yeah." He kissed her forehead, each eyelid and the tip of her nose. "It makes all kinds of sense to me."

When he leaned back, she snuggled up against him. Cheek to pec and said, "The feeling afterward reminded me of something."

"What?"

"It's stupid."

"Nothing is stupid where you're concerned. Come on, you can tell me."

"I—"

She hesitated so he gave her an encouraging squeeze.

"It's more like an observation but here goes. When I was ten my family went on a trip to Florida. After a few days there my dad said he had a surprise for me. I thought he was taking me to a water park, but that's not where we wound up. Instead we went canoeing down the Hillsborough River. This wouldn't have been so bad if it hadn't rained ferociously the day before. When the bus took us to the launching area the driver explained that there were downed trees and all kinds of debris in the water so we should follow the yellow ribbons and keep the oars down as the overhanging vines had snakes and spiders on them."

Aries was sure she didn't realize she'd shuddered at the memory. What kind of a fucking asshole was her father?

"So, you know the first time I saw a gator push off the rock he was sunning himself on and swim toward us, I forgot myself. I lifted my oar to change paddle sides and hit the branches above us causing an avalanche of Spanish moss, leaves and sticks crawling with all different sized spiders to land in our canoe. Spiders, even daddy-long legs freak me out, so I was ready to jump in the water and test my luck with the gators, but then I saw how pissed dad was and I knew I couldn't react. I had to deal with my fear. Swallow it and I did. I sat in that canoe and paddled the rest of the way, brushing aside the spiders that came too close. It was..."

He held her tight and whispered, "Was?"

"It was a weird experience for me. Being ten and surrounded by all those spiders, I was sure I was going to die until something strange happened. Eventually I went numb and by the time the trip finished I don't think I was even inside myself. Oh, I remembered docking and climbing out of that canoe, but I also remember I couldn't feel my legs and my muscles felt as if I'd expended them beyond endurance. Later that night I recalled bits and pieces of the ride not the whole time in continuum. That's what I feel like now. I remember being on that table and bits and pieces of what you said and did, but not all of it."

Aries frowned as he processed that comparison. "But you didn't like the canoe trip."

"I didn't say that. I said it was a weird experience for me."

"So tonight is weird for you too?"

"No."

"I hear a 'but'."

"With the canoe trip I was forced to reach beyond my limitations out of fear of my dad's wrath whereas with you, tonight? I was free to go beyond them because I trusted you."

God damn. There was nothing sexier than a smart woman.

"Although, now that I think about it, the end result was the same. Both times I felt more alive afterward than I ever did before. There should be a difference, shouldn't there?"

"Hm, if your dad wanted to take you on another canoe trip would you go?"

"No way."

He leaned down and whispered in her ear, "What about if I asked you to climb back up on that table with your shoulders down and your ass up so I could give you more of my attention, would you?"

"Yes."

"There's the difference and I'm glad for it."

"Me too."

"Jaxx?"

"Hmm?"

He should leave things as they were. He shouldn't push for more. "I haven't finished with all I had in mind to do with our session."

She sat up. "Did I spoil it?"

He reached for the O-ring on the collar and traced his index finger over it. "Of course not. I just didn't want to continue when you weren't all there. It's too soon for that. One day, but not today."

"What did you have in mind?"

He drew his bent knuckle over her nipples in a lazy series of loop-like patterns. Continuing the motion across the spiked center until he was sure he had her in the proper frame of mind. Then he said, "I want to write my words on your back in black permanent marker. After I do I'm going to bend you over and fuck you until both of us come hard."

She didn't miss a beat. "What kind of words?"

"Up you get."

"Why?"

"There's that word again." He shook his head. "How about I show you, but I need to get a piece of paper."

He took her by the hand to the cabinet and grabbed some paper out of one of the drawers. Then he walked them to the table. He wasn't going to let go of her. Not now. Putting the paper down, he shifted ready to lift her up but decided against it.

"Turn around."

"Why?"

"Because I want to see the marks I made on your ass, that's why. Seeing them really does it for me. I love the stripes."

She turned around and almost fell over trying to see behind herself to get a peek.

"Careful." He steadied her and then ran a hand over the hot strips. Over and over he rubbed in a circle until she quivered and grabbed for the table. "How are your breasts, are they tingly?" Her nipples would be in continuous spike mode for the next day or two. One of the benefits of being properly clamped for a time.

"Aries."

She leaned back against him, and a flashed image from his dream came to mind. He was so close to getting what he wanted from her. So very close.

"Let me show you what I want to write."

With her back to his front, he leaned forward and picked up the marker. Putting it to paper, he wrote, I belong to Ramsey Taylor. Not all the words he wanted on her, but enough for now.

When he was finished, he held his breath, hoping he hadn't ruined things. The last thing he wanted to do was scare her or make this too weird for her.

After she read the phrase she tilted her head and met his gaze. "I think I'd like that."

The air rushed out of him. "Beautiful. Bend over the table. Arms stretched up over your head and cheek pressed into the wood."

She did as he said without hesitation, causing heated adrenaline to race through his veins. He knew why he was feeling like he'd just conquered Everest. Owning a woman like Jaxx Gavin was a privilege. A blessing. A gift.

He kept his hand steady as he wrote his words across her lower back. In bigger script than he'd require if this had been a permanent tattoo. He wanted to enjoy this. Relish it. From hip to hip he claimed her. Marking her as his. And when she stood and he examined the words, her striped little ass and all that naked skin that belonged to him, something snapped inside. His restraint and the patience he'd been maintaining let go.

One minute he was standing there, looking at her, and the next he carried her over to the sawhorse and bent her over it. "Spread your legs." He was already covered with latex, so he didn't pause. Only took his cock out and then pushed it into her while he wrapped a hand around the collar and held her down. He tugged and pulled. Pumped and flexed into her as he stared at his words across her lower back. It was as if they taunted him to take, plunder and steal what he wanted from her. But then there was no need for thieving, because she opened herself up with a sigh and gave him all he wanted and more. She gave him everything, and he gladly took it.

Chapter Twenty

"Hey, sunshine." Aries kissed her shoulder. "Are you awake?"

Jaxx didn't answer him. She just rolled over and put her hand to his cheek. He looked so great in the early morning light. His big, tanned body was the picture of health, wrapped in the crisp white sheets. She threaded her fingers through his sleep-rumpled hair and pulled him down for a kiss. This led to more kisses until she was underneath him.

It was quiet and calm. Unhurried and wonderful. So different from the night before that she went with the experience. She lost herself in it, and in him. He was heartbreakingly gentle as he touched every part of her with his lips and hands. She never even opened her eyes when he broke contact and she heard him reach into the nightstand. She didn't want this newfound euphoria to end.

And when he entered her, it was slow. Easy. As he filled her up and consumed her. Rocking her in the cradle of the mattress. Steady and wonderful when the light came in. When the heat built inside her and the air got thin and all those lovely tingles wound around her. Pushing upward from her toes. Over her calves, knees, thighs and landing beautifully between her legs in a nice, tight squeeze.

She drew in a breath...until her inner muscles constricted one last time and gave way.

Her breath caught and held suspended for a blissful moment before she sighed it out. Deep and long as she rode the crest of this orgasm all the way home.

It wasn't until Aries collapsed on top of her and growled, "Damn," that she came back to herself. Loving the contact as his forehead rested on hers while he caught his breath.

It was a surreal moment. One she'd never forget. With his heart beating rapidly against hers and the early morning sunrise breaking through the shadows that fell on his bed, Jaxx Gavin realized she felt whole for the first time in her life. Both her physical and emotional state of being had just worked together as a team. Melding into one so she could enjoy herself instead of tearing her apart with guilt over all her failings.

So this is what inner and perfect peace feels like?

"Are you crying?"

"No." *Sniffle.*

"You are. Did I hurt you?"

"No. I don't want to talk about it."

"Why?"

"Even I'm beginning to hate that word. Never mind."

She went to roll away from him, and he wasn't about to let her go. He pulled her back until she was forced to spoon with him. "Oh, no you don't. I want to know what's bothering you."

"You're crushing me."

"Tough, spill."

She didn't fight him, but she wasn't talking either.

"Jaxx."

"I had an orgasm. Okay? Are you happy now?"

"Yes, I am, and I would think you'd be happy too. So why the tears?"

"I've never had an orgasm with a guy before."

Aries looked at the ceiling. The window. And then at the back of her head. "Ah, last time I checked I was a guy, and not to toot my own horn or anything, but you've had multiples with me."

"I meant nice guys."

"What?" He laughed and moved to make room for her to rollover. Shifting until they were nose-to-nose he stared her down. "I'm a nice guy."

"Not when we're screwing. You're usually mean."

"Mean?" He pulled back and scowled. "I'm mean?"

"Maybe bad is better, but don't worry, I like it. I just never knew that I could have an orgasm with a nice guy."

"Who's the nice guy?"

"You were this morning. The experience took my breath away."

Now he understood. This was important to her. A learning curve that would give her more power over her sexuality because now she knew without out a doubt she wasn't frigid when it came to vanilla sex either.

"I just worry too much sometimes."

"We all do."

"Not you."

He searched her face and then sighed, "Even me. It just may seem like I don't because I appreciate the power of a moment for what it is. I never stop to examine all the things it isn't."

When she grinned he pulled her in for a hug, pleased that she was happy. After a time he leaned back. "So I took your breath away, did I?" At her nod he whispered, "Want me to do it again?"

Damn there were those dimples when she smiled and said, "Maybe."

This is what he loved. A woman who was game for anything. He let go of her and leaned up on one elbow. "Rollover. I want to look at your ass." That wasn't all he wanted to look at. He wanted to see those words and know he hadn't dreamed all this. Especially the part where she'd said, "I'd like that." Of course, black marker was one thing and a bona fide tattoo another. But this was a good start.

When she shifted, he sucked in a breath. The immeasurable satisfaction he got spying the ink on her stunned him. The lettering looked and seemed so right. So perfect, as if his name should have always been there.

Just like in his dream.

Tracing his finger over the script, he knew this was no dream. And as such, he had to be careful. Bide his time for a little longer and he'd be able to make this their new reality. He told himself he wanted her for keeps because she surrendered to him like no woman had before, but that wasn't the real reason behind his feelings for her. He suspected the real draw for him was her mind. She was the most interesting woman he'd ever met. A little fucked up, sure, but then, everyone was, weren't they?

"Stay exactly like this. I'll be right back."

"Where are you going?"

"Don't move," he called and went into the playroom. Going to the cabinet, he found the item he was looking for and headed back. "Did you move?"

"No."

"Good. Now no squirming." He dripped some lube into the crease of her ass, and she clenched her cheeks together.

"Aries, what are you doing?"

"Relax. Don't tighten up."

She was putty in his hands as he used the tips of his fingers to spread the lube. Pausing to gently circle her tight little ring, pressing and testing to see how far he could go with her. When she didn't balk, he tugged on a condom and covered himself with the oil. "Very good," he breathed and positioned himself against her opening. "Relax," he repeated but her body automatically clenched. "Don't. Deep breath, babe. That's it. I'll go nice and smooth. It's going to feel good after this first part. Don't fight it. Bear down." He flex forward and pulled back and then pushed some more. "Relax. That's it. Just a little...a little more." Finally the tip of him went through the band of resistance and he slid all the way into her. "There." He leaned down and bit her shoulder blade.

"God. That kind of feels good."

"I know something else that will feel good. I'm going to make you come. It will be more intense now. Are you ready?"

"Oh, God..."

*****

A few hours later when Jaxx stretched awake and discovered Aries wasn't beside her she couldn't help feeling abandoned. She'd been literally crowded in bed with him earlier this morning as he hovered and hugged, and she had to admit she loved it.

Once she found her clothes and got dressed she went on a hunt. She didn't have far to go. Two steps out of the bedroom and she heard his hushed voice coming from the kitchen. He was speaking to someone on the phone.

"I told you I didn't want to ask her. Now what choice do I have? I'm committed. No. I said, no." He was standing by the counter and just finished wrapping tape around something he held in his hands. "Look, I have to go. Oh, hell yeah, you'll make it up to me."

Jaxx didn't move as Aries threw the phone and the tape on the counter and stalked to the front entrance. He was completely oblivious to her so when he left and slammed the door, she jumped and then headed to the window. She spotted him walking across the lawn with that wrapped-in-tape object in his hand. Looking beyond him she noticed an older woman fidgeting, sitting in the full morning sun on an Adirondack chair next door, while a younger woman sat on the doorstep behind her, messing with something on her phone. When the younger woman saw Aries approach, she stood and stepped out of the shade.

Trill

"Jesus." Jaxx nearly bumped her forehead on the glass when the ring sounded. Placing a hand over her heart and taking a deep breath, she ignored the call as she continued to watch what was taking place next door.

In less than a minute, Aries had the older woman sitting in dappled sunlight and whatever he'd given her, had managed to calm her down. Odd, but he didn't even speak to the young woman stood by. He just moved the older woman into the shade and got down on his haunches to talk with her. Jaxx was so busy admiring how great he looked she'd completely forgot about the caller until she heard the sexy voice on the answering machine.

"Don't be mad. I hate it when you're mad at me."

Wild Shar.

Jaxx was still frowning over the message, when Aries headed back to the house. She pushed away from the window and headed into the front hall, determined he wouldn't miss her this time.

"Hi." Although he smiled, it was a half-ass attempt.

"Hi back."

"I could put some coffee on, would you like some?"

"Sure." Following him into the kitchen, she was unsure about what else to say given his present mood. She watched him scoop the coffee into the machine and decided he was less mad than he was distracted. Over what? Wild Shar or the older woman?

"Aries?"

He didn't turn around when he spoke. All he did was continue with the task of getting out two mugs and bringing down the sugar bowl. "I know I promised to spend the day with you today, but—" he paused to still the spoon that rocked on the granite, "—something has come up that I have to deal with."

Not something. Someone. God, even his voice was distant. Cool when he'd spoken.

"I understand," she lied and continued right on fibbing. "It's just as well you're going to be busy. I am too. I have groceries to get, housework to do and I am on call this weekend."

He turned and came to the center island where she stood. With the width of that between them, he bent forward and braced his elbows on the counter. She nearly sighed noticing how good the days' worth of stubble darkening his jaw looked. It caused her heart to race and her pulse—damn, the more time she spent with him the more he affected her. Take right now for instance. She couldn't decide which was nicer. The tiger-eye granite or the steel-grey eyed man leaning over it.

"I thought you spoke to Maggie about working over the weekends?"

"I did. But it's my turn. No biggie." And before he questioned her further, she changed the subject. "Can I ask you something?"

"Sure."

"What did you give your neighbor? I saw you through the window. The poor thing looked upset until you handed it over. It seemed to have a calming effect on her. Does she suffer from dementia?"

He eyed her as if he were debating whether to go with the new topic or stick to the old. Thankfully he chose the new.

"Alzheimer's." He stood and stretched his back. "I did the paper towel trick. It always works."

"Trick?"

"Yeah. I noticed when my dad got agitated like that, he'd pick at things. His shirt or pants. Maybe specks on the table. It was as if his mind knew it needed to be occupied but it was too confused to make anything productive happen. Except for the picking. So you work with what you got. I rolled a bunch of paper towels like a pipe one day and then used masking tape to cover it all. I made a big show of needing his help, handing it over to him, and I asked him to unravel it. He spent hours trying. It kept his mind calm and he wasn't so stressed out all the time. Betty's at that phase in the disease."

"So, your dad has Alzheimer's?"

"Had. And yes." When the coffee machine beeped he went and poured them each a mug. "It's an awful illness. The only thing worse are naïve family members who live in denial. Betty's grandson thinks he's doing her a big favor keeping her out of a facility, but he's not. He and his wife work so much and travel that she's left in the care of a mish-mash of nurses. This one's a real problem, but they haven't fired her. They should. She's dangerous as Betty constantly wanders on her watch."

He finished stirring and handed her over the cup. She was surprised he remembered how she took her coffee, but then he was good at remembering things. "Geriatrics was the field I wanted to specialize in."

He got his own mug and joined her. "But you didn't."

"No, Maggie talked me out of it. She said there wasn't enough growth for someone like me. I needed to choose a field where I could build a client base, and with the elderly..."

"They die off. That's cold. Is that why you write your column?"

This surprised her. "You know about that?"

He leaned against the island. "Yeah, I used to read it to my dad. He thought your answers were funny."

"Not all of them, I hope. I do have the occasional senior concern that needs to be addressed."

"Sure. And I'm just going to put this out there. It really pisses me off that Maggie had any say in your career path. You and only you should choose what you want to do."

Jaxx was glad the tension was easing and things between them were beginning to feel normal again. After what they'd done last night and this morning she needed to feel normal with him. Actually, all she wanted to feel at the moment was wanted. "Maggie isn't all bad."

He snorted and put down his mug.

"Really, I know she can be a bear, but she's always been in my corner, you know?"

He nodded. "Yeah, I know."

Unfortunately, Jaxx finally owning that truth came with some unforeseen consequences. It forced her to come to terms with the fact that Maggie cared for her. She'd always tried her best to protect Jaxx from harm whenever she could. Admittedly, she was overbearing and, at times, overprotective, but she was never malicious in any form. Add to that her genuine concern over Jaxx heading for a huge fall with Aries and this thing between him and Wild Shar this morning going on and worry began to set in.

She wasn't going to let it rule her.

"I, ah, seem to be constantly talking about my family and problems. What about your family? You said your dad passed?"

"Both my parents are gone."

"I'm sorry. Do you have any siblings?"

"One."

She was trying to concentrate and not let doubts invade. Swirling her mug around and watching the liquid circle, she murmured, "Oh?"

"A brother."

She looked up. "Older or younger?"

"He's older. We don't talk much, but now that we're on the subject. He's having a company reception on Monday evening. It's more a party. There will be lots of prominent people there and I..."

"You...?"

"I usually don't attend—I get the company newsletter. But this year, I need to go. You want to come?"

The fact that he eyed his mug when he'd asked had her red flags flying and hearing the over-casual inflection in his voice? Hit her like a slap to the face. All she wanted was for him to look her in the eyes. He always looked her in the eyes. "Wh-where is it being held?"

"At our family home. You'd love the place. It's built into foothills of Tucker Ridge."

"That was where we parked the other night, wasn't it?"

He looked up and there was no mistaking his discomfort. Something was happening here and she had no idea what it was. She paid close attention as he said, "Yeah, my brother and I used to camp in that clearing. My mom and dad would always hike up at dinner time to make sure we were okay."

She searched his face. "That sounds nice."

"So you want to come?"

There it was. She saw the flicker in his eyes. He didn't want to—

I told you I didn't want to ask her.

When she recalled that part of his earlier conversation with Shar, she imagined her heart cracked just a little. Had he been talking about her?

Every instinct screamed for her to say no, but found herself saying yes.

"Great."

He put his mug in the sink and picked up his keys. "You can bring your coffee with you."

This was so abrupt Jaxx frowned. "Where?"

"I've got to get a move on so I'm going to take you home."

"Oh. I'll, um, get my purse." She turned to leave and he grabbed her hand.

"Hey?"

"What?"

"I'm sorry this came up. I had a great time last night." He didn't pull her in for a hug like he usually would have. He didn't even squeeze her hand as he said, "I'm glad you were finally able to open up this morning. That kind of release is exactly what I was hoping for before I...well—" he let go of her hand and stepped away, "—we'll talk about that when I get back."

"You're going away somewhere?"

"Yeah, I may not be back before Monday, but I'll call you, okay?"

"Does this have to do with—?"

"It's business. You want me top up your coffee while you get your stuff?"

She got the message loud and clear. He was practically pushing her out the door and there would be no discussion about his *business* on her exit.

Chapter Twenty-One

Aries waited for Jaxx to head up the front steps before he let out an aggravated breath and frowned. He never should have gotten that marker out. Never. Now all he could think about was getting that ink to be permanent on her silky skin. The sight did something to him. No, it created something within him. A need. A burning desire to own her for more than just a Scene.

She was the one. The only woman he wanted to keep. Knowing this he needed to set things in motion for a future with her. He'd been moving along nicely in that direction too, until Shar stepped in.

Fuck, he wanted to strangle her when he found out what she'd done. Sure he knew she was only trying to help, but thanks to her interference he had step-up all his plans with the complex and the club since he was committed to attending Gabe's party. He'd been leaning toward not going, but now he had to...with Jaxx even.

He snatched his phone off the dash and dialed his Architect. "Hi, John. It looks like I'm going to need the official plans sooner than later. No, I'll come to you. Can we get together tomorrow? Great."

He hung up and then called the airline. Once he had a ticket booked to Baltimore he headed home. It was going to be a rush, but he could do it. Now that he had to do it, he would. So when he found himself turning down a familiar road. Easing onto a gravel path and heading toward the clearing and his old campground, he scowled.

He didn't have time to waste and yet, here he was, once again revisiting a place from his childhood he hadn't been back to in years before being with Jaxx. So why was it, the harder he looked forward to the future he wanted to create with her, he found himself drawn back to this part of his past?

After he'd parked and took some time to scan the valley below, he knew why. Now that he had Jaxx, he was ready to put everything that came before, not only the club, but the fallout with

Gabe behind him so he could move forward with her. He wanted his dream to be their reality.

Probably why getting these things done without involving her was so important to him. He needed to close one chapter of his life before he opened another.

You already penned the first page of chapter two on her back.

He sighed.

First things first. He needed to get all his shit in order before he brought her into Gabe's place. With that in mind he worked out his plans.

*****

The second Jaxx walked through the reception doors she stiffened seeing Maggie. By the look of her she was loaded for bear. This wasn't a good time for confrontation. Although Aries had been polite on the way home and done all the right things she was close to having a meltdown. She'd never felt more distant from him than she did at the moment and she didn't want Maggie to see her fear.

"You stayed with him last night. All night. How could you? You know Gunther is arriving on Monday."

She had no idea what one thing had to do with another, so she ignored all that and said, "Good morning to you too."

"Don't you 'good morning' me."

Jaxx went right to her door and unlocked it. "Maggie." She didn't turn when she whispered, "Please don't do this now."

"Why? Are you too tired? Did he keep you up all night doing God knows what."

Jaxx closed her eyes and counted to three. If she were going to be stuck talking to her they wouldn't be discussing Aries. Maybe it was time they discussed something other than Jaxx's life. She opened her eyes, took a deep breath and spun around. "All right. You want to talk? How about we talk about you for a change."

"I'm not the one who was out all night with a man—"

"Leave Aries out of this. He has nothing to do with your guilt."

"*My* guilt?"

Jaxx crossed her arms over her chest and said, "I think it's time we talk about it."

Maggie nodded, "All right. I'm listening."

"You're feeling guilty because you chose not to adopt me and I got stuck with asshole parents that fucked me up."

Maggie scowled. "You're not...fucked up." She tripped over repeating that phrase and then cleared her throat. "Just a minute. You think I had a choice in the adoption process and if I did, I wouldn't have adopted you? Oh, Jaxx, I didn't have a choice. I was turned down."

"But..." This didn't make any sense. "I thought this was why you found me. Why you stepped in and—"

"There wasn't a day that went by that I didn't think about you. Of course I searched for you when I could. As to stepping in? Someone had to. You were going down the wrong path. Testing dangerous boundaries, just like you are now with that man."

"Leave Aries out of this. Please."

"Why? Did you guys have a fight or something?"

Jaxx couldn't help it. She looked away and the minute she did Maggie latched on to topic.

"You did. Did he break things off with you?"

"No." When that came out of her she wished it hadn't. She fully intended to go into her house and sort out all her feelings. Reexamine what happened this morning. But now that Maggie was prodding she worried if she didn't get behind that door, she'd break in two, right in front of her.

Maggie put a hand on her arm. "Are you okay?"

No she wasn't okay. She was so far from okay at that moment that something inside her snapped. All of her hard-learned control went out the window and she cried, "No I'm not. I'm not. I can't be the person you want me to be and I can't be the person I'm supposed to be. Don't you see?"

Maggie shook her head. "See what?"

"I thought it was you who liked the self-doubter, but it's not. It's me. I'm giving that person inside of me all the power."

The hallway echoed in silence following that outburst, and then Maggie said, "You're crying."

Brushing the frustrated tears away, all she could do was shrug.

"I've never seen you cry."

Jaxx took a steadying breath, hiccupped and then sighed. "That's because I didn't think I had anymore tears left in me, but I was wrong. So if you'll excuse me, I'm going into my house to wallow in them."

"My God, you're just like—"

Jaxx didn't want to hear her say "them". Not again. Not ever again.

She had turned away so she spun back around. "I'm just like me! I'm sorry if that disappoints you, but it's the truth, so you'll just have to live with it."

All Jaxx wanted to do was go inside and hide until she had control of her emotions. Now that Aries had helped unleash them, she was completely vulnerable. Scared. Angry that he'd abandoned her this way. It was almost as if...

Her ears started ringing, but through the noise she heard one word, "*exchange*".

"I was going to say you are just like your mother."

Jaxx stared at her. Unsure she'd heard correctly. "Excuse me?"

"She went after the wild ones too."

Suddenly Jaxx felt dizzy. She needed to lean back against the doorframe for support. "You're making that up to make me feel better."

Maggie took a deep breath as though she were bracing herself. "I'm afraid not, but it's high time I stopped making things up in other ways."

This was all she needed. She banged her head against the doorframe and whispered, "What things?"

"Memories."

That got Jaxx's attention and for a moment the situation with Aries was forgotten as she focused in and demanded, "What do you mean by that?"

"I thought it was for the best. Believe me."

"Maggie."

"Your mother. She...she..."

The sound of her own heart beating, nearly deafened her as she whispered, "Tell me."

"Your mother was a gypsy. She lived in the moment and on the edge. She tried every unthinkable thing. Fell in love with all the wrong men until one man, your father, swept her off her feet before he broke her heart. She was never the same after that."

"But..." Jaxx swayed and grasped Maggie's arm to steady herself. "You always said she was practical. That I should be more like her and less like—"

"I had to. I promised her that I wouldn't let you make the same mistakes. But after I found you, I realized I needed help. You weren't easy. And when I saw how much you disapproved of your adopted parents. Of the choices they made, I thought I could use that to help you stay on the straight and narrow. They were the bad to your mother's good. I needed to give you some frame of reference to get you back on track."

Dumbfounded, Jaxx let go of her. All this time. All the talks about how her real mother was a sensible scholar who... "You lied to me. For years I've been trying to live up to a ghost that never existed. Oh Maggie, how could you? There were times I thought I was losing my mind trying to be the person I thought I should be. Fighting my instincts because I thought they were all messed up. Doubting myself..."

"I was trying to do the right thing. And it was working until *that* man showed up."

The monumental hurt moved aside and outrage stepped in. "With *that man* I've been more myself than I ever have been before. You should be thanking him. I should be thanking him."

"I just couldn't—"

"You couldn't save my mother, but you thought you could save me, is that it?" Jaxx reached behind her and grasped the doorknob. "Here's a newsflash. I don't need saving. What I do need is honesty." She turned the knob and pushed the door open. "I also need some time to think about all this."

When she went to go inside Maggie stopped her. "I'm sorry. Wait. Please, you have to know that all I wanted was the best for you. I wanted you to have the bright future your mother never had the chance to have."

"I'm trying to understand. Believe me. But right now I have to go before I say something that we'll never recover from."

The last thing she saw before closing the door was Maggie's worried face. Yet as she climbed into bed and curled up into a ball, she was honest with herself, enough to admit. The pain in her heart, that was a deep and physical ache, had less to do with Maggie's revelation than it did with Aries strange and distant behavior.

Why hadn't she pressed him over it?

Fear.

She hugged herself tight. She couldn't let that rule her. Not anymore. One way or another she was going to have to face down the self-doubter within her, before it ruined the one relationship in her life she had come to cherish.

*****

By the time Aries showed up late Sunday night and woke her, she thought she'd had handle on her feelings. But she was wrong. He was brisk and to the point when he whispered, "On your tummy."

That's all he said before he stretched out beside her and traced his hand over the letters he'd put on her back. Over and over he followed the lines until she'd nearly fallen asleep again. But then the ice cold felt from the marker landed on her skin and she automatically stiffened. She would have complained, but he spoke before she got the chance.

"Don't move. Stay still. Yeah, just like that."

When he was done he put the marker on the night stand and pulled her up into the position he loved so well. She didn't protest. Not when he held on to her hips, not when he penetrated her and not when he slammed into her with a brutal need that burned. All she did was close her eyes and pray this wasn't his way of saying goodbye.

Later, after he'd tucked the sheets in tightly around her and stood by the side of the bed her heart raced at double time. She refused to open her eyes, afraid she'd see the truth. He was letting go of something here, she could feel it.

She held her breath as he brushed the hair from her forehead and chastely kissed her there. "I'll pick you up at six tomorrow night. It's cocktail attire. I'll be wearing a red tie."

She nodded.

"Jaxx?"

She opened one eye. "Yes?"

"After I meet with Gabe, we have some talking to do."

Her stomach did a flip without the flop. No, wait there it was. "Okay." She thought about Maggie and all she had to tell him in that regard. "Aries?"

He turned.

"I—" she sat up and pulled the duvet around her. To cover how nervous or maybe unsure she was, she scooped up the marker and fiddled with it. "I have a few things I want to talk to you about too." He stared at the marker in her hands, but didn't say anything. He just curtly nodded and then he was gone.

Chapter Twenty-Two

Jaxx put on a brave face, determined to make the best of the night. It certainly helped that Aries had practically lit up when he saw her poured into her little black dress. She'd accessorized her outfit with red, to go with his tie and he'd commented on that too. He still seemed distracted though, but she put that down nerves over the evening ahead. He'd already explained that he had a proposal for his brother to take a look at. And although she thought it was a strange time to be doing that, during a party, Aries had assured her he had his reasons and because of those, this was the only opportunity he'd have to present his plan.

She tried asking him about it, but he'd brushed her off saying they'd talk about it once there was something to tell her. So when they reached the high double front doors she'd let the matter go. Seeing their reflection in the huge panes of glass her heart swelled with pride. He looked like a million bucks in his Armani. But then in a flash the image was gone when both doors opened and an attendant greeted them.

"Aries. It's so good to see you."

Aries smiled at the older man and tightened his arm around Jaxx. "Thanks, Steven, glad to see Gabe hasn't fired your ass. This is—"

"Dr. Gavin. It's a pleasure." Steven stepped forward and took her hand. "I assure you, Aries brother was happy to see your name arrive on the RSVP list last week, I can tell you. He loves your column, as do I."

Her smile froze on her face. Last week? Aries only asked her two days ago. "Please, just call me Jaxx."

"Word to the wise," Aries leaned forward and spoke to Steven. "She doesn't like being called a doctor. Such a prestigious title, I'm hopeful she'll claim it one of these days."

Steven nodded. "I have my PhD in business and I still flirt with the idea of having people call me doctor. But then, you're a talented writer as well."

Jaxx's shook her head. "Truthfully, I had no idea my small advice column for the elderly was so popular."

"Why wouldn't it be? There isn't a person on earth getting any younger."

"You see? It's observations like this that had us calling Steven, The Philosopher. He was the strangest house-manager my family ever hired."

"Aries." She playfully swatted him on the chest. "That's not nice."

The two men stared at one another while Aries said, "Out of the list of other nickname options we used to have for him, I'm thinking it was the nicest."

"Prestigious?" She scowled. "Is that what my title is to you?"

"Oh yeah." He nodded to Steven before he led them away. "You should be bragging about it to everyone. I do."

She wanted to respond but then she spotted the ballroom. "I had no idea there'd be so many people." Her head was swimming with all kinds of thoughts. Looking down at the hand he had wrapped around her, she wondered. Why all of a sudden was he getting close to her? Being pleasant? Actually he seemed relieved. And why had he RSVP'd with her name before he'd even asked her to go? That's what she wanted to know.

"You okay?" He gave her an encouraging squeeze. "Let's find our table."

Once they were seated, Aries explained that although this was called a reception, it was no more than a glorified year-end back scratch for the higher-ups in his family's company. A company that his brother had run and, judging by the people and surroundings, he was doing a good job. She had just finished talking to a woman named Isabel, beside her when Aries caught her attention.

"I think it's time. I need to go track down my brother. You don't mind, do you? You'll be okay for a bit while I'm gone?"

"Sure."

"Great. But hey, if I'm not back in fifteen send out a search party."

Thankfully he winked, but there was a distinctive edge to the comment. Like maybe his brother would toss him out or something.

When he got up she grabbed his hand. "Aries? Why did you send that invitation back before you'd even asked me to come?"

"Invitation?"

She was sorry she'd asked. She could tell his head was someplace else. Suddenly they were back to the same disconnect she'd had from him over the last two days. "Yes, the RSVP to this."

He blinked. "Oh, I didn't send it, Shar did. Are you sure you'll be okay while I'm gone?"

I told you I didn't want to invite her.

She nodded and watched him walk off even as she wondered if she would be all right. So far she'd gotten a handle on her doubts, but jealously was the one thing she had no control over. Why was Shar always in the background? Always...

Just then a picture of Walter's engineer flashed before her eyes. That woman had sent an invitation too. One Walter knew nothing about. She'd been the one who instructed Jaxx to wait on the stadium lawn when she knew Walter wouldn't be showing up. Yes, that woman had always been in the background just like Shar.

Jaxx shifted in her seat and tried to put those thoughts aside, but the longer she sat and listened to the drone of chatter, taking in the sight of a crowd of unfamiliar faces, the more she recalled those hours while she'd waited on that stadium lawn. Surrounded by people she didn't know. Listening.

"*No.*"

"Did you say something?" Isobel asked.

"No. Would you like more wine?" Jaxx got up. She needed some air or something. She hadn't had a full-blown panic attack in years, but she recognized the unmistakable signs. She'd been so tightly strung over the Maggie situation and Aries, not to mention all her emotions in a jumble...what if he didn't come back? *Breathe.* Damn, if she didn't take some precautions she was going to have a meltdown. Now. Lovely.

That kind of release is exactly what I was hoping for before I...

Before he what?

She kept telling herself that she wasn't the thing that Aries was letting go of. He wasn't going to dump her like Walter had. She kept reminding herself that Shar was only a friend. And by the time she got to the entrance that led out to the front lobby she was almost a believer.

She was nearly to the exit when she bumped into a woman. "Sorry," she murmured and went to walk past, but then she heard the woman whisper to her friend, "That's her. She's Ramsey Taylor's date. A far cry from the last one that got him banned."

She took a step and then heard the other woman chime in, "I never thought Gabriel would relent. I heard this one's a doctor so I guess he had to."

Had to? Jaxx didn't want to believe it. Was this her part of the exchange? Getting him through the door tonight? Spotting Steven who was escorting an older lady through the crowd, she waited until he was free before she went to him. She didn't mince her words, she just pointblank asked, "Did you let Aries in tonight because of me?"

Although Steven was very polite when he said, "That's a topic you should be discussing with him, not me." The ruddy-red color that came to his cheeks gave her a different answer.

In a rush, all the texts, the mysterious business on holidays...leaving to see Shar those times? She tried to steady her breathing and get a grip, but by his own admission, he'd said he needed to see his brother and to do that he needed to get through the doors.

Steven excused himself and Jaxx nodded. At least she thought she did. It was true what Maggie had told her after all. Aries had needed her to bring respectable to the table. And now that she had and he got what he wanted? *If I'm not back in fifteen...* Oh no, she was feeling as if she were outside herself again. Only this time it was shock that carried her to the exit as somewhere in the back of her mind she kept telling herself she could handle this. She'd be okay with a little air and a moment to think things through.

But then she was waving down one of the company limos. Suddenly she was sitting inside it giving the driver her address. It wasn't until they drove around the fountain and headed down the long drive she examined why she was leaving without a word to him. The answer was obscenely simple. She wasn't going to be that girl waiting on the stadium lawn for a guy who had no more use for her. This time around she would carry home the pieces of her broken heart so no one else would see them.

Staring out at the darkened landscape the idea came to her that maybe she was just like her mother...

*****

Aries thought he'd be anxious, yet he wasn't. Not with Jaxx here with him. For the past two weeks he'd felt alive, needed and wanted. That was the best part. And now that he had all the arrangements made with the club? He'd make sure she'd know it. But first things first. He'd already decided even if Gabe wasn't willing to listen, he'd move forward with the build-out. It would just be smaller than he planned. Not the best scenario, but if Gabe was still on the warpath, it would be the only one he had open to him.

He'd seen his brother head through the second arch toward the back of the house and knew where he was going. Gabe liked his rituals, and tonight was no different. He'd head down to the wine cellar, open a bottle of Australian white and toast himself on another year's success. After a time, he'd come back up and play the gallant host until the last invitee was gone. Of course there were some out-of-towners who would be staying over, but his brother always managed to make everyone feel welcome.

Everyone but you.

That reminder got the old angst churning. Aries was almost second-guessing his decision to come, but then he walked through the line of wine casks and smelled the familiar aromatic scent and calmed down. Because there used to be a time he'd be here, waiting for Gabe. Ready to toast. Happy to share in the success no matter how much of a prick his older brother was. But his dad was alive then. His father always made things better between his sons while he was capable.

Aries paused, took a deep breath and let it out slowly. He straightened his cuffs and stepped around the last barrel.

"Gabe?"

"Ram?"

Gabe was the only one who called him that, and he'd always thought he hated it until he stopped hearing it. God, despite the brewing battle possibly to come, it was good to hear.

They stood several paces apart just staring at one another. It could have been seconds or even a minute, yet the silence was okay. Comfortable even, but then his brother cleared his throat.

"I'm glad you came." He turned and pulled a chilled bottle of white out of the bar fridge. Pouring two glasses, he scooped one up and held it out. "Should we toast the occasion?"

"No, thanks. I don't drink anymore."

"No?"

"That was the first thing on the list of 'have to goes' when I cleaned up my act. And about that acting, I want to apologize."

Gabe put his glass down and looked at him. The solemn expression on his face reminded Aries of their dad. Gabe had is eyes. "Why do you hate me?"

Clearly there'd be no beating around the bush tonight and Aries was very glad about that. "I don't hate you."

"You did and I want to know why."

This was something Aries had never considered. His brother was always sullen and silent, but now looking at him through the eyes of the man he'd become, he realized he was just a person surviving like everyone else on the planet.

"I never hated you. I hated myself and unfortunately, you're the one who got caught in that shit-storm."

"All those fights? The drunken binges? The women?"

Aries had plenty of time to think things through. It had taken him years to understand what drove him back then and he wasn't sure he could explain it well enough for Gabe to understand it now, but he was willing to try.

"I have no excuse for how I behaved. I do have reasons, but with those came choices and I continually made the wrong ones for a while. Maybe I did hate you a bit. If I did, it was because I thought you were the lucky one."

Gabe snorted.

"It's true. You were. Oh, yeah, we both lost Dad, but what I discovered—and this is something no grief handbook will tell you—

is that a primary caregiver loses everything they built the day the person in their care dies. For me, I lost Dad, but I also lost the insulated life I'd been building around him for years." Aries blinked away the sting these words brought to his eyes and continued, "That morning, the day in the cemetery after Dad was lowered in to the ground, you walked away with all your friends, your coworkers and the people you'd kept in touch with who had known him. Do you know what I did? I stayed there because that's where my best friend, my only friend was. I stood there and looked around at the emptiness and that's when I knew what I'd sacrificed in caring for him. As his world had gotten smaller and less complicated out of necessity, so had mine. Until there was only the two of us, but then he was gone."

"Jesus, I never knew. It never occurred to me."

Aries took a deep breath and let it out slowly. He wasn't finished. If there was ever going to be forgiveness between them, he needed to say it all.

"I had no friends and no life. I went from being on high alert 24/7 to nothing. It was as if I hit a brick wall that crumbled when I discovered we'd acquired the club. I know you were only trying to get me to focus, and I also know you probably regret the hell out of ever sending me there to run it, but in hindsight? It was the best thing you could have ever done for me. It gave me a chance to do the living I'd missed out on for so long. Hell." He walked over to the counter and picked up a coaster, turning it around in his hands. "It might have taken me a year to get myself back, but eventually I did. I'm just sorry that things between us have been bad."

"I was hurt too, you know. Especially by you."

Although stunned by that, Aries put the coaster down and was prepared to listen. For the first time in years.

"Do you remember what you said to me? How you'd always hold Dad's care over my head? Did you think it was any easier for me to step in and run the business? Do you know how many days—nights that I prayed I'd wake up and find out the pressure and stress was only a nightmare? It was a constant tightrope I had to walk to make sure our stockholders didn't find out too soon about Dad's condition. They couldn't know until they trusted me, and in order for them to trust me and for me to prove myself, I had to totally commit. I was 24/7 too. So when you started accusing me of not caring. Of taking off and sticking you with the burden, I'm not going to lie. I wanted to kill you."

Despite the seriousness of the topic and what Gabe said, Aries found himself grinning. Only Gabe would mention murder so casually and mean it. "You had a choice."

"Yes, and so did you. You could have run the company and I could have spent those last years with Dad."

Aries swallowed and looked away because when Gabe said that, his voice cracked. Both of them had been close to their father. A man among men. A role model who was larger than life to his children, until life intervened and turned that giant into the child and his children into giants. Both Gabe and he had to be better than they were in that moment when their dad was diagnosed. Gabe to run the business, and Aries to care for the father they loved, when it was decided there'd be no hospital or nursing home for Jack Taylor. His last few years had been spent here with Aries constantly by his side.

"I'm sorry you didn't get more time with him before things got bad."

"Me too."

They were quiet then, but it wasn't awkward. It was peaceful. And Aries wanted to believe if his dad was looking down from up above, he'd be pleased with his boys. Regardless of what came before, they loved one another. That fine line of love and hate? Aries knew for sure he'd just crossed back over it. Looking at his brother now, he couldn't imagine ever hating him, and yet not an hour ago that was exactly how he'd felt.

He thought about what had brought him here and was ashamed of himself. What they'd just discussed should have been the reason he'd come home. This was no time to bring up the complex. "I had another reason for coming tonight, but this is more important to me. I'm glad we had a chance to talk."

As he turned to leave he was stunned for a second time tonight, when Gabe yanked him in for a hug. "You stupid ass," his brother whispered.

Aries held on tight until Gabe laughed and released him. "Weird, isn't it?" Gabe put a hand on his shoulder. "It doesn't feel like so much time has gone by, does it?"

"No. No it doesn't."

"So what was the real reason that brought you here?"

"We can go over it another time."

"I've got time now. I'm not going upstairs until I finish my wine."

Aries smiled. Gabe always was a nosey bastard. "If you're sure?"

"Positive."

When Aries pulled the plans out of his breast pocket and smoothed them out on the bar-top between them, Gabe had his readers on peering down. "Architectural plans?" He squinted. "Should I invest? Is it another club?"

"It's a complex."

Aries waited and held his breath.

"The Jack Taylor Clinic?" Gabe examined the papers for a full thirty seconds and then shot a look up. "You're building an assisted living facility?"

Aries nodded. "Specifically for patients with Alzheimer's." He never doubted that Gabe would back him once he knew what the plan was. His only concern was getting through the front door so he could talk with him about it.

"This is brilliant. The location is perfect. Right between two hospitals. You must have scooped the warehouse next door. Probably cost you a pretty penny, but it'll be worth it once you get this going. I suppose we'll need to annex the company interest into the newly formed Foundation. Have you spoken to legal about this?"

He wasn't surprised his brother connected all the necessary dots so quickly. The guy was a brilliant businessman. But he was taken aback by... "You know about the warehouse?"

Gabe nodded. "Of course. Just because we were on the outs didn't mean I wasn't paying attention. You're my brother. Never forget that."

They briefly discussed the broader picture and then Aries said, "I have to get back upstairs, my girl is waiting for me."

"Yeah, I should get back too. What about these, can I take them?"

Aries looked at the plans and nodded.

"Great, my evening is looking up. I now have some work to do. Maybe I can scare up some possible donors for your venture."

"Donors?"

Gabe folded over the papers and tapped his thigh with them. "Yes, the way I see it, we shouldn't need to spend all of our own money on building. It's a good write-off for most of these guys, and all we'll have to promise is to put their names on a plaque. The more money they contribute, the closer to the top their name gets."

Aries hadn't considered that, but now that Gabe brought it up, he was beginning to see all kinds of potential.

"Stick with me. We'll get you the funds and then you can run with them." They had just gotten to the door when Gabe stopped and held up the plans, saying, "This makes me happy. You have no idea how proud I am of you right now."

Heading upstairs, Aries was buoyed by that comment. So much so, he was looking forward to sharing his great news with Jaxx.

Chapter Twenty-Three

"What do you mean she's not here? She has to be here."

Maggie stood at her own door and repeated, "She isn't home, but she will be soon."

"I was told she'd snagged one of the limos." He was sorry now that he'd taken that shortcut here. He probably could have caught up with them, but then, he wasn't the one who should be doing the chasing. *Right.* "She's okay then? I tried calling and texting, but got no answer."

"Yes. But why did you get here before her? If you were both together I don't understand."

Aries wasn't going to tell her. In fact, he was just ready to leave when he caught sight of something moving behind Maggie and his eyes narrowed. "She's in there isn't she?"

Her hand went to her throat as she unconsciously tugged on the white jersey material and scowled, "No."

"I saw something." He walked forward and craned his neck. "Who are you hiding in there?"

"I'm not hiding anyone," she sniffed. "If you must know it's Gunther Kreizeger."

Suddenly the space behind her was filled up with the form of a fucking Viking gladiator or something. The guy had to be six-foot-seven. "That's the German egghead?"

"Mr. Taylor!"

Maggie's scowl deepened, but the damned Viking smiled. Jesus H. The guy was a heartbreaker.

He snapped out of his man-crush moment and reached around to extend his hand. Oh sure, the guy did all the right things. He shook his hand back, nodded and mumbled some kind of accented nicety, so Aries was totally stumped as to why he wanted to pound the fucker into the ground.

He's here to steal your girl, remember?

Crush-time was over and in its place came cold-blooded suspicion. "Did you text Jaxx tonight about him?"

Maggie stepped back. It was a defensive move so even if she didn't answer he had the answer. "I did."

But not all of it. He could tell. "And?"

Her chin lifted a notch or two and she said, "I sent a picture of him too." Now she leaned forward and whispered, "You can't blame me for that. Look at him."

Aries wanted to wring her neck. No, he wanted to wring Jaxx's neck. This couldn't be why she left him tonight. Because of the Viking? It made no sense yet neither did her desertion.

He took stock of the guy and asked, "You're a nuclear physicist?"

When the Viking nodded a hunk of perfect blond hair slid over an eye. One look at him and even a blind woman would be drooling.

Now Aries really examined the guy. Trying to find some fault but there wasn't one as far as he could see. No wonder Maggie was trying to get them together. This guy was the perfect, respectable genius Jaxx deserved.

Fuck that. She was going to learn soon enough that he was now the only respectable guy for her. "She's mine Maggie. I'm not giving her up. Egghead or not, the Viking can go back to Finland."

"He's from Germany." She crossed her arms and leaned against the doorframe.

"I don't care where he's from. And why are you smiling?"

"Gunther, would you excuse us for a minute?" She didn't turn around. She just waited for the hulking shadow to disappear before she stepped out in the hall and shut the door behind her. "I don't want to offend the poor guy," she whispered, taking Aries by the arm and walking with him to the entrance. "After all, this is his first night in town."

"Yeah, well, if I have my way it will be his last night. What airline did he fly in on? I'll be sure to buy him a return ticket ASAP." He pulled his arm away from her grasp and growled, "What the hell are you laughing at?"

"Karma."

"You think Karma's biting me in the butt. Is that it?"

"No Aries, I know this Karma is mine alone."

She'd never called him anything but Mr. Taylor, so he was paying attention. "How so?"

"Gunther isn't the man for Jaxx."

Although he was surprised, he nodded anyway. "I'm glad to hear that."

"I think he's a man with your kind of... how should I put this? Sexual tastes?"

Great. This was all he needed. Now he was going to have to kill the guy.

"Well don't you have anything to say to that?"

He didn't as it wasn't prudent to discuss the crime before, during or after you commit it. "No—yes. Did you just find this out about him?"

She made a face. "Of course. Do you actually think I'd want Jaxx to be with...?"

Perfect. As if he didn't feel like shit enough already. "So what did you do, ask him? Or was he wearing a sign when you picked him up at the airport?"

"That is not funny Mr. Taylor."

"Well something is because your eyes are dancing with gleeful delight." He was trying to keep his aggravation in check. Would she ever spit it out?

"I made the mistake of talking about you in the hopes of—never mind about that, but you can imagine my surprise when I told him you were the owner of a sex club. I fully expected him to be disgusted and what did he do?"

Aries narrowed his eyes and shrugged.

"He asked me if I could get him an invite."

Now his eyes widened. "This is why you are practically glowing?" The woman was warped and that Viking wasn't getting an invite to anywhere but a ticket home.

"Oh, no. I'm pleased-as-punch over something else."

He pulled open the door and growled, "What?"

"You said you weren't giving Jaxx up."

"I'm not. So when she gets back here tonight, I want you to tell her I'm at home. And if she knows what's good for her, she'll march her little bottom right to my door with an explanation as to why she left tonight without telling me. She better not stay here with that guy at your place. That's all I'm saying."

"I'll tell her," he heard Maggie call after him, but he was too angry to respond. All he could do was simmer. Whatever the hell Jaxx was doing, she better work her shit out tonight. Tomorrow it would be too late, because he fully intended to call her on it. Even if he had to come back here to collect her himself, he would. Hopefully it wouldn't come down to that.

He got back into his car and turned things over in his mind as he headed home. Sure, he knew things had been a little strange between them the last couple of days, and he also knew that much of that was his fault. He should have told her he was anxious about his meeting with Gabe. Yeah, he could have blamed his bizarre behavior on that, but he wasn't one to lie. If only she hadn't bolted. How could he have the crucial discussion he planned on having with her when she didn't have faith in him?

She doesn't trust you.

Once she showed up all that was going to change. Big time.

"What the hell?"

He'd just turned onto his street and saw the flashing red lights from the fire truck while the strobe of blue and white coming from the cruiser nearly blinded him. He eased his foot off the gas and whispered, "Betty."

Jaxx had plenty of time to think as a fender-bender had traffic backed up for a half a mile on the highway leading into the city. What a nightmare. But then worse, was an hour later, when they pulled up to her house and she saw how Maggie's side of the building was all lit up. Seeing this, she knew for sure she didn't want to go in. And when she checked her last text from Aries confirming that he was on his way home, she made her decision. She was going to his place and have it out with him. How dare he use her to get into his brother's good graces.

She was in fine form by the time the limo turned on his street. She thought she was ready for anything, but then she saw the trucks. And as they rolled by, she spotted Aries arguing with a cop. At least he looked like he was. He was pointing and making gestures. "This is fine. You can let me off right here."

After tipping the driver and getting out, she decided she'd been right about one thing. Aries was mad. He was currently pleading with the policemen to no avail.

"Look, I may only be a neighbor, but I know Betty. More importantly—" he shot a look over at the crying caretaker, "—I know the young girl who watches her. Sometimes she gets distracted and Betty runs away."

The guy pushed his cap back and scratched his forehead. "I can't talk to anyone other than family members or someone who's responsible for her care. I'm sorry. Maybe if her son gets here and gives me the okay, then I can talk with you."

"It's her grandson. Have you checked the porch? She usually sits on the porch, and there may be a clue to what triggered her into leaving this time."

When the cop shrugged, Jaxx took note of his name on the badge that jiggled on his chest as he sighed, "I'm sorry, buddy. All I can tell you is we've got divers out in the pond."

And when she saw the distraught look on Aries' face as she came closer, she made another decision. "Officer Howley, did I get here before Betty's grandson?"

"No family has arrived," the officer said, suspiciously eyeing her dress. "And you are?"

She pulled her identification out of her clutch and flashed it at him "Dr. Jaxx Gavin. How long has Betty been missing?" She didn't give the officer the chance to better qualify her, so in her mind it wasn't really lying or breaking the law because she was Dr. Gavin. "Did you find any clues in the house? What she was looking at? Watching on television? Eating? These things are threads you can follow when dealing with dementia patients. Think 'tricky three-year-old' who's smarter than you are."

"I, ah..." The officer shifted on his feet. "We found a jar of coins on the porch. I think she was counting them."

"Coins, huh?" She turned to Aries. "Mr. Taylor, what do you think? It's nice of you to be here to help out," Jaxx said before she swung back around to face the policeman. "Mr. Taylor knows Betty very well." When that statement didn't seem to have any effect on the guy, she turned and gave Aries the "work with me" stare. "I see you were at some kind of a function yourself tonight. Did you get called as well?"

Despite how furious he was with her, Aries could have hugged her. "Yes, I did."

The police officer moved the crime scene tape aside and motioned them through. "Do you want to talk to the caretaker?"

Five minutes later, Aries determined that Betty wouldn't have gone near the pond. After he'd told her about the bugs, the caretaker said Betty refused to step on the grass even. So that meant concrete, and while all the manpower was dredging the pond looking for a body, someone needed to hit the bricks and find the person on the run.

He motioned to Jaxx to follow him. "Come on."

"Where are we going?"

"To the place Betty can spend her coins."

"A store?"

He helped Jaxx into his car. "No." When he got behind the wheel, he said, "To the bus stop. She used to ride the bus to the senior center for daycare. Now that she's gotten worse, they don't let her go anymore. I noticed she had the piles right. A dollar five in coins. Just what they'd make her pay to get on their bus. It wasn't a public bus. It was sent from the center, and the dollar five went toward supplies. It's a shot."

"Very good. You've obviously done this kind of thing before."

"I have. But just so you know, I'm not that distracted that you're off the hook. Did Maggie drive you here? I didn't see your car."

"No I took a limo."

"Here?" He did a double take.

"It's a long story."

"So you didn't go home to see the Viking?"

"Who?"

"Eric from True Blood. Your egghead sperm donor." He slowed his speed as they passed one of the two closest stops. "Damn, she's not here." He continued to drive up the street. Hopeful she'd be at the next one.

"You went to my house?"

"Yes."

"Why?"

"To tan your ass for leaving me the way you did. Look, maybe we shouldn't talk about this right now because I'm getting angry."

"I think I had good cause, but you're right," she said as he slowed down and drove by the second stop. "This isn't the time to have it out. Let's wait until we get home."

"Perfect." He scanned the second stop and when he didn't find her he pulled into a 7-11 to turn around. There was no way Betty could have gotten this far.

"What are you doing?"

"I'm going back. She couldn't have gotten this far. Damn. I was so sure about the coins. She could be anywhere and they're calling for rain."

"I know. Hopefully they'll find her sooner than later."

Aries doubted that. The police had a tendency of tripping over their own feet in most cases. The one time his father stole a set of car keys and drove off they had alerted everyone under the sun. They had questioned Gabe, who had fucked up the one time Aries had left him in charge, and then the officer had sat in the driveway waiting for Aries dad to hopefully return. Aries didn't even go home once he was called. He simply went to the grocery store to collect him. It had been an educated hunch back then, but now he knew better. The mind of a dementia patient only knows what it knows. So in terms of a search? You have to think inside the box instead of outside of it.

He was just about to turn on his street when Jaxx sat forward.

"Hey, here's a thought." He held up turning. "What about Monroe Park? You said there were three retirement communities there."

"Yeah, but the one Betty was always taken to was in the other direction."

"Well, it may be in the opposite direction, but I know there's a bus stop. We passed it that night before we, ah…"

"Son of a bitch!" He leaned over and kissed her hard. "Of course, they used to take the group to the park once a month for a picnic lunch."

And that was where they found her. Sitting alone on the bus bench, under the white beam of lamplight as she shivered. Aries was careful not to scare her. When he got out of the car, he could see how stressed she was. He had Jaxx drive them back and when the lights and people came into view, Betty got upset. She didn't cry or yell, all she did was furiously pick at her clothes. Once he got her into the house, he'd make her a towel roll.

"It's okay, honey. You're home now. We'll make all these people go away."

Chapter Twenty-Four

Jaxx used Aries' key to let herself inside. He'd stayed next door to fill in the blanks and wait for Betty's grandson to show up, as he was determined to speak to the guy about the situation this time.

She had taken no more than a step through the doorway and stopped. Someone was talking. She flicked on the light and called, "Hello?"

It was a woman's voice and it was coming from the kitchen. Keeping a firm hold of her purse—not that a clutch would do her any good in a possible cat fight, but you never know— she went inside.

The voice droned on, so she strained to listen. Going up the hall, she made a right. Then paused to turn on more lights before she stepped through the kitchen entrance and had a looked around. "Hello?"

It took her a second to realize someone was leaving a voice mail. And not a moment more, for her to put a name to the sexy voice.

Wild Shar.

"And Draco was good with the deposit. I made it a hefty one because he pissed me off last week when he stole all the Andes mints. Those are my favorite, as you know, and we're all out, so I'm going to order some more. Okay...I think that covers all the news about the auction and work stuff."

Jaxx had just exited the kitchen when she heard Shar's next words and shot back into the room.

"Call me when you get in and let me know how your vanilla arm-candy date went. Later."

The bastard. Just when Jaxx thought the situation couldn't get worse, it did...for him.

Wild Shar? She was fucking sick of hearing that woman's name! Vanilla arm candy, was she? Oh no, and Jaxx was prepared to prove it if she had to kick her ass. That would be proof enough.

*****

Aries wasn't even through the door when Jaxx came after him.

"Is everything okay with Betty?"

"Yes—"

"Good. Now." She poked him in the chest. "You wanted to have it out. I'm ready."

He stared at her finger being bruised against his chest. "If this is how you think this is going to go, you'd be wrong."

She gasped but he ignored the sound as he stepped around her and walked up the hall to the living room.

"Where do you think you're going?"

He didn't answer.

"I said," she rushed up behind him. "I want to have it out. I want answers."

She wanted answers? He stopped and she walked right into him.

"Ow."

"Tell me why you left without me if it wasn't to go see The Viking."

"I left because you were going to dump me if I stayed." She came around and stood in front of him. With her hands on hips and a scowl that could rival one of his, she spoke through her teeth, "But before we discuss that you are going tell me who Wild Shar is, and what she is to you. Got it?"

"I'm going to get something all right. Maybe the paddle or my belt."

Her chin came up a notch. "Go ahead. I dare you."

Damn she was brave. Gorgeous too. "You don't want to do that, babe. I love a challenge."

"Yeah, well so do I."

They stared each other down. Neither one of them budging as a full thirty seconds ticked by. Then her eyes narrowed.

"Tell me about vanilla arm-candy and exchanges."

Now his eyes narrowed. "Where did you hear about those things?"

"On your goddamn answering machine you creep." She shrieked that last word and tried to push him. When he didn't move, she raised a hand and would have slapped him had he not caught her limb mid-strike.

"Whoa, you really don't want to do that."

"Oh, yes I do."

He searched her furious face. "Answering machine, huh?

"Not just that. Maggie remember? You told her how you were doing an exchange with me."

He didn't let go of her arm, only brought it down so she'd be more comfortable. "I already explained why I said that."

Her belligerent snort interrupted him. "Yeah right. But forget about that. What about how weird you've been?"

He should have known this was coming. He'd seen her fiddling with the pen before he'd left her last night. And his disappointment was monumental. "You mean about the magic marker?"

"No. I mean about all your mysterious *business* and going out of town. After what we did Friday night and Saturday morning? It was a stab in the back. Totally cruel. And then Sunday night? Was that your goodbye fuck? It was, wasn't it? Ever since I cried. That was it. The end result of the exchange you were looking for before you dumped me."

Such a small word "no" but when she just said it and brushed over the subject of the marker he'd used on her without a blink? He was hopeful. Happy. Elated that she was pissed about these other things. "You little fool. I'm not going to dump you. Who said that?"

If he had to describe her expression he would say she mentally dragged her hands down the sides of her face before she ground out, "Wild Shar."

"Wild—when did you meet her?" Aries was trying to follow along, but Jaxx was huffing one minute and growling the next. It was difficult to keep up.

"On the fucking answering machine."

Now that wasn't hard to follow. "Okay, maybe I need to hear what was said, that has the spur under your saddle."

"Spur?" she choked out as he brought her along with him into the kitchen, "It's more like a mace and any minute now I'm going use it on the side of your lying, player-ass head."

He turned on her so fast she went still and silent at the same time. A good thing too, because despite being pleased over those other things, he had reached the end of his patience with the one subject. She needed to trust him. He'd given her no reason not to. Pulling her in by the shoulders, he drew her up against him as he curled down over her until they were nose to nose. "That's enough."

"No it's not. I—"

He tightened his grip and pressed her into him. So closely, she squeaked. He waited and when her gaze dropped to his chest, he spoke to her. Soft, but firmly, "As this is our first real argument, I think it's important I show you how I'm always going to win in the end."

She shot a look up. Her mouth opened as if she were going deny that bold statement, but then she must have thought better of it because she pressed her lips together and he actually heard her swallow.

"That's better. Now say you're sorry."

He didn't hear her gasp. It was more like he felt it, as her burst out breath rushed over him. He gave her credit though. She bravely clammed up even as she went cross-eyed, focused in and staring down her nose at him, instead of into his eyes.

"Jaxx."

He had less than a second to realize he'd misread her demeanor. He thought she was settling down. That she was ready to be reasonable so when she snapped, he briefly thought about the old saying, "the calm before the storm". She'd been the one, and now she was the other while he faced her storm.

She pushed and pulled. Jerked and kicked. Getting madder as he held her off. His plan was to keep her from harming herself while she got exhausted enough so they could talk. It would have worked too, if she hadn't cried out, "Win? This isn't a game. You stole my heart and you've crushed it."

It was shock that made him let go. Disappointment that caused him to step back. The idea that she had no faith in him was the reason he let her beat against his chest. Yet it wasn't until he saw the furious tears running unchecked down her cheeks that he gave into his own emotions. He had to, because those glistening tears were for him. He thought about the other tears she'd shed. How she'd surrendered so completely into his care last Friday night, and what she'd said about her limitations.

I was free to go beyond them because I trusted you...

She trusted him. That was why she was in so much pain now. It was herself she didn't trust.

"Aries!"

He ignored that when he grabbed her by the arms and hauled her up. He searched her face and then looked her in the eyes, whispering, "I don't want to crush your heart, babe. Never that. I want to own it."

When he swooped down and kissed her, she speared her hands in his hair and yanked, trying to escape him, but he paid no attention. Instead he continued with his sensual assault, knowing this was the only way the two of them could ever win. And when her grip eased, and she sank into his arms, he didn't let up.

He took hold of the strap of her dress and wrenched it. The sound of tearing fabric stroked him something fierce and when she shifted to shrug out from underneath it without complaint? He lost it. This was what he wanted. God yes. A woman who lived in the moment with him—no matter how that moment came. Happy, sad, right or wrong. As long as it was real that was all that mattered. And this? This was as real as it got.

Without breaking contact, he tossed her ruined dress aside and scooped her up. When her legs were locked around his hips, and her arms wound around his neck, he pulled back. The sight of her stripped down to lingerie with her lips dark and swollen from his attention did mad things to libido.

But then she groaned, "Don't stop." And he nearly fell to his knees with the overwhelming urge to get into her.

Everything went in slow motion then. He had one hand under her ass while his other peeled the black lace off her. First her bra and then the thong. The feel of her, warm and naked in his arms while he was still completely dressed, was empowering. Humbling. But if she didn't stop flexing and grinding on him he'd never have the strength to walk them to the bedroom where he kept his latex.

Jaxx wasn't letting up. Every nerve ending in her body was connected right to her heart. A heart that he wanted to own. She wedged a hand between them and traveled south. He was hard. Hot. And the way he was kissing her was as if he were staking claim, and she loved it. She wanted him to. No, she wanted him period. Now.

"Easy there, tiger. You keep that up and we may have a situation on our hands."

"Fuck me," she panted into his ear. "Fuck me now."

"I need—" He sucked in a breath when she wrapped her hand around his cock and lifted it out of his pants.

"Oh...oh, yeah." She moaned as she shifted and worked the tip of him against her clit. Warm wetness flowed, making a nice easy glide that she loved. She bit her lip and worked his velvet flesh against hers, harder. Panting and sighing. Groaning. "Oh, God. It would be so easy for you to slide right into me. Do it." She sank her free hand in his hair and tugged. "Fuck me right now."

"We can't—"

"It's okay. I'm on the pill if that's the only reason you—"

She didn't get to finish with that sentence as he walked them to the wall. He used his weight to pin her there until... "Mmm." The feel of him. The skin to skin contact as he penetrated her and went deep was toe curling deliciousness. "I love the feel of your hot cock inside me."

That was the last coherent thing she said as she clung to him. Relishing the feel of this kind of invasion. Taking it in and surrendering to it.

"Jesus, babe. I can't get enough of you."

This was perfectly fine with her. She buried her face against his chest and with one hand clutching his shoulder and her other wrapped around his red tie, she rode his cock. Shaking and trembling as the tingles came to life inside her. Faster and faster she flexed and pumped. Chasing the titillating waves. Breathing hard until she panted. Groaned. Moaned. God, the sensations were too much to bear. And when the suspended squeeze came? It stole her breath away.

"Breathe, honey. It feels even better when you breathe."

His gravely whisper pushed her right over the edge and then she did as he told her. She took a breath and the light came in as she cried, "Aries."

"So fucking warm...and wet."

"Aries..." She wound her arms around his neck and hugged him close. Welcoming him. Encouraging him to find his own release. And when a few minutes later he did, by giving one final thrust and whispering her name, she smiled. Even as she acknowledged that if this was the way he was always going to win when they argued, she figured she could live with it.

"I owe you a dress."

After all the whispering this deadpan pronouncement sounded like Hannibal Lecter saying "Hello Clarice". It struck her funny-bone and she laughed.

He pulled back and shook his head. "You are the oddest woman."

"Then we make a good pair."

Although she was joking, his eyes darkened and his expression turned intense. "I know. And about that? There are a few things I need to tell."

"What?"

"You'll see."

By the time Aries had her wrapped in his robe and sitting on the bed waiting for him, he was ready himself. He'd changed into a pair of sweats and a T-shirt and he knew exactly where he wanted to start the conversation.

"You're lucky I don't put you over my knee."

"For?"

He brushed her bangs aside and said, "For being foolish enough to think I'd be so callous as to have orchestrated an exchange without discussing it with you first. And a vanilla arm-candy plan to execute?" He shook his head. "Ridiculous."

"You can't blame me there. Wild Shar, remember?"

"Do you honestly think I would go through all of the planning and putting up with your less-than-stellar—on more than one occasion—behavior for just a date? Ludicrous. Shar lives in a bubble. I love her—"

"That's it, she's a dead person." She nearly came off the bed.

He held up a hand and chuckled, "Whoa. Relax and put away the claws." When she settled he grinned, "I love Shar as a friend. Only a friend. She's great at business, but she sucks at the personal stuff. Unfortunately, she doesn't know it. I try to keep her out of mine as much as I can, so I tend to agree with her assumptions as long as those assumptions keep her off my back and out of my shit."

He folded his arms over his chest when it came to him. "But the voicemail message wasn't why you left the party."

"No." She blushed and looked away.

"Jaxx."

She looked back and admitted, "I had a panic attack—"

"What?"

"Entirely *your* fault."

He threw his hands up. "Of course it was. Do tell."

"You made me open up and now I'm...I'm an emotional wimp."

"That's why you had a panic attack? Because I got you to open up?"

"No," she grumbled. "It was just all too familiar. The feeling and the fear. And when I thought you weren't coming back something happened and I freaked out."

He scowled down at her and she scowled right back up but didn't say anything.

"Jaxx, why didn't you list this on the questions I gave you. At the very least you should have told me you suffer from these kinds of episodes."

"Why? So you'd know how completely fucked up I am?"

"No, so I'd be aware of this when we did our Scene."

"Oh." He was right about that, but then until tonight she hadn't had one in years. Thinking about that, she sighed, "At least now I know why I'm screwed up."

"I suppose that's my fault too?"

"Nope that's Maggie's fault. But I don't have the strength to talk about that right now. She and I are working it out. It's just going to take some time." She looked up at him. "So I was wrong about you planning to end things?"

He shook his head. "If only you knew. Stand up." He gave her a hand and held on to her as she kicked the bulk of terrycloth that pooled at her feet aside so she could walk with him to the chair. Sitting down, he pulled her over his lap. "Maybe it's time you know the truth. We still have to have that talk I mentioned."

She sank against him. "As long as you're not going to dump me, I can handle pretty much anything. So talk away."

"I plan to." When she looked up he tapped her nose. "You were right about me, Jaxx. I never told you, but you were. The Rorschach test? You nailed it. I loved my father and I was always afraid I'd never live up to his expectations. And as you found out tonight, I did have problems with my brother. You were even right about the mask. I knew who I had to be to get where I am. I knew, and I was comfortable with it. Only now I've met this woman, you see..." He took hold of her jaw and rubbed her chin with the pad of his thumb. This was it. Confession time. "She's perfect for me I think, but I haven't taken off the mask for her."

"I knew it." Jaxx smacked his shoulder and kicked her feet with glee. She loved being right. "You're not as kinky as people believe you are."

"How could you possibly say that after all the shit you and I have done?"

He had a very excellent point. "All right, I'll keep quiet."

"You back off too quickly. That's a terrible flaw for a therapist."

"So I'm right about the kink?"

"To some extent. I may not want to spend lots of time at a local sex club, or mine even—"

She threw her arms up in the air. "I knew it."

"But—" He grabbed hold of her hands, which got her attention, "—I do want other things from you."

"Like?"

Unbelievable. His gaze dropped. It actually dropped for a split second, but that second was long enough for her to gauge how serious he was before he looked back up. "I'm taking that mask off now. This is my reality, okay?"

"Okay."

"I want you. I want to own you. I want you to know that you're mine. Completely and utterly, so there's no question and no room for doubt between us. Ever."

Her heart raced at those words. Hell, even her toes curled in unadulterated pleasure. "I'd like that too."

"You would?"

When he drew back she didn't know why he was shocked. "Yes." She put a hand on his cheek and tried to keep her voice steady. Low, so it didn't crack. "I've spent my whole life waiting for someone to want me. Really want me, and I'm glad it's you."

He held her gaze and his was so intense she was almost mesmerized, when he whispered, "I want you to wear my collar."

She waited for him to say more, and when he didn't she frowned. "I already did. Friday night, remember?"

"No, not that collar." He reached down and pulled a flat box out from between the upholstery and chair cushion. With a snap he opened it right in front of her. "This one."

The tri-colored necklace looked like delicate lace. "It's beautiful." The gold, copper and silver threads were so intricately woven it was hard to tell where one ended and another started. She traced the outline with her finger while she thought about what he was really asking.

"I don't want the special to end." She looked up at him. "This will be for you and me. No one else. The rest of the world goes on as they do, but you and I will have this secret between us. A commitment that's deeper and more meaningful than most couples ever share in a lifetime."

She knew what he meant now and she also knew she wanted it. "I think...I think I'd like that."

"There's something else." He put the box beside her and grabbed both of her hands again. She'd never forget the look in his eyes. If she lived to be a hundred she'd always remember it. Hopeful and wary at the same time. "The marker? I want to make it permanent. I want my name, tattooed on you. Low on your back where only I can see it. I can't tell you why I have this need for tangible proof that you're mine. Especially when no one else will see it. I just do, and I know this is a hard limit for you, but I want to be honest with you because I won't stop asking. I'll always be hopeful that you'll change your mind one day, but until you do, I'm positive we're going to go through a lot of markers."

"And cleaning bills. Those letters leave black smudges on all my clothes."

"Oh."

He looked so crestfallen she couldn't keep him dangling on the hook any longer. "So I think I'd prefer to make it permanent too...on one condition."

His gaze burned her up when he swore, "Anything. If it's in my power to give it, I will."

"I want you to get one for me. I want my name on you."

Huh. There was another expression of his she'd never forget. But then he hauled her in for a bear hug and she didn't have time to examine it.

"Absolutely. Where? Below the belt or above it somewhere?"

He seemed so pleased that she smiled against his chest. Happy for no other reason than he was. "You know those barbwire ones that people wear around their biceps?"

"Yes." He rubbed a hand up and down her back and it warmed her.

"Well I was thinking we could have an artist design one like that, only it would be a stylized version of my name in a repeat pattern as you've got a lot of bulging muscle to cover."

His hand stopped moving. "That's a phenomenal idea, babe. Did you just come up with it on the fly?"

She took a deep breath and purred, "No, I've been thinking about this since last Friday." This was the truth. He had great biceps and her name would look stunning strangling one of them.

He held her off him and scowled, "But I thought you hated tattoos?"

"Hate is a strong word. I just think they mess with a woman's fashion when they're plastered all over the place. Roses and vines up against plaid? Drives me nuts."

His scowl deepened and so did his voice, "But you struck a line through the word on your limits list and added exclamation points even."

"I did?"

"Jaxx."

She tried to fight back the cheeky grin, but failed as she finally admitted, "Oh all right. I knew this was one of your weaknesses, so I forced you to have deal with it. At least I got you thinking about it, right?"

"Now you're just messing with me, aren't you?"

"Yeah, it's fun."

"Well, I hope you'll still think it's fun when we get to the point in our relationship that I put down some rules and create some rituals. Oh, and I'll still surprise you whenever I want, only instead of using your key I'll be coming home to you to do it. I want you, Jaxx. All to myself. I'm selfish like that. No sharing and you don't get to leave me. You'll be all mine. My woman, my love, my wife."

Her heart nearly beat out of her chest. "Are you...are you asking?"

He didn't blink. "No."

Right. "I accept." She threw her arms around his neck and ignored his exaggerated grunt as she whispered, "I hear it."

He gave her a squeeze. "What?"

"The song for my soul. It's you."

"God, I love you."

She buried her face against his shoulder and said, "What a wimp I am. You're going to make me cry."

"Well, before you do, could you say it back so I'm not left hanging here?"

It was such an off-the-cuff question that she laughed, "God, I love you back."

"You really are quite the parrot when you want to be."

She was quiet for a minute. Thinking about all that they'd been through. Where they started and how far they'd come. That's when she remembered something. "Hey," she sat up and pushed her hair back off her face. "I think I need to offer you my condolences."

He took her chin between his forefinger and thumb and rubbed. "For?"

"Losing?"

He frowned. "I didn't lose. I got you, didn't I?"

"Yes." She fit her cheek in his palm and pressed in. "But at a pretty hefty price—your bachelorhood. So, if I'm not mistaken I do believe my magical vagina just TKO'd your magnificent balls."

She waited for him to process that and when he did, he grinned. "If I had to lose to someone, I'm glad it was you."

Before she let him kiss the hell out of her, she replied, "Great. You better get used to it, babe, because I see someone crying on the golf course in the very near future."

He laughed and scooped her into his arms. She loved the rumbling sound of it. But then there was nothing but the sound of her heart pounding as he made her forget about every magic, but the kind he spun all around her when she was tucked safely in his arms.

Epilogue

Life was good. Maggie and Jaxx's relationship was on the mend and Maggie had a new boyfriend—Q—and a new project—the Viking—which meant she wasn't interfering in their lives very much. The complex was almost completed, and Jaxx was back at school to get a specialty degree in Geriatrics like she always wanted. Once she was done with that, she was going to open up a practice of her own at the Jack Taylor Clinic. Aries was not only pleased, but proud about that.

Things with Gabe were better than he'd ever imagined. They were working on another real estate deal together, and Aries had even stepped in to help with the company now that Jaxx had set Gabe up with a woman. Aries never knew how alike he and his brother were when it came to the opposite sex until his brother got shitfaced one night on a guy's night out. Aries, being the sober one out of the two them, heard a lot of interesting stories about the women in his brother's life, but Gabe and Lisa Monroe's first meeting topped them all. He still wasn't sure he believed it. It kind of reminded him of one of those jokes. There was a nun, an elevator and a vibrator... Damn, if that really happened, Gabe was going to hell. No doubt about it.

Aries stopped the cart and took a deep breath. Two minutes later he was standing at the first tee, secretly stressing over being whipped at golf by his gorgeous wife. He was very competitive, and golf was his game. But he was prepared to take it like a man.

"I like your clubs," he told her. "They look new." They were top-of-the-line ladies Ping's with a custom putter and a driver that looked like something engineers at NASA had constructed. "Did you bring enough balls?"

She turned and gave him a saucy look. The sun shined beautifully against the tri-colored metal around her neck. "Did you?"

"Jaxx."

She sauntered over to the blue markers and bent to push in her tee. Was she shooting from the blues instead of the whites? Holy fuck, he was screwed if that were the case. He needed to calm down. Take another breath. There wasn't a chance she could out-drive him. No way. "You're going to drive off the blues?"

"Blues? I'm not upset. I'm feeling good, actually. And I brought a ball. They're pretty expensive."

Okay, this he had to see. One ball? If she managed to play with only... "If you play the whole game with one ball I'll get on my knees and bury my face between your legs on the eighteenth until you come all over me."

She picked up her driver and held it straight out, pointing it at him. "That's a deal." Slowly lowering it, she winked. "And if I don't win, I get to suck you off at the eighteenth until you see stars, okay?"

He nodded. Thinking this arrangement could work out better than he'd been anticipating. "I think I've just found myself a new golf buddy. Okay, proceed. Let's see what I'm up against."

"Alrighty."

He wasn't paying much attention to the way she addressed the ball because she had the cutest little ass wiggle as she got set, and he was mesmerized by it. He thought he heard her whisper, "Here goes nothing," but that couldn't be right.

She swung and then rushed forward a couple of paces with her hand cupped over her eyes. "Oh, I forgot my glasses. I can't see. Where did it land? Ohhh! Is that it?"

Frantically she pointed, no doubt fixating on the white rim of the cup, because it definitely wasn't her ball.

Furiously she scanned the distance. "Where is it?"

"Right where I want to be."

She jerked to attention and squealed, "It's on the green?"

"No." He crossed his arms and narrowed his eyes. "It's between your legs."

Priceless was the only way to describe her, when her head snapped down. "What? Wait, how did that happen?"

"We golfers call it a whiff. You probably know it better as a swing and a miss."

She tilted her head to look at him. "No."

Okay, he couldn't contain himself. All this time she'd lied and strung him along exploiting another one of weaknesses. He dropped his arms, shook his head and laughed, "You have absolutely no idea how to play golf, do you?"

Her grin was so wide her dimples appeared as she spun around to face him. "No, but I do like to drive the cart, though."

That perky announcement sobered him up. "Yeah, well, it will be hard for you to drive anything when you can't sit down. You are so getting a spanking for this one."

"Great." She dropped her club in her bag and came right over to him. He thought she was going to try to talk him out of the spanking and he was prepared to deny her, but then she walked her fingers up his chest, stopping at his collarbone, and said, "Since it's a foregone conclusion that I've already lost, would you like to see those stars now?"

"Nothing would please me more. But we can't hold up other golfers. Even if we could be discreet. And we'd have to be discreet because I don't want to lose my membership."

"Men." She snorted. "Where are your magical balls now? Don't worry. There won't be anyone else on the course this morning."

His adrenaline spiked. It'd be great if she were right. "How do you know that?"

She popped her brows. "We own all the tee times until noon."

He gave a low whistle and said, "That must have cost a pretty penny."

"Yeah, but you can afford it."

She was sliding south when it occurred to him. "Jaxx, did I buy all that fancy equipment for you that you don't know how to use too?"

"Yeah."

He was going to argue, maybe tack on another spanking, but then just as she promised, he saw stars. And they were the brightest kind that had him totally speechless.

His only thought when he groaned and sank his hands in her hair was the magical vagina had fucking scored another one. Damn.

About The Author

I love to write sexy, humorous and emotional romance where a happy ending is guaranteed. I'm an optimist, who believes life is awesome, people are complicated— but in a good way— and we should never stop learning. I currently call Florida home with my gorgeous husband (Honey). I have two wonderful kids and one very bossy English Bull terrier. When I'm not writing, I'm either reading, oil painting or getting to the Sunday crossword puzzle before anyone else does. I really love to do that as, you know, you get to look smart filling-in all the easy answers first.

If I weren't an author? I'd want to be an international spy with top-level security so I could have a peek at Area 51 and decide for myself if those green guys are for real. Failing that? I'd probably go with chicken sexer.

All kidding aside, I love my characters and I hope you do too. You can visit my website at http://www.Authorrileymurphy.com where I blog about life, but mostly Honey. Or, if you like, shoot me an email and say hello. I love to hear from readers! You can catch me @ write2rileymurphy@gmail.com I promise I answer all my emails because you guys rock!